Angels on a Tombstone

J . F .   F O R A N

PAGE PUBLISHING, INC.
New York, NY

First originally published by Page Publishing, Inc. 2018

ISBN 978-1-64214-779-7 (Paperback)
ISBN 978-1-64298-137-7(Hardcover)
ISBN 978-1-64214-781-0 (Digital)

Printed in the United States of America

Prologue

July 17, 1891

Stradbally was a quiet, peaceful village nestled between two hills facing the Irish Sea. The members of its only club, St. Grellann's, were mostly rugby players. Some were short and powerful; others long and lean. They crowded the bar, their uniforms dank, sweaty, and stained by the grass or caked in the mud that was ever present on the hilltop pitch that overlooked the sea. After practice, they enjoyed a glass or two of stout, and a racket at the door caught their attention as a new group entered the club. Towering above the others, they saw Jeremiah. Hellos cascaded out chiding him for missing practice, arms raised in welcome. Jeremiah Knox was a member, a rugger, a fine striker, but several of the men with him were not members. One voice from the bar said, "Shit, that's O'Farrell."

Passing by, Jeremiah said, "Easy, lads. We're here for a short meeting in the card room. I'll catch a pint with you later."

Another voice from the bar, head down, said, "Nothin' but trouble will be cocked up back there. Gonna oust the Brits from Erie? Fuckin' Fenians are nuts."

O'Farrell ignored the comments and walked beside Jeremiah straight to the backroom. O'Farrell was well known from Cork to Dublin and feared. He was the head of arms procurement for the Fenians.

Twelve young men, all talking at the same time, gathered in the wood-paneled room, some in their rugby togs, some in workclothes, and some, like Jeremiah and O'Farrell, were in suits. Of the men, Jeremiah at nineteen was the youngest. O'Farrell at twenty-five was a Fenian veteran. The oldest in the group, at thirty, was Johnny

3

Fitzgerald. O'Farrell raised his arms to quell the noise; it sounded edgy to him. "Settle down, lads. We've got some big news." The rumble of voices lowered. "Settle down I said!"

The room became quiet. "The raid at the Brits' Waterford Barracks was a major success. The fire damage to their barracks and munitions storage was substantial. Keep in mind, though, you killed a few of the regulars."

The room burst with applause and yells. "Death to the fuckers."

O'Farrell put his hand up. "They'll be seekin' revenge. Keep yer eyes open and watch yer backs." With a huge smile on his face, his arm swept the room. "The next attack will be even bigger. Jeremiah's done all the planning. I'll turn the floor over to him."

Jeremiah stood, his tall lanky frame dominated the small wood-paneled room. He explained how the master of the Cork Rail Station approached him a few weeks earlier after one of his speeches on Irish Independence. The station master described that an eight-car freight train loaded with arms and munitions will be headed to the Waterford Barracks in a few weeks. The Brits needed to replenish what was lost from the raid. Jeremiah picked up a paper from the table and waved it to the men. "This is the timetable, and our train is the nighttime 10:02 out of Cork three weeks from now. The station master said it will be lightly guarded because the British don't wish to attract attention to what's on board. We're going to side-rail the train, and I'll show you how it's to be done and who's doing what." Questions flooded the room.

"Do you trust the station master, Jeremiah?"

"What do we do with the weapons once we've unloaded them?"

"What about guards on the train?"

"Where do we do the planning?"

Jeremiah held up his hands. "One at a time, lads. It's all in the plan." He picked up a slender document from the table so they could see it. "We'll meet here every Monday. The club's virtually empty on Mondays, so it's safe. Today, I'll outline the plan so you understand the strategy and your personal responsibility. Next Monday, we'll dig hard into the details."

At the conclusion of the meeting, the men adjourned to the bar, and O'Farrell lingered behind. He faced Jeremiah. "You know most of these men well. Who do you worry about?"

"After hearing their questions, there's two of them that I should drop from the raid. I'll need two replacements."

"Who are you questioning?"

"Did you get a good look at Tommy Makeen's face? His question indicated fear. He seemed scared to me, and that's unusual."

"Yeah, well, Makeen got the shit kicked out of him last November by the Brits for some crap he pulled. Maybe he is scared. Okay, he's out. Who else?"

"I don't think Rippy O'Toole's got his head on straight. I don't know what to make of him except he's totally crazy with the risks he takes. At the Waterford Barracks raid, he ran in the front door before he tossed the fire bomb. He could have been seen as well as killed. He's ..."

O'Farrell laughed. "I like crazy people like that, but it's your call."

Jeremiah said, "We can't afford crazy right now. This is too big. Every man's got to be trusted."

O'Farrell clapped Jeremiah on the shoulder. "You sure don't act like a law student Jeremiah. You're a tough Fenian, a Fenian leader at that."

Jeremiah didn't seem to acknowledge the comment. Dead serious, he replied, "When I finish at Edinburgh, I want to use the law for Irish independence, like Joseph Callahan. But now, I want the British and their loyalist Irish friends to know they're in a fight."

Chapter 1

August 1, 1891

The knock on the door was loud and startled him. Sean was on the second floor, running water in the bathroom sink. Carefully, he finished filling the glass, putting it aside to listen. The pounding at the door spoke of a male's hand, a noisy male at that. His wife, restless with fever, was in their bedroom two doors away. He was rarely home at this hour; late afternoons found him in the pastures overlooking his black Angus herd or at his inn and pub in the village, but today he'd come back to the rambling farmhouse to see her. She had remained in bed, unusual for her, and he was concerned. Her voice came softly into the bathroom, "Get that, will you, Sean?"

Quickly he moved through the second floor hallway. "I'm a-comin'!" he hollered. In his fifties, he was still lean and muscular. His tall angular frame descended the stairs two at a time, his powerful hands slapping the banister as he left the last step. He strode across the wide entryway and opened the heavy black oak door to Colin Reilly.

Constable Reilly took off his hat and bowed slightly. He was shorter than Sean by a head or more, and his rumpled gray suit was tight over his powerful body. His shoulders and arms reminded all that he gained his current position with a natural ability to handle the roughest drunks in the village. "Forgive me fer interruptin' yer day, Sean, but it's important." He paused, taking in Sean's tall body filling the doorway. "May I come in?"

"Of course, come. Take a load off. What's botherin' yer today, Colin?"

"They said at the pub that yer'd be here. The missus having a touch of a cold, they said, didn't they? How is Fiona?"

"She's fine, Colin. She'll be back on her feet in a day or two. Iffins yer don't mind, I'd like to get down to business as I've got to tend to her, then get out to the barn. My man is worried about Connor."

"That bull of yours, Sean, is a pride to us all. A champion again this year." He shook his head, pulling his thoughts together. "Damn bull, I'm scared to death of him. Went near him year or so ago, never again."

Sean laughed. "I seen you, Colin, yer thought he was a cow, didn't yee? Tried to pet him." He uttered a small chuckle. Sean watched the constable shifting from one leg to another. He said, "Bulls of his size and caliber move fast and are known to be pissed off most the time, so it's good to stay clear." He waved Colin to a plain upholstered chair near the wide stone fireplace and sat across from him. His body was heavy on the three-seater divan. "But more importantly, what's on yer mind today. Is this a social visit, or do yee come on constabulary or town council business?"

Colin Reilly clasped his thick hands in front of him as if he was unsure what to do with them. He shifted uneasily in his chair, his eyes not ready to give Sean the attention he sought. He was younger than Sean, somewhere in his late thirties. His face was pale and lightly freckled, free of wrinkles except for slight creases around his mouth, hinting that he'd seen hard times. "I'll get right to the point, Sean. Last night, with the help of the British Regulars, we raided the St. Grellann's Club."

"The football and rugby club?" Sean began to chuckle. "What fer? Yer constables or the regulars need some footballs or uniforms?"

Reilly's jaw was set. His features, normally drawn and dour, were especially well suited for the challenges in his job. "Nah, on a tip we went there, didn't we? Found footballs and dirty shirts, true enough, but more important, we found a book, a plan, Sean." He paused to look at his hands, rough and big. They belonged to a larger man. He glanced back up at Sean, his lips pursed. "Yes, Sean, plans ... plans to raid a munitions train, and more importantly"—his stern gaze held

Sean's eyes for a flicker of seconds—"plans to steal the weapons and ammunition from the train."

Sean exhaled. "More goddamn trouble from the Fenians and in our town, shit. Pushin' the British problem agin, pitting the Irish against the Irish."

He said, "That's bad business. Usin' the club for their trouble-makin'. I'm pleased, Fiona too, that you're on top of this trouble. These boys here, getting all riled up by that goddamn Parnell, the Unionists, the Fenians. Best to stop 'em here before they get into real trouble."

Sean rose from the divan. "Is that it?" He glanced down at the Constable still seated. "Good work there, Colin, although I don't know why you needed the British Regulars. We got to keep them out of our affairs."

"Please, patience, Sean. There's more. The Regulars called us in because they suspected from one of their informants that a dangerous raid was being planned. The papers we found in the hall confirmed it."

"Jesus." Sean sat back on the divan. "Well, you don't need me or the rest of the council on this, do ye? It's yer jurisdiction, or is it the Regulars? By the takin', any of the lads we know?"

"Yes, Sean." He lifted his head to stare directly into Sean's eyes. "The plan we uncovered was written by yer son, by Jeremiah." He saw Sean was too shocked to comment, so he rushed on. "Clear directions on what train, the number of raiders, the time and place for attack, what cars had the guns and ammunition, and so forth. Very well done, this plan."

Sean sat bolt upright in the divan, his fists curled. "No, no … can't be. He's clerkin' for Judge Wicklow over in Waterford as yee know."

"We know, but we know also that he's been seein' Jimmy O'Farrell in Dublin, the Fenian leader there."

"Nah, nah, he'd never associate with the likes of O'Farrell. He's doin' law work with the judge."

"Sean, the Dublin police and the British Regulars are workin' together like never before. They're seein' another rise of Irish nationalism, and they mean to stop it. In this situation, they have seen Jeremiah and O'Farrell together at the Dungarvan Club in Dublin, and O'Farrell's been handin' out pamphlets written by Jeremiah on Home Rule and Irish Independence. His name's on the booklet."

"He's just gotten back from Scotland, his summer break from the university. Are yee sure yee have the right Jeremiah?"

The constable rubbed his large hands and kept his eyes steady on Sean's face. "We've known fer years before he went to Edinburgh, of his opposition to the British rule in Ireland. He's the only lad around here who could plan something this elaborate. And as I said, we know he's been working with O'Farrell and the Fenian people in Dublin." Colin studied the man across the hearth from him. Gently he shook his head and, in a quiet voice, said, "We've got to bring him in, Sean. We've got to talk with him."

"Jesus, Colin, he's clever for sure, but he's too smart to do something illegal or criminal. Why bring him in? This all's a big misunderstanding or mistake."

"That's what I thought, Sean, and want to believe, but he's been writing those pamphlets and essays for the past two years. The Crown prosecutor in Dublin has read his writings and called it treason and sedition, he's serious. The county police from Waterford and Dublin wanted to come here, but I said no. I'd talk to you and Jeremiah first."

"So you've come here today to do what?" He pointed a long finger at the constable. "You're going to turn my boy over to the British? Jesus, Colin, yer own people."

"I don't have choice, Sean, it's the law, and Jeremiah's broken it. These are dangerous times, you know this. The old acts of the Fenians are with us agin. And it looks like the boy's in the middle of it. The British and Irish loyalists in Dublin want him."

Sean shook his large head and thought back. He remembered when he first heard the about the group of radicals, the Fenians. It was in his childhood when the Irish who wanted to expel the British were pitted against those who supported British rule. With regret that still lingered, he remembered that his Irish neighbors spied, informed, and killed other Irish; there was no trust among neighbors. And now the violence was back with his youngest involved?

Sean said, "Well, I think you and the British are half-cocked, but we'll see. Jeremiah should be here any moment. He leaves Judge Wicklow's chambers at four each day. His train should be in any minute. We'll get this cleared up fast."

Sean stood up muttering under his breath, "Jesus H. Christ." He cupped his hands and hollered, "Mary! Mary O'Donnel."

Doors opened and closed. A young maid in a plain gray dress that flowed from her thin shoulders to her ankles shuffled out from a backroom, a whiff of cooking flavors followed her into the sitting room. She glanced quickly at the two men and curtsied. Her lank colorless hair flopped lazily against her shoulders as she bobbed up and down. "Yes, sir?"

"A cup of tea for our guest and me, Mary." She curtsied again and left the room quickly.

"Ye said you raided last night. The boy was here all night a-workin' on a case for the judge."

"We know that, Sean. We picked up ten of them last night, half from Dublin or Waterford and a few boys from Stradbally. You know the type. The Collins brothers, Allie Dolan, Timous O'Malley, Tommy Makeen, and a few others—all with a long history of troublemaking."

Aye, thought Sean. Making trouble for the British. The thought troubled him. He thought back to the Fenian insurrection of 1867. It was the political fever of his youth, but he'd had no part. He didn't believe that violence furthered the Irish cause and was pleased when those days were over. Yet his boy favored the Fenians and their strategies for independence. He wasn't surprised but was disappointed. He and Fiona knew Jeremiah, their youngest by many years, was the smart one of their five children. He knew Jeremiah had political ideas that were different from his own, but the boy was quiet about it, at least at home. The boy liked reading, a bookish one. A boy who liked being alone, very comfortable in solitude.

He thought about his other children, all much older. Jeremiah was most different from the oldest. Tommy, in his mid-thirties, had the farm now. A good farmer who increased the herd of top-grade Black Angus. Edmund, the third-born, would take over the pub and the inn where he worked, and James was in the seminary and would soon be ordained. Agnes, second-born, was a teacher in nearby Waterford and married to an engineer at the glassworks there. From his earliest years, Jeremiah picked up books and taught himself to read and write long before he started school. He asked questions while the others followed the family's rules. Jeremiah always asked why. Why this rule of bed by seven? Why not six or eight or nine? Why church on Sundays? Why not Wednesdays and give workers a break midweek? On and on. He excelled in every school, and they decided to send him to law school, a natural place for his inquisitive and argumentative mind.

Because of his strong opinions on Ireland's political squabbles with England, they decided to send him to Edinburgh for university rather than to Trinity College in Dublin. In Scotland and away from the Fenians, they believed he would gain a better perspective on British rule in Ireland. But it hadn't worked. After two years at Edinburgh, his readings of Locke, Hume, Burke, the US Constitution, the peasants' revolts in Russia, and others that Sean couldn't remember, the boy was fully convinced that British rule over Ireland was wrong and should be removed. That his son favored the Fenians over the Unionists or Parnell's people was perplexing to Sean and devastating to peace-loving Fiona. Violent expulsion of the British would never work in his mind, nor was it the right course of action to Fiona. But what had the boy really done?

The doors swung open, and Mary came in with a tray she held nervously in her hands. "Place it on the table, Mary," Sean said. "The constable and I will take it directly."

She curtsied. "Will there be anything else, sir?"

"Not at the moment, Mary." She turned, and her eyes darted from the constable to Sean as she left the room.

Colin sipped the tea. "It's a sorry business I do, Sean, but it must be done. We can't have our boys holding up trains and stealing weapons and ammunition. Somebody could get killed. We've got to talk to Jeremiah. I hope you and Fiona understand."

"The boy wants what many of us want, our own Home Rule. That's all."

"I know, Sean, but the way he and the Fenians are goin' about it hurts the cause." He rubbed his hands together. "After the bombing of the barracks in Waterford a few weeks ago, the British have increased their troops here and their special investigators. The plot to rob the train of weapons only convinces the magistrate in Dublin that it's the time to put down the Fenians. And they've got a new magistrate in the Four Courts, who's reputed to be real tough on the troublemakers."

"The boy's political in his interests, not in military violence like the Fenians, you'll see."

The constable let his eyes rest on Sean. *My life's been good though,* he thought. *I got off the farm, got into police work, have good living, have a house with a roof and plumbing. What else does a man need? Why's this kid stirring things up? If he's political, why is he with the Fenians? They're pushing for a war to expel the British and the aristocratic Irish amongst us. The kid's a warmongering political. Why doesn't he like the British and wealthy Irish? He's one of the rich Irish. The Brits and people like the Knoxes have been good to me.* Colin sipped his tea, his eyes blinking as if sending a message but remained quiet. *Be careful,* he thought. It seemed to him that Sean Knox was being clever or devious, but he didn't know. Was it possible that Sean didn't know what his youngest son was doing?

Chapter 2

Both men turned as the front door opened. Sean rose. "Aye, Jeremiah, here yee are, lad. How was the day?"

His body filled the doorway. Large hands hung by his side, dangling out from the coat whose sleeves were an inch too short. His tie was askew, a sharp blue against the white of his shirt, and had been pulled away from the collar to give his sinewy neck room to breathe. His lush brown hair fell in a wave over his forehead. In a predictable habit, he pushed it back with his left hand. He was still breathing hard from the brisk walk up the hill from the station, and he regarded the constable warily as he caught his breath.

"It was fine da." He took in Constable Reilly's presence and thought, *Oh shit.* He walked to the coat pegs on the wall and placed his coat there. He turned to Reilly and said, "Constable Reilly, it's a blessing to see you. What brings you out to Knox Farm on a blustery day?"

"Normally, it's good to see you, lad, but these aren't normal times, are they?"

Jeremiah was beginning to feel nervous. He glanced at his father, who remained by his side, yet his father remained quiet. Jeremiah asked, "What do ya mean *not normal?*"

The constable stood, and as he rose, he pulled a thick document from his satchel. He waved it at Jeremiah. "I've come to talk about this plan, lad. It has your name all over it plus all your Fenian friends. It guides the Collins boys and others to side-rail a train, hold the guards hostage, and take away box loads of rifles, machine guns, and ammunition. It's a clever plan, Jeremiah, but it's against the law. Of course, yee know that, laddie." He stuffed the document back in his satchel. He pointed at Jeremiah. "I have an arrest warrant for your participation in an act of sedition." His stubby finger was shaking toward the seat of the chair.

Jeremiah flicked a hand toward the constable. "A warrant, really. Let's see it. See what evidence you have."

His face feeling flush, the redness becoming evident, Reilly blurted, "I don't have it yet, but these plans are all the evidence the Crown needs. We can get your confession here, or we can do it at the station. You choose, Jeremiah."

"This is all very vague, Constable Reilly, do what? What is this confession you refer to?"

"Don't get cute with me. I'm not impressed with your learning at the fancy university in Edinburgh. We can go over this plan here, or we do it at the station."

"Station, aye. You don't have a warrant for me? So come back when you have one, and I'll have my lawyer here to see where I go, if I go."

Constable Reilly took a deep breath. Normally, he was not confronted or challenged, his evidence in question. The lad was too self-assured for him. Softly he said, "You're in deep trouble, lad. I have the right paperwork. So it's better to come now or talk here. Make it easier on yerself."

"'Tis true, Jeremiah," his father interrupted. "Colin wants to help yee. Better here."

"Da, I don't agree. He ..." Jeremiah pointed a long arm and a single finger at Constable Reilly then glanced over to his father. "He's a tool of the British. He's no longer Irish. He's one of them."

Jeremiah laughed at the constable. "Those papers yee have there, anybody could have put my name on them, including you. You have nothing, and you know nothing."

"You're wrong, Jeremiah. Tommy Makeen rolled on you and the rest of the boys. We have the local boys, the Collins brothers, and Allie Dolan in cells right now, and I was awaitin' your return from Waterford. The Dublin and Waterford boys have scattered, but we'll catch them. They're all talking."

"A cat's ass they're talking."

"Careful, son. Watch the language in my house."

"Sorry, da, but the constable is out of order and saying things when he has no proof. He doesn't know whether they're true or not. Before I talk to anyone, I'll talk to my friends in Dublin. I'm not talking now, and I'm not going anywhere." With that, he sat in a chair near the wide stone fireplace.

Sean walked over to his son and said, "Perhaps if you talked now, we could get this all cleared up. Clearly, they don't think you planned this train robbery. The constable here is a family friend. He came here. He didn't want the British inspectors here. Talk to him."

"No, da, if he wants me to talk, he can get the proper notices, and I can get the proper help. It's the law, and he must observe it. Even the British know that."

The constable stood up. "I tried, Sean. I did. But the boy is strong-willed, and the British think he's a ringleader, that he's danger-ous. The Crown prosecutor's done his work, yee see. He's convinced that Jeremiah became radical from his days at the university and his association with Jimmy O'Farrell. My duty and responsibilities are clear, so I'll be back." He tipped his fingers to his forehead and said, "I'll let myself out."

Sean walked Colin out. The two men stood outside the front door as a soft mist began to collect around them. Sean raised his jacket collar. Constable Reilly whispered, "Always a chill in the after-noon mist." Then he paused. "Sean, please bring him to the station in the morning. We have the proper papers there. If yee don't, the Crown's deputies from Dublin will come here to get him."

Sean nodded, waved the constable goodbye, and returned to the hearth. He took a seat across from his son and said, "Now tell me what happened. What's going on?"

"I can't, da. It's too dangerous, and you and mum and the others should not be involved in any way. So yee must never know."

"But something bad's happened. A train robbery and the Makeen boy rolled on you. Can that be? Is he telling the truth?"

Jeremiah's clear green eyes, the eyes of his mother, darted down then up to his father. There was calmness in those eyes. It was a young face, the face of a nineteen-year-old, but the eyes were much older.

"Da, Makeen's scared and is probably trying to save himself, but yes, I've been involved, and yee should not know more. Trust me, da. Trust my legal training. No more questions."

"I can't have that in my house, son. I need to know what's going on. I don't want a criminal here, and I don't want your mother and I to be embarrassed."

"Da, I'm so proud of what you and mum have done. While everyone else in Stradbally was stewing over what to do with the land bill, you went to Lord Fitzgerald and got the option on the acres here. It was so amazing, with the land came that damn bull ... Connor the First."

Sean acknowledged the compliment with a nod.

Jeremiah said, "Now it's my turn, and the country needs people like me as your generation needed men like you to take our lands back from the British."

"Good enough, son, but remember, we need to pay off the Fitzgeralds, and it's almost done. I don't want to lose that by any illegal actions."

"Trust me, da, they can't take what you've paid for, and they can't change the contract unless you default. It's the law, and the Brits do stick by their laws. Now what I've got to do is change the law on Home Rule. We need to govern ourselves. We need to be a nation. We need to secure our rights as free men."

"Later, son. I don't want the university lecture on the rights of man."

"Da, yer goin' to hear nasty talk about me, and it may sound bad. But if yee listen carefully, they'll seem right if yee'll hear my thinking."

Sean stood up and shook his large head. "This sounds complicated, son, so we'll get to it but later. I'm goin' to the barn to see Marty. He's got some problem with Connor. We'll gather the family at dinner and discuss this fully." He turned abruptly and went out the front door, slamming the door behind him.

Jeremiah sank back in his chair and stretched his long legs in front of him. *Damn that Makeen,* he thought. *He's put me, all of us, in a helluva spot. I've got big trouble and the old man's mad. The fam-*

ily will disown me. He shook his head then pounded his fist into his other hand. *They raided the club. How did they know to do that? Somebody showed them where the plan was hidden. Makeen or others panicked. Was Makeen a mole, or do the Brits have another mole in their unit who put them onto Makeen? Somehow, they found the plan. This could be bad,* he thought. They could never pin the raid on him. There were too many names on the plans. But if someone talked, they could claim the idea, the information on the trains, the information on the military cargo. All the planning was his. He stood up and paced the room. He wondered if Makeen tied him into the raid, bombings, and shootings at the Waterford Barracks. A lot had happened in the past few weeks; it was good, needed, but not if they were caught. If they talked, as Constable Reilly indicated, that would be a bad problem. He pounded his right fist into his left palm again. He walked to the front door and went toward the barn. He walked rapidly around the property, his long legs eating up the rolling ground, trying to make sense of what happened and what to do about it. He walked until he felt sweat on his chest and confirmed his only action. He must call Callahan.

Years later, Jeremiah would recall the family dinner with a shiver and chills. The dinners were always noisy, full of talk and laughter. This evening it was quiet, nearly morbid, as if a death in the family had occurred. There were disagreements in the family, and like all families, there were differences in skills and temperaments, but mostly the Knox clan was boisterous, supportive, and close-knit. The silence was broken by his oldest brother, Tommy. He was thirty-five, built square and powerful unlike the tall, lean Jeremiah. He was a bachelor but not from lack of trying. He was simply unpopular with the ladies, arrogant, opinionated, brusque, and often rude when dealing with women. And mirrors, unlike the other members of the Knox clan, did not favor him kindly.

With no introductory comments, he said, "Jeremiah, what in hell's wrong with you? You've always been bookin', getting strange ideas, and written them down in those pamphlets. Da says yee cocked a plan to rob a British military train. You've always been crazy, but now you've really done it. We've got a good life here, and you're goin' to wreck it with your Fenian beliefs and actions. Yee's embarrassed us all."

Fiona, the family matriarch, was slender. Her black hair pulled back was flecked with gray, her face still red from fever while her long thin hands played nervously with her napkin. She gazed around the long board table and took in her family. It was a varied lot, she acknowledged. There were wide differences in temperament, in skills, and even in appearance. She'd pulled a long dress over her bedclothes, resolute to address the situation regardless of her health. "Tommy, that's enough. He's your brother." Her eyes stayed on his face until he looked away. She smiled faintly and gazed at the faces of her family. "We'll go around the table as always. I'm sorry, Agnes is not here with Timothy as she'd speak next, and I know she'd support what Jeremiah is trying to do."

Red-faced, Tommy broke back in, "Mum, yee don't know that. The boy here was planning to kill people. Agnes would never countenance that. Never."

Jeremiah, his voice soft yet clear, said, "You show your born ignorance, Tom. Leap to conclusions you do without knowledge, without a shred of proper information. It's no wonder da took you out of school at thirteen."

"Yer the one ignorant, Jeremiah, our dear grandfather—bless his soul—John Francis, he told yee to be a stonemason like him. Yee cut the stone with him on the new barn a few years back. He admired yer skill there. Our granddad wouldn't agree with all yer book learnin'. Waste of damn time."

"He's the one that encouraged me to go to Edinburgh. He liked my scholarly side. He never pushed stonework. You don't know what you're talking about and never did." Jeremiah had fire in his eyes as he stared his older brother down.

Tommy stood up. "Yer holdin' your big education over me. Yee always did. Look what it's gotcha. Smart boy goin' to jail, that's what."

Sean slammed his hands down on the table. "Sit down, Tommy. Enough, yee two. We go around the table as we always do, and Tom, yee had yer say. So shut up."

Tom's napkin was twisting in his hands, his face even redder. He bit his lip and looked at the meat on his plate, his head shaking.

Sean said, "Edmund, what say yee?"

Edmund was shorter than the rest, a quiet man of thirty, still a bachelor who lived in an attic room in his inn. He managed the inn and pub with a tight fist on the purse strings and a careful watch over his help. Fastidious and precise, he hid his intrinsic shyness with a welcoming personality at the pub and inn. When with his family, he preferred to listen rather than talk. He bit his lip as he looked at his father and at Jeremiah. Slowly he glanced at them then spoke down to his plate. "The boys at the pub knew the story, da. Yes, they did. They said Tommy Makeen's a snitch, been under the finger of the constable and the British for some past trouble. Don't surprise me none if he told tales of Jeremiah and the others. Get himself some leniency, ya see." He looked up to see all eyes riveted on him, and he bit his lip again.

"Is there more, Edmund?" asked Sean.

"One more thing, da. Jeremiah's my brother. I love him, and I admire him. He's so smart, but I wish …" He turned to look directly at Jeremiah, his eyes soft with moisture. "I wish you'd use those brains to be a lawyer and not to put them at the disposal of the damn Fenians."

Jeremiah met his gaze and nodded.

"And, James, what say yee?" asked Sean.

The fair redhead, slender like his mother with the same soft features, tugged at his clerical collar. He glanced at his mother. "Da, Mum, I wish Jeremiah would feel peace in his heart, forgive the British for their wrongdoings, and know in time they will recognize that their ways are wrong and even sinful." He looked across the wide table into Jeremiah's eyes and said, "Jeremiah, I wish you'd follow the words of Christ and not the words of Kant, Hume, Locke, and those other Protestants. They're leading you astray."

Jeremiah leaned forward and opened his mouth. His father put up his hand. "Hold on, Jeremiah. Wait yer turn."

"Fiona," Sean addressed his wife with a kindly smile. His eyes sparkled as he gazed at her. "It's so kind of yee to leave yer sickbed to address yer son. Give us yer wisdom, love."

"Miah, she was the only one in the family that abbreviated his name and the only one he did not correct when called Miah. You've always given me reason to think. Yer thoughts often troubled me as they are different than mine, different than your father's. Yee never could stand cruelty, ignorance, or unkindness to others. Even as a little boy, yee could never understand why there were poor and dirty children. Why some townsfolk had a house that was falling down. Yee never could forgive a slight. Yee always wanted to make it right. Is that what yee done here, done this time with this action against the British?"

"It's true, Mum. The British were bringing guns and ammunition to the local police and to their own troops, to oppress is further. They don't care about our problems. They want to silence us. If they want to bring more guns into our land, we planned to stop them. We Fenians believe that we need those weapons for our own protection. I agree if they have guns, we need guns. They want to keep the absentee landlords holding the peasant farmers down, and they're doing it with military force so we advocate military force to remove them. It's the only route we have."

"Protection my foot," blurted Sean. "Those Fenians want the weapons to start a war, Jeremiah. Are you ready for war too?"

He ignored his father with a long sigh. How often did he hear his father find reasons to support the actions of the constables and the British owners in the county? Too often. *The old man wants the status quo*, thought Jeremiah. The current life of the family was good. Their land was bought fairly. The farm and the Angus herd had been very successful, and the inn and the pub were solid moneymakers. *Good for da*, he thought, but not so good for most of the other people in the country.

Slowly, he glanced from his plate and placed his fork on the boiled potatoes and said, "Da, the poverty here is atrocious, much higher than in England, Wales, or Scotland, and it's because 90 percent of the land is in the hands of the British or a few Irish aristocrats. You bought our land, da, but you're the exception. You all know that for the past century the absentee landlords collect rents and don't improve the property. They don't allow the land to be used by more imaginative farmers or turned into industrial projects like in England. The laws stop us from making progress. We need our own Home Rule, laws by the Irish for the Irish."

"Damn, son, where do yee get yer facts, get your theories? Is that what they're teaching you at Edinburgh?"

"We're taught the law and who has the rights to pass laws. I've learned that most of the laws in England advance the interests of the English. They're not for us or the Scots or the people in India and so on. Further, at the university, I've read about the rights of man and how they're turned into law. The English have these rights, and the Irish don't. That's wrong! Look at the American Constitution, they protect the property rights and hosts of other rights of their citizens. We've nothing like that in Ireland and won't as long as the English rule this country."

James pointed a finger at his father. "Da, if I may."

Sean nodded, and James twisted his clerical collar again then said, "Jeremiah, I've always found the writings of Augustine, Aquinas, and Paul to be more helpful than those Scottish Protestants of yours. They seek understanding, patience, and forgiveness before change can come."

"Like blessed are the poor. Well, the poor aren't blessed here … are they, James! They're starving and wretched. You've seen our villagers every day, kids with no shoes, same for the women, and half-starved they are. Over two million people have left Ireland in the past twenty years because they were starving. What do Paul or Aquinas have to say about that? That the meek shall inherit the earth? Well, the meek can't inherit when they don't own their home or their land or any other possessions. Where is your god on these matters?"

Sean glanced around the table. "Anyone with more to say?" He absorbed the quiet faces, edgy, nervous, and red. "Well, we'll learn more tomorrow what Constable Reilly and his British friends plan to do with Jeremiah. Until then, let's finish dinner."

"Before we leave my situation," Jeremiah inserted, "let me say one more thing. I'm sorry if I've embarrassed you. That's not my intent, but I must do what I believe is right. And I believe our own police and the British occupiers are arming up for a real shutdown of people like Parnell, the Fenians, and any others who are working toward Home Rule for us. They will jail us, kill us when it suites them, and try to turn peace-loving folks like all of you into an opposition and against those who want an Irish country, one that's free of British rule. The Americans freed themselves for such rule. We should do it."

Sean shook his large shaggy head; Fiona wrapped and unwrapped her napkin. She looked at her husband, her eyes beseeching him to remain quiet. Instead, he said, "If you agree with what the Fenians have done here, or were the brains behind the plot, then God bless yee, son, 'cause I can't help you if you've broken the law."

"Bad laws need to be broken, da, to show they're bad laws."

"But theft, robbery, and possible murder is what the Fenians do. That's god's law they're about to be breakin'."

Jeremiah studied his father's hard face. He could see and feel the man's frustration. The old man was in sharp disagreement with his own position on these issues. He knew then, and it would be confirmed over the years, that he had created discord in the family, created wounds that he discovered, over time, would be slow to heal. If only John Francis were here, his grandfather would have supported him and made them listen. His grandfather would have forced them to admit that they had given in to the English in order to sell their beef at high prices in the London market and later made agreements that provided them with the only license for a pub and inn in the village, thus enabling them to own this fine house. His grandfather provided balance and perspective at the dinner table. It was now that Jeremiah realized that John Francis had been the glue in the family structure, holding it together in good times and bad. If a rift or fracture in family matters appeared, he'd fix it and heal it. He missed the old man, now dead three short years and already Jeremiah's sense of a family was being disrupted. His confidence in the purpose of a family, the value of his family to him was being tested, and he did not like the sensation. He felt an emotional gap between him and his family. He didn't like it but was surprised that he felt a cool, detached attitude toward them.

Chapter 3

The telephone call came as the dishes were being cleared. Sean raced to the telephone and snorted into the receiver, his responses gruff and unintelligible. As he listened, his face turned red. He turned to Fiona, who had watched him from the edge of the dining room. She spoke before he could get a word out. "Sean, what is it?"

"Get Jeremiah, my love. We're a-goin' to the constable's office tomorrow at ten."

"Oh dear." She turned away. With her handkerchief, she dabbed at her cheeks as she went toward the kitchen. Something deep tugged at her. It was just a meeting to clear the air perhaps, but her instincts told her something different. Her senses, fueled by the fever, were on fire. Deep down, a feeling began to swell. She tried to push it aside, but it wouldn't budge. She had a knowing feeling that once he entered the constable's office she'd never see Jeremiah again. The thought made her heart flutter, and she placed her hand on her chest to calm it down. She steadied herself as she opened the door to the kitchen. She hollered up the stairwell, "Miah, your da has gotten a message from Constable Reilly."

He ambled down the stairs to the living room to learn there was a warrant for his arrest, and voluntarily, they would go to the constable's office in the early morning. It was clear from his father's attitude that all discussion would be at Reilly's office with the arresting officers and not at home. They discussed the meeting time; it was a short exchange. His father was too angry and confused to offer more conversation. Sensing the silence would endure, Jeremiah broke away, "Da, I'm going to my room and prepare my thoughts for tomorrow, but first, may I use the telephone and call my friends in Dublin?"

Sean nodded and left the room in search of Fiona, muttering to himself, his language unintelligible. Confused by his father's garbled language, Jeremiah asked, "Da, do you have more thoughts?"

There was no response as he watched his father walk away. He felt irritated and was certain that his father was so angry he couldn't speak. Alone in the empty room, Jeremiah took a few deep breaths and picked up the phone. He gave the operator the number of Joseph Callahan, attorney and lead lawyer for the Fenians in Dublin.

Callahan had a busy practice, mixing criminal and civil cases with a small staff, and it was made chaotic when the Fenians needed him. He'd been handling telephone calls all day, and despite the late hour, his clients were stacked in his waiting room, all chairs occupied with several people standing, hoping to see the man. He ushered his client out of the office while reaching back to his desk for the ringing phone. He listened to the barking voice before he responded, "Jeremiah, ahh, I knew I'd hear from you. The big news is about Makeen ... Did the police tell you that?" He listened for a second. "Yeah, that's right, the little bastard Makeen spilled the beans. Everyone has been rounded up. Some son of a bitch is a snitch down there. I believe he put them onto Makeen. Any ideas who?"

"No." Jeremiah paused for a second thinking. "Well maybe, but not sure. Do you know why Makeen rolled?"

Callahan said, "It appears the police had something on Makeen and offered him leniency if he talked."

"Yes, I've heard that too."

Jeremiah suppressed the anger he felt. "So the snitch knew of Makeen's weakness, and that got us exposed." He paused for a second. "You said they have everyone. Really?"

"Yeah, they got your whole group. It's a disaster for the organization. Martin's worried about the leadership, thinking he might get exposed by O'Farrell and you. He's hollerin' mad, callin' this a major fuck-up. He told me to let you all hang. You get the idea."

"He's not serious."

"Well, you know him. He's all fire, so yes, he is at the moment. He's not going down for this so if this falls on you and your crew, it's your necks. He wants to make sure it's not his neck."

"We get I get no legal help from you or other Fenians?"

"Nah, we won't abandon you, Jeremiah, but I can't help much, given the document they found and the squealing of Makeen."

"How bad does it look?"

"We'll talk more tomorrow, but the judge is out for blood. He wants to link this to the firebombing of the barracks, so he wants jail time for everyone." Then he rushed next comment, "But that's his bluster. We'll talk more tomorrow."

Jeremiah knew his actions with the Fenians carried risk; he knew he was violating the laws, but the consequences, if caught, were mere abstractions to him. Callahan's comment made it personal. He was nineteen, his life in front of him, and now he had to realize that his life was about to change course. He felt as if he'd been punched in the stomach. His family, his education at Edinburgh, his life going forward could be irreparably altered. He felt his knees go weak. He took a deep breath to restore his composure; he said, "My meetings at ten in Stradbally. Can you make that?"

"Nah, too much to do here. I've got to clean up what I can from the horrendous mistakes of your crew. But I'll meet you at the train station at two. We can talk there. I'll have some ideas by then."

"Meet at Dublin, why?"

"No choice, Jeremiah. They're going to read you the charges at the constable's office in Stradbally then load you on the eleven-o'clock train to Dublin. You'll be sequestered in a special police car. You'll not be with other passengers. You're to be arraigned in court in the late afternoon."

"They can't move that fast, Joseph. We can slow them down with procedures."

"Not so on this one, Jeremiah. You're all being charged as terrorists as threats to national security. They're invoking the Treason Felony Act of '48 plus the Explosives Act of '85 in order to wave all due process for what they call terrorists. By tomorrow night, your fate will be clear. You face a big decision right now. Do you want to run—and I mean run—tonight, or do you want to be a martyr? By being a martyr, I mean going to trial, doing jail time, and getting the kind of press that Parnell gets. You need to decide, lad."

Jeremiah wiped his forehead. The beads of perspiration were trickling down his cheekbones. His breathing was audible. *Holy Jesus Christ*, he thought. The Treason Felony Act implied a long prison term, not the short sentences Parnell and his people typically served. He shivered at the thought. He brushed his face with the back of his shirt sleeve, leaving a wet stain near the cuff. He'd seen this situation in some of his classes. The speed of the police and judiciary was incredibly swift when it needed to be or the authorities wanted it to be. This was the situation now, he surmised. He felt committed to the cause for Irish Independence, and the cause was right. Cowards back down or run—not me. He swallowed quickly, his voice now firm. "No, I won't run. I want the people to know what we've done and why. I need a courtroom and the press for that."

"Be careful, Jeremiah. Don't let your idealism overrule your reasoning." Callahan glanced down at the pile of arrest warrants on his desk and shook his head. "Here's the situation. You and others have gotten the attention of the British. They plan to lock all of you up and throw away the key. Hear me on this. While I try and get court dates and judges lined up, you'll see no press. You'll be tucked away, like Parnell and others before him. Are you ready for that? Or do you want to run? Think about it."

Jeremiah remembered *tucked away* was Fenian slang for jail time. "I've thought about it. I'll see you in Dublin tomorrow."

"One more time, Jeremiah, running is an option. I can get you help, and we'll get you on a boat to Germany. But you'll have to leave tonight. O'Farrell's on his way. You can join him, but I need to know now … if I'm to get the right papers."

"No, Joseph. I'm going to stand tall. No running for me."

The day broke with gray skies; a fog hovered over the Irish Sea. After pecking at a bowl of oatmeal, each mouthful tasting worse, Sean placed a cap on his head and motioned to Jeremiah. "I can't eat. Before we go to the constable's office, let's walk the farm."

His father loved to walk around the edges of the acreage and particularly by the barns and feeding pens. When he was home from Edinburgh, Jeremiah would often accompany him as it was the only time when he and his father were alone.

When it was clear that his father planned to walk the land and not talk, Jeremiah said, "Da, I know you're angry, but let's talk about it. I want you to hear my side."

"I know your side, Jeremiah. You said so at dinner. I canna understand it. Yer throwin' your life away and hurtin' the family too. I'm sure you'll see your mistake."

"It's not a mistake, da. Action like mine must be taken to release us from the British. I don't like being caught, but that won't stop me or the others."

"Yer willin' to go to jail like Parnell and them others? That's nuts."

"If that's the price I must pay to move our vision of home rule forward, so be it. I'll survive like Parnell and finish up at Edinburgh when I'm released if it comes to that."

"You're makin' a big assumption, laddie." He stopped to stare at Jeremiah, meeting him eye to eye. "Do you think I'm willin' to continue to pay for your education to become a radical and overthrow everythin' I've worked for? This plan of yours has been a great disappointment to me, so you better think again."

"Is that the way it's goin' to be, da? You'll stop my education."

"Hear me clear, Jeremiah. I'll not pay to educate a radical."

He could feel his insides tighten, his blood rising. "One more word to you, da. I'll find a way to complete my education. You just wait and see." With that, he turned from his father and walked rapidly back to the house. As he strode away, he acknowledged, for the hundredth time, that he and his father were different people. Conversation between them was infrequent and often awkward. This conversation, like many others, was brief but sufficient to highlight the gap between them. He knew his father loved the land, and Jeremiah recognized the attachment was emotional; the fact that the sale of beef had made him rich was incidental. He tried to understand his father's words on his radicalism, but all he could fathom was the old man wanted the current political arrangement to continue. Jeremiah rounded the corner from the water trough to the handsome stone barn that housed the large herd.

Jeremiah looked up at the wide doors to the barn. The anger that was burning inside him released as he thought back to what he and his grandfather had done. He was fourteen at the time, and his mom said, "Carving a bull couldn't be done by a fourteener," but he did it. His eyes rested on the wide stone support beam above the double barn doors. There the carved image of Connor I dominated the entrance. Five years later, it was still in his mind a beautiful rendition of that gorgeous bull. And to his grandfather's delight, he had done all the fancy stones for the corners and the roof supports as well.

John Francis had said those many years ago, "Yee really knew the stones and how to use that chisel."

Jeremiah thought back to that pivotal year; he was fourteen, and between his father and grandfather, they had accumulated sufficient capital to build a large stone barn to protect and feed Sean's growing Angus herd. Ever since his grandfather had come to live with them, the farm grew faster, and the family seemed to live better. Jeremiah had just turned ten when his grandmother died, and John Francis arrived with his suitcase and his box of tools. Later, wagon loads of goods, chairs, tables, dinnerware, and rugs arrived, but Jeremiah's powerful impression was set when the rangy, big-boned John Francis knocked on the door with two bags in hand. Almost immediately, he and Jeremiah became constant conversational companions. Together, they sketched then planned an expansion of the house to accommodate John Francis, and next they planned expansion of the outbuildings and especially the design and construction of a new stone barn. Sean was happy with their partnership. They relieved him of work where his skills were limited.

John Francis was a well-known stonemason in Waterford County and had done the statues and the fine stonework in the bell towers for churches as far north as Dublin and as far south as Cork. He taught Jeremiah how to cut limestone, sandstone, and even granite. By age fourteen and the foundation of the barn in place, John Francis had said that Jeremiah was ready for cutting the blocks for the barn and maybe even capable to do some fine trim work. As they worked together on the barn, John Francis's confidence in Jeremiah was proven; the work exceeded the older man's expectations. His compliments gave Jeremiah a sense of pride and joy in this newfound skill.

John Francis had said, "Yer goin' to be better than me, Jeremiah. This could be a career for yee, but yer like the books, don't yer, lad?"

Jeremiah remembered his reply, "I do grandfather, and I'm good at that. I like the thinking. But I like the working with stone too. Very satisfying."

John Francis had said, "Yee have lots of skills Jeremiah, but let's remember what the country needs. It needs smart fellows like you more than it needs good stonemasons."

Jeremiah took one last look at the barn then turned up his collar. The fog off the sea had drifted up the hill and chilled him. He hastened his pace back to the house. Their workmen, Ken and Trian, had walked the carriage to the front of the house. Ken was holding the horses, which were snorting, restless at this early hour. Wisps of fog wove around the two horses, putting a light veneer of moisture on their shiny coats and on the sides of the Knox's carriage.

Trian said, "We're ready when you are, Mr. Knox."

He nodded. "I'll get my satchel and be right back."

When he returned to the carriage, he was surprised, his father was sitting in the rear seat.

"Da, no need for you to come. I'll be back shortly or, at worst, the end of the day."

Sean said, "I want to see, I need to understand what's going to happen."

Jeremiah slid in beside him. "As you wish, but I don't want to tie you up. Callahan and I can take care of this."

Absently, Jeremiah pulled his coat across his chest, sensing the cooler air outside as the horses trotted toward the village. He glanced back at the handsome stone house; a chill raced through his body as the house receded from view. He cleared his eyes; on the steps to the house, he thought he saw the ghost of his grandfather with tears in his eyes, waving goodbye.

* * *

The police station and the chief constable's office was in a small single-story stone building with a thick thatched roof in the center of town. The police station was next to the larger town council building. Both faced the town green where Sean's driver had parked the carriage, the horses at rest, shaking their heads then bending over to nibble the grass. As Jeremiah stepped into the building, the police station seemed very small and cramped. Two desks faced him, empty of the town's two officers. He and his father stepped around the paper-strewn desks and went to the open door of Chief Constable Reilly's office. Reilly greeted them with an outstretched hand and guided them to a barren room next to his office. As they sat in the chairs positioned around a battered rectangular table, scarred from years of abuse, Reilly said, "Thank yee for coming in peacefully, Jeremiah. It'll make things easier." The pale light from the overhead bulb in the windowless room made Reilly's face appear haggard and old. Jeremiah glanced at his father, whose face was frozen, barely concealing his agitation. The chief constable took a sheaf of papers from under his arm and placed them on the table. "Sean, if you and Jeremiah would read these papers from the Crown prosecutor, I'll come back in a moment and answer your questions. In the meantime, I must greet our visitors." Sean and Jeremiah stared out the door as Reilly exited but could not spot any visitors yet heard him extend greetings as he said from the outer room, "They're reading the charges."

There was a movement of chairs creaking against the floor as Reilly reentered their room. "Who's out there?" asked Sean.

"In a moment, I'll explain. But first, what questions do you have from the Crown's charges."

"It appears that I've broken two laws, and I'm being charged with treason. This is crazy and can't stick," said Jeremiah.

"Sean, Jeremiah, I'm not the judge, nor the grand jury, but the Crown prosecutor believes he has sufficient evidence to try you and many others under the Treason Felony Act and the Explosives Act. You will be going with the two officers from the Dublin Court on the next train. At Four Courts in Dublin, you'll be formally arraigned on these charges." He stopped and was quiet. He gazed at Jeremiah, sadness in his eyes. "It's hard for me to do this, but my job is done.

I've delivered you to the court officers, and you'll proceed to Dublin with them."

Sean, sitting back in his chair, his head held high, asked, "Can I go to Dublin with him?"

"Of course, Sean and I understand that Jeremiah has a lawyer waiting for him so yee need not worry about that."

"Is that true, Jeremiah? Is that the Callahan you mentioned?"

"Yes, da. Last night, I called my friends in Dublin, wanted to see what they knew. I learned that we're all to face the prosecutor somewhere in the next few days. There's no case, da. They're citing a criminal law, and we're acting in a political manner. We've done nothing criminal."

Sean eyed the chief constable. "Is that how they see it, Colin? Is that how you see it?"

"I'm a police officer, Sean, not a prosecutor or a judge. George Hill, the Crown prosecutor, is a tough man and he says the laws have been broken." He turned his eyes to Jeremiah. "Criminal and civil laws have been broken, and it's my responsibility to enforce them. I'm just doing my job by informing you of the arrest warrant and turning Jeremiah over to officials from the County Court in Dublin."

He escorted them to the outer room, and the two constables stood up. They were short compact men, their shoulders bulging under their long, dark overcoats. On their heads, they wore dark gray, nearly black bowler derby hats squeezed onto their full heavy faces. They nodded in solemn acknowledgment of Sean, and one of them turned to Jeremiah and said, "Extend your wrists."

Constable Reilly injected, "Billy, I doubt that will be necessary. This a law student, a scholar."

"Donna give a damn, Colin. George Hill says bring him in, and I'mma gonna make sure he gits there."

Jeremiah said, "I won't run, Constable. I'm innocent of these ridiculous charges and will be on my way back to Stradbally later today."

"Yer our prisoner, Mr. Knox, and we'll sit with yee, eat with yee, pee with yee, and walk wherever you need to walk. We're stuck to your side, do you see? So if Constable Reilly swears by yee that yee won't run, then I'll put the cuffs away. One funny move though and on they come. Clear?"

Jeremiah nodded. He turned to his father and said, "Da, yee don't need to come. Joseph Callahan is going to meet me at the station. He'll clear me with the court today."

Sean wanted to hold his feelings back, but it was not his nature. He was angry with his son, and his frustrations had been accumulating for years. When Jeremiah was sixteen, Sean didn't want university for him. He preferred to have him on the farm or working the inn or the pub. Yet he agreed to the pressure from John Francis, his wife, and his fourth child, James, the Catholic priest. They had convinced him that Jeremiah could use his many skills to help the people of Waterford County, be a first-rate barrister in the county and maybe run for Parliament at some point. He agreed that the boy was a natural leader, but unfortunately, he saw the boy as a natural agitator as well. Nothing was ever quite right for him. Teachers were stupid, police were corrupt, and the decisions of the British landlords robbed the poor. The British rules and regulations in Ireland bothered Jeremiah from an early age. Now, he'd pushed too far, Sean feared. "Nah, son, you've made a mess, and I want to know how big a mess."

Jeremiah could feel his father's anger and wanted no part of that in the train or in interactions with Joseph Callahan. He knew the seriousness of the plot. He knew the law the constable referenced and knew it could be used for acts of treason and even for plans of treason. The law was loose, and it depended on how aggressively the Crown prosecutor and judge interpreted and applied the law. He didn't want his father to understand how far he was willing to go to fight for Irish home rule and the release of lands from the absentee landlords. He'd lost faith in his father, knowing that they could never agree on his ideas. Now, the old man planned to pull him out of Edinburgh, expanding the gap between them.

In his mind, Jeremiah knew the Crown prosecutor's charges were serious and the consequences could be very bad for him. He said, "Da, Joseph Callahan knows the Crown prosecutor and the judge. He'll work his magic. Don't worry, I'll be home for a late dinner. Go home and comfort mum. Tell her I'll be fine."

"Come now," said the Constable called Billy. "We need to catch the eleven-o'clock train to Dublin. We're goin' now."

"Da, go home. I'll be all right."

Sean said, "There'll be phone somewhere. Call or have this Callahan fellow call as soon as there's news."

Jeremiah shook his father's hand. It was a strong hand pump, and he stared hard into his father's eyes. "I'll see you later today."

Chapter 4

Jeremiah stuffed the papers defining the charges against him into his satchel and searched through his law school memory for cases of treason where the defense was political differences. He thought of Parnell's constant troubles with the British and his imprisonment. He thought of historical examples and the trials of Socrates, Joan of Arc, and the English parliamentarians and kings who had been imprisoned and beheaded for differing political positions. Martyrs for a cause—the thought that once impressed him now frightened him. Did he want martyrdom at this age? He wanted the stage, he wanted to be able to show the Irish people that there were those in the country who were brave enough to fight, clamor for Irish independence, and rid the country of the British oppressor. His confidence and comfort in his current situation tended to ebb and flow. In a change of attitude, he turned to the two constables escorting him and asked, "Why are you not on my side? Why support British oppression?"

They walked as if on a morning stroll from the police station across the green to the edge of town. There they mounted the steps to the train station and waited for the express to Dublin. The packed gravel of the platform crunched under their feet as they stood quietly. Jeremiah stared at one then the other, his eyes asking for an answer to his question.

Billy shifted his squat powerful body to face Jeremiah. His fellow constable just looked at Jeremiah with a dismissive grin. Billy said, "Laddie, yer a troublemaker. Yee make it hard for all of us when you do these things. If we're going to get what you Fenians want, we'll get it peacefully, and we'll get it when the British conclude we're ready. When they're convinced, we can govern ourselves."

They stood on both sides of Jeremiah, ensuring he would not leave them, ready to secure him with handcuffs if necessary. Billy's fellow officer, more taciturn and quiet, simply responded, "Yeah, that's right. Yer trouble, and we make sure trouble doesn't happen."

They mounted the steps to their car. Other passengers were currently seated, some chained to their seats. This was the police car as Constable Reilly had mentioned. Jeremiah glanced at his fellow passengers—some were his age, some older. There were about fifteen of them in the thirty passenger car, apparently all prisoners headed to the Dublin Four Courts. He took a seat across from his two guards, staring at them, and undaunted, he continued his lecture. "We're working for your rights, for a better life for you and your children. A time when you can buy your own land, buy a house, pay taxes that stay in Ireland. The British want to retain the land and extract all the income our people produce. They want to leave us poor by taking our tax income to London. They want to control us with their police and courts and keep power over us. Don't you see that?"

Billy lifted the paper back to his face. "Shut up, laddie. We don't need a lecture from you. Yer goin to jail." He fluffed the paper twice then put it down and studied Jeremiah's face. "You know, laddie, yee made strong enemies with the Waterford Barracks raid. Never mind the plan to rob the train. Men were killed at the barracks. We knew some of them, good men all. Those men got long memories, won't surprise me none if they come after yee, no matter what the court does. Keep that in mind." Then he burrowed his head in the newsprint.

The land flew by as they crossed patches of open pastures, deeply green under the overcast August sky. They passed thatched cottages where barefoot children in ragged clothes played outside sagging stone cottages with tiny windows, chasing the chickens pecking in the dirt or playing with sticks and baked clay balls. As the train steamed into Dublin's station, the profusion of tracks and bays for the trains had Jeremiah confused, searching left and right for the presence of Joseph Callahan. He was nowhere to be seen. All Jeremiah saw was a cordon of police officers gathered by the tracks. Clearly his car was not the only one receiving a police escort. With both arms held by the two constables, Jeremiah stepped down onto the platform and was greeted by a uniformed officer. He said, "Billy, Donny good work. The wagon's over yonder, a short walk. Did this skinny shit give ye any trouble?"

"Nah, he's an intellectual, a university boy fuckin' up his future. Let's go."

Joseph Callahan appeared as if from a cloud. Out of nowhere, he was suddenly walking beside them as they made their way to the police wagon. "Gentlemen, I'm the barrister for Jeremiah Knox, and I wish to speak with him."

"We don't know nothin' of the kind. Keep yer distance, he's goin' to the Castle."

Callahan, in a smart plain gray suit cut to fit his trim body, touched his clean-shaven cheek. "I have here the assurance from the Four Courts that I can talk with my client upon his arrival."

"His arrival at jail, Counselor."

"No, no." Callahan waved a piece of paper in Billy's direction. "This is from George Hill, the prosecutor, describing my client's rights and mine as his barrister."

Billy ignored him glancing at the paper but not reading it. "Okay, you can walk with us to the wagon. After that, you see him when the judge says you can see him."

Callahan exhaled, his hot breath pushing the cool fog at the tracks. He leaned toward Jeremiah and whispered, "These bastards ... we'll talk more after the prosecutor meets with you and your charges are stipulated. You'll be going to Kilmainham Gaol. It's not a good place, and I have a plan to get you out."

Jeremiah stopped and looked at him. But the uniformed policeman and Billy pushed him forward. "Move it, laddie."

Jeremiah said, "What plan? It's a plan for everyone, yes?"

Callahan ignored him. "Jeremiah, I need to talk with yer da and mum. Are they in tonight?"

"They're always in at night unless it's Saturday. But I want no deals, no special treatment. I want my day in court."

The guard accompanying them was getting irritated. Staring directly into Callahan face, he said, "Keep it for the courtroom, Mr. Callahan. That's all yer getting now."

They approached the wagon, and the guard opened the locked door at the rear of the vehicle. Inside sat five other young men who started to move toward the door, and the police removed their batons. The young men returned to their benches, and Jeremiah joined them. He glanced at their faces, hostile, unfriendly, their eyes sizing him up. Their clothes were worn, their shoes battered and in need of polish. No one moved to make room for him, and he sat in the most obvious open space. He crowded the man next to him who said, "Watch it, young dandy. I'll give yee more than you can handle."

Jeremiah nodded and moved to assume the least space his long body needed. The five men continued to stare at him from time to time; it made him uneasy. One man stood up and tried to reach him, but the chains on his wrists and feet contained him. "Fuck," he said, "I wanna see yer money. Dressed like yer, yee got money. Let's see it."

Jeremiah was not chained or handcuffed. He stood up to the man. "I've got no money, and if I did, it wouldn't be goin' to you." Although slender in build, he towered over the man. His large hands flexed into fists, then relaxing, then flexed again.

"Tough, are yee? We'll see when the chains come off."

They both sat down. Jeremiah brooded. This was a tough and unpleasant lot. Would these be his cellmates if he was held over? He didn't like that idea, and it ate at him. Nervously, he flexed his hands again and again. The other men watched him in silence.

A man who appeared to be near Jeremiah's age pointed at him. His unshackled hands were dirty, and his knuckles were raw with cuts. He said, "We're a bunch of thieves and murderers here. What the fuck do they want with a pretty boy like you?"

Jeremiah thought his Fenian association would impress them, perhaps quiet them and leave him alone. He said, "I'm a Fenian, and they think they have me on several charges."

The five of them looked around, and then the laughter started. One said, "Did yee bring yer bombs with yee? Yer goin' blow us all up?" They seemed to be quite amused at their wit.

Jeremiah said, "We're doing this for you, to take the country anyway from the British so you'll have better chances for jobs and a decent life."

"More people to rob, that's okay with me." More laughter filled the wagon.

The five continued to stare at him as if he were an animal in a zoo. The attention made him nervous again, and he flexed his hands. Why was he with this crew? Common criminals, why was he travelling with them? Would he have to fight his way in the holding pens? The prospect of the next few hours began to stir fear and uncertainty. For the first time in his life, he was not surrounded by friends or people like him.

A small window at the top of the wagon let in the gray light. Barely, Jeremiah could make out the upper stories of stone-and-brick buildings as the wagon clattered through the streets. Each bounce of the wheels over the cobblestones jarred Jeremiah's back and kidneys, and he sought to find a comfortable position, but none was located. He heard the clank of a gate opening then closing, and the wagon came to a halt. As the door opened, the police, with batons drawn, yelled move to the open door, pointing at large double doors across the courtyard. The men ran fast to avoid the waving batons. Inside, they were directed toward different hard wooden benches as manacles were attached to their feet. Their wrists were checked to ensure the handcuffs were tight. The group shuffled down a long corridor and again sat on a hard wooden bench and told to wait. And wait they did. It seemed like hours to Jeremiah, who had no food or water since early morning. He asked the guards for water, and they joked about his request. "Would yee like yer tea now, Mr. Fenian, one lump or two?" He laughed heartily as did his fellow guards. A taller, surly-faced guard with thin black hair and a pocked marked face stepped close to Jeremiah and whacked him hard on his wrist with the baton. "That's for talkin'. More to come fer yer kind."

The other guards laughed; one said, "Ah, Timothy, he won't be able to hold his tea cup. Shame on yee."

Jeremiah closed his eyes and willed the pain to calm down, but the wrist pulsed and screamed. Don't antagonize them, he thought.

They're not his people. They didn't know or care about a freer Ireland. For the first time in years, he asked the question, "Are these people worth it?" He kept his eyes shut and went to his inner self. It is worth it, and they'll appreciate it later. He kept repeating, "They'll appreciate it later," again and again.

He lost track of time, but he measured it by the pain in his back and buttocks from sitting on the bench. He opened his eyes and looked at his fellow prisoners carefully for the first time. The surly crew from the wagon were not there. He had been placed on a bench with twelve others. Four were associated with his plan to rob the train, although he did not know them well. They were older, in their twenties, and had been in the Fenians for years. The wink of an eye was all they acknowledged, and it said to him they would not implicate each other. The message was clear, and he looked away.

At last, the door nearest to them opened. It was a wide double door, and they were pushed down a central aisle to a set of benches in front of a magistrate who sat on a high platform behind a desk high above them. It was Judge Hardy, and he glared through his half glasses at the motley crew below. His mouth was turned down as if he had indigestion. It gave his face a severe appearance, his ice-blue eyes cemented the impression. Jeremiah stared at him, trying to get a measure of the man, concluding he was tough and unsympathetic with this set of prisoners.

Judge Hardy surveyed the twelve prisoners, his eyes deadly cold. "What have we, Stevens?" he asked the bailiff.

"They're all charged under the Act of '48 for inciting treason and terrorists acts."

"I see several familiar faces in the crowd. It must mean they want to be put away for even longer stretches this time. They must miss the good food."

The courtroom was silent. All eyes were on the judge. There was no reaction to his attempt at gallows humor. Jeremiah stole a glance around the room. Behind him, several rows back in the gallery sat Callahan, who caught his eye. He lifted his right finger in a signal that Jeremiah did not recognize, but the gesture relaxed him. As the judge began to speak, Jeremiah returned his gaze to the front of the courtroom.

Judge Hardy asked each defendant to stand as he called their name; he gave the defendant a brief glance then glanced at his notes and read, in a dead voice, a date. Jeremiah came to understand that the date was for a formal hearing. At that time, the charges against each man would be finalized. He was aghast. Connally, the first called, was an older Fenian, and his hearing date was set for two months away. Connally would spend two months in jail. As a risk to the community, he was not eligible for bail. The charges, if any, would be levied at that date, and then a trial date would be set. This judge, Jeremiah thought, was going to put this group out of circulation for a long time. His name was the seventh called, and he stood up.

Judge Hardy lifted his head to get a good look at Jeremiah. Unlike his quick view of the other prisoners, his glance rested on Jeremiah for several seconds. He removed his half glasses, polished them on the edge of his robe, and replaced them on his nose, his eyes never leaving Jeremiah. Jeremiah could feel his gaze, and he met it directly, not blinking. The judge snorted and said, "September 7, next is Loughlin. Stand up, Mr. Loughlin."

Jeremiah sat with relief. Only a week but then he realized he would spend it in jail with these others. But only a week, it must have been Callahan's doing.

After the last name was called, the twelve were led from the courtroom and back to another prison wagon. Crowded on the benches, curse words in Gaelic were mumbled, some bit their lips, twisted their hands, or pushed their heads back and stared at the scarred ceiling of the van. All were lost in their own thoughts, their dates for trial, the possible sentences for violations of the Act of '48 as the wagon rolled back over the cobblestones to Kilmainham Gaol. As they tumbled out of the wagon, the sturdy prison appeared in the day's mist as a grim medieval fortress. Its tall stonewalls spoke to the myths of no escapes, of permanent confinement of harsh separation from the lively life of Dublin, and from the lives they had recently led. "Jesus Christ," a burly, compact prisoner sitting next to

Jeremiah commented, "I was here years ago, and it looks worse than I remember."

Jeremiah stared at the older man. His hair was lank and thin on top. His ears were the most prominent part of his head, and they stuck out like wings, his mouth was wide, the lips tight, giving an appearance of impatience. He was a longtime freedom and home-rule fighter, a long-term Fenian. Jeremiah wanted to ask about the gaol, about time on the cells, about the food and life inside, but his instincts told him to be quiet, be observant, and be ready to protect himself. No one commented on his early date for trial, nor did anyone mention the differences in trial dates. It was understood without expression; they were to protect each other, beware of snitches, and be uncooperative with the authorities.

The wardens, joined by six others with batons at the ready, escorted the men into a holding pen. Again, they sat on benches until their name was called. Jeremiah learned that this form of booking was to assign each prisoner to a cell and to separate the Fenians as best the facilities at Kilmainham would allow. Jeremiah was walked down several flights of stairs to a dark, dingy chamber where cells were located on both sides of a damp stone corridor. At last, the jailer grabbed his ring of keys and opened cell 86. In the eight-by-ten-foot cell were two metal bunks with dirty straw mattresses and thin gray blankets. The air in the cell was rank with the sweat of male bodies and rotted garbage. The beds were occupied by two large men who stared at him as he entered, five other men sat on the floor against the walls. Their clothing was, for the most part, a simple shirt, pants, and jacket. The clothing was shabby, thin, and dirty from sitting and sleeping on the floor. One of the large men, prone on the mattress, his bulky arms linked behind his head, asked Jeremiah, "Fenian?"

He nodded.

"Welcome to the West Wing, the prisons' worst. It's got no heat. It's damp, and we have no window, no light." With that, he rolled over and faced the stone wall.

Other heads in the room nodded or said "Aye," and they left him alone. No one moved to make room for him in the cramped cell, so he searched for space along the stone wall and found a small niche where he could squat and sit. He pulled his body against the wall and tried to find a comfortable position. He closed his eyes, shutting away the stench and dense mass of humans in the cell. Voices emerged around him. Small talk in soft tones resumed as soon as the guards left. He could not make out who was talking or what the conversations were about. He tried to put his thoughts on better topics like his trial and how he and Callahan would present his case, but the stench in the cell distracted his thoughts. He was nudged in the ribs by the man next to him. Startled, he looked at him. "I s-s-s-said," said the short emaciated man with a slight stutter, "what are y-y-yee here for?"

He leveled his eyes into the gaunt face where streaks of grime mingled with scabs. His face was hard yet the eyes were wise and seemed to have compassion. Jeremiah glanced around the room; it had become quiet. All eyes were on him, including the two men on the beds. He replied, "The Act of '48, treasonous acts, they've brought in twelve of us."

One of the men in the bed sat up. "What da fuck you'd do?"

"We didn't get it done. We were planning to derail a munitions train and rob it. We were snitched out, nabbed before we could do it."

"Oh shit … no bloody English killed. Well, ain't that the shits." With that, he fell back on the bed, resting his head on his arms again.

Jeremiah turned back to the man beside him. "What's he in for?"

"M-m-m-murder, k-k-k-killed the man who f-f-fucked his wife."

"And the man on the other bed?"

"M-m-murder also, k-k-killed a man in a b-b-b-bar fight."

Jeremiah nodded, his head bobbing as he glanced around the cell. Others had returned to their own thoughts or prior conversations. The cell was quiet again. He said, "I'm Jeremiah, and why are you here?"

"I'm G-George and I'm a th-th-thief."

"There no Fenians in with us?"

"Naaaa, y-y-yer the only one so f-f-far."

The wheels of a cart rattled in the corridor, and the custodian announced, "Soup's a commin.'" There was a clang on the cell bars, and a small gate in the door was unlocked. A large urn slid into the cell, followed by eight cups tossed on the grimy floor. The scramble for cups was like a rugby scrum to Jeremiah, and he reached then grabbed then pushed to get a cup. "Wait yer turn!" the man from the bed roared.

The big man rolled off the bed, took a cup from another man, and dipped it into the watery stew. In an order, elusive to Jeremiah, the men took turns dipping their cups into the urn until it was bone-dry. His first sip on the stew nearly gagged him, but he fought the impulse and swallowed. *I need the nutrition*, he thought. Another cart rumble by, and two loaves of white bread were tossed through the small gate, and then it was locked. The men on the beds took a loaf and broke them into pieces, and the chunks of bread were quickly devoured.

Jeremiah learned that water came by after the stew and bread. And once a week, a pail and mop were brought into the cell, and the men cleaned the floor and walls. After the cell was cleaned, each cell was emptied, and the men were taken to a room to bathe and clean, yet they retained and remained in their own clothes until their case was called.

That night, Jeremiah curled in a ball on the cold, damp stone floor. Restless, he moved and nudged other bodies. He was pushed back when he entered another's space, and the complaints about crowding and space interrupted what little sleep he was able to get. Amid the discomfort of the stone floor and body crowding was the strong stench of eight unwashed men, rotted food, and moisture that dripped off the walls. He woke, tired, stiff, and aching, after little sleep and horrid dreams.

In the afternoon of his second day, a guard came to the cell and called for him, and he was taken to a small windowless room two floors above his cell. As he climbed the stairs, his legs yearned to move faster and to kick the confines of sitting and sleeping in one position in the cell all day and night. As he entered the room, the manacles on his wrists were secured, and he was seated at a chair on one side of a modest-sized desk. The two chairs and desk were the only items of furniture in the room. The door had a window at the top where he could see the guard, and the guard could see clearly into the room. The guard had been uncommunicative as to where he was going and the purpose of the change in rooms, so Jeremiah sat perplexed, wondering what would happen next. After five minutes or so, the door swung open and in walked Joseph Callahan. He clapped Jeremiah on the back and settled into the chair across from him.

"How are you, lad?"

"It's beyond description down there. Eight men in the cell, no room to walk, stand or sleep, no beds and disgusting food. Otherwise, it's just like Edinburgh."

Callahan laughed. "It'll get better. That's a holding tank down there, and it will thin out. Eventually, you'll get a bed, a couple of roommates, but hopefully, by then, you'll be gone."

"Christ, I hope so. What can be done?"

"It's tricky, lad. They want to come down hard on the Fenians, and this caper of yours is going to be used as an example. Judge wants to tie all of you into the barracks raid as well as the train raid. All you lads are going to do time."

Jeremiah took a deep breath. What does that mean? How long? Where? Was there no hope of case dismissal? His mind was in a tizzy. He was about to talk when Callahan put up his hand. "Wait, lad, I have two pieces of news. First, the judge has no information to tie you into the barracks raid. So whoever snitched on that one, he didn't mention you. The second is even better news. I talked to your parents last night, and I talked to the judge this morning. We may have a deal."

Relief swept through him, but he pushed down any sense of optimism. "Say more."

"For background, let me start with." He paused for a moment, ensuring he had Jeremiah's full attention. "The judge knows you." Jeremiah expressed surprise but remained quiet so Callahan continued, "Yes, he went to a Republican rally in Dublin last summer and heard you speak. He was ... I guess the word is *impressed*, so he read some of your articles. He thinks you're very persuasive, very convincing. That's a nice compliment, but he comes to a hard conclusion." Callahan coughed and wiped his mouth with a monogrammed handkerchief. "In a word, he doesn't want you in Ireland. He thinks, even in jail here, you'd be converting the inmates, sneaking out articles, attracting newspaper coverage. He doesn't want any of that."

"What does he want?"

"He wants you expelled from the country." He waved a finger at Jeremiah, "And not to Scotland. He wants you far away. Australia, Canada, America ... somewhere like that, if they'll take you."

"Jesus." Jeremiah shook his head. It had drooped down to the desk. He was muttering, "No, no, no, good God, no." He lifted his head to stare at Callahan. "Not that. I want to be more like Parnell. In and out in a year and then back to the fight. Finish my degree and go after them in the courts."

"Sorry, Jeremiah, the judge can put you away for life under the Act of '48, so you don't want that. He's offering a very good deal. Go abroad for a few years, let people forget about the train incident, then come back. It's the best outcome for a very tough case."

"But how long will it take before you find a place and situation that will take me. I want to continue my education or at least find work, a place to live, and so on. There's a lot to be arranged."

"That's the good news." Callahan allowed a small smile, his satisfaction evident. "It's done. A deal, an arrangement has been found. When I talked to your parents, I mentioned one possibility was that you'd leave the country. This morning, they called and said they'd spoken to your uncle, your father's brother in Boston, in the United States. He's agreed to sponsor you, and he can work the immigration agency in Boston. He apparently knows those people well."

"America." He blew out a blast of air. "For how long?" He knew nothing of the country. Its distance from Ireland and its uncultured reputation bothered him. Again, the sinking feeling crept over him.

"I'll need to work on Judge Hardy, but I think I can get him to agree to five years before you could petition to return."

"What about the other guys? What deals can they get?"

"Only you and Will Lampley will get a deal like another country. Will's a lawyer, like you, young and persuasive, and he has relatives in Australia. The rest of the boys are looking at long prison terms. For most of them, this is the fourth or fifth offense and the most serious one. Hardy wants them stopped cold. This is your first offense, but the judge is worried about you. He's thinking you're another Parnell, but worse because you're more militant."

"Will Lampley's been terrific. I like working with him. I'd hate to lose that."

Callahan laughed. "He will too, but he's practical. He said he'd go to Australia to avoid jail. And he said he'll be back."

"Yeah." Jeremiah seemed lost in thought. His eyes surveyed the barren room then stared down at the desktop. His mind sorted through the little he knew of Boston, of the United States. Were there lots of Irish in Boston, his uncle was there, so maybe. What would he do there? Be a common laborer in a factory or in a roadside, digging ditches? The unknowns still tore at his soul. The court was ripping him away from his country, his family, from Edinburgh, from his well-planned future of a barrister fighting for Irish independence.

Callahan let the moments pass in silence. Finally, he said, "What do you think? Is the US better than jail time?"

Again, he waited as the silence extended. "Oh yes, I nearly forgot, yer da said yer uncle will take you into his law practice as an apprentice so you can finish yer studies and become a bona fide attorney."

"My uncle agreed to that?" He shook his head and ran his fingers through his bushy brown hair. The idea provided an immediate lift to his spirits. "Hmmm, that's a special twist."

"Think of it, Jeremiah. Five years away, you've seen and experienced another country. You'll come back an attorney. You'll have experience and some money. You'll be more valuable than ever. You might be ready to run for parliament."

Jeremiah rubbed the side of his face. The bristles of his beard were noticeable after two days of no shaving. "What do mum and da think of all this?"

Joseph Callahan had been with Fenians expelled from the country before and the parents had wailed and moaned, everyone unhappy. But Sean Knox was different. Callahan could tell the father was angry at the boy. Callahan had concluded that the old man believed the boy was a problem and had embarrassed the family. His father seemed happy, even relieved, that Jeremiah would be out of the country and away from such militancy. The mother, he couldn't tell. She was more quiet on the phone. "Well, they seemed relieved that there was an alternative to prison, and your da said his brother owed him many favors. It was a good time to collect on those."

"How about my brothers and sister, do they know? Can I see them before I go?"

"Since you seem to be agreeing, these are the things I can discuss with Judge Hardy. He has a lot of power now with all this rebellion happening, and he has lots of flexibility too. I'll work with him to see what can be done."

"When do I see him?"

"Your date for filing charges is in three days. It may come sooner, but it will not be later."

"I understand. But how quickly will I be shipped to Boston, and where do I stay until that happens."

"You'll remain in Kilmainham. I'm pretty sure of that, and I'll work to get you a better cell. I'll try to get you to the East Wing, cleaner cells, no dampness, windows and heating, I understand."

Chapter 5

When Jeremiah returned to his cell, there were three prisoners milling around the small space. "Where are the others?" he asked.

"Off like you, and maybe they won't return. Maybe we'll have more room."

As the day progressed, a book cart went by, and Jeremiah chose a Bible from its stack. He sat to read, others talked quietly or rested against the wall. As dusk neared, only four remained in the cell, and Jeremiah suggested they play Irish Four Fingers to determine who got the beds for the night. He was unlucky in the game and spent the night again on the cold stone floor. The urn of stew arrived and the identical slop of the night before was the evening meal along with one loaf of bread for the four men. The four men ate hungrily, the stew and bread disappearing in minutes. Their talk explored what happened to the other men. Questions arose over what prisons or sections of this prison were used for thieves, for murderers, for political prisoners. If their cases were settled quickly, did it mean long or short sentences? The experienced prisoners regaled Jeremiah with tales of punishment, the length of prison terms, details on the cells of Kilmainham, prison food, the lack of exercise and visitation. Slowly, the information about life in prison became more real to him, less idealized. It became less appealing as a place to write, to reach the public and bring attention to the issues and consequences of British rule. He began to recognize that a prison term was a hard way to earn a badge of honor for revolutionary activities.

He thought again about Callahan's proposed deal, and it became more compelling. The aspects of a different country and new living conditions began to settle more acceptably in his mind. His loss of Fenian activity, university life, and education in law dismayed him.

He'd planned to work in a prestigious firm in Dublin upon gradu-ation. Judge Wicklow had assured him of a spot in his former firm. With his income from law, he planned to devote all his spare time on Fenian activities. To lose that was a big loss, but he'd made his bed through his activism. He knew that and had to accept the con-sequences. That was the price of pushing the fight aggressively at the British. Now the news from his uncle was promising, an apprentice-ship in his law office. He'd still be able to work in the field of law. Leaving Edinburgh was hard, but he had to be realistic. The offer of America was better than jail. As he tried to sleep on the cold floor, he was restless and uncomfortable. The same dream kept occurring throughout the night; he was walking down an empty country road devoid of all life, no buildings and no vegetation. A storm was brew-ing ahead of him, and there was no place to shelter him from the storm. He woke with a jolt, shaking his head to erase the images, but as he rubbed his eyes, his thoughts were becoming clear. He resolved to tell Callahan at their next meeting that he would accept the pro-posed deal.

The next day, the four men in his cell were led up the stairs and out a door into an enclosed yard. There other prisoners walked, talked, while some ran around the enclave, and others did push-ups and other exercises. This lasted about an hour by his estimate, and the four were collected and brought to a large meeting room where they were seated at benches. Across from them and separated by a five-foot barrier sat their visitors. Jeremiah saw Callahan sitting, awaiting him, and assumed the other visitors were barristers as well. With their heads appearing above the barriers, Jeremiah conveyed his conclusion on the deal to be sent to America.

Callahan could see that the decision was not easy and had come with hard thought. They discussed how to inform his family and how to handle the forthcoming hearing with the judge. Callahan thought Jeremiah would face the judge in two days, and there would be time for family visits before deportation.

Callahan was wrong. Early the next morning, a guard rattled his keys on the cell door as he opened it and called for Jeremiah. He placed manacles on his wrists, and they walked up several flights of stairs into a brightly lit room filled with long tables. Although the room could seat hundreds of men, only a few of the long tables were occupied by prisoners. No one looked up as he entered; their heads were down devouring their food. Jeremiah could smell hot meats cooking and porridge steaming in large vats. He was ushered to a wide bathroom off the main room and shown to the sinks where toothbrushes, shaving cream, shaving brushes, and blades were sacked. His manacles were released, and he was told to wash up, shave, and return to the main room. Guards watched him carefully, ensuring that he did not attempt to slit his wrists or steal one of the straight-edge razors. Clean and with his hair neatly combed, his pants, shirt, and jacket brushed clean from the dirt and grit of the cell. He and his guard walked into a room where the food was assembled in deep trays of eggs, porridge, bangers, breads, pots of tea, and water. He was given a food tray and told to help himself.

"What's next?" he asked the guard.

"First, yee'll eat, then we go to see your barrister. That's all I know. So be quick about it."

The food was not the same quality of his mother's or their cook Mary O'Donnel's, but it was the best meal Jeremiah had in days, and he devoured the breakfast in minutes. His guard saw him place down his fork and said, "Let's go," and hauled him to the staircase. Following a few other prisoners on the stairs, they made their way to a corridor with doors on either side. The guard studied his notepad momentarily and pushed Jeremiah toward room 608. The room was windowless and filled with six sets of benches; there were no attorneys in the room. Several guards stood around the walls of the room, and Jeremiah counted ten prisoners seated on the benches. He joined an empty spot and glanced for familiar faces and saw none.

"All right, laddies, let's go!" shouted a guard after they had been seated for fifteen minutes. They were brought out to a courtyard and led to a paddy wagon much like the one that had brought Jeremiah to Kilmainham Gaol several days earlier. The clip-clop of the horses seemed eerily familiar to him as he stared out the narrow window to determine their direction and to find a familiar landmark. He found none until the horses slowed, and he could see the dome of the Four

Courts in the distance. *Damn,* he thought, *could I be going in front of the judge today? It's too early. It's too soon.* He worried. *Has Callahan's plan broken down? Is the deal off?* He began to sweat and stir nervously in his seat. Next to him, the prisoner commented, "Calm down, laddie, the worst they'll do is kill yee." And he laughed heartily.

He stared hard at the man. His gaze severe, and the man turned away from him. But the interaction had calmed him. *I can take whatever they give me,* he thought. *I've done this for my country and have nothing to be ashamed of. Nothing but pride in my work. And I'll tell the court that.*

They left the wagon and were led into the chambers of the Four Courts. The massive entry hall was overwhelming to Jeremiah. It was majestic, and it was a goal of his that one day he would plead cases in the building. But now, he came under different circumstances and was herded into a waiting room with the other prisoners. One by one, they were called to their respective court, and Jeremiah had not seen or heard from Callahan. At last, his name was called, manacles removed, and he walked into a spacious courtroom where the judge, Judge Hardy, sat above him behind a beautifully carved desk, his firm gaze watching Jeremiah. Callahan stood up, and Jeremiah was led to a chair beside his barrister. The chairs were off to the side of the court and below the dais of the judge.

Jeremiah's mind rushed into the change of time. What were the reasons for an early date with Judge Hardy? It was days earlier than Callahan had predicted. He shuffled his feet left to right, had the deal fallen through, and was the judge going to jail him permanently? There were no other Fenians in the court, and he'd seen none as he proceeded to the judge's courtroom. Did the absence of fellow Fenians have any meaning, any significance? He glanced at Callahan for some signal, some form of reassurance, but got none. His body felt weak, and he started to sit.

"Remain standing, Jeremiah," Callahan whispered as Judge Hardy peered down at them.

The bailiff from the far side of the court announced, "Jeremiah Knox, Your Honor, has been charged by the Crown prosecutor under the Treason Felony Act of 1848 for actions taken against the Crown on the dates of July 15 through July 25 of the year 1891."

"Be seated," the judge said.

Judge Hardy continued to stare at Jeremiah as if he could not believe his eyes. It seemed like an hour to Jeremiah before he spoke. Finally, he cleared his throat. "I have reviewed the facts of this case with the Crown prosecutor and with Mr. Knox's representative, the honorable Joseph Callahan. It is my considered judgment that Jeremiah Knox, despite the young age of nineteen, is a danger to the peace and security of Ireland."

Jeremiah could hardly believe what he was hearing. He thought the damn judge was going to put him away forever. He arched his head, stretching his neck. Callahan leaned over and whispered, "Relax."

Judge Hardy continued to stare hard at Jeremiah. "When considering the advantage of a fine legal education at the University at Edinburgh, his actions on the dates cited by the bailiff show a marked indifference to the laws of Ireland, indeed a callous disregard of said laws. By dent of his education, his inflammatory, and I reluctantly admit, his very persuasive oratorical skills, I deem Mr. Knox to be a danger to the country. Thereby, and with the agreement of the Unites States and the city of Boston, I expel Mr. Knox from Ireland, and he is to be deported to the city of Boston at the soonest possible date."

"If his sponsors in Boston and the United States discover that he continues his rebellion toward his native country, they have agreed to return him to Ireland and this court for resentencing." He stopped to sip at a glass of water by his right hand. The hand was firm, Jeremiah noted, no trembling. The judge then glanced again at Jeremiah. "Under special conditions, Mr. Knox may apply to Ireland for restatement of residential privileges in five years. The special conditions are to include and not be limited to no active involvement with the Fenian movement while in the United States, no participation in any societies in the United Sates that advocate or fund the removal of Great Britain from Ireland, and full adherence to all laws of the United States." Again he paused to sip from his glass of water. "Mr. Knox, please stand."

Jeremiah rose. "Mr. Knox, with your signature on these documents, you will agree to leave this country on the next available ship departing Liverpool for Boston. I have notice from my office there is such a ship sailing on September 1, 1891, and my office has booked you on that ship. With your passage on this ship, I hope, in all sincerity, to never see you in this courtroom again. Bailiff, present the papers to Mr. Knox and secure his signature and that of his representative, Mr. Callahan."

He watched as Jeremiah signed the agreement then slammed his gavel down and said, "Case closed."

Jeremiah sunk in his chair and grabbed Callahan's arm. "You did it—no jail. Thank you. How can I ever thank you?"

"It's okay, Jeremiah. You can thank me by staying clean in the US and coming back here in five years to continue the fight. I see you in parliament, lad, I really do."

"Jesus, Joseph, I've lost track of time. When is September 1?" He looked at the sheaf of papers the bailiff brought him from the judge; his eyes riveted to two pages.

Callahan said, "It's tomorrow, Jeremiah. Judge Hardy's booked you on a ferry out of Dublin this afternoon. You'll board the Boston bound ship in Liverpool tomorrow morning. As I said to you a few days ago, he wants you out of here. It's an incredible compliment to how impressed he is with you, but he's moving fast because of that perspective."

"Oh god." Jeremiah wiped his brow. "Part of the deal is no visits. I leave without seeing any of my friends or my family."

"That's what he wants, Jeremiah. No big or small farewells for you. He thinks you could start riots."

"What now, then?" Jeremiah asked.

"We'll get a ride to the port, and you'll get on the next ferry to Liverpool." Callahan had worried privately that Jeremiah might run at this point, but Judge Hardy had covered that possibility with a well-drawn plan.

Two burly wardens of the court had joined them at their chairs and were directing them out of Judge Hardy's courtroom. Their blue suits were an odd mixture of a suit and a uniform, and they spoke with authority. "Mr. Callahan, your client is still a ward of the court until he has boarded the S/S *Caledonia* in Liverpool and is on his way to America. We will be with him from Dublin to Liverpool and from Liverpool until the ship departs."

"Yes, yes," Callahan said. His memory forced back a few years. "I remember now. It's the procedure we followed with the Sullivan lad a few years back."

"Yes, sir, it's the exact same procedure. The judge wants to ensure his decision is fulfilled. We'll accompany Mr. Knox here to the ferry, on the ferry, and to a hotel at dockside and on to the *Caledonia* tomorrow."

"I'd like to stay with him at least until he's on the ferry."

"At your pleasure, sir."

Jeremiah was slowly awakening to the prospect of leaving the country and felt totally unprepared. "What'll I do for money? Good grief, I have no change of clothes, no kit of any kind," he blurted.

"Yer passage is paid for by the Court, and yee'll have two meals a day with yer ticket. Yer in steerage, but the food's okay. Yee'll go to America with the clothes on yer back, just like everybody else." The warden chortled.

Callahan said, "I'll loan you some money, Jeremiah, and I'll get it back from yer da, and you can pay him back as soon as you get settled."

The wardens moved the two men quickly into the courtyard where a carriage awaited them. They moved rapidly through the streets to the port at the River Liffey.

"This is moving very fast, Joseph. I won't be able to see my … my brothers, sister, will I?"

Callahan said, "As soon as you're on the ferry, I'll call your home and tell them what happened in court. Maybe some of them might be able to get to Liverpool."

Jeremiah snuffed at the thought. *Not to worry*, he thought, *that won't happen. It's too sudden, too fast for da or mum. I'll write from the ship and send it when I land.* "Joseph, tell them not to worry. I'll send a letter as soon as I can."

The carriage came to a halt at Dublin's harbor. Callahan searched through the window for the ferry pier and spotted it. "Let's unload here, Jeremiah." The young man laughed.

"I have nothing to unload." He spread his arms wide, emphasizing the emptiness, the absence of any belongings. "I go to America with the shirt on my back."

Callahan reached into his vest pocket and retrieved a money clip thick with British pounds. He peeled off a host of notes and gave them to Jeremiah. "Use this money to buy some clothes in Liverpool. Hopefully, you'll have some time there."

The two wardens had left the carriage and stood beside Jeremiah. One spoke in cold tones, "If we have time, we'll go to a shop. Otherwise, it's straight to the ship." He looked at the papers in his hands and said, "The *Caledonia*. When this paper says Mr. Knox is to board, we're walking him on the ship whether he has clothes or not."

Jeremiah and Callahan laughed. Jeremiah studied the two guards briefly. No humor in them at all, he thought. He wanted to find lightness in the moment; he was being expelled from his country, and he wanted to find some degree of levity, some buoyancy of spirit that this was not the end of life. Sadness would come, but he didn't want just now. His mind was whirling. He fought for clarity from the shock of his sentence, but deportation was hard to digest. He struggled to grasp what would happen on the ship. How would he find his uncle's home? How would he survive in a new country despite his uncle's promises? He summoned his courage, reaching deep inside for the confidence that had always been a strong part of him. "Gentlemen," he said, "I've accepted my fate, wrong as it is, and I won't embarrass you. I won't run or jump in the harbor. But I do want to get a fresh shirt or two, some undergarments, another pair of pants, and maybe a jacket."

Unruffled, the lead warden said, "I'm repeatin' myself. We'll find a shop iffens we have time. We're stayin' overnight at a rooming house on the wharf, and the ship leaves the dock at seven tomorrow morning, so we'll not have much time to find a shop, but we'll see."

Callahan inserted, "Fine, gentlemen, fine … Now, I'd like a moment with Jeremiah before you board the ferry."

"Hurry it up, Mr. Callahan. The ferry's tootin' her horn already. She's ready to go."

Callahan took Jeremiah by the arm and led him two steps away. "Laddie, I'll call your parents and tell them what happened. You should call too once you're settled overnight in Liverpool. Now here are my final thoughts. Once you're on board the ship and when you land in Boston, people from the Fenians and other Irish nationalists will know your name. You're a hero to them, and they're likely to look you up. Stay away from them Jeremiah. They're trouble and will get you sent back to Judge Hardy. We don't want that, do we?" He searched Jeremiah's eyes for understanding, for agreement. All he could see was thoughtfulness. So he repeated, "Don't break the judge's agreement. Don't get active with these people, okay?"

"I understand," Jeremiah replied. "Do the Irish in Boston and elsewhere in America know what's going on here and support it."

"Yes, they do, and a considerable amount of money for the cause comes from the Irish in New York, Boston, and other Eastern cities. So beware. Wait till you get back before you get active again."

Jeremiah clapped him on the shoulder, expressing a comfort he didn't feel. "Fine, Joseph, fine … I'll be a good boy. Thank you for all you've done, and I'll write to you once I'm settled. I hope the five years goes by fast."

"Callahan grabbed Jeremiah by the shoulders and shook him gently. You're a brave lad, a smart lad. Be good and come back soon." He turned his head away quickly, "Better get to the ferry, the steward's waving the last passengers on board."

Chapter 6

Jeremiah, his shoulders hunched under a summer jacket, walked the deck of the ferry and watched the coast of Ireland disappear. Not normally emotional, he had a sinking feeling about leaving Ireland. The country didn't want him, didn't approve of his ideas and strategies. He felt a flood of sadness wash through him, and he got angry with himself. Was it his fault the plan was discovered at St. Grellann's? He'd hid it well. Who snitched the location of the plan to the British? No need to mope, no time for remorse—it was over, and now he'd live with the consequences. He liked what the Fenians had said about him, "Cool as a cucumber, cerebral and quiet," yet these images didn't feel right at the moment. He felt emotions rushing through him of loss, failure, and loneliness. He was a criminal but couldn't admit that. He was alone on this voyage, no friends with him, going to a country where he knew two people, distant relatives. He pushed these feelings down and willed them to become silent. *You're bloody and bruised, old boy*, he thought, *but you're still alive, not in jail, so you have choices ahead of you.* He admonished himself as he strode the deck. *You can rise again.*

It was late in the day; the sun was beginning to recede through gray clouds. As the ferry pushed through the waves of the harbor, the breeze from the ocean chilled his face, and his long hair was swept back away from his broad forehead. He ignored his two wardens as he nodded to passengers who tipped their hats to him but did not see anyone he knew. After an hour of pacing around the deck, he went into the passengers' lounge and took an empty seat on the wooden benches, his watchers close behind. The murmur of voices flooding the lounge were pleasant. He let the noise wash over him and closed his eyes for a moment, slowing the whirl of thoughts in his mind. He began to let the drama of the day drift to a quieter place. He knew he was beginning an important journey, an odyssey that would change his life, move his life from one platform or trajectory to another. What that new platform would be was unknown, yet in the soft timbre of voices around him, he sensed comfort. It was as if they were telling him to not be afraid.

The two guards were never far away, and as the ferry docked in Liverpool, they joined him side by side as escorts to the shabby boarding house two blocks away. The worn white shingles with chipped paint had withstood harsh winter storms for years, and the old structure was a sturdy harbor site for sailors and a farewell lodging for deportees from the English court system. Jeremiah's room had two beds, one for him and one for a warden. The other warden took a chair, placed it by the door, and sat protecting the egress from the room. Jeremiah glanced at him and said, "That's an uncomfortable place to sleep."

"I'd take your bed, but the judge said no to that. Judge Hardy was clear, so I'll switch with Harry after a few hours."

"I want to call my parents."

"We'll see if there's a telephone in the lobby, and we'll watch you make the call."

He knew they worried that he might be arranging an escape, and he laughed quietly at their concern. There was no way he could avoid going to America. They shadowed him so closely they seemed like part of his skin. In the room, they sat against the door, and at night, they said they would handcuff him to his bed. There was no way could he escape.

Jeremiah talked at them, wearing them down with his logic and good sense. There were two of them. How could he run away? His guards annoyed him, but they didn't push their authority. They were like a suffocating smoke, always there and hard to get rid of. He badgered them with his requests, plebian as they were, until they gave in.

"I'll make the call tonight when my parents are most likely at home. And now can we walk the streets, find some clothes?"

They strolled the streets of the harbor where they found a clothing shop. Carefully examining his money, he purchased two sets of underwear, socks, two shirts, a jacket, and pants. He wanted to look decent, presentable on board the ship, and with fresh new clothes, make a good impression on his uncle and aunt. The shop provided him with a small cotton sack where he placed the new items along with a shaving kit. "Anything else, Your Highness?" The lead guard asked.

Jeremiah remained in the doorway of the shop and pulled Callahan's remaining money from his pockets and sorted through it, counting carefully. "No, gentlemen, unless you wish to carry my purchases." He smiled at them.

"Up yours, laddie. Let's get off the street. My feet are killing me."

Jeremiah studied the roll of currency in his hands and kept them shielded from the bills. He had a substantial set of funds from Callahan. He said, "I must husband what's left with care. I have a long journey ahead of me."

"Yee won't be buyin' cocktails for the ladies on the boat, the judge sent yee away with no money." The warden laughed.

"You're right, I'll have to forego any ideas of romance."

"Best be," the other warden offered. "Yee bein' a major criminal and terrorist. Yee'll scare the shit out of everyone." He laughed long and hard, edging his companion with a hit to the ribs to enjoy his wit.

Jeremiah frowned as they plodded back to the boarding house. They stopped at a dockside cafe where his wardens had glasses of ale, greasy fish with boiled potatoes; he tried the same but found the oily food disgusting. He swallowed a few mouthfuls, then his mind drifted to the *Caledonia*. He wondered what the ship's captain and crew knew about him. Were there others on board sent away from the British Isles by the courts? It worried him, and he decided then and there to stay by himself and avoid contact with other passengers.

As the sky darkened, they left the cafe, returning to the lobby of the boarding house. From the telephone in the matron's office, he called his parent's home, and there was no answer. That was unusual, he thought, so he tried twice more, and connections could not be made. His wardens, sensing he was trying to get a message to the Fenians, said, "That's enough, Knox. Back to the room with yee."

He felt empty; he missed discussing the events at court over the past few days, the sense that some kind of closure would fill the void in his soul. He was still thinking about his father's harsh words. He wondered if his father had calmed down. Would he be surprised or pleased with the judge's decision? He worried about his mother. She'd been sick, unusual for her. Would his exile make her worse? She was strong in spirit and mind, and that thought relaxed him. He'd write to them once on board and mail the letter as soon as he reached Boston. He'd make it a long letter describing the voyage and his first impressions of his uncle's house and law office. The idea gave him some comfort. With these thoughts, he stretched out on his bed, turned his back to the wardens, and tried to sleep. His right wrist, handcuffed to the edge of the metal bed, limited his movement and pinched his wrist each time he moved. After a short time, the wardens stopped talking, and the room went quiet and dark. Jeremiah, constrained by the handcuff, moved carefully on the lumpy mattress and was unable to find a comfortable spot. Sleep would not come as thoughts of the voyage, of five years away from Ireland, of being separated from his studies at Edinburgh, and being removed from the Fenians raced through his consciousness. His mind played with these worries over and over, interfering with his desire to relax and sleep.

Dawn came slowly for him, and he welcomed the walk to the *Caledonia*. He was getting on with his prison sentence. Leaving the shores of England was no longer an abstraction; it was real. The gangway to the ship was in front of him. When he boarded the *Caledonia*, his expectations of steerage were confirmed. It was a crowded hold with rows of bunks along one side and long tables on the other for dining or sitting between meals. He noticed small cabins at either end of the hold and queried the purser about their availability. The purser, his blue jacket over gray slacks with the quasi-military cap on his head, regarded Jeremiah with thoughtful up and down screening. "You're an educated man, aye?"

"Yes, sir, Edinburgh, law."

"Have you a pound sterling on you?"

"I might just have one, yes, sir."

"Well, it seems that we've had a cancellation for that cabin down on the far right. It's yours for a pound. With that cabin, you'll have rights to go to the other decks, go to the library, the main lounge and bar in first class. It's a good deal, sir."

Jeremiah turned his back on the man and fished in his pocket for the roll of Callahan's money. He found a pound note, turned and handed it to the purser.

"Done," he said. "Here's the key. You'll enjoy the other decks."

"Well worth it, and thank you."

Jeremiah unlocked the small cabin, placed his cotton bag on the bed, and went to wash his hands in the bathroom. Ah, a bathroom of my own, a bed with privacy and access to the library. He stretched his long frame on the bed until he heard the whistle and went to the lower deck to watch the ship pull away from the pier. Below him, he saw the two guards, hands behind their backs, talking to each other as the ship moved slowly out of the harbor. They saw him and pointed, and he returned their observation with a salute, the Irish salute. He walked around the lower deck, gaining familiarity with the ship, then moved to the upper deck. He was stopped by a crew member who then let him pass once Jeremiah displayed his cabin key. Circling the main deck, it was evident that the passengers were better dressed, older and more convivial than in the deck below. He searched out the library; it was roomy. At least twenty by twenty, he thought. And the highly polished wall shelves were stacked with books. He found many to his liking and planned to return in the evening and dig into the works of Immanuel Kant.

It was late afternoon, and the ship had moved into the open ocean. He heard noise in the steerage cabin and went to explore the activity. Beer was being served from a large barrel, and he selected a tankard and filled it. He met several fellow passengers and sat down to talk, but had to avoid the reasons for his stay in the United States. He hadn't prepared answers to these questions, so he started joking with other passengers and swilling more and more beer. A lass with a lovely face and long body came to the table and sat next to him. "Coleen," she said and introduced herself. She appeared friendly and tried to get him to slow down his drinking. He toasted her beauty and continued to drink. Shyly, she asked him why he was drinking so much. Was he sad about leaving Ireland? Was there an injustice, a lost love or no hopes for work that were bothering him? He was slowly descending into a stupor and knew he might say too much. His assault on the beer keg was unusual for him, normally a moderate drinker. He knew he was drinking to drown his loss, his mistakes with the Fenians that placed him at this table. He mumbled to Coleen that he needed to go to his cabin. She helped him to his feet and guided him to the door.

At that moment, she said to him, "I'll be back with yee when you're right. I know yee'll want to talk about what botherin' yerself."

He didn't remember a word she said when he saw her the next morning, his head pounding, his hands shaking. She smiled at him and moved aside so he could join her for breakfast at the long communal table.

The first few days of passage were smooth, the air clear, the winds low, and the *Caledonia* cut easily through the waves. The fourth day brought a storm. The ship tossed, which kept many passengers in their cabins, and Jeremiah was alone in the library, reading Kant's *Critique of Pure Reason*. His head down and riveted on the meaning of Kant's work. He barely heard the words. "My, you're a serious soul. I've seen you here every day."

The conversations with Phoebe Cronkite in the library began to open him up to meeting others. He found he could talk of his plans in Boston without revealing the reasons for his departure from Ireland. He began to trust these interactions, and they began to occur with greater frequency. In the evenings, he drank beer with Coleen or had cocktails with Phoebe or her friends on the upper decks. He did not talk about himself, which was refreshing to them, and gave him an air of mystery. These afternoon and evening sessions helped pass the time and enabled him to shift from moments of painful remembrance of the botched Fenian raid to hours of gay conversation. The days began with reading in the library, followed by walks and conversations with one of the young women. Then in the late evening, he took pen to ink and paper and wrote his letters.

After penning notes to his family, he wrote to the dean of the law school, informing him of his travels in America and that he would not return for the fall term. His next letter was to Ian McCracken at McCracken & Sons of Edinburgh. He met the sculptor when he entered his studio to admire a statue of Apollo. The sculptor's shop was located near Jeremiah's apartment, a few blocks down the hilly street. On a Saturday in early September, with little to do, he entered McCracken's studio to search for the proprietor. Hearing noise in the back of the shop, he discovered a host of students working on a variety of stone carvings. A thin, wiry man clothed in a dust-covered smock gazed up from one student and waved to him. They talked about Jeremiah's law studies and his interest and experience in stone-work. Jeremiah had found, with good organization in his class work, that he had ample free time on weekends. McCracken invited him to his Saturday instructional sessions, and Jeremiah attended each Saturday faithfully for two years, slowly earning great praise from the well-known sculptor. During these Saturday sessions and in the late afternoons when possible, Jeremiah advanced his skill beyond what John Francis had taught him. He thought stonework was a wonderful hobby and one he hoped to sustain all his life.

In his best longhand, he wrote to the sculptor:

> Dear Ian,
>
> It is with great sadness that I inform you that I'll not be attending Edinburgh Law at next term. My plans have been radically changed this summer, and I'm on my way to America. More on that later. For the moment, I'd like to thank you for your instruction in sculpture and your kind comments on my progress. You enabled me to work in your studio at my own hours and convenience, which was most helpful given my studies at the university.
>
> I'm still astounded from your comment in June when you declared that I should give up law

and work as a sculptor. That comment, that compliment will stay with me forever. Thank you. Somehow, and the feeling is deep inside, I sense that I will return to sculpture at some point in my life, and it is your instruction that has made it more than a hobby to me.

Sincerely,
Jeremiah

He placed the addresses on the envelopes and sealed them. He thought about McCracken's parting comment one day when he said, after complimenting Jeramiah on his work, "Nations, laws, and lawyers come and go. *Only art endures.*"

The thought made him smile as he pushed the letters to the back of the desk. He'd mail them from Boston. He glanced at the envelopes and thought, *This is the end or at least an end.* He put his head down on his hands and rested both on the tabletop. A deep sadness washed over him. He let the memories of his law school classes, his university friends, and the days at McCracken's studio flow through his mind. He remained in that position until the bell rang for dinner.

Chapter 7

As he shuttled down the gangplank, he looked for signs yielding his name and saw none. With guidance from the customs agents, the herd of passengers went into Boston's customs house for processing. In the melee of passengers, he lost track of Phoebe and Coleen and concentrated on securing the proper documents for admission to the United States. The documents were stuffed in his cotton sack, and he rummaged through his clothes to find them. He glanced over them, examining the court documents and his uncle's agreement of sponsorship. The passengers were herded into pens where agents asked questions. They separated travelers with obvious health issues and briefly examined the documents of all passengers. The customs agent seemed unconcerned with Jeremiah's papers and whisked him through by checking him off the *Caledonia*'s passenger list. He left the pens and entered a large reception hall; his eyes wandered around the vast room, looking for his uncle. He hoped to recognize him after a gap of ten years. Instead, he saw a poster held by a young man with curly brown hair, his name printed boldly on the whiteboard. Jeremiah waved to him, and the young man yelled, "Mr. Knox!" He offered his hand as Jeremiah approached. "I'm Henry. Follow me. Your uncle will meet you at a restaurant nearby."

With his small cotton bag in hand, they crossed the cobblestone square to a narrow street. Two-story buildings on either side blocked the September sun, producing a chilly breeze on Jeremiah's neck. They walked a few blocks to the Union Oyster House. Jeremiah thought he was back in Ireland. The restaurant's weathered exterior, the deep-red bricks pockmarked with age spoke to its founding in pre-revolutionary days. Its wide board floor covered with scattered sawdust, polished wooden walls, round wooden tables with iron-backed chairs reminded him of the pubs in Dublin. The waiters in white aprons slung low on their waists and draping down to their knees moved quickly around the tables. They carried round trays of beer glasses or plates of oysters balanced on one hand held above their heads.

Jeremiah smiled at Henry. "This is like the pubs in Ireland."

"Your uncle thought so. He wanted you to feel at home on your first day."

"Ah, Henry, hello. I see you have a guest." The greeting came from a well-dressed man in a suit with a striped shirt and tie. He had a confident and knowing air; he stood at a tall receiving desk, his elbow on a book of reservations. He studied Jeremiah carefully and asked, "Is this the young man from Stradbally?" Henry nodded.

"Welcome to Boston, young fella," said the receptionist. "May your stay be pleasant." He left the reception stand and pointed, "This way to Mr. Knox's table." He seated Jeremiah, and Henry took a seat beside him.

Henry said, "I'll stay until your uncle arrives, then I'll return to work."

The restaurant seemed to become more alive when James Knox walked in. Jeremiah recognized him right away. He was as tall as his father and had similar facial characteristics, but it was his walk or strut of confidence that Jeremiah remembered, and that was in full display. The reception man was all manners, bowing and scraping. A few gentlemen from other tables rose and waved to his uncle. He acknowledged the greetings, shaking a few hands as he proceeded to the table. There, he stretched out a big hand. "Welcome to America, Jeremiah. What's it been, ten years since I last saw you? You've gotten so tall."

His uncle didn't seem as large to him now as he did back in Stradbally those many years ago. He was nine at the time, no wonder. Now he was half a head taller than his uncle, and the older man was much heavier. "Aye, Jeremiah, you're tall and dark-haired like the Knoxes, not fair like your mother's clan."

"Da claims we must have some Viking blood in us bein' so much taller than other folks."

"Whatever it is, it works, son. We stand out everywhere, just as you've done." He glanced at Henry. "Thank you, Henry. I'll see you back at the office. I should be there by two."

"Yes, sir." Henry picked up his hat and quickly departed.

"Hard-working boy, that one," James Knox mumbled as he picked up his napkin and wiped his mouth. "He'll do all right."

"Is he a lawyer in your firm, Uncle James?"

"No, son, no, he's not got the brains for that, but he's good at all the messengering we need done around town and with the courts. Let's order as I need to get back, and I want to tell you what's up here in Boston."

"I'm all ears, sir."

James gave him a quick look then turned to the waiter. "I'll have my usual, George." Turning to Jeremiah, he said, "That's a dozen oysters and a draft beer. What would you like?"

"I'll have the same."

The reception man had returned to their table and said to James, "Mr. Knox, there's a man at the front door, see him." He pointed to a short swarthy man with thin black hair dressed in a worn suit standing next to his desk. "What I mean is he wishes to speak to the gentleman with you."

"By Jesus, already." James stood and strode over to the reception desk and spoke to the man, his hands pushing out in sharp gestures. The man raised his right hand in a half fist and waved it in James's face, turned on his heel, and left.

"What's that all about?" Jeremiah inquired.

"It's what I worried about when I agreed with your dad to sponsor you. We'll talk more of it at dinner tonight." He brought his eyes up to Jeremiah's and held them there. "He's a well-known troublemaker among the dock workers. He scans all the lists coming in from Ireland, so he knows about you. I'm guessing he knows what you've done. I told him to stay away unless he wanted big trouble."

Several questions came to Jeremiah, but he decided to wait. "Well, perhaps tonight when you have more time, I can hear about this."

"Yes, definitely. For now, I want you to take a carriage over to a place called South Boston. You'll go to the top of the hill near a park. Tell the carriage man that you're to go to M Street number 48. There, your Aunt Sheila will settle you in our guest room, and we'll meet at dinner to discuss your next few weeks and months in America."

"Do you want to know what happened in Ireland and why I had to leave?"

"I know your situation, Jeremiah, and I'll hear your version, but as a lawyer, I've talked to your lawyer, Mr. Callahan, and to Judge Hardy as well as to my brother and your mom. I have a good picture." He lifted an oyster to his lips and slurped it down in one gulp. "But to be continued at dinner."

"Will I see any of the cousins?"

They're all out of the house and away. "Tina's in New York with her hubby, as is John, who's working on Wall Street. Benji's in the law firm with me, but he's in Washington on a case right now." As they ate the oysters, conversation slowed down, and Jeremiah was hesitant to initiate new topics. He didn't expect to carry the conversation, and his uncle seemed quite content to finish the oysters and finish his beer in silence. It seemed awkward to Jeremiah, but his uncle had covered the topics he wanted. The rest would come that evening.

James paid the bill and escorted Jeremiah to a waiting carriage outside the restaurant. He gave the driver the fare. Jeremiah watched the waterfront pass by as they clopped south around the several channels that separated the heart of Boston from South Boston. James Knox had come there thirty-five years earlier. Having been second in line in the family, the farm went to Sean, his older brother, and Jeremiah's father, and he had no interest in going into the clergy. At first, he lived in boarding houses along the South Boston waterfront. Evenings he would walk alone up M and N streets, admiring the handsome stone townhouses high on the hill above the harbor and Fort Point Channel. He vowed that he'd own one of those houses and was prepared to work toward that goal. First, he found a job as a runner and petty clerk for a law firm on Custom House Square. He studied the firm's law books at night, and after two years, having spotted errors in the partner's use of case precedents, he convinced the managing partner to allow him to apprentice law there. For six long years, he toiled at pedestrian tasks of research, studying the growing code of law in Massachusetts and the type of law that the growing middle class in Boston needed, deeds, titles, property rights and the maritime law affecting the goods traded in and out of the harbor. At age thirty, he married and moved his bride to an apartment on Farragut Street, overlooking the harbor. He was moving up. In those years, he took Sheila on his evening walks up M and N streets, showing her the houses he liked, and they shared the dream of ownership someday. By age forty, he had his own law firm, had a lock on all the Irish businesses in Boston, and the private legal work of all the owners. He moved Sheila and their three children to a four-story stone townhouse on M Street and hired a maid to help her with the cooking, washing, and cleaning.

As Jeremiah gazed at the houses around James's fine home, he knew his uncle had done well. His father had done as well, but it was clear, his uncle was a success in the new country. From the conversation with the carriage driver, he gathered his uncle was well known in Boston and not only in the circles of the Irish. He also observed at lunch that his uncle was hard driving, much like his father. He stepped from the carriage, his small cotton bag in his right hand, and rang the doorbell on the house. A pretty maid in a gray cotton dress with a white apron opened the door and called for Mrs. Knox.

Sheila Knox was as quiet and reserved as her husband was loud and brash. Her petite body disguised her strength of mind and a willingness to use it when her husband was too confident or willing to take risks with the family's well-being. Graciously, she led Jeremiah to a sitting room and ordered tea inquiring about his trip on the *Caledonia* and the health of his parents and siblings. They traded stories for a half hour, and then she showed him to his bedroom, one of the rooms formerly used by her son, the lawyer. The lone window had a wide view of the harbor and beach below. He opened the window, and a cool breeze off the ocean provided a fresh and sharp sea fragrance to the room. Jeremiah thanked her, drank in the cool air, stretched his long legs on the bed, and went instantly to sleep.

A knock on the door roused him. The light was dim as he walked to the door. The maid told him the family was in the sitting room, awaiting his arrival for a cocktail before dinner. He straightened out his pants and shirt and descended the broad staircase two steps at a time. In the sitting room, Sheila and James were in plush armchairs facing each other, and he surmised they had been in earnest conversation. Her face was slightly flush as though upset, and his mouth was tight and firm as if they'd been having an argument.

"Jeremiah, did you rest well? We're having a drink. Would you like one? I'm having some good old Irish whiskey." He lifted a handsome cut glass with a small amount of whiskey at the bottom. "And Sheila's having a glass of sherry. Would you like what we're having, or would you prefer a beer?"

"A beer would be fine if it's not much trouble."

"Hazel, please get Mr. Knox a tall glass of that fine Canadian ale we have. I think he'd like that."

She bustled away, and James turned to Jeremiah with a stern gaze. "Jeremiah, that fellow at the restaurant that wished to speak to you, I want to talk about that, and we'll continue it over dinner."

Jeremiah nodded, already sensing a more serious James. He'd only known the man from his few visits to Stradbally and from the meal at the restaurant, but he remembered the man could change moods faster than his father. It was intuition, he knew that, but there was something about his uncle that told him to be careful. He glanced at his aunt who was gently biting her lower lip, her hands twisting in her lap. Clearly, his uncle did not want to hear about his family or the court case or about his work at the law firm. Or maybe that was what this was about. He said, "Yes, sir, please go ahead."

"That fellow, the one you saw at the restaurant. I've concluded that he'd been told to look for you. He knew the ship, the date of arrival, and that you'd be meeting me. He had a lot of intelligence on you, on us. Do you know where he got that information or how he got it?"

"No, sir, I do not. Never saw him before."

"Well, as I said, I've been in contact with your father, with your lawyer and the judge. I've concluded that the Fenians, your crowd of political radicals, contacted this man to meet you and keep you active with Irish activities here in Boston."

"What in the world would I do here that would be useful in Ireland?"

James wrestled in his chair, an awkward movement to get comfortable. "I think it's mostly to raise money and to send guns to help your Fenians in Dublin."

"That's a lot of organization, a lot of coordination that seems unlikely to me."

"That fellow, I know of him, big agitator, labor organizer on the waterfront and a member of a society like your Fenians here in Boston. You need to know that the Fenians are active up and down the East Coast and in Canada too."

He was aware of the Fenian movement in the United States and Canada but did not acknowledge that. He said, "What would he want from me? I have no connections here except you and Aunt Sheila. I have no money." He was perplexed, confused, and shook his head in dismay.

"Ah, lad, you underestimate yourself. They know about your speeches, your skills at organizing, your passion for political action. They want your skills in their organization here, the one on the docks."

"But, Uncle James"—he leaned forward in his chair—"as you know, I've been charged by the court to stay away from political activities and to remove myself from the Fenians. I don't want any involvement, at least not right away."

"That's smart, Jeremiah." He took a sip of his whiskey and leveled his eyes at Jeremiah again and let the glance linger. Jeremiah met the gaze and held it, but the man's intensity caused him to shift his eyes to Sheila. Pleading, she asked, "Jeremiah, how was the voyage? Did you have any bad storms?"

"Now damn it, Sheila, the boy and I are having a serious discussion about political radicals here and how he looks to them."

"Of course, James."

"Well, as I was sayin', this fellow—and I'll go to my grave on this one if I'm in error—but yes, he wants to recruit Jeremiah. I'm guessing he has a job all lined up for you to, maybe even a place to live. They're like that, make it easy for the newcomer. Buy them off. You know that, Sheila."

"I do, James, but on the good of it … They give the new arrivals a start in life that helps."

"Oh, horsey … woman, I didn't want to say this, but now I must." He took a big gulp of his whiskey and cleared his throat. "Jeremiah, your dad, your mom, they know you're special, smart. Unfortunately, so does Judge Hardy."

"He's never talked to me." Jeremiah inserted surprised.

"No, but he's heard you speak at meetings, rallies, and he's read your writings, your pamphlets, and whatnot. He told me that." He sipped his whiskey again then got up and poured more into his glass from the crystal decanter. He returned to his chair and sat down with an awkward thump. "You know what he said to me on the transatlantic. He said you're better than Parnell ever was, and you're only nineteen. You're a problem for the English, but you're too aggressive, too radical for the Irish. Basically, he thinks you're dangerous."

"Yeah, he said as much at my hearing."

"You got it, boy." He took another big slug of his whiskey; he seemed to be rushing. "You haven't touched your beer, son. Drink up."

Jeremiah sipped the beer, watching his uncle as he sat back in his chair. He understood the comments, and in a way, he appreciated the observation the judge had made about him. But something in James's whole approach on the subject worried him. *Let him talk,* he thought. *His intent will be revealed.* "It's a good beer, sir, much appreciated as I appreciate your hospitality in your beautiful home."

James waved the comment away, "Of course, son. Now where was I … Oh yes, now this big talent of yours is what that man at the restaurant wants to capture, to use in the push to get more rights for the Irish on the waterfront. He's after better working hours, higher wages, safer working conditions, and so on. He probably needs someone who can speak and write as well as you can."

"And you think that's a bad idea. To help our fellow Irish here?"

"Easy now, son. I didn't say that, and I'm not indifferent to my own." He froze Jeremiah was his eyes. "But what I am sayin' is that

I've put in a lot of work and had a lot of success, if I don't say, in making my own mark here in Boston. And my mark's not just with the Irish. I've made headway with every group, including the damn Brahmins. Yes, sir, I've cracked the top here, and I don't want to lose it or get it compromised by associatin' with some radical politics."

"Uncle James, I believe in helping the poor, the working man who can't make ends meet, but I'll calm it down here. I have to, and I told the judge I'd stay away from politics for a while to protect myself from being sent back to Ireland."

"Jeremiah." He glanced over at his wife, who had hung her head down. Tears had begun to stream down her cheeks. "I'm going to follow the judge's advice, and your dad concurs. We want to get you away from the fever the Irish are creatin' here in the city. Sorry, son, but we need to get you out of Boston. Being an apprentice in my law firm is too risky." He stopped for a second, worried that Jeremiah might leap out of the chair and punch him. The boy looked ready to pounce.

James avoided eye contact and rushed on, "With your powerful reputation, it's not a good time for you to be here because the Fenians will find you, use blackmail to get you involved. You'll be harmed. My name will be hurt, and you'll be deported back to Judge Hardy." He waved a finger at Jeremiah. "And that damned judge told me clear he'd put you away for a long time. We don't want that do we?" Finally, he looked at Jeremiah, his face—at the moment softer—seeking understanding, agreement.

Jeremiah's suspicions were confirmed; he had a sense that something bad was coming, and it had. He sat calmly in the chair while his mind was in a whirl. With a distaste for both of them that was growing as each minute passed, he studied his aunt and uncle and sipped his beer. A slow-burning fury began to rise in him, and he fought to control it. Racing through his mind was that he been lied to, betrayed. The quiet in the room was unlike the roar of anger in his heart and head.

Sheila had become pale and in a faint voice offered, "Jeremiah, getting away till things calm down here might be good for you, then you can come back."

Her confirmation of what James had said was devastating. He sunk in his chair; the comments from both of them had accumulated, and he could not believe what he had just heard. His ears were ringing. He could feel his heart racing. He wet his lips to enable him to speak. His mouth felt so dry. He rushed out the words, "So this was the plan all along. No apprenticeship in your firm. Done without conversation with me. It's my life. Why was it done this way? What I want to know, Uncle James ... who did the lying here? I was never going to stay in Boston, was I? So was it my da who lied? Was it Callahan? Or was it you? At least have the courage to tell me who the liar is."

Slumped in his chair, James said, "There's been no lies, Jeremiah. Lots of new information was developed between me, your folks, your lawyer, and the judge while you were on the *Caledonia*. You've been given a real break by the judge, and I've been asked to ensure the Knox end of the bargain."

"It's clear and simple to me. I've been lied to, and I would never have agreed to this deal. Sending me away from the practice of law is enormous punishment. It's my future, and you've taken it away without consulting with me, without my agreement. I'd have taken my chances with a jail sentence and been out in a year like Parnell."

"You don't know what the judge would have done and your lawyer, Callahan, wasn't sure either. Your dad and I felt this was best."

Sheila said, "Jeremiah, you're very gifted, and your gifts have gotten you in trouble. We're saying be quiet for a while before you decide exactly what you want to do. I believe that you've been led astray by Charles Parnell. Do you really want to be in and out of jails all your life like Parnell and the other leaders in the movement? Please take time to think it out."

"I've not been led astray by Parnell or any of the others. I have thought hard about the cause, but I'm smart enough to know now is not the time, and I can wait. But I want the legal background to be stronger and more effective when I return. Now you've taken that away."

"It's for a while until things calm down," James said. "I've arranged a job for you in an area where your father says you have a rare skill, and it's not teaching, speaking or writing. It's in stone cutting."

"Stone cutting, well … Jesus H. Christ. I've heard it all." He fixed his eyes on his uncle. "Is this my da's idea? It sounds like him, his form of punishment. He never wanted me to do law." He cursed his father silently, then said, "So I'm to be a slave in a stone quarry. How is that different than a prison? Where is it, Canada, Australia?"

"You're upset, Jeremiah, I understand, but your language—please," pleaded his aunt.

Jeremiah ignored her, his mind spinning with thoughts. He said again, "Who's the liar? Who did me in?"

"Lad, lad, calm down. I've told you," James said. "There are no lies. It's just the situation, and it's time for you to recognize that. Perhaps you can get back to Ireland in five years and finish law school then. You'd be only twenty-four. Way younger than when I got my law degree. So let's talk about getting you settled in Worcester. It's not in Canada or Australia. What do you take us for?"

"Worcester?" Jeremiah asked. "What's this Worcester? Where in the devil, is it?"

His uncle responded, "It's a good place, Jeremiah. It's the state's second largest city. Lots going on there, and it's about fifty miles from here. An hour by train. We'll be able to see you often."

Quickly Jeremiah rose from his chair. "I'm not staying here another minute. Give me the address of the company, and I'm on my way." He stared hard into his uncle's face radiating the contempt he felt, disgusted at the betrayal of his uncle and his father. "I'll go there, so you don't send the police after me and ship me back to a jail in Ireland." He reached down and took a final sip of his beer. "I'll get my bag while you get the address, then I'm gone."

"You need a meal, some rest. Stay a few days at least," Aunt Sheila said.

"It's always clear when you're not wanted. You can relax. I'm leaving."

He trotted up the stairs and placed his small cotton bag under his arm. He counted out the money left from the cash Joseph Callahan had given him. Perhaps it's enough for a boarding house tonight and then enough left for transportation. He'd see what his uncle had arranged.

At the base of the stairs, Sheila waited. "Please stay for a few days. This has been a shock, too sudden. It will seem better in the morning. I'm sorry, but this is the way James does everything. He means well, but it comes out poorly at times."

"It's not just Uncle James, Aunt Sheila. I see the clumsy hand of my father and older brother in this." He thought back to the acrimonious dinner the night before his meeting at the constable's office. "My da, my whole family disagree with my politics and want me punished." He fought back the tears that wanted to flow down his cheeks. He took a deep breath. "That wasn't clear to me before, but it is now. I'm on my own."

James had joined Sheila at the base of the stairs. "Jeremiah, I heard that. You're not on your own, so don't turn your back on your family." He had an envelope in his hand and gave it to Jeremiah. "In the envelope is the name of the owner of the stone works, his address, and a brief description of the work he does. He's done good work for our local archbishop. Also, there's some travel money, enough until you get your first pay."

Jeremiah took the envelope and stuffed it in his jacket. "Family—what family turns its back on a son? You, my father, my oldest brother ... some of you, all of you, whoever it is just sold my life's ambition, my dreams down the river. For what? To distance yourselves from a fervent Irish patriot fighting for the rights of others?" He paused, fighting back the fury he felt. "If that's my family, who needs them?"

"Jeremiah, easy, lad. We're doing our best for you." He extended his hand.

Jeremiah pushed his uncle's hand away. "I want no more from you." Quickly he turned, slammed the door, and descended the steps and onto the street.

Chapter 8

He couldn't get way fast enough. He half ran, half stumbled down the hill, his lone cotton sack under his arm. It was getting dark. The sun had disappeared over the horizon, and a soft gray light settled over the water in the harbor. As he neared the piers, he slowed to a brisk walk, something chafed his leg and he stopped. Jeremiah pushed his hand into a pant pocket and felt a roll of paper. He pulled out a wad of dollar bills; surprised he counted them. Dozens of them, in a mix of dominations. There were ones, fives, tens, and a few twenties. How'd they get there? He thought of Aunt Sheila's tearful embrace as he left; she must have stuffed it his pocket as she hugged him. He stopped to count them, looking around carefully for other walkers who could see his wad of cash. It was over a hundred dollars. In a sad day, this was a ray of good news. *Wow*, he thought. Then he opened the envelope. James had enclosed fifty dollars along with the address of the stonemason. For the first time that day, he smiled and thought, *This is too good to be true.*

At first, he was bothered by the intrusion of the gift. He wanted nothing from these people. But he thought about it; this was guilt money, and he'd damn well use it. He added up the remaining British pounds from Joseph Callahan and the money from his aunt and uncle. He knew he had adequate funds for lodging that evening and for many evenings plus plenty of money for train fare and food.

A cool breeze came off the water, and he felt the chill on his face. It sharpened his senses, awakened him from the harsh exchange with his uncle. He felt some new sensations, with some money in his pocket, a sense of freedom began to well inside him. This was his adventure now; he was not tied to his uncle and his law firm. He was beholden to no one but himself. He was alone in America with a job in Worcester, and he'd see how that went. Then he'd decide whether to make contact with the Irish activists in Massachusetts or maybe New York. He had names and could get more from his friends in Dublin. His first day in the new country was a major disappointment, but a change had happened, and he realized it freed him. His step picked up, and he moved more quickly. His head swiveled as he took in his surroundings, observing the different clothing and faces of the people he passed, the schooners and steamships anchored in the harbor, and the newly constructed warehouses built with large blocks of granite dominating the piers. Clearly, it was his life now, and it was up to him to make something of it. He began to see the withdrawn apprenticeship as more of a disappointment than a loss, because he'd find a way back to the law if it were right for him. There was plenty of time for that.

With a new spring in his step, he began to search for lodgings and a bank to convert the British money into US dollars. Then on the next morn, he would be off on the first train to Worcester. He'd do that to stay clear of any infractions that would send him back to Ireland and jail. And he'd work there until he found something better. A slave in a stone quarry had little appeal to him, but he mused that could change quickly. He knew he had a logical mind, one that worked well, and he'd use his mind to find the right kind of work for his talents. He could cut stone, but that was not the best use of his talents. It was a job and a start here in the new country, but it was a transition until he found a way back to the law.

It was his first evening in the new country, and he was alone. Being alone didn't bother him; unlike many of his friends, he welcomed solitude. He thrust his shoulders back and increased his stride. It's just me he acknowledged, and he wanted to record every moment, every experience with precision. The harbor at dusk was cool. The soft slap of the waves against the stone jetties had a predictable, reassuring rhythm as he walked along its shoreline. He passed endless rows of piers and decided to follow the waterfront road into the heart of Boston. It was a longer walk than he remembered from the carriage ride, but it was interesting to see the unloading of ships, the bustling trade on the docks, and the teeming bars that lined the street. As he neared Rowes wharf, he spotted an attractive boarding-house, the Mayo. Its Irish name gave him comfort. Its clapboards were freshly painted. Its blue shutters provided a sharp accent to the white clapboards. It had the overall appearance of well-managed lodging. He went inside and booked a room for the night.

The desk clerk said, "No women in the rooms, no cigars in the rooms, and for an additional twenty-five cents, you can have a full dinner and breakfast."

Jeremiah turned down the offer and asked directions to the Union Oyster House. He had enjoyed his luncheon there and was looking forward to their fish dinner and a strong ale. He settled into a small room on the second floor. There was no rug on the wide boarded floor. The single bed in the corner was barely long enough for his tall frame. The mattress was a bit lumpy as he pressed his hands into it. A wooden chair sat against the wall next to a very small desk, and a single window peeked out over an alley below. He placed his cotton sack on the floor, slid it under the bed, and stretched out to think about the day before going to dinner. The treachery of his uncle rose to the front of his mind. He felt the heat of anger once again then pushed these thoughts quickly aside. He'd deal with them, through letters to his family and Callahan, when he reached Worcester.

He rolled off the bed and walked down the corridor to the com-munal bathroom to wash before dinner. Returning to his room, he changed into a clean shirt and gazed briefly into the cracked mirror on the wall. He pointed a long finger at the mirror and wagged it vigorously. He said to the mirror, "You're on your own now, laddie. Earlier than you expected, but so what? Damn it now." He pulled his finger back into a clenched fist. "Make something of it." He left the room in a rush and plunged into the crowded street teeming with carts, horses, and people. He dodged the crowds and manure scat-tered on the cobblestones as he made his way toward the restaurant.

The stench from the waterfront was keen in his nose as he entered the boisterous room. At the bar, the patrons stood two deep and the mixture of men in coveralls, men with aprons splashed with sea grit or blood, and men in suits with white shirts and ties all mingled together, jousting for attention with the bar keep. *This is America*, he thought, *you wouldn't find this mixture in a Dublin pub.* He stared at the bar until the manager addressed him.

"Hello, young man, back again. I'm Harry O'Neil. Where's your uncle?"

"At home, I wanted to try your dinner as the lunch was so good."

"Do you want the bar first or table."

"I'll take the table but wouldn't object to a wee ale or two."

"Are you here for the duration with your uncle, or are you movin' on?"

"Movin' on … Worcester."

"Be careful up there, lad. Different crowd in Worcester. Everybody lookin' for factory work. The French got there first and are quick to fight off other nationalities. Not too many Irish up there, yet so they're havin' trouble. Are you from east or west of Ireland? I'm from a cottage off the Ring of Kerry?"

"Like you"—he smiled—"south and east, Stradbally near Dublin."

"Of course, your uncle's territory. Well, it's the poor Irish from Connaught and Mayo that's botherin' the Frenchies. That's the problem in Worcester. You'll need to stay away from them for your own safety."

As he sipped his ale, he thought of O'Neil's comment on the Irish. *We are a contentious lot*, he mused, *with many differences.* We argue and do it all the time. Some of us take our grievances into violence to get our way. Others, like my family, talk the differences to death. His uncle warned him about his own kin as Harry O'Neil had just done. He saw the loneliness of the Fenian battles in Ireland with more clarity. It was no wonder that his Dublin group had trouble getting widespread support. The Irish couldn't agree on anything. Even his own family was split over home rule and the notion of Ireland as an independent nation. He was never certain whether it was his difficult conversation with his uncle or the innocent conversation with the manager of the Union Oyster House that slowly moved his mind to be open and careful about political involvement in Worcester and away from active political involvement anywhere. Already, he'd been exported for his beliefs and actions and to continue in this vein would likely bring the possibilities of physical harm and, worse, deportation and jail time. Yet Ireland remained strong in his mind. The desire to go back was keen, and he wanted to return to the study of law, but that would have to wait. Edinburgh and Ireland were five years away.

The next morning, his cotton bag beneath his arm, he found the station for the Boston & Albany Railroad. Once seated, he passed the small villages of Brookline, Wellesley, and Framingham and was charmed by their well-tended land, well-built cottages, and in places, fine homes. When he arrived in Worcester, he asked directions to the McGuinness Stone Company and supplied the address. He was guided to the E Street Trolley Line, told to ride it to the end and then be prepared to walk a mile. The sun was warm in early September, and he removed his jacket, wiped his brow walking the dusty, dirt road toward McGuinness Stone as it was called. Dripping with sweat, he reached a sprawling shed of dark brown wood. It was more of a ramshackle building than a tightly constructed barn. He asked for George McGuinness, and the stonecutter walked him over to a short stocky man with wrists and arms of a tree trunk. His handshake nearly crushed Jeremiah's hand.

"Well now." McGuinness paused to wipe his brow with a red handkerchief. "You're the terrorist, are you? You don't look like a terrorist to me. James Knox's nephew, are you?"

"Yes, that's me."

"I hear you can cut stone, show me." He pointed to a large block of limestone about six feet across by Jeremiah's estimate. "Cut that in half, no ragged edges, and in a straight line." He gave Jeremiah a hammer and a chisel and walked him over to the stone slab. Other workers in the shed stopped their work, watching.

Jeremiah drew a mental line down the center of the block and traced the chisel over it. He placed the chisel on the stone and began to tap. He opened the stone in two perfect halves. "Okay, what's next?"

"You'll do. Here's what I want. Get yourself some work clothes, boots, and gloves at Johnson's Hardware in town. Then if you don't have a place to stay, go to Mrs. McCaffrey's Boarding House on

Millbury Street. It's right off the E Street trolley line, the line you took to get here. She's got a good clean place, spacious rooms, and good food twice a day. Good place to get you started."

Jeremiah nodded. "Okay, when do I start? I can start now. I need the money."

"Get your work clothes first. Then I'll see you tomorrow morning at eight, right here. One of our carriages will take you to the quarry, and you'll cut rock … like the slabs here." He pointed to the limestone block at their feet. "And load them on a sled. That'll get you used to the work, then we'll see what else you can do. Now, if you need money for the clothes, I can advance you part of this week's pay because I trust your uncle. I don't do that for everyone."

"No, I'm okay for the clothes and a week at Mrs. McCaffrey's. When is the first payday?"

"Every Friday at five."

Mrs. McCaffrey regarded Jeremiah warmly. She'd come from Cork, a short journey south from Stradbally. Her trip to America had come from sadness having lost her two children and husband to a Typhus epidemic fifteen years ago. She had immigrated to Worcester and, with her husband's savings and a loan from her family, she had purchased an abandoned house on Millbury Street. Slowly she took in boarders while she brought the ten-bedroom house back to its original quality. As the rooms took shape, she increased the weekly rents to the point where they were the highest in Worcester yet she had no difficulty finding tenants. But, as Jeremiah was to find out, he would have no trouble meeting this expense because McGuinness paid well, but he paid on the basis of productivity. Jeremiah's challenge was how to become productive in his new work. He wanted to be well paid.

The first week in the quarry was a nightmare. The blazing September heat, the hammer and chisel in outstretched arms exhausted him as he cut slab after slab of stone off the walls of the quarry, placing the slabs on rollers then lifting them with others onto the bed of the cart. His back ached, and his legs quivered from lifting the big stone slabs. His hands were bleeding from misplaced hits with the hammer and chisel. By noon on the first day, he sank exhausted against the wheels of the cart, seeking shade from the heat of the sun and tiredly munched on a sandwich from his lunch pail. He was convinced; he couldn't finish the day. Yet when the other men moved, he moved with them. On the second day, the thoughts swirled through his mind. Could he finish the week? As each day passed, he was convinced that this was his prison sentence, the pain in his back, and arms were worse than his discomfort from the stench and crowding at Kilmainham Gaol. This was indeed the punishment meted out by his father and uncle. He felt that they wanted him to suffer, and he was suffering. He wondered if they had any idea how backbreaking and difficult it was for a law student to hammer at walls of rock in a stone quarry all day. He thought, a year or two in Kilmainham Gaol might be much easier than this. After all, Parnell was in jail, and he was getting his writing done and still active with political influence. By Friday, when the cart hauled the tired workers back from the quarry and he was handed his first bundle of cash, he felt of surge of excitement and energy. One of the younger workers, Cary, suggested meeting at Dooley's Tavern after dinner, and he agreed.

The tavern was crowded and noisy, and the violins were beginning to play lively Irish Reels. The noise became louder, and the energy in the room swelled in good feeling and friendship. Jeremiah felt the contrast from the quiet often mournful nature of the pubs in Dublin as they discussed politics and other world events while the mournful ballads darkened the mood in the room. There was none of that here. The talk was all about women, their sport teams, and sport events generally and amusing anecdotes at work. As far as he could tell, he was the only one in the pub with education beyond grade school. At first, this did not bother him, but he realized that he needed more penetrating intellectual topics and would wonder where to find them.

After a late Friday night full of conversation, Irish whiskey and ale, he fell fast asleep as soon as his head hit the pillow. He woke in a turmoil; a dream had frightened him. In the dream, he was climbing up the walls of the quarry, hand over hand, seeking holding places on the sheer stone surface. The climb was hard and slow. His arms were exhausted. His back ached. His hands were bleeding. A fall would kill him. Finally, he reached the top, and as he gazed out at the scenery in front of him, he shuddered awake soaked in sweat. He shook his head, wondering what it meant as he returned to sleep.

Through the fall and into the colder months of late November and December, Jeremiah carved the huge blocks at the McGuinness quarry and other quarries in the local area. He shaped them skillfully to meet the size of tombstones or long slender slabs for ornamental uses. Occasionally, in rainy weather, he worked in the large shed shaping a tombstone or reducing a large stone slab to the outline of a statue, but he was not asked to do the fine cutting for lettering or ornamentation. Over these months, the work became easier for him as his blistered hands gained calluses then hard tough skin. His wrists and arms added muscle to the points where they felt like steel bands to Coleen, who saw him on occasion. Working outside gave his skin a permanent tan and lightened his dark-brown hair with streaks of gold. He began to fill out his long frame into a powerful body, and by December, he became capable of putting in long hours of grueling work on the stones. At times, in the shed on colder days, he worked alongside Antonio Biasi, McGuinness's senior stonecutter, who Jeremiah considered an artist, a sculptor. The elderly Italian had taken a liking to the lanky Irishman. He taught him how to use the smaller chisels and cutting tools to make designs, to do fine lettering on tombstones, and to shape the arms and legs of statues. Often Jeremiah would remain in the shed past working hours and practice carving the shapes Biasi had taught him. He would draw a leaf or flower on a scrap of paper. Then working with discarded shards of stone, he would cut the stone to match the drawing. He thought of his earlier carving of Connor I on the barn's entrance in Stradbally, and he was pleased with his progress in advancing these skills. The days in McCracken's studio had helped him immeasurably. He told Biasi about the bull, about the days at McCracken's, and the older man laughed.

He said in his broken English, "You see, Jeremiah, this is your destiny. This is what you were meant to do. It was always there, and now it's just beginning to come out."

Heavy snows that winter drove the cutters inside, and from their inventory of granite, marble, limestone, and sandstone, they worked on shaping the stones into final forms for buildings, cemeteries, and statues. With Biasi standing over his shoulder, the older man complained of a pain in his stomach and asked Jeremiah to finish the printing on a tombstone. It was done well and fast, and Biasi called McGuinness over to examine the work. The boss gave Biasi an odd look, and the older man waved again, an insistent gesture for McGuinness to join him.

Biasi said, "I'm quite sick and weak, so Jeremiah finished. See ... very good."

McGuinness said, "You want him out of the quarries and to be your assistant, don't you?" He looked at the older stonecutter. "Antonio, I want you to see a doctor. You complain about this stomach too much."

"I will boss, soon. I must say though, Jeremiah does some things I don't do. He draws well, then he cuts to that design. You always get what he designs. No surprises. Very valuable."

"Excuse us, Jeremiah." He pulled Biasi aside and whispered in his ear. "Two things, I want you to go to the doctor—I mean it." He shook the stonecutter's shoulder. "And second, I can't do that. Trimble, Hogan, Pierce have all been here much longer than Jeremiah. They all want to do the fine work with you. I can't jump him over them."

"You need to, boss, because, he'll leave. He's that good, that fast."

"We'll see," McGuinness replied.

McGuinness walked away with a wave to Jeremiah indicating good work. Biasi turned to Jeremiah and said, "Let's work on a spire for St. Timothy's church in Barre. That's a good challenge."

"I don't know what it's supposed to look like," he replied.

"Tonight, after work, go to the library and choose some books on churches in Europe. You'll see all kinds of spires then bring me a couple of your sketches tomorrow, and we'll get started."

That night, he visited the Worcester Library and poured over books documenting the design and construction of churches. He marveled at the intricate work in the windows and towers at Mont St. Michele and Chartres. He marveled at the spires and bell tower of Westminster Abby and the Duomo in Florence. He sketched several designs of spires taking the features he liked best from each cathedral. He assembled these to show Biasi in the morning.

The older man was delighted. "I see these in my head." He pointed a gnarled finger to his temple. "But I can't explain it to anyone else. You make it better for both of us to work to the same purpose, yes?"

But McGuinness needed Jeremiah for more basic work. And he was assigned to cut Carrara marble for the interior pillars of a bank lobby. Shaping the square slabs into circular discs was not as intricate as shaping a spire, but Jeremiah was delighted to be working with marble. It seemed to glow back at him as he chipped and shaped each disc, eighteen inches in diameter. He'd never worked with marble before and hoped McGuinness would give him more work with this gorgeous stone.

Jeremiah's first winter in Worcester was a trial. He'd never experienced such cold nor the endless accumulation of snow. It was never like this in Ireland or Scotland, he mused, and he missed both countries. He was delighted when spring arrived. The blossoms were beginning to emerge. The birds had started to come back, and their songs were louder every day. They flew in and out of the eves of the big shed, their songs adding to the music of the hammer on chisel and the click-click of falling stone. He'd been working in the shed during the winter months and was worried about being dispatched back to the quarries as the weather improved. When he heard the rumble of a carriage in the outer drive, he glanced out the open door. It was drawn by two large black horses, their harness matched the color of their coats and was accented with silver discs. The color of the horses was a perfect match to the glassy sheen of the black carriage. Out stepped a middle-sized man assisted by another—perhaps his butler, Jeremiah thought—and he stopped work to watch the man. His face was colorless, appearing dour. There was no hint of smile as he greeted McGuinness. His black top hat and black suit were formal, and his face conveyed sadness. McGuinness was deferential, most unusual for him, as he bowed to the man in greeting. They talked for ten minutes or so, and the man was helped back into his carriage, and they left as quickly as they had arrived.

McGuinness called for Biasi, and they talked for several minutes. Biasis gestured toward Jeremiah, but McGuinness shook his head indicating no. "You do the tombstone as Mr. Cawley desires. I have something else for Jeremiah to do."

Jeremiah was sent to Boston to pick up a shipment of Italian marble from the waterfront and bring it back to Worcester. Unloading the cargo and processing it through customs, checking it for damages, and transporting it to a freight car would take a couple of days. Jeremiah was told to stay with the marble until it arrived at the shed. When he arrived at the shed a few days later, he found the shop in an uproar. Hogan, one of the more experienced stonemasons, was ripping mad. "If I can't satisfy that son of a bitch Cawley, nobody can."

He was referring to the man from the black carriage. In the meantime, Biasi had taken ill. His stomach had acted up again, and he was too ill to work and was in the hospital recovering. Mr. Cawley had ordered a tombstone for his granddaughter. She had died suddenly from pneumonia, and the family wanted a special tribute to the ten year old. They had decided that her tombstone would include an intricate design of angels. Jeremiah learned that Hogan had etched out an example on stone, and Mr. Cawley became red in the face, bellowing at McGuinness, "Is this your best! It's awful! You've put us in terrible bind. We're having her funeral Saturday, three days away. She'll be buried with no tombstone, unthinkable!"

McGuinness had gone to the hospital to get Biasi released, and his doctor refused the request. He came back to the shed bearing Biasi recommendation, assign the job to Jeremiah.

In the hospital, Biasi, to avoid irritating the stitches in his stomach, had whispered to McGuiness, "Have Jeremiah sketch what Mr. Cawley wants, then show the drawing to him. Make certain Mr. Cawley agrees with the sketch, then let Jeremiah do the carving. He'll get it right."

McGuinness had no such confidence, but as soon as Jeremiah arrived, he gave him the problem. He assigned others to unload the marble and pushed Jeremiah into his office. "Sketch some angels for me. They're to go on the header of the tombstone."

Jeremiah sat, placed his fingers on his temple for a minute, then began to draw. He completed five sketches and showed them to McGuinness. He watched his boss as he reviewed the artwork.

McGuinness studied them one at a time, then laid them out in a row, comparing them. He picked them up, shuffled them into a neat stack, placed them under his arm, and said, "Come with me."

They piled into his worn carriage and drove at a crisp, trotting pace to the mansion of Harold Cawley. After making it clear to the butler at the door that this was an emergency regarding the forth-coming funeral, they were shown into Cawley's study. The old man was at the end of the long room, seated at a massive desk, he glanced up then rose to meet McGuinness and Jeremiah. He crossed the cream-and-blue Kirman carpet and pointed the two men to chairs facing a wide stone fireplace. He took a chair across from them, the leather creaking from his substantial weight.

McGuinness offered an apology for intruding but said he had some designs for the gravestone he thought Mr. Cawley should see. The old man nodded and asked if they'd like some water, then extended his hand for the drawings. Jeremiah and McGuiness shook their heads, and Cawley, ever sparse with words, said nothing and began to examine the drawings. His mouth was drawn tight, his fore-head showed slight beads of perspiration, his breathing was labored and he moved as if impatient. There was no expression on his face. He said in calm tones, "Well, these are much better, and I like this one best." He waved it toward Jeremiah and McGuinness. "Let me get my daughter and see if she agrees."

He pulled a cord near the fireplace, and a butler appeared at the door. "Charles, please get my daughter and tell her the stone people are here."

Moments later she arrived, dressed in black. Her eyes were red, and her grief was obvious to Jeremiah. He expressed sympathy, and she smiled at him, tears leaking down her cheeks. She reviewed the drawing selected by her father then asked to see the others. She placed them back in his hands. "Yes, Daddy, I like this one best too although there all very nice." She turned to Jeremiah. "Yes, this one is particularly lovely," she said. "So much like Suzanne, light and floating." She began to cry again.

Cawley reached out to comfort his daughter. "Who can do this, McGuinness?" He turned his eyes to Jeremiah. "Can you cut as well as you draw?"

"Yes, sir, I cut better than I draw."

Cawley's eyes widen and stared at Jeremiah for a second then took a handkerchief, wiped his mouth, and held it near his nose. "Unfortunately, the funeral is Saturday." Cawley turned from Jeremiah and faced McGuiness. "You know this McGuinness. I'm not pleased with your mistakes." He sighed. "I guess we can place the finished memorial at the grave site later."

"No need, sir," Jeremiah interrupted. "If you need it by Saturday, I'll have it ready for your inspection by late afternoon on Thursday."

McGuinness leaned into Jeremiah. He whispered, "Easy, lad."

"As long as I have a clean stone with the printing done, I can place the two angels above fairly quickly."

Cawley glanced again at Jeremiah and almost broke into a smile. "Get this lad back to work, McGuinness. Thanks for coming here. I'm much relieved. Are you okay with this, my dear?"

She sniffled into her handkerchief and nodded, then patted Jeremiah on the arm and left the room.

"One question, sir." Jeremiah gazed into Cawley's tired eyes. "In the drawing you selected, the angels are looking down at the grave site. In that rendition, there is no expression on their face or lips, no smile nor any sign of sadness. I want to make sure that sense of heavenly neutrality is okay with you, with your daughter and her husband."

Cawley turned to McGuinness. "Where'd you find this young man? You have depth, son. You've captured what I feel." He stopped for a moment. "Your art recognizes that there's an indifferent god up there ... Only an indifferent god would have allowed that beautiful child to die."

As they walked backed to the carriage, McGuinness said, "You did well in there, but you made a big promise. Old man Cawley will be out at the shed at tomorrow afternoon, looking for that tombstone."

"I know that. But what I can't figure out is how Hogan screwed this up. Two angels on a tombstone, it's not that difficult."

"One thing about you, Jeremiah, you don't lack confidence."

"Ah, yes, my father often made the same comment."

Chapter 9

When Harold Cawley and his daughter arrived at the shed the next day, they did not expect to see a finished tombstone. They entered the large barnlike room, shielding their eyes from the dust searching for Jeremiah. They spotted him sitting in a battered wooden chair, dusting residue off the carvings at the top of the tombstone. They walked toward him as he moved the brush delicately around the faces of the angels, flicking marble dust and small stone chips away from their faces, his concentration riveted to the carving. He didn't move or acknowledge them as they approached; he kept staring at the tombstone.

For him, the two angels had come out of the stone. He was there to release them so they could look over the young girl for eternity. The cutting and placement of them had been effortless for him; his eyes and hands spoke to the heart of the stone. They spoke to each other, the desired form flowed back and forth. Harold Cawley broke the silence. "Mr. Knox, hello." He stared at the stone then turned his head sharply toward his daughter. "My god, it's done."

Jeremiah lifted his head as if awakening from a trance and looked at them, not seeing them at first. Slowly he rose, as McGuinness bustled out from the back office to join them. Jeremiah bowed his head slightly. "Hello, it's a pleasure to see you again." He rubbed his right hand on his trousers, removing the dust, and extended it to Harold Cawley, then bowed slightly toward his daughter.

McGuinness had been in a nervous state all morning. Every fifteen minutes, he darted out to observe Jeremiah's work. When he spoke to him, the young man answered without moving his hands and eyes from the hard granite surface. McGuinness recognized that the sculptor's concentration was intense; he wondered if Jeremiah even heard him. He glanced at Harold Cawley and pointed to the two angels as if he just discovered them, his face expressing surprise. "What do you think?" McGuinness blurted.

"Oh, the angels are so delicate, floating in space, beautiful like Suzanne," said Cawley's daughter. "They're welcoming her into heaven, Daddy, don't you see." She pulled her handkerchief from her purse, dabbing her eyes.

"I see that, and something more as Mr. Knox, and I discussed yesterday." He halted and gave his daughter a light hug, his arm wrapped around her slender shoulders. "This is beautiful work. A sad moment captured exquisitely." He stared at the stone for a long time, his quiet stance becoming uncomfortable for Jeremiah.

"Would you like a private time with the stone Mr. Cawley and Mrs. Harrigan?" Jeremiah offered.

"Nay," Cawley answered. "Stay here, lad. I wish to talk more with you."

"I've thought about the angels, and I've captured what I intended." Jeremiah paused, letting his comment sit with them, eager for a reaction. Nervous with the lack of response, he added, "I'm ready to make some changes if you and Mrs. Harrigan would like to suggest them."

Cawley looked at his daughter, and she shook her head. Tears were again beginning to form in her eyes. Delicately, she wiped them away then reached out and touched Jeremiah's arm. "I can't speak just now. These angels take my breath away."

Cawley said, "Can we find a place to sit and talk? I wish to settle accounts with Mr. McGuinness on the memorial."

McGuinness said with a smile on his broad face, "My office is a clutter, but I have two chairs. You and Mrs. Harrigan can sit. Jeremiah and I can stand while we talk." He pointed to the small office in the corner of the shed, secured Harold Cawley by the arm, and led them into the cramped space.

Cawley was surprised and delighted with his granddaughter's tombstone. He settled the account quickly with McGuinness and paid handsomely for the work. They completed the arrangements for delivery of the tombstone to the cemetery, and Cawley and his daughter exchanged glances. The death of the child was painful for the old man and devastating on his sensitive daughter. She moved restlessly in the old wooden chair seeking the courage to speak, to break into the family tradition of letting her father control all conversation.

Finally, she spoke, "Daddy, tell Mr. Knox what Frederick said. He's my husband." She looked at Jeremiah. "Tell him what he wants to do for Suzanne."

Gently, Cawley put his hand on her knee. "I have some new ideas on this." He lifted his hand away and smiled at her. "I'd like to talk with you and Frederick before we talk with them." He gestured toward McGuinness. "Can we wait until after the funeral?"

She stiffened, uneasy with his change of their plans. "Of course, Daddy, but I like what Mr. Knox has done."

"And that won't be forgotten, darling."

Puzzled, McGuinness and Jeremiah let the conversation close with no further questions. They walked the Cawleys to their carriage and bade goodbye. As the dust flew from the departing carriage, Jeremiah turned to McGuinness. "Boss, do you think we'll ever hear the rest of that conversation?"

"We've done many things over the years with Mr. Cawley, and he's always been satisfied. There's no question. Your work here has pleased him greatly. Whatever it is they're thinking, I expect they'll be back."

Two weeks later, the handsome black carriage rolled into the McGuinness Company's parking area, and McGuinness sprinted from his office to greet them. Harold Cawley helped his daughter descend, and he gazed around the lot as he shook McGuinness's hand. "Is Mr. Knox here by chance?"

"He's just back from Groton. He's inside. Shall I get him?"

"Yes, I'd like him to be part of this conversation. We have some new work to discuss."

They gathered in McGuinness's office. Cawley whisked dust off a chair and sat down as did his daughter. He initiated the conversation with background about his son-in-law. He informed them that Frederick was a strong character and poured his grief into his work. His daughter nodded as he spoke, and he revealed that Frederick was most pleased with Suzanne's memorial and how fast and elegantly the sculpture of the two angels had appeared. Cawley seemed lost in his own thoughts as he related Frederick's understanding of the causes of his daughter's death. He said, "Frederick blames the sewage system in our neighborhood for his daughter illness, and he plans to move my daughter and their other children to the outskirts of the city. He will build a house there, and perhaps more importantly, he wants to build a church there too. They want to name the church after Suzanne, a memorial to her."

He paused to glance at his daughter, who had placed a handkerchief to her eyes. As she wiped her tears away, she said, "Yes, we'll call it St. Suzanne's."

Cawley released a long sigh. "Yes, the little one was the closest to a saint I've ever met." He pounded his hands on his thighs. "Indeed, we're going to do that for her and for the other Catholics in the area. Currently, all the Catholics in the neighborhood must travel into central Worcester to go to church; it's a great inconvenience. Between Frederick's funds and mine, we can build a very nice church. The bishop has agreed to the need for a church and has approved our plan. This was all happening before Suzanne's unfortunate illness, and her death accelerated the process."

He stopped to look at McGuinness and Jeremiah. He recognized he had their full attention. "I'm almost finished. We've not yet hired an architect nor a builder. Before we do, I want to make certain that you're willing to do what the Cawley family wants." He paused, his eyes darting back and forth between McGuinness and Jeremiah. "Here's the family's plan, and it involves your firm Mr. McGuinness and Mr. Knox. I imagine that you'll need time to think it over and time to talk to each other."

"What we'd like to do is hire you"—he pointed at Jeremiah—"just you … for two weeks this summer. I liked the sketches you did for the tombstone, so I'd like you to go to Italy and sketch the best-looking church exteriors and interior features you can find. I suggest you start in Rome, where you'll meet Bishop Grimaldi, an old friend. Then he'll guide you to other cities, most likely Florence and Siena. I'm not interested in the big cathedrals, but the smaller or midsized neighborhood and parish churches. Then my family will work with you to combine the best of what you sketch into a single design for the church. Then we'll get the architects and builders involved." He smiled. It was the first time Jeremiah saw the man smile. It wasn't warm, but it was welcoming. "What's in it for the McGuinness Company, you may ask?" He pointed a long finger at McGuinness. "I promise that your company will get all the stonework. Or at least all the stonework you're capable of doing." He kept staring at McGuinness. "Now, part of our plan is that we want Mr. Knox, when he returns from Italy, to create a statute of Suzanne to be displayed at the entry to the church. You may assign him to other tasks in the church, but I want your word that he'll be responsible for the statue of Suzanne."

McGuinness opened his arms. "This is wonderful, Mr. Cawley." He leaned forward in his chair, his face beaming. "I'm most pleased with your confidence in my company. We'll need to discuss the particulars as we go along and establish our usual contract for the work." Cawley nodded, and McGuinness saw the agreement. He said, "One question comes to mind regarding Jeremiah's trip to Italy. How will that be financed?"

"I'll pay you directly and add 50 percent above his normal wages for time lost in Worcester. Plus I'll pay for his living expenses in Italy." He laughed. "I know people in the Vatican. Bishop Grimaldi, as I mentioned, is an old friend. He'll find quiet monasteries for Mr. Knox's lodgings and meals—that'll keep the costs down and this handsome young man away from Italy's temptations." Again, his cold smile appeared, and he allowed himself a short laugh.

In the weeks after Suzanne's funeral, McGuinness examined the prospective loss of revenue from Jeremiah's work in Worcester. He met with Harold Cawley to discuss the calculation in hope that his request for additional funds would not derail the project. The two men rectified the difference, and Cawley agreed to compensate McGuinness for the full loss of income while Jeremiah was away. Then Cawley began his communications to Bishop Grimaldi to schedule Jeremiah's visit.

With the two angels on a tombstone behind him, Jeremiah pushed for more intricate sculpting work, and McGuinness agreed. When Biasi returned to work, he shared some of his projects with Jeremiah. The speed of the two men and their quality of work expanded the type of work the McGuinness Company could do and business increased.

With his success, Jeremiah received a pay increase, and after ten months at Mrs. McCaffrey's lodging, he moved from the boarding house to an apartment on the third floor of a three-decker house. As he prepared to move, he sorted out his possessions. He laid them on his bed and grinned. "Not much here." He chuckled. "The damn letters from his family were the largest bundle," he muttered, staring at the assorted goods. Everyone had written. But his father's letters were the most memorable, and they annoyed him. The old man was a clumsy writer, his frequent letters were brief, a few lines at most, and he repeatedly emphasized that the stone quarry work was essential for Jeremiah to get his head straight over his Fenian addiction. Letters from his mother were more informative of the goings-on in town and about their family, but she made it clear, she supported her husband's thoughts on Jeremiah's separating himself from the Fenians and being faithful to his responsibilities in Worcester. The letters from his siblings were less frequent and limited to a general curiosity about life in America.

Although it was never stated by a family member, he surmised that he was not missed. Or he thought his activities with the Fenians and his conversations about his political philosophy were not missed. Was he strange? He wondered. What might cause a sharp pain in others, he thought, did not disturb him. The attitudes of his family were their feelings and thoughts, not his. Their letters didn't bother him. He didn't miss them; it seemed odd to him that he didn't miss them, but there it was. He was comfortable in this distant land, at peace in his solitude. It was true, he caused pain in their lives, but not intentionally. More important to him was the betrayal of his father and uncle. His father's letters were clear. A hiatus from the education and practice of law was good for Jeremiah. A letter from his uncle provided additional irritation; he demanded a weekly accounting of his work at the McGuinness Company. He wanted to know if Jeremiah was following the stipulations established by the court in Dublin. Was he adhering to the prescriptions agreed to by his father and by him? This letter convinced Jeremiah that his father and uncle had conspired to shape his exile and define the walls of his prison. He crumpled his uncle's letter, his blood pounding in his temples, and fired it into a wastebasket. Still not satisfied, he went to O'Doul's tavern, and with several shots of Bushmills, his normal calm returned. When the next letter from his uncle arrived, he decided to deposit all mail from that address into the trash, unread.

On his final day of packing, he took the bundle of letters to the large trash bin behind the boarding house and dropped them in. It's baggage from the past, unneeded, not helpful, he concluded. He didn't want these memories in his new apartment.

Chapter 10

His apartment had two bedrooms, for one room he purchased a double bed to accommodate his long frame, a simple curtain for the window and a battered old oak bureau for his clothes. He scrubbed the wide board floor until the pattern in the wood gleamed and decided to add a rug in the future. In the other bedroom, he established a studio purchasing a ten-foot-long hardwood table where he worked with clay models and smaller stone sizes to test new ideas for decorative work and statues. In the evenings, he continued a simple routine of work in the studio or study at the library. Daily, he had a small breakfast of eggs, toast, and coffee. He brought a lunch with him to work, and his dinners were in local restaurants where the food was abundant and inexpensive. His clothing needs were simple. He purchased one good suit, two white shirts, and tie, which he rarely wore. His rugged work pants, shirt, and boots completed his wardrobe. His needs were simple, and he lived frugally. On average, he put half of his weekly pay under the mattress using the other half for rent and living expenses.

The weeks passed quickly, and the date for his departure to Italy arrived. He had purchased a second hand, battered leather suitcase for a dollar and packed it with the items neatly lined up on his bed: his work clothes, work boots, the new suit, and shirts. He didn't have enough clothing for foreign travel, he worried, but he didn't know what else to buy. He departed Worcester on the train to New York, wearing his new suit, white shirt, and blue tie above black shoes. To fellow travelers aboard the ship to Genoa, unaware of his modest wardrobe, he appeared to be a dapper young man with a strong presence and an air of confidence.

The initial schedule of two weeks away from McGuinness and Company became six weeks as Jeremiah calculated the time aboard ship and the days of travel in Italy. McGuinness reluctantly agreed, and although the young man had been with the company less than one year, the boss recognized Jeremiah's presence in the shed would be missed. McGuinness expected that Biasi would have more work than he could handle and attractive contracts for decorative work would have to be turned down because of Jeremiah's absence.

When Jeremiah approached the wharfs in New York, he thought about his arrival in Boston less than a year ago, how disappointed he was in his uncle and the cold reception that followed. He'd ignored them since his angry departure and the Fenians had not found him in Worcester. On that part, his uncle had been right. As he boarded the ship, he acknowledged the court order curtailing travel to Ireland, but the restriction didn't bother him. At some moments, it felt odd that he didn't need or want to see his family yet. Most of the time, it felt right. They had lied to him and clearly wanted him away from Ireland. As the year went by, the isolation from his family bothered him less and less. He had become comfortable in his isolation and had accepted the hard facts of his family's disapproval. He would not suggest they visit him in Italy.

When he boarded the ship and located his first-class stateroom, he was astounded at the difference from his passage a year earlier. It was more spacious and had a porthole with a view of the sea. He walked the corridors and first-class deck, hoping to see some young female passengers. He'd had little time for women in his first year in America. He met a few young ladies at church socials, and he visited Coleen on occasion, but mostly he worked, saved his money, and studied church art in the Worcester library. With time on his hands while crossing the Atlantic, he hoped to meet some interesting women as he had on his voyage to Boston. In the dining room the first night, he scanned the passengers seated at all the tables and was disappointed. He didn't see any single women nor any women that attracted him.

The largest cities Jeremiah had experienced were Dublin and Boston. When he arrived in Rome, he saw a city at another scale. He wanted to roam its streets, find the specialty clothing shops admired in the newspapers, try the much-vaunted food, and get a feeling for the city. But the Cawley family had set a schedule for him. He was to meet several Vatican officials. His main contact was Bishop Grimaldi, the Vatican's Supervisor of Buildings, who was accommodating, friendly, and conversant in English and four other languages. Grimaldi was curious about Jeremiah. To the bishop, this seemingly nonreligious young man was given the large responsibility of finding design ideas for a church in the United States. And the church was being financed by one of the Vatican's major American donors. He supplied Jeremiah with list of churches in Rome with different levels of artistic complexity and offered to visit these sites with him. From the ornate Italian style in the larger churches in Rome to the smaller simpler churches in the teeming neighborhoods, Bishop Grimaldi produced numerous examples of religious art. He enjoyed the young man and marveled at his sketches of the church exteriors and interior spaces, especially his detailed renditions of the altars.

Jeremiah felt an immediate kinship with the winding narrow streets in Rome, where churches, centuries old, were tucked into compact neighborhoods. The open windows hiding the women calling to each other intrigued him, and he wanted to visit with them, stay in their homes. He was rapidly becoming comfortable in Italy. The ancient apartments and official buildings were all around him, familiar and welcoming. He recognized that he was still in many ways a European.

In Florence and Siena, the narrow streets flowed into large plazas, and the bishop would nudge Jeremiah to pay attention to a local church. "I see, young man," the bishop observed, "that the pretty ladies attract your attention as well as our majestic cathedrals."

Jeremiah blushed. "Everywhere I turn in Italy, I find my senses overwhelmed."

"Nicely said, Jeremiah, but I'm not blind. The ladies find your giant size and fine looks most appealing. You must not forget our purpose."

"You've seen my book of drawings, Excellency, I'm recording all that we've seen. The Cawley's will have much to choose from."

"Yes, yes, I agree. You've been industrious." They walked quietly for a while, the bishop's head down in thought. Finally, he broke the silence. "Remind me, Jeremiah, to introduce you to Maria. She is the daughter of my cousin, Andrea, a banker here in Siena. She'll get your mind off these others who keep gazing at you."

Jeremiah laughed, he thought, a catholic bishop introducing him to a woman. This was not done in Ireland. "As you wish, Excellency. You are my guide in all things here in Italy."

He left the thought as they approached a small church in a cramped plaza near the Via Campo. A set of boys were playing soccer in the stone courtyard, the ball errantly caroming off the walls of the shops around the plaza. The bishop waved his hand at the boys to whisk them away, and they ignored him.

As a law student, Jeremiah had not spent much time in art galleries or pondering the artistic splendor of the interiors or exteriors of churches. In Rome, he marveled at the work of Michelangelo, at one time staring at the Pieta in St. Peter's until his knees buckled. Now in Siena, an ambition began to grow inside him. His love of law was slowly being etched aside by a passion to design altars and to build them. He was not especially religious, but there was something in an altar, the focus of thought or prayer that moved from that locale in a church straight toward a higher being. The altar was the focus of the beliefs, of the messages that went from the lowly parishioner to God. The altar was the center of attention in the church. He wanted to focus his skills on creating altars most fitting for the type of people who worshipped in each community. He knew he was not ready to create an altar like those in Italy, but he now had a goal. He wanted to build the skills to be able to do that at some point. He wanted that time to be fairly soon.

The small church, known for its frescoes, was charming but offered no new design ideas for Jeremiah, so they exited the church, dodged the soccer game, and wended their way back to the Palio. The day had become sunny and hot. Wiping their brows, they stopped at a shop for relief from the sun, or so Jeremiah thought. The main room was cluttered with pots, urns, and small statues. The bishop called for Pietro and a shaggy-haired man covered in dust emerged from a backroom. The small wiry man covered in white dust was young yet older than Jeremiah. He nodded to the bishop and studied Jeremiah. His eyes moved up and down the much taller man.

Grimaldi said, "This is Signore Knox from the United States. He is a sculptor and works in churches. He will build one upon his return. Signore Knox meet Pietro Antonino."

Jeremiah blanched at the bishop's interpretation of his purpose in Italy but smiled and remained quiet. Suddenly, an avalanche of Italian flooded the room. Pietro shook Jeremiah's hand several times then ran into the backroom, returning with a pad of artist paper, where he scribbled his name address and a telephone number. Bishop Grimaldi urged him to slow down and began to interpret. "Pietro wants to tell you he built the altar, pulpit, and the communion railing at Saint Giacomo's here in Siena and in many other churches. They use him frequently to do repairs at the Duomo here. And he would be honored to work with you in America at any time."

"Thank him, and we may call upon him and other artisans like him that wish to work in America. The country is growing fast, and many churches are needed."

As the bishop explained this to Pietro, his smile revealed a wide set of very white teeth. He started bouncing up and down, and he shook Jeremiah's hand several more times. "When do you build? I can go, I can help," he pleaded through the Bishop's translation.

"May I see your work?" Jeremiah asked.

The bishop, laughing, translated again. "Of course." Pietro rushed out the door, the two men following as fast as they could move.

He brought them to the Duomo and pointed out his work and why it was done. It was mostly repairs of the communion railing and work around several of the windows, which required highly ornate carvings to match the carvings done years, if not centuries, earlier. In a neighborhood church, he walked them onto the sanctuary, and he ran his hands over every facet of the stonework on the altar. "All mine," he said in garbled English. It was of modest size, but the design was intricate, elegant, and the marble gleamed in the delicate coves, archways, and spires. Jeremiah turned to the bishop. "Tell him, this is exquisite, and if I can find a way to bring him to America to work on the Cawley's church, I will."

The bishop translated then said to Jeremiah, "I thought you two were quite similar. He's older, more experienced, but you have parallel ambitions and artistic skills. You will do well together."

Pietro listened quietly to the conversation between Jeremiah and Bishop Grimaldi, his finger resting on his temple. "Your Excellency," Pietro asked the Bishop, "I wish to ask Signore Knox a question."

Pietro talked nonstop for several minutes, the Bishop listening intently. When he finished, the bishop turned to Jeremiah. "This gentleman"—he gestured toward Pietro—"invites you to work in his studio for a week or two to help on a church bell tower, his primary stonemason has an injured wrist. That way, you can learn each other's skills. Are you able to stay in Siena and help?"

Jeremiah said, "Is this true? If so, I will need to get agreement from my client Mr. Cawley and my employer Mr. McGuinness. If they agree, I will stay."

The bishop conveyed the message to Pietro and explained it would take several days of telegraph cables before an answer was possible. Pietro indicated he understood and shook Jeremiah's hand violently up and down as before.

Pietro asked the Bishop, "Will you please, Excellency, you and Signore Knox join us for dinner?"

"No, no, my friend. I promised Signore Knox that we'd meet my cousin Andrea, his wife, and daughter for dinner."

"Maria," exclaimed Pietro. "Is it true what they say, Excellency. She's to marry Count Benedetto Fazio?"

"Yes, sad, but nonetheless true my friend."

"Yet you will introduce Signore Knox to her?"

"Do you believe in miracles, Pietro?"

"Oh yes, Excellency, I surely do." His eyes scanned Jeremiah from head to toe. "Perhaps I see your wisdom."

Jeremiah had not absorbed enough Italian to understand the conversation between Pietro and the bishop, but he understood a serious exchange had taken place. The bishop explained as they walked back to the hotel. "Jeremiah, I want you to meet Maria because it will be interesting for you and for her if you are to stay and work with Pietro."

"Why interesting, if I may, Excellency?"

"You are young, she is young. You should meet some women from our country that are similar to you in culture and intelligence. Not those young girls who ogle you on the street as we walk."

Jeremiah chuckled. "I see."

"And important," he added, unsure if Jeramiah understood what Pietro said about her forthcoming marriage. "Maria is engaged to marry a man who is much older. My cousin and I have low opinion of him."

"I don't understand my role here."

"You and she are the same age, twenty, if I'm correct. The count is in his mid-forties, rich with an odd, perhaps exotic lifestyle. By meeting you, perhaps she will see what she is missing by ignoring younger men. Thus far, my cousin tells me, her head has not been turned by any of the young suitors in Siena."

"Hmmmm."

"Are you willing to accompany me?"

"My curiosity is sky-high, to use an American expression."

Andrea Grimaldi's palazzo was a sprawling building of several stories, from the wide-open entryway, a curving staircase led to an upper story. Spacious rooms opened off the hallway with intricate blue patterns inlaid on white marble floors. Twenty-foot ceilings gave the rooms the appearance of immense space, and large windows overlooked a grove of olive trees. Andrea greeted them in Italian and English, escorting them into their sitting room. They sat on matching white-and-gold brocade couches near a fireplace that was six feet wide and five feet tall. A white-jacketed servant entered the room, offered drinks from a tray; and Jeremiah, glancing at the bishop's choice, made the same selection. When Maria and her mother entered the room, Jeremiah was stunned.

Unlike most of the Italian women he had met or seen in the churches, cafes, or walking on the streets, Maria was not short, not dark-haired nor full-bodied. She was quite tall, long in arms and legs; her face was pleasant but not beautiful. What struck him most was her hair. It was lush, shoulder length, and brilliantly blond. Her blue eyes flashed with energy. She looked more German or Scandinavian than Italian. Her father had fair hair, what was left of it, and that was her heritage thought Jeremiah.

She greeted him with a kiss on each cheek and said in perfect English, "A sculptor and an American, what brings you to Siena?"

He wanted to be witty, clever, maybe even flirtatious, but chose to be polite, careful. He described his project and the assistance of the bishop then described the features of Siena that had most appealed to him. She nodded and urged him to sit next to her as she took a seat on the couch. She leaned forward, indicating she wished to hear more, and they talked until dinner was served.

The five-course meal had many highlights for Jeremiah, but the veal preparation was memorable. The pasta was the best he'd ever had, and the Tuscan wines, red and white, were delicious. He consumed them with gusto, laughing while answering their questions. The bishop added to Jeremiah's purpose in Italy entertaining the Grimaldis with tidbits of Jeremiah's history as a political radical. It was evident to Jeremiah that the bishop and his cousin were from Italian aristocracy, and he realized that more time with this family and Pietro could be interesting and beneficial. He gazed upward to the frescoes on the ceiling, wishing that the extension for his stay in Italy would be approved by McGuinness and the Cawleys.

As he and the bishop departed, Maria reached for his hand. "Jeremiah, when will you learn if you are to stay and work?"

"In a week or two, perhaps sooner."

"Would you like to walk the hills this weekend, see some of the older, more ancient villages?"

The bishop turned to Jeremiah as they left the Palazzo. "Did you enjoy the dinner and my cousin's family?"

"I did."

"Well, don't be coy, young man. What did you and Maria discuss at the door."

"Oh, that. We're to go hiking this weekend."

The bishop smiled, said nothing, and pointed to the carriage that would take them back to their hotel.

Chapter 11

Agreement to extend Jeremiah's stay came after a few days. Cawley was pleased Jeremiah was working on the statue of Suzanne in Siena, so he cabled, "As long your work on the statue can progress well, stay on, young man. Stay on."

McGuinness had different needs. He wrote, "Jeremiah, in addition to the statue of Suzanne, you'll be working on the floor of the altar and the communion rail. I need you here as soon as the exterior of the church is done and we begin working inside. Maybe a month or two, no more."

Jeremiah found that behind the little storefront off the Palio was a large studio where a dozen stonemasons worked on a variety of urns, friezes, statues, and repairs of damaged altars. Jeremiah made immediate contributions to a bell tower and to large stone base supporting a statue of Jesus Christ. While in the studio, he observed the artisans working on various sections of altars, pulpits, and statues. Pietro demonstrated his technique on how to convert a sketch into a statue, how to create realistic faces on the heads of saints, and how to create motion or establish stillness in statues. His advice was constant, and Jeremiah struggled to keep up with the unending flow of instructions. He felt slow and inadequate, yet Pietro was never critical; his mode of teaching was through inquiry and suggestion.

On a cloudy day, when the light in the studio was low, Pietro said, "Jeremiah, when the light is poor, I choose to work on the large appendages. When the light's better, then I'll work on the delicate features like the hair or eyes."

Jeremiah nodded. "I find that moving from, say, the arms back to small details like the eyes to be difficult. I can't get the precision I seek. It's not only poor light that bothers me."

"Understandable, what I do is work the arms or garments with my larger chisels and hammers. Then stop, get a glass of water, stare at the statue for a few minutes, then get my smaller instruments to work on the finer details like the hair or fingers. I need a break in time to shift from the large to the small."

Jeremiah didn't want to admit it to himself, much less to Pietro, but he questioned his skill. Normally very confident, he faced the stone each day with apprehension, the chisel often trembled in his hand. He wanted success with his statue of Suzanne and worried that it was unattainable. Would he have to depend on Pietro to save him?

When he'd been in Pietro's studio for a month, he rose one night from a terrifying dream. It was black outside, and he had no idea of the time. He found his watch; it was 3:15. Oooh, he sighed as he thought about the dream. He reached beneath his night shirt; his chest was covered in sweat. He went to the bathroom and toweled off, thinking about the horror that had awakened him. He'd been shaping the face of Suzanne, and the chisel hit his little finger, cutting it off above the knuckle. Blood streamed over Suzanne face; it spurted over the sleeve of his shirt before he could cover the severed digit. He looked to the floor for the tip of his finger and woke trembling in a deep sweat.

That night, he had dinner with Maria at a trattoria near the Garabaldi's palazzo. He told her of the dream, how it disturbed him.

She smiled and reached across the table, taking his hand. "You're new to our country. You're learning our language, our customs. You're working with strangers. And my uncle Carlo, your friend the bishop, says your work is amazing." She stopped, watching him, wanting her words to be heard. Worried, she added, "You don't believe me, do you?"

He shook his head.

"Pietro told Uncle Carlo that he's never met anyone who learns so fast and produces exactly to the desired design. Yet you feel overwhelmed. When I'm with you, I can see it. I feel it."

"Pietro said I'm fast, good?"

"Absolutely," she said it with such conviction. She laughed. "That was aggressive, wasn't it? Sorry. You're good, you must know it."

"How did you get so wise at twenty? When I listen to you, I feel like a child."

"It's been fascinating watching you, getting to know you. The adjustment's hard, isn't it? I can't imagine going to your country and doing something in my field."

"It is a challenge, but it's a matter of necessity."

"That's courage, Jeremiah."

"You're the one with courage, Maria."

"What have I done to show courage?"

"Your engagement to the count. It's against the wishes and expectations of your family, is it not?"

She looked down at her hands, pursed her lips as she raised her eyes to his. "Yes," she said slowly. "No one seems to approve. No one seems to understand my reasoning."

"Is it misunderstanding, or is it disagreement with your logic?"

"What do you think? I never heard your thoughts."

"It's not my business, Maria."

"Jeremiah." She rolled the sound of his name, her accent giving it emphasis. "I just made it your business. I want to know what you think."

"If I must, I don't want to be rude."

"Stop delaying, Jeremiah."

"Okay, I'll say it like an American, I'll be direct. Why marry at such a young age and to a much older man?"

"That's everybody's opinion, isn't it? I know my father and Carlo pushed you toward me. Did you know you were a pawn in their game?"

"The bishop asked if I wanted to meet you. I agreed because I wanted to experience the upper class in this country. His intentions, if I knew them, wouldn't have altered my choice."

"Ah, it's true. Carlo wanted the handsome young sculptor to turn my head." She laughed, a rich and throaty tone.

Jeremiah blushed, and she squeezed his hand. He liked the reassurance and caressed the back of her hand with his long thumb. "Unlikely Maria, I'm aware of the class structure in Italy. I'm not appropriate for you."

"From what I know of you, Jeremiah, if you wanted a woman, class structure wouldn't stop you. Be honest, what's really at the heart of your observation?"

"We're twenty, Maria, sweet Jesus." He shook his head. "Way too young for marriage."

"I thought you just said I was very wise for my age. You can't have it both ways." Her eyes were lively as she scrutinized his face.

"I'm not ready for family responsibilities, not remotely. Are you?"

Her expression shifted from playfulness to a message he couldn't decipher. There was something in her eyes, the way they seemed to look inward when he asked questions. A dreamy look crossed her face. At that moment, she seemed far away. He sensed she reached back to centuries of female knowledge.

She said, "In this country, in the world." She opened her hands extending them beyond her body. "How many women have the opportunity to become a contessa? I may be only twenty, but I know this is an unusual situation. One that is not likely to come again. He may be older. He may wander to other women from time to time. He may drink too much, gamble too much, but I'll have status in our country that most women would die for."

"Yet, with your intelligence, you can do what you want. Be your own person rather than acquire status or prestige via marriage."

"Maybe in England or your Scotland or Ireland, that's possible. But not here."

"I met Antonia DiComo, the author, she's …"

"Oh, her, one of the bishop's friends. A true exception, Jeremiah. Trust me." She placed her other hand on top of Jeremiah's, enclosing it with her long fingers. "Look, I feel ready for a life with a man. That may be unusual, but that's where I am. I know that you're years away from that life. I might want to wait for man like you, but for how long? It's too uncertain."

"Darn." He laughed. "I like this sensation." He gazed down at their hands. "You've aroused my interest."

"Bad timing, Jeremiah." She laughed. "But when you decide what you want from a woman, come find me. I may be a widow by then." He started to chuckle, then they exploded in laughter.

During his stay in Siena, they saw each other often. In their walks, they went hand in hand. In parting, there were brief kisses, yet their physical exchanges were chaste communicating friendship more than love or passion. He valued her insights on his struggles with the language, the culture, and the demands of his craft. Speaking with her and with Pietro's stonemasons on a daily basis, he gained facility and eventually comfort in the language. It's lyric beauty. It's resonant tones had a calming effect on him, adding to his enjoyment of Siena and appreciation of all things Italian. Her comments on his work, along with those of Pietro, increased his confidence.

After two months had passed, even Jeremiah had to admit that his skill as a stonemason had advanced dramatically. Slowly he began to accept what McCracken, his Edinburgh instructor, had said, "He could be a sculptor."

When he boarded the George Washington in Genoa, Pietro was with him. A cable from McGuinness indicated that the contract with the Cawley's had been signed and the exterior construction of the church had begun. One day as they stood on the deck, the cool salt air whipping at their faces, Jeremiah said, "When we arrive Pietro, we'll begin work inside the church. But first, you'll meet McGuinness's crew, and we'll find a place for you to live."

The short Italian placed his large bony hands near Jeremiah's face. "We will make a magnificent floor and altar. Like no other in Wooster."

Jeremiah clapped him on the back and in his best Italian said, "We'll dazzle them."

Their arrival in McGuinness's shed was the cause of much celebration. The exterior shell of the church had been finished signaling the beginning of the interior work. McGuinness had several hungry stonemasons eager to start on the new project, and they greeted Jeremiah and Pietro with joy. Hands clapped, backs slapped, shoulders shaken with strength and enthusiasm, the smiles wide on the crew's faces. The large shed, normally known for click-click sound of chisels working and frequent cussing gave way to a new frequency as McGuinness's crew wheeled out a keg of beer and the drinking began. The men wanted to celebrate the launching of a new and major project—the Church of St. Suzanne. Using every form of drinking glass available, they saluted and toasted Jeremiah and Pietro.

Unused to beer and such buoyant energy, Pietro was bewildered. Confused, he asked Jeremiah in Italian, "What is going on? Why are these men drinking and celebrating on a workday. Is it holiday?"

Biasi sidled up to him. "Pietro, I'm from Montepulciano, so I can help you with the language." He grasped Pietro's shoulders. "They're excited to welcome you and to start this work. It has been too quiet here for too long. When Jeremiah left for Italy, work slowed down."

After several glasses of beer, the hand shaking, and backslapping ceased, the men lost at what to do next broke into song. The only song they all knew was "Ta Ra Ra Boom Deay, Ta Ra Ra Boom Deay." They bellowed the verses over and over with their glasses held high. Jeremiah had never seen the crew so ebullient. His eyes were as wide as Pietro, and he was pleased with the reception.

He said to Pietro, "I'm not sure the celebration is for us. I think they may be delighted that several tons of marble have come with us. They know the marble will keep them busy for a year or more."

As the celebration wound down, McGuinness brought Pietro and Jeremiah into his office. "Good lord, lad, the boys missed you. I guess that's obvious." He chortled—his short barking laugh was his main form of expressing joy—then he looked solemn. "Gentlemen, let's get down to details."

He explained, with Jeremiah translating, that Pietro would work under contract to the McGuinness Company and be responsible for the altar of St. Suzanne's. Jeremiah and the McGuinness masons would make the flooring, the communion rail, the window adornments and the bases for all the statues. Pietro's workers in Siena would make the statues of the saints. Pietro would also guide Jeremiah in his work on the statue of Suzanne.

Pietro nodded; agreement was easy for him. He trusted Jeremiah, and his only questions brought smiles to McGuinness and Jeremiah. "Where will I live? Where will I eat? How long will I be here?"

Jeremiah offered, "Until you find something better, you may stay with me. I have a spare room, and it's simply but fully furnished. And I think the Italian food in Worcester will surprise you. You'll find many friends there."

McGuinness's response was more terse. "How long you stay is up to you. It depends on how fast you work."

Pietro's housing started as a temporary lodging with Jeremiah and became an easy, sustainable arrangement. Jeremiah and Pietro worked on separate projects during the day, Pietro on the altar, Jeremiah on the statue of Suzanne; and in the evenings, they dined at local restaurants or with friends from the McGuinness shop. Later they would work in Jeremiah's studio, discussing the techniques or design changes they'd employ the next day. Without discussion, the weeks rolled by, and Pietro stayed with Jeremiah, the two men comfortable in each other's company. The work on the altar progressed rapidly with Jeremiah assisting Pietro on the carving of the spires.

Stepping back to examine his work on the altar, Jeremiah turned to hear the voice of Marty O'Malley. He said, "You and that Italian, the work is beautiful. This will be the best altar in Worcester."

Jeremiah placed his hammer on the altar base, his chisel in his hand, he glanced at O'Malley then back to the spire. "You think so, that's nice to hear."

Pietro, not understanding the man's comment, glanced at him, smiled, and continued his work.

O'Malley said, "Jeremiah, I've come to admire you as a sculptor, and now I learn I'm to admire you as a fighter for our cause."

Jeremiah twitched inside, his stomach flipped. "What's this, O'Malley?"

"Boys in Boston and in New York have spoken to me about your work in Ireland. You're a hero there. They've just discovered where you are."

Jeremiah sighed. "Sweet Jesus," he muttered. "Probably confusion. Wrong man."

"Nay, lad. You're from Stradbally, deported by Judge Hardy. You got a five-year term, four more to go. The description fits perfect. Tall, rugged-looking, and working for McGuinness. No, I've got the right man."

Jeremiah walked away from the altar, walked past O'Malley to the entrance of the church. O'Malley followed him.

Jeremiah turned. "Okay, you found me. So what? What do you want?"

O'Malley was a large man. He was a wide as he was tall, and he was quite tall. Below his blue work shirt, his massive hands were gritty with dirt and sawdust. Jeremiah estimated they were the size of a small ham. One punch from him would finish most men.

O'Malley said, "Easy, lad. You're with your own people. We fellow Irish must stick together in the new country. Help each other. Plus"—he studied Jeremiah, taking a measure of the man—"I have information you need to hear."

"What's that?"

"The boys from my city, Dublin, tell me some crazy British thugs that lost a brother at the Waterford Barracks raid are seeking the killers and want revenge. They have your name along with a bunch of other names."

"What?"

"Yeah, don't know how they got the names, but they got them and are traveling around Ireland, looking for your fellow raiders." He smiled. "The good news is that our boys will kill them before they hurt any of ours."

"*Our boys*, you just said a mouthful. What do you mean *our boys*?"

O'Malley said, "As you might guess, I'm with the Fenians here in the US. We're a good group, making sure we get good wages, get hospital care when hurt, get decent schools for our kids. We're not trying to overthrow the US government. We're making sure the Irish get a fair shake here."

"I appreciate your information of the thugs. Do you know their names?"

"Yeah, they're the Milton brothers. Thomas Milton was the one what died."

"Well, I'm pretty safe here. America's a long ways away."

"Don't count on that, and I'll keep my ears open."

"That I appreciate, but back to the Fenians. You must understand that I'm under very restrictive orders from the court. I can't do anything political here, or I get sent back to the judge, and it's prison for me. I'm not going to risk that."

"I hear you. All I want is to stay in touch, and I'll make sure my friends know your situation with the court."

"As long as we understand each other."

"I'm on the job here, so we'll see a lot of each other. From time to time, I'd like to talk."

Jeremiah went quiet. "I appreciate your help with news of the Miltons." He gazed into O'Malley's large face. "If I can help the Irish here, you show me the action to take. If I agree, I'll take the action, but on my own and independent of the Fenians. Do you understand?"

"Relax, Jeremiah. All I ask for is the opportunity to talk from time to time."

"We'll see. Tell me the topic, and I'll let you know."

O'Malley's work crew completed the brick exterior before the snows fell, and their interior carpentry work was superior. He offered Jeremiah a sandwich from time to time, and the two men talked. O'Malley's main concerns were for better housing for Irish laborers and what to do about practices in shops and factories that discriminated against the Irish. He appreciated Jeremiah's thinking, his creative solutions to labor problems, and his willingness to draft persuasive letters to Worcester's City Council on housing and discrimination practices in hiring. Otherwise, he left him alone. Jeremiah never knew what O'Malley said to his compatriots in the Fenian organization in Worcester, other East Coast cities, or what he sent to Ireland. But it appeared that O'Malley honored Jeremiah's request, and he heard no more about the Milton brothers.

The speed of O'Malley's crews on the exterior of the church put pressure on the McGuinness crew working the floor, alcoves, statues, and Pietro's altar. As the year ended and the new year began, St. Suzanne's was taking shape. Pietro worked feverously to complete the altar and return to Siena; he missed his family. He pressed Jeremiah to assist him on the altar, and they worked in close tandem, creating identical figurines on the spires with little conversation. Each knew what the other was doing. Biasi, seeing the demands on Jeremiah, assisted with the statue of Suzanne. The work flowed fast. Visitors, including members of the new clergy assigned to the church, stopped by to inspect the work. The new monsignor introduced himself to Jeremiah. "Young man, your crew here works so quietly, so much industry, and the result, as I see it now, is beyond any beauty in my prior churches."

Jeremiah thanked him and, each night, before leaving the partially completed church, kneeled before Pietro's unfinished altar and thanked God for Pietro and for the altar he was creating.

One year after the start of construction, the small church of Saint Suzzane's was blessed by the bishop of Worcester and the first Mass celebrated. The four foot statue of a young girl mounted on a shelf in the wall of the entryway took people's breath away. Some stared and didn't leave and had to be pushed away. The girl with soft ringlets in her hair, her slender body erect as her eyes gazed upward to the heavens, was luminous in white marble. Pietro's Carrara marble was evident elsewhere in the statues along the walls next to the confessionals. And Pietro's marble altar glowed in the soft light directed on it. Its soaring spires matched the spires on the exterior of the church, the marble work intricate and highly ornate. Jeremiah was asked by the Cawley family to join them for the first Mass, and he watched the reactions of the parishioners as they entered and left the church. He was pleased with what he heard, and he gathered it was the same for the Cawleys.

It was late that Sunday when he returned to his flat. He went to his study, the second bedroom reclaimed after Pietro's departure, and leafed through his book of sketches. It was quite full and filling every month. He moved the bulky volume to a new bookcase, which he had recently purchased. On the desk was a new folder, the beginning of a new book, and the first entry was a photograph of "Angels

On A Tombstone," and next to it was a picture of the statue of Saint Suzanne. His first year in America was behind him, and in his mind, he'd made the adjustment fairly well.

I've kept out of trouble, he thought, *kept away from the radicals in Irish politics and managed the contact with O'Malley carefully.* Yet the Fenians had found him. Somehow, he knew he wasn't completely free from their needs.

He was most pleased with his place at the McGuinness Company. He felt secure there. He looked at the two photographs and thought, *It will be rewarding to add more of these to the book.*

Chapter 12

Jeremiah, learning the craft beside Pietro and Biasi, advanced rapidly at the McGuinness Company. He would spend two more years at McGuinness Stone, advancing his skill in the decorative features of new buildings and on statues. By his twenty-second birthday, with the statue of Suzanne behind him, he was beyond carving inscription on tombstones. He was sought to do statues of saints, decorative work on buildings, and on the interiors of churches. Requests came with increasing frequency to McGuinness Stone for Mr. Knox to work on a statue for a particular saint or for a pulpit. Often, the requests were for other difficult and demanding sculptural designs. Jeremiah found the work added up rapidly, and there was more of it than the McGuinness Company could do. On his twenty-second birthday party, McGuinness, who had organized the celebration, took him aside. The burly owner had enjoyed several glasses of Jamesons and was exuding friendship to all. He approached Jeremiah and put his arm around his shoulder.

He said, "Jeremiah, you've gone further and faster than anyone I've seen in this business, and you're pretty good at the business side too. You've become a sculptor. We're stonemasons here. Our skills are complimentary and different. I think you should have your own business like your Italian friend Pietro. I'll send you work, you send me work, and we'll both get very rich." He laughed loudly and opened his arms wide. "Whattaya think? People are moving into Worcester in droves and in Massachusetts generally. There are churches and buildings going up everywhere. There'll be more work than we can ever do. We can't miss." He gave Jeremiah's shoulder a hard tug. "It's your time, isn't it?"

This required more thought than McGuinness knew. Jeremiah had been in Worcester for three years. In two more years, he could return to Ireland, or at least it was a possibility. If he went back to Ireland, he could return to law school. He could find a way to be active in politics again. But in the past three years, the news from Ireland had not been heartening. Home Rule had not come, and the police pressure on the Fenians had continued. Many of his former friends and associates were in jail. Letters from Joseph Callahan were bleak. Being away from legal work and political strategy for three years had, at times, tugged at his mind. He missed the action in politics, the importance of it. But the memory of it was slowly receding. His satisfaction and successes with sculpture had crowded into the space he had for law and for Irish independence. He had begun to question the effectiveness of the Fenians. Was their approach to the cause the right course of action? Were his skills best suited to the cause, or were they more appropriate to the artistic field of sculpture? He needed to think about it.

At home, in his third-floor flat, he kicked off his shoes and lay on his bed. His hands behind his head, he took stock of where he was at twenty-two. He had become a first-rate stonemason and a reasonable and rapidly improving sculptor. He had made a fair amount of money and, after two years, had the confidence to trust a bank where he had over a thousand dollars stored. He had worked hard, and his work was all he had. A few friends touched the edges of his life. His social activities were limited to Friday nights, on occasion, at local pubs and the socials on special holidays at the Erin I Club. On weekends in the spring and fall, there were the rugby games with the club's team. These sporadic outings had been sufficient for him for the first three years. In thinking about it, he was satisfied with his social side life.

He was not married, nor was there a serious woman in his life. A few women, like Coleen and Maria, had come and gone. He'd never made contact with Phoebe from the *Caledonia* although he thought of her from time to time. He was in no rush to meet women and, particularly, in no haste to marry one. In letters from his father, he had gathered, from reading between the lines, that his presence in Ireland was not missed, and his past actions had not been forgotten by the police, the courts, and the conservative-minded folks of Stradbally, Cork, Waterford, and Dublin. He found the letters from his father to be annoying and wondered why the old man bothered him with such unpleasant news. He considered reducing all contact with his family to the bare minimum. He had stopped all communication with his uncle, giving up any intention of pursuing a legal career in his firm. He would not work with the man.

He rolled onto his side. What about McGuinness's idea? His own company doing fine design work in churches? Was it possible? How did one get started? He thought, come Monday, he'd talk to McGuinness at their lunch break. He stood up. He liked the idea of working with his hands to create objects of beauty and objects that were useful to others as they prayed, as they talked to God. This was doing something good for people, and he was finding this path rewarding, perhaps more rewarding than the hard path of politics in Ireland.

On Monday morning, as George McGuinness arrived to open the shed, a tall man, well dressed in a black topcoat and bowler, was waiting for him. Standing beside a rented carriage, the man said, "You're late."

"And a good morning to you, sir. What can I do for you?"

"I'm Casper Soames, a weekend guest and friend of Harold Cawley. Regrettably, I'm in rush. I must catch the nine-o'clock train to New York." He paused to catch his breath. "Would you be so kind to give this to Mr. Knox? I assume he's not here as your business is locked up." He handed McGuinness a business card and an envelope.

McGuinness tipped his fingers to his cap. "Will do." And he waved the man goodbye.

Jeremiah started his day at St. John's Church in Worcester. The pastor wanted a new pulpit, more elevated and ornate than the current version, and he consumed much of Jeremiah's time with a lengthy review of his sketches and design. Finally, securing agreement on the design, Jeremiah left for McGuinness Stone at mid-morning. He went straight to his workbench and, putting the pulpit project aside, conferred with Biasi on a statue of St. Paul. The pastor of St. Paul's Church in Auburn wanted St. Paul to be moving toward a crowd, and he presently appeared locked in a stationary position. While talking with Biasi, Jeremiah saw the envelope and business card on his bench and promptly forgot it. The flow of St. Paul's tunic was not quite right, and he and Biasi worked the limestone together to get the proper effect of the wind on the garment. He had planned to talk with McGuinness about his business idea, but the flurry of work pushed that plan to the back of his mind. The sharp ring of the bell signaled lunchtime, and he and Biasi put down their tools. "To be continued," Biasi said. And they both laughed.

McGuinness, a glass of water in his hand, approached Jeremiah's bench. "What was that envelope and Mr. Soames's card all about?"

"Oh, I forgot to open it. Let's see." He tore open the white envelope and read quietly for a moment. He looked at the business card and read the letter again. He glanced up at McGuinness. "This man, he's the senior member of some church in Connecticut, Simmstown. It's down near New York, he says." Jeremiah snickered. "Get this, he wants an altar like the one at St. Suzanne's. He'd just spent a weekend with the Cawleys and went to church at St. Suzanne's on Sunday." Jeremiah shook the letter; the smirk face remained. "Jesus, George, somebody told him I did it. That's crazy. He's sending his architect up to see me. This is a mistake. That's Pietro's altar."

"It's yours too. You did a tremendous amount of work on it, so don't look a gift horse in the mouth. This is just what we talked about at your party. It will be the first contract in your own company."

"Well, I clear this up in a letter to him."

"Don't do that, Jeremiah."

"Can't mislead the man. It will only come out in the quality of the altar. There's no fooling a work of art. What Pietro does is art. I cut stones."

"I've been trying to tell you, my brick-headed Irish friend, you're an artist too. You've developed into a first-rate sculptor."

Jeremiah finished his lunch quickly and returned to the statue of St. Paul. He worked the garment for a while then went to his bench and worked on the design for the St. John's pulpit. He worked through the reminder of the day, the hammer and chisels working deftly up and down the marble. Toward the end of the day, his wrists and hands tired, he washed in the shed's large communal bathroom, removed his smock, and donned his jacket. He walked the mile to the trolley and got off at Third Street for Caccione's Trattoria. It was a favorite of his. The room was dark, the red-checked tablecloths and the candles on the tables provided the only brightness in the room. The aromas of garlic and rich tomato sauce filled the room as he wound his way to a table in the back corner. He ordered a large plate of spaghetti with garlic shrimp immersed in a rich tomato sauce and a glass of chianti. The wine was young, sharp, and hard. It gave heat to his parched throat. It was an early dinner. He left before the crowds came in, and he strolled down Third Avenue toward his flat. He came to the large glass ball marking the entry to O'Doul's Pub. The faded yellow of the ball and black print of O'Doul's Pu always brought a chuckle from him. Old O'Doul was too cheap to repaint the sign and put the *b* back in *Pub*. Jeremiah hesitated for a moment then entered. He slid onto a well-worn wooden stool. His elbows rested on the highly polished bar top. He placed a dollar on the counter and caught the bartender's eye. "I'll have one Charlie." While sipping the neat Jameson, Terry Sweeney, a neighbor, saddled up to the seat beside him. Sweeney was a contractor and had supplied several work leads to Jeremiah and to the McGuinness Stone Company. Sweeney had been encouraging Jeremiah to go independent for some time. He felt that a new firm was needed for the ornate work in buildings. As they talked, Sweeney admitted that he didn't know about churches but that Jeremiah should take the meeting with the architect. Jeremiah came away from his conversation more confident about a company of his own, seeing the possibilities as something concrete, not just an idle idea. The Jameson lifted his spirits, but as he walked home, he decided to tell Mr. Soames the truth and let that opportunity pass. He'd start his firm with clear principles: the work would be confined to what he wanted to do and could do, and the client would have complete understanding of a specific design. He'd draft Soames letter when he got home, yet when he'd climbed up the three flights of stairs, sat in his only chair for a few minutes scanning the evening's news, he felt fatigued and decided to do the letter the next day.

His first task in the morning was to repair a frieze at the city library. Biasi could finish the garment on St. Paul. The frieze was a limestone border across the front of the building and had been damaged by a winter ice storm. He cleaned away the debris and rechiseled some of the damaged limestone and, by noon, had completed the work. He placed his tools on his shoulder and walked to the trolley. When he reached the McGuinness shed, the architect, as Casper Soames had said, was waiting for him.

McGuinness was unusually polite to the architect and introduced Henry Vaughn with a lengthy monologue, making it clear to Jeremiah that the man was one of the foremost church architects in the States.

Vaughn laughed. "Thank you, Mr. McGuinness. That was over the top. Don't want to scare this one off."

Jeremiah said, "Mr. Soames indicated that you'd be in touch, and I thought that meant by letter or cable."

"No, Mr. Knox. When Casper Soames says, see someone, I jump." Again, he laughed, a deep throaty tone. He clapped his hands. "Can we sit somewhere and talk?"

McGuinness offered his office, and they moved scattered papers to his desk and found sitting space. As they settled down, Jeremiah said, "Mr. Soames has the wrong impression. I didn't do the altar at St. Suzanne's. That was Pietro Antonino of Siena."

"We know that, and he doesn't want an Italianate altar anyway. He finds the Italian sculptors way too ornate for him. He wants the pillars, tabletop, and tabernacle that you did in the sanctuary. Plus he wants a bell tower like St. Suzanne's and maybe the pulpit."

"I see. Well ..."

Vaughn raised his hand. "I'm pleased Mr. McGuinness is here, because Mr. Soames is very clear on this." He paused, focusing his eyes on McGuinness. "He wants Mr. Knox. He doesn't need the whole McGuinness crew as we have the equivalent artisans nearby in Connecticut. Will that be a problem?" He kept staring at McGuinness.

McGuinness shrugged his shoulders; a slight grimace crossed his lips. He said, "No, that's not a problem. Mr. Knox and I have been discussing separating his type of stonework from ours."

"That's grand. So what do you think, Mr. Knox?"

"Assuming we can agree on the fees and the type of stone I'd recommend, I'm in." *So this is how you start your own company,* he thought. It was easier than he expected.

"You'll find capable artisans to help you in the local area, and we can assist you in that process. You'll stay in a local hotel in Simmstown, which we'll pay for, and here's our offer on fees." He handed a sheet of paper to Jeremiah.

Jeremiah had enough training in the law to learn of negotiating styles, card table faces, and calm demeanor. He maintained a passive face, but inwardly he could hardly contain himself. The offer was nearly double the fees paid to McGuinness Company for the St. Suzanne altar. He glanced from the paper to Vaughn's eyes. "This is fair, I accept."

"Good. Well, better than good. Now, Mr. McGuinness, may we borrow your office for a few more minutes? Since you've freed Mr. Knox for this work, I'd like to discuss something else with him."

McGuinness laughed as he exited the room. "Keep your shirt on, Jeremiah. You're dealing with New Yorkers now."

Vaughn settled in and smiled. "Normally, Mr. Knox, I don't do my clients negotiating and selling, but Casper Soames is special. I've designed a chapel—by the way, that's my specialty—for Soames's alma mater in Gridley Mass, a private school not far away. The St. Suzanne's bell tower is perfect for the school there. I'd like you to do that too, plus I'd like you to do the stone frames for several large stained-glass windows. On that one, you'll be under contract to me, same terms. Is that agreeable?"

"Can the timing of the two jobs be managed to avoid conflict?"

"Since I'm in charge of both—yes." He watched Jeremiah for a second, "Do we have a deal?"

"I think we have two deals. I'm delighted. When do we start?"

"As soon as you can get loose of your obligations with Mr. McGuinness. Shall we go talk with him?"

The conversation lasted all afternoon. By its end, Jeremiah knew more about the intricacies of business than he knew existed. And he realized there was much more to learn. And it was now clear—he had his own firm, his own work to win, his own fees to negotiate. His work future was entirely up to him. He kept insisting on two principles for the work: first, as far as it was practical, he wanted the stone work done on site so he could work at the site or in a shed near the site. He did not want to run the risk of damage during shipping. And secondly, he would spend most of his time on site.

McGuinness pleaded for him to retain a shed for his work in Worcester and that the McGuinness Stone Company would rent permanent space to Jeremiah to use on his projects. Although delighted with the offer, Jeremiah resisted insisting that he would prefer to work with local artisans as long as they were up to the task. Ultimately, he agreed with McGuinness and was grateful for his insight on Jeremiah's need for local workspace.

On travel to sites, Vaughn laughed. "Welcome to the vagabond world, never home. That'll be tough on a young man like you, no social life."

"I'll adjust, but being on top of the work is key. That's most important."

"I like your sense of priorities. We'll work well together," Vaughn added.

The trains from Worcester south toward New York were frequent, and the Simmstown Depot was a few stops prior to the city. The church was in construction, and the architect was asking for the bell tower sketch as soon as he arrived. It was clear the altar was going to be needed in the near future, so he settled down to find a work shed, the artisans he needed and order the marble. Here, Soames and Vaughn were ahead of him. The marble had arrived in the port of New York and was ready to be inspected and shipped to Simmstown. During his first week, he selected his crew, secured the marble from New York, and began work on the altar. As the work progressed, Vaughn, seemingly satisfied, brought Jeremiah via train to Gridley, Massachusetts, a small rural town about fifty miles from Worcester. On the outskirts of the tiny village was the elite private school. The chapel was under construction, and Vaughn showed Jeremiah the design of the large arc-shaped stained-glass windows. The stained glass was to be set into stone arches within the overall arc of the window. Jeremiah's eyes widened, and he glanced from the artist's rendering to Vaughn.

"Mr. Vaughn, the size of these windows and your concept of the stained glass will surpass many of the fine churches I saw in Italy or in Dublin."

"Ah, thank you, Jeremiah, and now let's look at the design in terms of what I want you to do." He laid his hand on the drawing of the main window. "I want you to craft all the stonework for the overall arch and for all the individual panes you see that are designed for stone. Then"—he moved his hand to the design of the chapel's exterior—"see these spires on the bell tower and on the edge of the roof? I want you to shape those as well." He stepped back from the drawings and placed his hands on his hips. He chuckled as if he had a private joke going on inside him. "The problem is how to get you to do the two projects done simultaneously, and I have an idea."

Jeremiah shared the man's chuckle, although the source of the humor, at the moment, was elusive to him. "This I must hear."

"Well, you claimed that travel is no problem for you, so how about this? You spend one highly concentrated month in Simmstown and one here in Gridley until we're done. If one has an emergency, you can alter the schedule. But as a general rule, one month here, one month there. What do you think?"

Jeremiah scratched his head. "I dunno. It seems like the altar at Simmstown is simpler. Why not do it first, get it over with, and then come here?"

"Very practical, young man, except Mr. Soames wants the chapel done for some ceremony next year. And of course, he wants the church done quickly too."

"Yes, he made the church schedule very clear to me, which is why I suggested it first."

"I understand, but you grasp our predicament."

"Yes, of course. He's paying and is demanding. Well, how about this? I do the chapel spires in Simmstown in between my other work there. There is gap time in the altar work when I have my crew doing some of the simpler sculpting."

"You'll ship the spires via rail to Gridley?"

"Yes, I may even travel with them when I come here for my month. How does that sound?"

"I had the sense you'd figure this out." He extended his hand to Jeremiah. "Let's work ahead on this basis and talk every week."

As his third year in the United States came to a close and his fourth year started, the passing months flew by. He was so absorbed in the Simmstown Church and the Gridley School Chapel, the issues of home rule in Ireland and the completion of his legal studies in Edinburgh receded from the front of his mind. The letter from his mother informing him of the coming marriage of his older brother Tommy came as a surprise. It was special news because he had concluded that Tommy's personality would never appeal to a woman. His mother conveyed her sadness that he could not return for the wedding. She had appealed to the court for a short stay for Jeremiah, and Judge Hardy rejected the petition. She talked about how time had passed and her happiness that he was in his fourth year and would soon petition for return. He had received her letter in Worcester on a weekend between visits to Simmstown and Gridley. On the train to Simmstown the following week, he thought about his reply to her. In recent months, the appeal of law school and a return to Fenian activities had continued to trouble him. On one day, he would bristle with enthusiasm over a return to the old fight. On other days, it was totally unappealing as he thought of the jail terms of his friends, of his own deportation, and how that paled with his success in the United States. What should he say to his family about living and working in America? Should he admit that it was more satisfying and had become more appealing than he ever expected?

As he worked on the final pillar for the altar, the chisel delicately adding the last fluted lines to the pillar, one of his artisans stood by him.

"Aye, Jeremiah, yer touch is gentle yet sure. How do yee do it?"

He kept at his work, undeterred by the comment, yet said, "Billy, my boy, your accent is a giveaway. Donegal, is it?" Billy had unsettled Jeremiah from the start. He'd heard good recommendations about the young man's stone-working skills and hired him. Yet there was something in his gruff manner, his distance from other workers that worried Jeremiah. He watched him carefully at first then relaxed as Billy was good with the stones and kept to himself.

"Yes, sir, and I have a message for yee."

"Do you speak it, or is it written?"

"It's to be spoken."

"Ah, can we do it at the lunch break?"

"We can but in private, yer see."

Jeremiah, concentrating on the pillar, let the request die there. Why private? He wondered but did not consider it further. He focused on the marble. "Okay."

Billy munched on his sandwich as he sat on the edge of a slab of limestone. Jeremiah walked toward him, hitched his pants up, and sat beside him. "Okay, what's so private?"

"Yee didn't tell us. Yee didn't tell me that yer famous. Yee were a fierce man with the rifle at the Waterford Barracks bombing, and yee planned the Cork Rail Station ambush. A brilliant stroke, I heard."

Jesus, he muttered quietly. Other than the few exchanges with O'Malley, he'd avoided all contact with the Fenians for over three years. He felt free in America, and his uncle had disappeared from his life. "Well"—he laughed as he gazed inquisitively at Billy—"that caper got everyone else jailed and two of us deported. Not a successful moment for the Fenian movement."

"But we need that kind of courage and thinkin' here." Jeremiah started to talk, but Billy put up his hand. "Please, hear me out, Jeremiah. It's our land, our families I'm talkin' about."

"Quickly, Billy. I've pledged to stay away from such matters while in the US."

"We know yer helped Marty O'Malley up there in Worcester with housing for the Irish. My brother-in-law, Terry, Terry Litton, he knows all 'bout yee."

Jeremiah took a long swallow from his jug of water then shook his head. He conveyed discouragement, but it did not deter Billy. He said, "Yeah, Terry needs some help with thinkin' about a strike on the docks of New York and about raisin' some money for some works by the family in Donegal."

"What do you mean by works in Donegal?"

"Can't say."

Here we go, thought Jeremiah. The works in Donegal were likely to be disruptive, possibly dangerous, and if they're caught, his name would appear—his chance of return compromised or, quite likely, ruined. "Who's Terry workin' with in New York?"

"I'm not supposed to tell yee."

"If you don't tell me, I plan to ignore this whole conversation."

"Okay, they're called the Hibernian Brotherhood."

"Ah, US branch of the Fenians. Are you a member?"

He seemed pained to answer the question but finally admitted, "Yeah."

"I'll give you an answer in the next day or two. But first, I know that I cannot help on the strike. I'll be sent right back to jail in Ireland on that one."

"I'll tell Terry."

He spent the next two evenings on a telephone, trying to reach a friend, Charley Kaneel, at the Erin I Club who was a lawyer. When they finally connected, they discussed Jeremiah's new projects and his commitment to stay away from the Irish troublemakers. When he mentioned the contact made by the Hibernian Brotherhood, Kaneel was informed of the group and emphatic.

"Stay away from them, Jeremiah. They're Fenians, making trouble about working conditions here in the States, organizing marches and strikes, and beating up other workers who don't agree with them. And they're always raising money to fund the Fenians in Ireland. And it's been a lot of money according to my inside sources. So I'd suggest you stay away."

Chapter 13

The next day, Jeremiah called Billy aside. "Here's the news. I talked with my lawyer. If I get involved with this New York Hibernian Brotherhood, I'll be sent back to Ireland and to jail. So the answer to Litton is no."

"He's not going to be happy."

"That's not my problem, and if you bring this up again, I'll fire you as fast as the words come out of your mouth." He saw that the man had backed away, a snarl on his face, his hands tightened by his side. "I don't want to fire you, Billy. You're a good stonemason, but I can't have politics in my work."

Billy tugged at his cap, his hands relaxed. He turned away from Jeremiah and returned to his work. No further words were exchanged, but Jeremiah could see the man was not pleased. Jeremiah knew he had not heard the end of this situation.

Later the next day, he left for Gridley. An emergency had arisen on the limestone carving for the big window arches. When suspended high on top of the supporting pillars, the arch showed cracks. He felt he knew the problem. Vaughn wanted slender arches for the peaks of the windows, and they could not hold their own weight and certainly not the stonework above them. Jeremiah had to convince Vaughn to allow the arches to be cut wider and with greater density. They met, and Jeremiah convinced him to try three different depth and width levels until they found one that had the strength to support the weight above it. Jeremiah insisted that from a distance or even on close inspection the different thicknesses would not be discernible to an observer.

Vaughn snapped back, "Maybe you don't see it. Maybe others don't see it, but I do. This last arch is not elegant. It's not for a church. It's more for a stadium."

Jeremiah sighed. "Okay, I'll see what we can do. Can you come back tomorrow?"

"Only in the early morning. I need to be in Boston by noon."

They worked through the night. With a set of kerosene lamps for illumination, Jeremiah labored through the night, carving intricate patterns on the face of the arches for the main window. The size of the arch was unchanged. It was much larger than Vaughn's desired dimensions, yet the effect of the patterns on its face seemed to soften the impact of its natural bulk. That was Jeremiah's opinion and it was shared by the two stonemasons who worked with him through the long evening. As the dawn broke and the carving completed, they went to the school's dining hall for coffee and eggs and ate with the students. Their young faces turned to Jeremiah, asking questions about the chapel and how old he was. How did he get this job? Jeremiah thought about his age and realized he was only five or six years older than these students, and a sense of energy and satisfaction surged through him. The older Italian stonemasons laughed with the boys and claimed that he was the architect's son. That's how he got the work.

When they returned to the site, Vaughn was there pacing back and forth. "What did you decide, Jeremiah?"

"It's here, sir, inside the building under the canvas."

Vaughn's taciturn facade restrained his normal surge of feelings. He believed that bursts of emotion were not helpful to those who worked on his buildings. An early amount of praise could summon slack work later while sharp criticism could instill indifference or hostility among the workers producing mediocre results. He preferred to be hard to read, even stoic, an enigma to his workers. He was having a hard time of that with the young Mr. Knox.

Jeremiah lifted the tarpaulin, revealing the two sides of the matching arches. Vaughn stood in front of the arches, then walked along their sides and then to their back. He returned to the front and stared again, taking his time. "You've cut them down substantially, haven't you? They'll never take the weight."

"Sir, measure them if you will. I think you'll be surprised."

Jeremiah handed Vaughn a tape measure, and he walked to the arches, stretching the tape across their front. He looked down at the tape then went back to the arches and measured them again. "They're the same size as yesterday. How did you do this?" he asked. "It's a bloody miracle."

"It's just an optical illusion. The carvings on the face of the arch soften the impact of its size and make it look smaller. I saw examples of this in Rome, so I thought I'd try it here."

"I'll be damned. This is amazing." He lifted his hat to scratch his head. "I've got to run as you know. Have the construction crew raise them into place when they can. I'll be back later in the week to see them in the building."

"I'd like to refine the decorative art more if that's okay. Maybe a day or two more of additional detail will enhance the beauty."

"I trust your judgment, Jeremiah. I think I owe you one on this innovation."

"I'll take that chip, sir. I may need it later."

Vaughn turned to the whole group of stonemasons, his arm waving farewell. "Well, I'll see you boys later in the week, and if we're ahead of schedule as you and Mr. Knox expect, I'll see those arches in place."

When Jeremiah made the "chip" comment, he was thinking ahead. He believed that he was not through with Billy, Terry Litton, and the Hibernian Brotherhood. An inner sense alerted him. He felt he'd hear from Billy or others again.

The following week, he was due in Simmstown, and the exterior shell of the church was nearly complete, and the basic shape of the altar was in place. The delicate carvings around the base of the table, the intricate work of the arched coves around the tabernacle, and the peaks of the spires were all that remained to be done. The statues at the altar and in the entranceway would come last. Billy asked Jeremiah to join him for dinner at his favorite diner in the village. It was crowded for a Monday, the wood-topped tables and the red leather booths were jammed with road workers, contractors, and rail workers. The work crews were drawn to Simmstown to support the town as it absorbed the influx of wealthy professionals seeking the quieter surroundings of rural Connecticut to the crowds and filth of New York. As Jeremiah slid into the booth, a stranger extended a powerful hand. "Hello, Jeremiah Knox. I'm Terry Litton, Billy's brother-in-law."

Jeremiah took the hand; the grasp was iron strong. Jeremiah could see that Litton's fingers, and knuckles were raw and cut as if he just finished a bare knuckle fight. His face was young, a little older than Jeremiah's, he surmised, and there were scars above the eyes. Along his left cheekbone was a jagged scar, giving him the face of a pugilist. His black hair was thinning and lay flat against his scalp. His eyes were a cold blue, and the effect was one of power and supreme confidence. His massive shoulders and thick chest strained against the confines of his blue work shirt. He was big man and used his physical appearance as a partner in his conversations.

"Jeremiah, may I call yee that? I must get the next train back to New York, so if yee don't mind, I'll git right to the point."

Jeremiah face sank into an expression that his father and his fellow Fenians deplored. His eyes went narrow, his lips were thin and tight, and he kept opening and closing his hands. He stared hard at Litton and said nothing. For his father, it was the stony silence that bothered him, and it seemed to have a similar effect on Litton.

Litton stammered, "Well now, I need yee and yee don't seem interested in helping a fellow Irishman."

"Not true. I will help any Irishman in a just cause. As Billy probably told you, I'm required by law not to associate with any group agitating any political activities, especially radical Irish causes here in the US or in Ireland."

Litton waved his massive hand. "Yeah, yeah. I've heard all that. Don't mean schist to me. We're not doin' anything illegal. We just want our rights."

Jeremiah said, "Hear me out. The judge could not be more clear on this subject and on the consequences for me if I transgress." He leveled his eyes on Litton again and then continued, "If I transgress, it's back to jail in Dublin. Is that clear?" It was not meant to be a question, and he rested back in the booth.

"What we need is for you to talk to the police about the US Constitution, about our right to assemble, and so on. Yee just go in and visit with them. Nobody will know. Very simple."

Jeremiah laughed. "Nobody will know I talked to the police? You're joking, am I right? Perhaps you're aware that the police have a few Irishmen on the force. Be realistic." Jeremiah hesitated for a second. "Billy mentioned raising money. That's not possible either."

"I don't like the way yer going, laddie. Careful now … perhaps you're not aware, but people don't bullshit me." His cold eyes stayed fixed on Jeremiah's face. "You mentioned money, let's get to that for a minute, and we'll come back to your help with the law. I promised to raise a certain amount of money for the Fenians in Donegal and elsewhere. We want to make sure yee'll contribute too."

"First off, I'm starting a new business, anything I earn goes into the business. Before that, I arrived here in the US with only the shirt on my back. That's all. I have no funds."

"Bollocks, yer running a big expensive construction here and elsewhere. You're in league with Soames and Vaughn and that crowd. All very rich. Don't tell me yee have no cash." He placed his large bruised hands down hard on the table.

Jeremiah pointed a long finger in the direction of Litton's face. "I'm telling you two things so you better listen good. I have no money, and second, if I had it, I can't give it to you with my court order. If I send any money to Ireland, it can only go to my parents or to a church."

"Listen here, Mr. Knox. I'm not buyin' yer shit and don't like yer tone." He pointed a crooked finger at Jeremiah. "I know a lot about yee that the courts don't even know. I know for a fact that you carried a rifle for our cause, the Gewehr 88 that our ladies brought from Germany by yacht in 1889. And you carried that rifle at the Waterford Barracks bombing. I can claim, and there's no proof to the contrary, that yee shot at and hit British Regulars in that ambush." He stopped and pointed a thick finger at Jeremiah. "I also know that the Milton brothers are looking for yee, for revenge. I know they're on the run for attempted murder of your crew from the Waterford Barracks raid. They're headed to the US, so I'm told. You need my protection, and you need me not to tell the judge about your role in the barracks raid."

He'd hit Jeremiah in the stomach with that comment. No one in the Fenians would talk about the rifles, how they got them, who carried them, who took shots at the British. The internal code of the organization was strong. So how did Litton know this? Even Judge Hardy had not mentioned it in his trial. Shaken, Jeremiah rose from the table. "I don't give a rat's ass what you think you know or what you like or don't like, but you better think twice when you threaten me."

"Before you leave, Knox, I want yee to know that if yee don't help as I've nicely asked, I will tell your fucking court—wherever they are in Ireland—that you're a solid member of the Hibernian Brotherhood here in New York. And I know more about your actions in Ireland than your court knows. They'll welcome my information. Let's see what they think about that one."

Jeremiah was stunned by the threat. He fought fear. His breathing became labored, and he fought to control it. He didn't like the feeling of tension and willed himself to slow down. "You heard me. Don't fuck with me unless you want some very bad consequences. You've mentioned blackmail. Perhaps you don't know it, but it's against the law here." He moved his face close to Litton's. "Perhaps you don't know this, but I know how to use the law." With that, he turned and left the restaurant. While he worried about the Litton's threat with the court, he was troubled by the news that the Milton brothers were headed to the United States. He believed he knew how to deal with Litton, but what to do about the Miltons was elusive to him.

Billy shook his head and said, "Jesus, why did yee do that, Terry, threaten him? He don't take threaten, and he's got powerful friends like Mr. Soames and Mr. Vaughn. At the site, they mostly talk to him. They talk more with him than the overall boss of the construction."

"Wake the fuck up, Billy. He's just a Mick like the rest of us, but a Mick that can help us as the bastard should. Besides, the rich boys will drop him like a bad habit if they find a better sculptor."

"Yee heard him. He's screwed with the courts."

"They'd never know. Yee tell him tomorrow, Billy, if he doesn't join me in the strike and provide some the money, I'll rat him out like I said."

"If I tell him that, there goes my job."

"He wouldn't dare, threaten him with damage on the building site."

"He'll do it. He'll fire me, and I'll never work in Connecticut again. I'll have to come back to New York."

"Yer exaggeratin', Billy." He slammed his fists in the table. "You tell him tomorrow what I said."

Billy nodded, stared down into his glass of beer, slowly shaking his head.

Jeremiah's legal studies had prepared him for the likes of Terry Litton. Court cases on labor agitation in the mills and construction sites in London, Manchester, and Birmingham had provided many examples of the wiles and strategies of labor agitators. At the end of the week in Simmstown, Vaughn appeared on site to inspect the week's work. After discussion of the progress on the church, Jeremiah asked Vaughn to step aside. He said, "I mentioned I may want to cash in that chip. The favor you mentioned in Gridley earlier in the week."

"How so, Jeremiah?"

"We may have trouble on the site here. One of the workers here has ties with the Hibernian Brotherhood in New York, and their leader came here looking for support."

"Why you and support for what?"

"As you know, I have some legal education. They're planning a strike in the docks and want my legal arguments to make it legitimate. And they want money to support similar activities in Ireland."

"Well, that's not our problem, Jeremiah. You're a sculptor, not a lawyer, so ignore it. Plus, the New York police will take care of any striking mob faster than you can blink an eye. And the money thing, that's the Brit's problem."

"Well, sir, their leader has threatened this site with destruction if I don't help them with their legal strategy and with some funds."

"Why you, Jeremiah, do they have something on you?"

"Sir, they know I was politically active in Ireland before I came to the US. They think they can use that to hurt me."

"And your donation to their cause, that's up to you."

"I think we better protect this site until the actual church people take it over."

"Yes, I see." Vaughn placed his hand on his eyes and rubbed them vigorously. He mumbled again, "I see, I see." He removed his hands from his eyes and looked at Jeremiah. "Who's the person on site that got this started?"

"His name is Billy O'Rourke, a nice lad, good stonemason but easily led by others."

"Fire him, don't you think."

"Yes, I agree. However, that may incite some locals and, quite likely, the New Yorkers. They'll seek revenge for firing Billy and for my not playing their game in New York."

"Well, Jeremiah, these problems are not new to us. My construction sites in New York and some other Eastern cities have had similar threats. We'll handle this my way. Don't worry."

"What about the trouble in New York, the strike on the docks?"

"I'll leave that to Casper Soames. He's very close to the mayor and police chief. They'll know how to handle Mr. Litton … that's his name?"

"Yes, thanks for listening, and you've eased my mind. I'll get back to my real work."

He met with the construction manager and described his conversation with Vaughn. They agreed that Billy would be released that day, and the construction manager indicated that a team of Pinkerton's would be hired to protect the site day and night. He claimed that Mr. Vaughn and Mr. Soames had to bring that type of help on other jobs. They walked to the bench where Billy was working and asked him to pack his tools. The construction manager was a short compact man with a kindly face, but when he needed to be firm, a new face appeared. He said, "Billy, you're a good worker, but you made a couple of bad decisions. First, you brought a well-known New York troublemaker to our site, and second, he threatened our site with damage if Mr. Knox here doesn't cooperate. Well, I've got good news for you Billy and bad news. The good news is that we're not going to have you arrested and put in prison for five years because you've threatened extortion and damage to private property. The bad news is, you're fired as of today and this minute."

"You sons of bitches. You …" He pointed a finger at Jeremiah.

"Oh yes, one more thing. Any disruption on this site by you talkin' to other workers, any nuisance you might have in mind for Mr. Knox, and we'll get the police on you for criminal charges pronto. Do you hear?"

Billy looked straight at Jeremiah. "Wait till Terry hears about this. You'll get yours."

The two men escorted Billy from the church site. That night, the Simmstown police placed five guards around the church construction site. The following night, a team of Pinkerton's appeared and stayed with the property until it was formally installed as a church in the diocese of Norwalk. The threats from the Hibernian Brotherhood was passed from Vaughn to Soames. Even Vaughn was surprised. The news of threats was a relief to the New York financier. The Hibernian Brotherhood had obstructed other Soames projects, and the information about Terry Litton on the dock strike was all Soames needed to contact the mayor. A series of charges, fourteen in number, were brought up against various members of the brotherhood, and five of Litton's top henchmen and Litton himself were arrested without bail as dangers to the safety of the city. They were held for several months before trials began, and the dock strike and the threats to Simmstown Church site by Terry Litton were never realized. But Litton did make one threat good. He got the message to Judge Hardy's court in Dublin that Jeremiah Knox was involved with the Hibernian Brotherhood.

While the letters were crudely written, the judge was concerned that Jeremiah's political activities had continued in the United States.

He thought that the charges might be false, that this complaint from Litton might be some form of retribution among Irish gangs in the East Coast, but he couldn't ignore the information and decided to examine it further. To be careful, he wrote to Jeremiah, extending his suspension from Ireland for another two years or until the facts behind this allegation were better understood.

When Jeremiah received the notice, he was furious, stomping around his apartment in anger. He didn't know how to proceed. He wanted the flexibility to return to Ireland, but the need to go home and the desire to return to the politics had become less compelling. Yet when the judge postponed his return, he was, nevertheless, agitated. In letters from Callahan and his friends in the Fenian organization, he sensed his expected return generated more worry and concern than enthusiasm. With Parnell dead, the primary activists were in Irish jails or, like O'Farrell, in Germany, Australia, Canada, or New Zealand. The independence movement was in disarray as second-tier activists fought for leadership. Callahan hinted it was not a good time to return. Jeremiah stewed, aware of his own indecision on returning to the fray of Irish politics.

Letters from his family had dropped off. His letters were also infrequent. It was clear to him, after four years, the family's disapproval of his Fenian association and the scars from his painful exchange with his father had not subsided. He had distanced himself from his family, and those ties had become weak. Contact with them was declining in frequency. Why did he want to return? He wasn't sure and was rapidly coming to the point where staying in America had grown in its appeal.

Letters from his uncle and Aunt Sheila were a nuisance. Each time he saw their address or letterhead, the memory of their treachery infuriated him. Without giving them a second glance, he dropped their letters into his wire wastebasket, unread.

He contacted the Four Courts in Ireland, and the slow process to address Judge's Hardy's extension began. He sought affidavits, documents, and letters from employers, landlords, and clients, and eventually filed a response to the judge's ruling. Assembling the material took him through his fourth year, and it was in his fifth year that Judge Hardy finally responded.

In Jeremiah concerns with the Milton brothers, he contacted immigration officials. He found agents in Boston and New York who had relatives in his Erin I Club in Worcester. After many discussions, they agreed to keep an eye out for the arrival of Burton and Harry Milton from England.

Chapter 14

A late February snow blew into his face, stinging his eyes, the harsh storm ignored his hat, his scarf, and found ways to freeze his cheeks and eyelids. He didn't mind the snow or the cold weather. He found the air bracing and the snow exquisitely beautiful. He could not convince the lovely Kathleen Cooney that this was a beautiful day. He tried in his jocular way swinging his arms at the blizzard of white declaring the power of winter beauty while she dismissed his attempts with a brief wave of her small hand. She insisted they get to the tea house as quickly as their legs would carry them. Once inside, the steam on the windows obscured the swirling flakes of snow, and they rubbed their hands before securing the cups of tea. Jeremiah actually hated tea, preferring a good whiskey on a day like this, but Kathleen liked her tea. He enjoyed her company, and it was rare to have her alone without the constant presence of her sister or aunt. At age twenty-two, she was interested in finding the right man, and her family was organized to support her quest. He knew he was not the right man. At twenty-four, he was far from ready for marriage. He liked her looks and her passion, but she controlled access to her body, saying, "Once we're engaged." He'd been hearing that phrase a lot lately, and it was his signal to move on.

He thought back to Coleen and Phoebe on the S/S *Caledonia* and to Maria, now a countess. They were his age and had sought and found permanence. Marriage did not fit him, at least not now. His drive, his energy was directed toward his work. And his work entailed two important requirements. He had to keep advancing his skills to get the interesting and lucrative work from sculpture, and he had to be free to travel to the work sites. There was little time for a deep involvement with one woman, so he continued to live a semi-monastic life. While he experienced moments of loneliness, he preferred the simplicity of a single life; it made his days easier. Weekdays he was on the work sites in various cities and towns in the northeast. On the weekends, he'd return to Worcester. Occasionally, he would journey to Boston or New York when he sought wider social and cultural experiences. Although the women he courted asked about his solitary life, he dodged the question. His life was quiet, and he liked that. He thrived in his work and enjoyed his own company when at leisure. He preferred no company to the nonsense chatter he experienced from some of the women he knew and from the late drinking evenings with the lads at O'Doul's. To him, there was nothing missing from solitude. It gave him time to develop his thoughts on the design of altars, to enjoy his travels to Italy, to pour into literature, and it enabled him to restore energy for his work.

After the heated exchange with Terry Litton over the Hibernian Brotherhood, he felt reluctant to take work near the cities where the Irish radicals were most active. Vaughn had suggested they look at an opportunity in Boston and Jeremiah begged off, "Too busy and too near the Irish who wish me to be active with them."

Vaughn suspected there were other reasons, but didn't press Jeremiah for further clarity. He knew, somewhere, somehow, the young man had a secret or two to keep, and he decided to refrain from further inquiry. He'd found a strong talent, and although Jeremiah didn't know this, Vaughn had found his talent at a very reasonable price. Vaughn knew the gap between Jeremiah's fees and the fees of top sculptors and stonemasons in New York would soon close. He wanted to lock Jeremiah into his work before other architects and builders discovered him, and he became too expensive.

Jeremiah was resting his legs, seated on a stool in the work shed at the Simmstown church. He was ripping pieces from a loaf of bread, his luncheon favorite, and combining the bread with large wedges of cheese. He bought the bread and cheese from a grocer in Simmstown in the early morning before the other patrons came to the shop. It was a wonderful discovery. The small town grocer was also a baker who prepared fresh bread every day. It was a treat that made the lunchtime break a special moment, one he looked forward to all morning. As he ate, the large automobile that ferried Casper Soames came to rest outside the shed. Vaughn stepped out first, straightened his jacket and pants, and approached him. Jeremiah hadn't seen him in over a week and was surprised at his arrival. Following him from the vehicle was Soames. Jeremiah slowly rose, placed the bread on the stool, and waited. *What's going on?* he wondered. *These men never come mid-week.* And Soames, he hadn't seen him in over a month.

Vaughn extended his hand. "Sorry to interrupt, Jeremiah, but we both wanted to see you."

"Yes." He eyed both men carefully, trying to hide the concern that crossed his mind. "How can I help you?" His shoulders slumped slightly as he shifted his weight from his left to his right foot.

Soames laughed, aware of Jeremiah's suspicions and ignored them. "Good to see you, Jeremiah. Good God, man, you've helped us. We got that bugger Litton dead to rights. He's been a nuisance, in fact a disruptive danger to many of my projects violating a host of New York laws. He'll be in jail for the next five years once the New York police and the courts are through with him. I want to thank you personally. You'll have no more trouble from him."

Ah yes, thought Jeremiah, *maybe no trouble from Litton but the Brotherhood may want some revenge.*

But Soames was happy, smiling. "You see, Jeremiah, by trusting us you've protected this church from damage, and you've stopped a ruthless New York gang that's bothered many of my building sites. And Litton caused major problems on the New York docks, theft, extortion, etc., and that's getting cleaned up. You've done well."

"I really don't understand their tactics, sir. I mean they have work here compared to no work in Ireland. If they could get work in Ireland, they would not be paid what they're getting paid here. Their logic eludes me."

"As it does many of us in the city. But thank you again, lad. This site will be safe with the Pinkertons until the church can take it over. You've done far more than just making beautiful works of religious art. If you need anything, don't hesitate to call me." He extended a business card to Jeremiah and shook his hand.

At that point, he turned to Vaughn and said, "Henry, I want to see the chapel at Gridley so please arrange that. I understand from the headmaster that it's coming along quite well."

"It is Casper, I think you'll be delighted."

"Well, I want to make certain that this church is done and the Gridley School work is completed before you run this young man up to New Hampshire."

"Nothing changes until your satisfaction is complete," said Vaughn.

Soames left as quickly as he arrived. He walked with unusual speed for a man his age and entered his car. He sat in the back seat and gave a cheery wave to Vaughn and Jeremiah as the car roared off toward New York.

Jeremiah watched the car accelerate away from the church, dust flying in all directions. He shook his head. "Is he always this busy, always in such a rush?" Jeremiah asked. "And what did he mean by sending me to New Hampshire?"

"Oh dear, yes." Vaughn wiped his eyes from the swirling dust. "I've just won another school chapel. It's the Concord Abbey, much like the Gridley School chapel, and it's in Concord, New Hampshire. I'd like you to work with me on that one too. They like your design at Gridley and have some different ideas as well. Can I interest you in that?"

"When I looked at my schedule and saw the empty space after these projects were finished, I did plan some work in Worcester."

Vaughn seemed to stiffen in Jeremiah's eyes. He became more erect. His posture was straight and perfect. "Are these projects major efforts like the Gridley School or the church here?"

"Oh no, sir, I have a couple of statues to do. McGuinness continues to send me work, which I share with one of his fellows."

"Let me make my request more clear. From my discussions with various church groups and schools, I can keep us both very busy over the next few years. As long as you keep your work at this very high quality, I can promise you all the work you can handle. Well, at least for the next couple of years."

Jeremiah's response was slow. "Really, you can do that? McGuinness is a good businessman, but he never knows what's going to come in."

"I'm at the front end of construction planning, so I have more notice, and I lock my work up first. And I can pick the people and companies best suited for the job. Or at least I have a strong say over that."

"Well." Jeremiah reached out and shook Vaughn's hand. "Nothing would please me more." He held back for a second, jelling his thoughts. "If I may, sir, I do have a couple of concerns."

Vaughn seemed unsurprised. "Of course, tell me."

Jeremiah said, "I'd prefer not to work in a major city where the Hibernian Brotherhood is active, and second, I'd like to have a month off here and there to go to Italy and work on my craft with people I know in Siena." In the back of his mind, he wanted to see Maria again, curious about her life with the count. Pietro had informed him of the marriage, and between the lines, Pietro had intimated that Maria was having early misgivings.

Vaughn leaned against the door of the church, hesitating over Jeremiah's concerns. "Those conditions are okay with me. The next few buildings I have in mind are in New Hampshire or on the border of Massachusetts and New Hampshire—mostly new churches, seminaries, and school chapels so you'll be a fair distance from Boston or New York. Now, Europe's another matter. Italy's probably more like two months with all the travel, but across the three years I'm thinking about, we should be able to find the time."

"This sounds good to me. I need to do some planning … May I respond in a week or so?"

"Of course, let's keep discussing this as I want to convince you that the work is there. The risk to you is small, and the rewards will be great."

After finishing work that day, Jeremiah passed up a gathering of his fellow workers at Coyne's Bar & Grille in Simmstown. He took the evening train to Hartford with plans to go to Gridley the next day. At the Hotel Statler, he took a hot bath and soaked in the tub for thirty minutes. He dressed in his new suit and went to the hotel's

Bonning's restaurant and ordered a Jameson. They did not have Irish whiskey, so he ordered a Scotch and thought about Vaughn's proposal, swirling the amber liquid around in his glass. What to make of Vaughn's plans, to be captive to one man's projects for the next three years? Was that a good idea? What about returning to Ireland? He tossed these ideas back and forth as he drank the Scotch. He signaled the bartender and had a second. He ordered the roast beef with potatoes and green beans, and as he ate, he deliberated.

He had not yet heard from Judge Hardy's court on his petition to keep the original suspension. Five years would be completed by August this year. He did not want it extended as the judge had proposed. His head began to spin. What if the judge allowed him to return in August? Would that make a difference? He found the thought troubling.

The prospect of returning to Ireland had always been his goal, his dream. The return to Edinburgh and completing his law degree had sustained him over the years in America. Now he thought, what would he do with a law degree? What would he do in Ireland? He thought of Joseph Callahan's case load and working in Callahan's office, he thought about his work with the Judge Wicklow in Waterford, and as these experiences came to mind, he was surprised. He was less enthusiastic than he expected.

The more he thought about Vaughn's offer, the more interested he became. He had come to love the artwork he created. The altar at the Simmstown Church was stunning. He'd heard that from Vaughn, Soames, and the regional bishop in Hartford, plus all his fellow workers. The pulpit, the frames on the windows, and the bell tower were highly complimented as well. He knew his work was good and getting better, and he desired to explore and try more complex stonework. And the pay was glorious. Due to his travel schedule with all expenses paid, he had no time to spend his earnings. He had his weekly rent and his weekend meals; that was all. With his observation that immigrants were flooding to the United States, he purchased shares in a few steamship companies and in the telephone company. He banked the rest. Occasionally, his evenings with the ladies or his lads ran into a few dollars, but this did not happen that often—he was too busy. Saturdays and Sundays found him pouring over art books in the public library, examining the cathedrals of the world or rummaging through magazines for ideas on buildings, statues, and garden adornments. In the early evenings, he sat back at O'Doul's Pub, and while he was sipping his Jameson, his mind roamed to the artwork he studied. He framed the picture of an altar or a statue of a saint onto a piece of marble or limestone and let his mind carve the image from a substantial stone block. He worked the technique in his head. Then later, as the evening darkened and the street lamps ignited, he'd rush home to sketch his ideas in his burgeoning notebook then test these ideas on the blocks of clay in his spare bedroom. He'd work until he fell asleep, exhausted.

As the winter slowly gave way to spring, the church in Simmstown was nearing completion, and the chapel in Gridley was making progress for a fall completion in time for the start of a new academic year.

Vaughn had set the schedule for the chapel at Concord Abbey. He suggested a summer start, and Jeremiah had agreed. Yet he was unsettled over the plan. He wanted a decision from the court and needed it to settle his future path. Like most events in Jeremiah's life, a determining influence came from an unexpected source. He returned from his week in Gridley, and the monthly bill for rent was marked final. The meaning of *final* was unclear to him, so he wrote to the owner, seeking a better understanding. The return letter came later the next week and indicated that the bill he received would be the last from the owner. He was selling the building, and Jeremiah's next bill would come from a new owner. Jeremiah blanched at the news. This might mean an increase in rent, possible eviction if the new owners preferred different tenants—the uncertainties bothered him.

He wrote again to the owner, asking him for the address of the new owner. The reply was that the buyer had just backed out and the building was back on the market. He could stay another month or two with no worry. Jeremiah went to his bank and talked to the manager. He inquired about the purchase of apartments, of single homes, and of the bank's programs to assist new buyers. Fortified with the information, he wrote again to the building's owner and communicated his interest in purchasing the building and asked for the sale price. He returned to his banker, showed him the sale price, and asked about the price of similar buildings. The banker advised him of a good offer below the asking price, then said, "Mr. Knox, you can purchase this property with your savings and still have plenty left in your account. The bank will be delighted to lend you capital, but you don't need the added expense of our interest."

Jeremiah made his offer, and the owner agreed instantly. Once the papers were signed, he informed the existing tenants that he was the new landlord and they could stay at their current rents. He would collect the money each Saturday morning. His new responsibilities included managing the building, handling the maintenance, and ensuring the key operating systems of heat, light, plumbing, repairs, and snow removal worked perfectly. Given his travels, he scratched his head. How could he manage emergencies and weekly maintenance while he travelled? He asked his banker for references on maintenance men and talked to several of them—too expensive. They all wanted a full-time position. Later in the weekend, he was sitting at the bar in O'Doul's Pub and asked Charlie if he could post a job offer. O'Doul asked, "Sure, Jeremiah, but what fer?"

"I bought my building, and I'm going to need help to operate it and do the basic maintenance. You know, fixing faucets, toilets, sweeping the walks, shoveling snow, and so on."

"I got just the man for yee. Young man was in here just last week. Arrived from Glasgow, hungry for work, a carpenter by trade, but can't find work. Getting desperate. Seems like a good fellow."

"Give him my name, I'll find him."

Instead, Hamish McDougal found Jeremiah. In his workroom, Jeremiah was working on a clay sculpture of Saint Aquinas for the college of Holy Cross about a mile from his house. The knock on his door startled him; no one ever came to call. He wiped his hands on his work cloth and answered the door. A man stood in the doorway, younger than he and a foot shorter, his cap in his hand, his face serious. He nodded, his head bobbing in a gesture of respect.

"Sir, Mr. O'Doul sent me as he said yer looking for a maintenance person. I can do carpentry, anything yer need. And I'll work cheap."

"Come, tell me your name and let's talk."

Hamish McDougal's story intrigued Jeremiah. Worcester was teeming with work in factories, in the construction of new three-decker apartments and office buildings. Why couldn't the young man find work? As he told his tale, Jeremiah wanted to laugh but kept the humor to himself.

"So," Jeremiah said, "you were told to come to this area because there is so much work, but once here, you found that the French and Irish had all the jobs and gave the new jobs to their own kind."

"Yes, sir, that's what's been happening."

"Why'd you come to America?"

"Same as you, sir. More work, better work than in Glasgow or anywhere in Scotland."

"And you want to work right away?"

"Yes, sir, I'm getting low on funds. I need a place to stay, and I'm getting mighty hungry."

Jeremiah stoked his chin. He liked what he saw but had to be honest. "I have this one building, so it's probably just a part-time requirement."

"That's okay, sir. It'll get me started. What does a maintenance man git fer pay?"

"I was planning on five dollars a week."

"That's not much, sir, but I'll take it if I can have a cot in your basement."

"You'd sleep in the basement? You'd better look at it first."

"Sir, it'll be warm in the winter and cool in the summer. If it's dirty or dusty, I'll clean it spick and span. Yes, sir, I can do that."

"Well ..." Jeremiah paused while he considered how to phrase his next condition. "I like you Hamish. You look like a hard worker. But I travel quite a bit. I need you to stay a while and not leave me on short notice. You know, when a better offer comes along."

"I can do anything yer need while yer gone, even collect the rents. Just about anything." Hamish twisted his cap in his hands.

"You wish to say more, Hamish."

"Yes, sir, and I don't mean to be bold, but folks at O'Doul's Pub talk about yee all time, yer success as a sculptor and all. They think yer'll buy lots more buildings. I bin thinkin' maybe yer can get me on some of your big rebuilding jobs. Yer know, fixin' up the places yer buy. When Charlie O'Doul told me about yer, I said that's the man for me."

Jeremiah laughed. "Okay, let's look at the basement, and if that works for you, you have job. Then we'll see what happens next."

"You won't regret this, sir. I'm ready to work today."

As he went down the steps into the basement with Hamish, he smiled. The smile was still on his normally serious face as he turned toward Hamish. "As you see, the room's spacious. It's empty, it's dark, it's fairly clean, but it is a basement. What do you think?"

"It's got a toilet, and I'd wash the floor some, but otherwise, I could live here if yer let me."

Jeremiah extended his hand. "It's a deal. Get your stuff Hamish and move in. Here's some money for a cot, a lamp, some towels." He reached into his pocket and counted off a wad of bills. "Here you go."

Hamish's eyes widen at the stack of bills in Jeremiah's large hands. "Thank you, sir. I'll be right back. Other than the bed, everything I've got is on my back."

Jeremiah laughed and nodded. Five years ago, he'd arrived in the same state although he made no note of it to Hamish.

Hiring Hamish was a small step for Jeremiah, but it was a significant one. He had acquired an apartment building; he had invested in Worcester. For the past four years, progress in sculpture had defined Jeremiah's life, but without fully realizing it, the building on Vernon Street established another root for him. In choosing Hamish McDougal to manage the building, Jeremiah was strengthening his connections in America.

While his initial success with sculpting provided work and income during in his exile from Ireland, it did more. It illustrated to him that he had other talents beyond his intellectual abilities, which had originally pushed him toward law. His growth from stonemason to sculptor confirmed what Ian McCracken had said to him in Edinburgh, "Why are you doing law when you have this skill?"

Sculpture had become a fascination, a passion, a reward in its own right that had surprised him. He couldn't wait to get at the stone each day and release the designs within. And there was the second surprise. Sculpture provided an income beyond his wildest dreams. The purchase of the triple-decker, the hiring of Hamish, and the new work with Henry Vaughn cemented a new platform, a new profession for Jeremiah. When he first arrived at McGuinness's Stone Company, the isolation of cutting stone in the quarries seemed like punishment until the illness of Biasi created the opportunity to cut the angels on Suzanne's tombstone. His experiences in the new country were accumulating in a clear direction. The country was growing rapidly, and the demand for new churches was evident throughout the northeast. For these churches, he could not ignore the desire rising in him to build the most beautiful interiors or exteriors in stone whether it be an altar, a window, a bell tower, a pulpit or statues. Alone in his apartment, he reviewed these developments over the past few weeks, and the information was pushing him toward a longer commitment in America, but he was not ready to acknowledge that. Thoughts of the Fenian cause still lingered, the drive to get the British out of Ireland brought back the thrill of rebellion, of action that could change history.

His thoughts about the Fenian movement would come and go for him, yet they never lingered in his mind for long. His thoughts would then shift to practical matters, his work and what to do about Hamish. He could see the young Scot washing the basement floor, putting his bed and chair in the room, making the boiler room his apartment. He merged these thoughts into a wish. He hoped that Hamish would work out well and give him ample notice when he found a full-time job. He liked the young man and wanted him to succeed. Jeremiah recognized he needed help if he was to manage this apartment building and sustain his demanding work schedule. He wanted both and realized Hamish, or someone like him, would be essential as long as he was in America.

Chapter 15

The letter that arrived that week reminded him of one of his favorite novels, *Les Misérables*. After five years of exile, the country's agents and his enemies continued to hound his existence. The persistent presence of Judge Hardy and the Milton brothers in his life was like Javert's never-ending pursuit of Jean Valjean.

In a letter from a former Fenian colleague in Dublin, Jeremiah learned that the organization's *toughs*, as he called them, had hounded the Milton brothers out of Ireland. They were headed to New York. *Beware*, the letter emphasized. He could only assume that he was on their list and purchased a pistol, a Colt 45, then proceeded to learn how to fire it at the police range in Worcester.

Judge Hardy's letter, when it finally arrived, was irritating. He thought the judge had two options, either allow his return or mandate a two-year extension. It was neither and the letter seemed so odd to Jeremiah that he was forced to laugh. The judge wanted him to come to Dublin for an interview and a discussion concerning "essential conditions" for his return to Ireland. Jeremiah thought he'd benefit from another opinion on the judge's *conditions* and Hamish came to mind. Taking the three flights of steps in a fast descent, he went to the basement and roused the young Scot. "Come with me to O'Doul's. We'll have a tipple of whiskey."

In the immaculately clean room, Hamish was resting on his cot. Along with a plain wooden chair, it was the only piece of furniture on the cement floor. Hamish was reading an old tattered book, the title faded and hard to see. His shoes were off as his feet rested on the bed. Jeremiah could see the holes in his socks.

Hamish said, "I hope you're buyin', boss. I'm a little low on cash."

Jeremiah laughed. "I can see that. Do you need an advance for some new socks?"

Hamish swung his feet off the bed and sat up. "Okay, okay, I need to be more careful with my clothes. I understand that, but my socks are telling you I need a raise."

"What I see is that you need to plan your expenses more carefully. Let's go to the pub and talk this over."

They entered O'Doul's Pub, and Charlie greeted them heartily as they took a table at the rear of the room. "One Jameson and one Glenfarclas." Hamish added, "Or maybe you have the new one—the Mackinlay's?"

Charlie, his white apron slightly wet from washing the glasses, wiped his hands. He said, "Now, goddamnit, Hamish, yee know I don't have Scottish brew here. Yee've got to drink our whiskey, Irish whiskey, the real stuff."

This continued a banter that had started weeks ago, the young Scot slowly fitting into the work and drinking culture of Worcester. The whiskey came, neat, a rich amber, strong. Jeremiah and Hamish lifted their glasses in a salute and sipped. Jeremiah had an idea and wanted to test it. He'd discovered that Hamish was not only clever with his hands, he had a quick wit and sized up a situation with unusual speed. Jeremiah saw, from the first days of work, that the Hamish anticipated where and when repairs were needed on the building. Without prodding from Jeremiah or even complaints from tenants, he fixed the roof and gutters that had been damaged by the ice from a long winter and totally replaced the old plumbing in Mrs. McCready's bathroom. He alerted Jeremiah whenever a new building was on the market; his eyes and ears were always open.

Jeremiah watched the young Scot, amused as he pursed his lips. A sense of slight distaste crossed Hamish's face as if he sipped a dram of cod liver oil. Jeremiah said, "You'll get used to it, laddie."

Hamish added, "I'd better if I'm goin' to keep working fer you." He sipped again, and pleasure began to relax his face.

Jeremiah said, "I've had troubles in Ireland as I told you. Today I received some new news." He sipped his Jameson, taking his time.

"Now the judge wants me to come to his court and talk about conditions for my return."

Hamish coughed, nearly spraying his last sip across the table. "What … yer not leavin', are yee?"

"No, no. I have a response in mind, and I want your thoughts." He waited for a response, and getting none was not surprised. He was coming to the conclusion that Hamish was a good listener yet a man of few words. He liked that in a man. There was something about a quiet Scot that inspired confidence and trust. He observed that trait in his fellow students at Edinburgh. They could be trusted, could be counted on to do what they said. With each passing day, he trusted Hamish more and more. "What I plan to do is say no to a trip to Ireland. But I won't stop there. What I'll do is invite the judge to interview me here in Boston or New York or perhaps Siena, where I'm going this summer. What do you think of that?"

Hamish sipped the Jameson one more time, trying to get used to its sharp bite. *Why can't the Irish get a better mix of peat and sherry in their whiskey?* he wondered. It would soften the bite, pop the flavor a wee bit—smoother to the taste. Do they lack imagination? Jeremiah had too much imagination, but he wasn't a whiskey maker. Too bad, the Irish needed him in a malt factory. Hamish stared at the glass as if willing it to offer up a faint hint of Speyside, something more familiar to his Scottish taste. He raised his eyes to Jeremiah and spoke slowly. "Well, I'm guessing since it's from the court, you'll have to respond. And given that"—he stalled, thinking carefully about his next few words—"I think it's a jolly good response. Almost as good as tellin' him to take his conditions and stick them up his arse."

Jeremiah sniggered at first then tossed his head back and erupted in laughter. Hamish, delighted at Jeremiah's reaction, joined him in laughter.

The mail across the Atlantic was slow, and it was many months before Judge Hardy realized that Jeremiah had little intention of returning to Ireland. It was a relief to him in one way and a concern in another. The young man had well developed philosophical and legal positions to support Home Rule for Ireland. That he was willing to fight with arms for his cause was disturbing to the judge, but deep down, Hardy thought that Jeremiah could become a voice of reason among the radicals in the country. To lose him to the United States was a loss to Ireland. The judge recognized that, in Jeremiah, he had rid the country of an intelligence it needed and was left with a rough and tumble lot of Fenians in Dublin who knew how to fight but not how to think.

Judge Hardy's return letter left Jeremiah with the impression that if he initiated a meeting and a desire to return to Ireland, the court was open to the idea. He didn't reply to the letter and put it in a safe deposit box for future consideration. Letters from his family drifted in sporadically. In their letters, his mother, brothers, and sister were curious about life in the United States and how he was getting on. But his father's letters had a different tone.

Dear Jeremiah,

These days are quite hard. My back has given me big trouble again, and I now need help with the cattle. That reminds me that your Fenian friends have angered the British enough that they're not buying products from Ireland anymore. My sales of beef are way down. Are these Fenians trying to ruin the country? Callahan tells me the judge learned you're still in touch with the radicals in America. When will you learn that these people are nothing but trouble?

Da

He tossed the letter on the floor and stomped around the apartment. *Well, goddamnit*, he fumed; he wasn't missed except to be cursed. His father had made it clear in prior letters that his work with the Fenians was an embarrassment to the family and had hurt business in the pub and the inn. Now, it has hurt the farm as well. He stared out the window at the bustling traffic below. *It's so much more active here*, he thought. Trolleys and carriages meandered up and down Vernon Street, the clatter of wheels and voices rising up to his third-floor window. He pushed that thought aside and thought about his family. Largely, they had ignored him once he arrived in Boston, and then he'd been sent by his uncle to Worcester. He admitted that his passion for Irish independence was his own, not shared by his family and perhaps was even selfish. But it was authentic, and the consequence was that it separated him from his country, and it was clear to him now, it separated him from his family. If he wanted a family around him now, it would be his alone. Should he form it in the United States?

Family matters were a fleeting concern; he had little time to dwell on them. Telephone calls and telegrams from Vaughn prompted him to travel, to begin new work, to arrange artisans to support his efforts, and to secure work sheds to protect the marble work from weather and from theft. The new set of projects were distributed across the southern sections of New Hampshire and the border towns of New Hampshire and Massachusetts. A church in Fitchburg and a seminary in Peterborough seemed to flow one into another as the work continued. Jeremiah was buried in work with no relief in sight when a financial problem arose at the Concord Abbey School. Vaughn had sent a telegram to Jeremiah to stop work; the school had not paid its bills in two months. He sighed in relief as he read the news; it would give him more time to accelerate work on the other projects. With the telegram in hand, he left his hotel and went to the worksite. He announced the news amid much grousing among the stonemasons and the other construction workers. His team of stonemasons clustered around him.

"Damn, Jeremiah. What's going on?" asked Eli. He was of middle age, robust in build and short in temper. He was the most outspoken member of his stonecutters.

Jeremiah didn't know the man well but explained to the group what he knew from Vaughn's message and advanced the idea that the school was famous, its alumni rich, and the work would be continued. He advised the men to go to other projects on a temporary basis.

Eli coughed and spat on the ground. "Goddamn, Jeremiah, that don't work for me. This is my job for the summer and beyond. If I don't have summer work, my family don't eat."

Jeremiah raised his hand. "Everyone … raise your hand if you can't find some short-term work to tide you over." About half the group raised their hands.

"Okay, you fellows with your hands up, come with me." He brought five of them into the work shed and pulled a sheaf of papers from his satchel. He spread four sheets of paper across a tabletop. Each sheet defined work to be done in different churches in the coming months. "Let's look at St. Peter's seminary in Nashua." He glanced up at the faces around him. "Who wants to go there and can get there reliably every day?"

"That's two statues, Jeremiah. That's your work."

"You can do it Albie. I'll check in with you from time to time. It'll give me a break."

The next three projects were in towns in Massachusetts. They were not far from Concord but would require travel and overnights. Eli protested again, "I can't travel away from the missus just now. She's been sickly, and we've got five young'uns to care for. I need to stay in Concord for the summer."

"I'll come back to you, Eli. Let me take care of the rest."

He made certain that each man knew the location, who to report to, and what part of the stonework would be their responsibility. Heads were nodding and faces were becoming more relaxed. "Is everybody but Eli set? Okay, you call or telegram me whenever you have a problem. I'll call the construction boss at each site. Tell him who's coming and what you're to do. The bosses will be thrilled. They were worried about a shortage of skilled masons. Off you go." He waved them away.

"Now, Eli, there's nothing here in Concord. Your former employer has no work?"

"That's why I came to you Jeremiah. He's been hurtin' ever since you won the Concord Abbey job. He wanted that bad. He needed it and had to let lots of people go."

"Well, Mr. Vaughn has very specific requirements for his stonework."

"Nah, that's not what my boss said. He said Mr. Vaughn wanted a sculptor, and that's what you are. Plus you know how to guide us masons. That's why he lost."

"Let's solve this. I want you back on this work as soon as Vaughn and the school clean up their financial mess. I think it will be pretty soon because they'll want the building enclosed by the time the snow falls."

"But what can I do? I want to work with you. I've learned so much in a short time and want to learn more about how to do this fine work."

"Here's an idea. If you can't find some short-term work, grave-stones, or whatever, I'll pay you your weekly wage until we start again. How's that? It'll be a loan."

"No, no, Jeremiah. I can't have no loans. How'd I pay it back?"

"You have good skills, Eli. I can use you again, and I will. You'll pay me out of each week's wage once the job starts, just a little bit each week. It'll work out."

"How can you afford that, Jeremiah? You're not workin' either."

"Remember, Eli, I've got four other projects going right now, and I'm not married. I have no children to feed or dress."

"But I saw you. You gave away your work to Albie, Carl, and Toby and others."

"There's still plenty for me to do on those jobs. But more important right now, it gives me a break, and I sure could use one."

They shook hands on their agreement. Eli, normally taciturn and sullen, seemed remarkably happy to Jeremiah. Eli waved good-bye and sauntered off down the road toward the town and home. His wife would be delighted to see him, Jeremiah thought, and the man would be eager to return to work as soon as it started again. Jeremiah thought about the offering of wages; it was an impulsive move but the right one he decided. If the work delay was between two to six weeks, he would not notice the loss of income. It was a good bet, and he'd won the loyalty of a strong worker. He stepped out into the sun and shielded his eyes.

Gary Hawkins was waiting for him. He was about the same age as Jeremiah, compact and strong with a thick shock of brown hair that needed cutting. Jeremiah liked him. He was eager and a fast learner, displaying solid skills in cutting stones for the arches in the doorway. A partial arch was done; it was graceful and would provide strong support for the brickwork above. The decorative work on the arch was an elegant weave of branches. Jeremiah was delighted; his own work on the arch would be minimal. He only had to add the delicate school crest at the top of the arch.

"Get that troublemaker all sorted out, Jeremiah. He certainly seemed happy. In fact, I've never even seen him smile before."

"He's got great skills, Gary. Don't want to lose him from the project."

"You won't. He may grouse, but he loves what he's doing here. We all do. You and Mr. Vaughn really challenge us. It's very rewarding. By the way, what are you going to do with your free time?"

"I feel so good about my work right now. I may take a wee vacation. I've got all our boys helping on my other projects."

"I'll tell you what I'm doing. You may want to join me."

He did not know Gary well. In fact, Jeremiah wasn't particularly close to anyone, especially those who worked on his jobs. He thought of himself as more or less of a loner, to use the American term he'd once heard. "Are you going to have a holiday?"

"Yes, indeed. Every summer, I go to a place called the Ocean House in Rye Beach. It's not far from here. The hotel's right on a beautiful beach, and it has grand swimming if you can stand the water temperature."

"You're what, early twenties, and you go to the beach for cold water swimming?"

"I guess I left a little out. The Ocean House is a big hotel, and it attracts hundreds of single girls from Boston, even some from New York. It's heaven."

Jeremiah regarded Gary closely. *This could be a good idea*, he thought. *It's near my work if things need attention. Better yet, it's closer than Cape Cod.* "Yeah, I may join you."

"Time's a wasting. We can catch a train in Concord if we hurry. Be there in time for a late afternoon swim."

Compared to his monastic existence in Worcester, Rye Beach was a cornucopia of woman. Gary was correct. Store clerks, secretaries, and nurses flooded to this tiny community with its enormous white sand beach and hotels. The Ocean House was the queen of Rye Beach, housing hundreds of guests, offering tea dances in the afternoons and a lively bar in the evenings. The balance between men and women was about even according to Jeremiah's eye. The mating process was active. Apparently, everyone was there for the same purpose. As he did in Stradbally, Jeremiah found the sea relaxing and inspiring. He loved to walk the long, flat beach down near the edge of the water. While Gary introduced himself to every cluster of girls on the beach, Jeremiah would walk the white sands alone. With a beige panama hat on his head, a long sleeve white shirt, and full-length white pants, his long strides strolled the beach as the waves crested at his feet. He shed his shoes and let the end of the wake rush over his feet as he walked, his mind on his projects, his sculptures and particularly his work on altars. The girls watched him, protected under their beach umbrellas, talking to Gary as Jeremiah walked.

"He's your friend. Why is he always alone?" they asked.

Gary would describe the work they were doing and Jeremiah's role. It drew attention, interest, and many questions; his response was never altered. "He likes to think, and he does that best when he's alone. And out of his thinking comes the greatest ideas on design. He carves the most beautiful items."

A petite brunette, her eyes following Jeremiah as he walked down the beach, said, "Oh, he must be very religious."

Gary replied, "No, I think not. I'd call him spiritual, not religious. Once he said to me that he believes in beauty and wants to create it where people gather to think, to pray or worship."

The brunette turned her attention to Gary. "Should I go and join him on his walk? He's right down there." She pointed at the tall angular figure striding at water's edge.

"I don't know him that well, but I'd guess not. This is his thinking time. If he invites you, it'd be fine, but he'd have to invite you."

Gary was eager to please and secure a place for himself with the young ladies, so he would suggest, "We can meet you for tea or a cocktail later on the porch or bar if you'd like, and we can all get acquainted."

So Gary introduced a process, and Jeremiah agreed. Each afternoon as the sun began to set, they would drift to the porch of the hotel and mingle with girls that Gary had met in the afternoon. In the warmth of the sun and the geniality of the crowd, Jeremiah would shed his reserved mien and entertain them with stories from Ireland or from his experiences in America. Often he and Gary would find a suitable companion for dinner or dancing and occasionally for the night.

Gary found a young lady in their second year of visits to the Ocean House and later that year married her. Jeremiah enjoyed many of the women there and, unlike Gary, enjoyed variety over a permanent association.

It remained quiet at Concord Abbey throughout the summer. Jeremiah discussed the situation with Vaughn, and they decided it was a good time for Jeremiah's trip to Italy and Siena. The staff from the Concord project was able to do the work at the other projects, and they would save the more intricate sculpting work for him. Two months away would not interfere with any schedule. He boarded the SS *Britannia* in New York bound for Genoa and took trains from there to Siena. He joined Pietro and settled in doing some basic carvings on marble statues of saints. He continued to learn much from the Italianate stylist, and that began to expand when he was asked to work on altar in Florence.

He was invited to the palazzo of Count Fazio for cocktails and dinner. Maria greeted him at the door with kisses on each cheek then she held him, staring into his eyes for what seemed like an hour to Jeremiah. The count lingered in the background and finally asked, "Maria, darling, let the man breathe."

Introduced to the count for the first time, Jeremiah was surprised at his age. While in his forties, he appeared much older. The count's bald head, flabby cheeks, rosy-red face, and a paunch that pushed his waistcoat over his belt aged him. His walk was hesitant, giving Jeremiah the sense of too much alcohol or a serious infirmity. Maria, while quite lovely, was subdued during dinner, her face a bit drawn and tired. At the end of the evening, she walked Jeremiah to the door and, in parting, took his hand and held it firm. "You are one of my dearest friends. You must write to me often and promise to see me every year when you come to work with Pietro. You must promise." She held his hand tightly, her eyes boring into him until he nodded.

"Of course," he said. "Nothing would please me more."

The next day, he and Pietro left for Florence. Before work each day, he visited the Duomo to gain insight from the stonework done centuries earlier and to secure ideas for his own work. At the end of each day, he added new sketches to his book. Pietro suggested that they work together on a highly decorative design for a new altar at Santo Gabriel, one full of intricate carvings of spires soaring up behind the tabernacle. The back of the altar and its spires would rise twenty feet above the floor of the altar. The marble was pure-white Carrara. The design was an intricate concept, daring, highly detailed. As they carved sections of it, it was quickly evident that the detail in each spire was precise with religious significance. The altar was very busy with detail, but the effect was stunning. It was the most beautiful work he'd ever done. Jeremiah called it his Italianate style, and he was to use it again and again when the budget of a church enabled it. As the altar took shape under his chisel and Pietro's, he wished to see its completion.

It was late August, and the altar would likely be finished by late September. A cable from Vaughn altered this plan. The board of Trustees of Concord Abbey had found and approved the remainder of funds for the chapel and wished for work to start immediately. As Jeremiah surmised in July, the trustees wanted the chapel enclosed before the winter took hold. That meant his work on the doorway arches and stained-glass window frames needed to be completed by late November.

Pietro understood yet was saddened. Jeremiah was a joy for him, a different soul, an unusual man in work ethic. His artistry was advanced from his own staff of artisans. He trusted Jeremiah with the altar, a trust he could not extend to his own people. Jeremiah was from the United States yet not American. He was European yet not Italian and Pietro not only observed the difference but benefitted from it. For him, Jeremiah's technique emphasized function over form, movement over stasis, and he merged these into an Italianate form without harming the unique nature of that design.

When they parted, Jeremiah promised Pietro work in Massachusetts the following spring. One of Vaughn's new contracts called for an Italianate style altar in Springfield, Massachusetts. As they shook hands at the train station in Siena, Pietro said, "A messenger gave this to me. It's for you. Be well, my friend. Send me news and hopefully a contract for the altar in Springfield."

Jeremiah opened the note on the train. It was brief and from Maria. She admonished him to remember his promise to write. Write every month, she emphasized.

Chapter 16

It was a sunny September afternoon. The leaves on the elms and maples were beginning to turn, the emerging colors of reds, yellows, orange, and brown decorated the branches of the trees on the Concord Abbey campus. The change of seasons came earlier in New Hampshire. Already there was the touch of morning chill that initiated the sparkling beauty of Indian summer. By midday, Jeremiah had shed his sweater and was working in his shirtsleeves, the cuffs of the shirt rolled up to his elbows, revealing the sinewy muscles in his forearms. He was carving a statue of St. Paul, a patron saint of the abbey, which was to be placed in the entryway of the chapel. Dust from the marble creased his hands, and some had come to rest on his cheekbone when he'd attempted to remove a few beads of sweat, the white dust forming a tight line from his cheekbone to his ear.

A voice from the yard outside caught his attention. It sounded like Eli. "Jeremiah, a man here wants to see you."

He placed his hammer and chisel on the bench and walked to the open end of the church. It had become a shell with three walls and a roof. The open end would be the entryway when the arches were finished. There waiting for him, his face partially obscured by the shadows cast by the roof, was his uncle.

"Jeremiah, it's been way too long." James Knox extended his hand, and Jeremiah took and quickly released it.

Jeremiah stared at his uncle, his face calm and quiet. He let the silence linger.

"You look good, lad. Bigger, stronger. The work goes well, I hear. You've become a celebrity."

"Aye, you've heard that, have you?"

"Yes, and more. The *Boston Herald* had an article with pictures about one of your churches. Sheila read it to me." He waited for a response, but Jeremiah simply stared at him. "I hear you're in high demand by the best architects in the east. This is a Henry Vaughn Chapel, isn't it?"

"Why are you here?"

"Let's walk, chat a little. It's been a long time."

"That's true. I haven't heard from you in several years, but I wonder, since you're older, are you getting hard of hearing? I asked, why are you here?"

"Easy, lad. We're family, and your family hasn't heard from you. And I've been in touch with Judge Hardy. I want to talk about that."

"Let's be clear, Uncle. My family's embarrassed by me, and you included have been delighted to see me out of the way."

Nearby, the stonemasons and some of the construction crew had put down their tools. They made the appearance of taking a break but were listening to the conversation. James Knox moved a few feet away, waving Jeremiah toward him. "Let's walk a little. They're listening over there." He moved his head in the direction of the crowd of workers.

"I'm fine right here and need to get back to my work. I was in a good rhythm when I was interrupted." He started back toward the interior of the chapel.

His uncle grasped his arm. "Please, Jeremiah, stay a bit. Hear me out."

He pulled his arm away, giving his uncle a sharp look, his eyes bristling with hostility. "I'm tired of saying this, why are you here?"

"Okay, I'm here because your family has not heard from you for over a year. You've never responded to my letters or Sheila's, never accepted our invitations for visits. Recently, Judge Hardy has contacted your parents because he hadn't heard from you. And through them, he eventually contacted me. They've all asked me to find you. They want you to come back. The five years are up."

He stopped at this point and watched Jeremiah. His nephew was quiet, staring at him, the silence slowly became unsettling, yet he waited for Jeremiah's response. He thought he'd brought good news, thought that Jeremiah might rejoice or at least appreciate what he'd done. He assumed his nephew would be thrilled about a return to his homeland. He waited, yet it was a strain on his patience.

Finally, Jeremiah said, "I don't remember my last contact with the family, but it was fairly recent, maybe a year ago. In the letter, my father blamed me for his loss of beef sales. Who needs this?" He stopped, shaking his head with a disgusted laugh.

"And you wanted me out of Boston and away from your law firm." He raised a finger and shook it in his uncle's face. "An apprenticeship, that I'd been promised. And then you sent me, a top law student, to a remote granite quarry to work as a common, unskilled laborer at a subsistence wage."

He paused for a breath.

His uncle seemed lost for words, then stammered, "But, Jeremiah …"

Jeremiah said, "So yes, contact with my family has been infrequent. I'm healthier for putting them aside as they've put me."

"Your mum and da don't feel that way, nor do your brothers and sister."

"Balls, you should read their letters. That's not what's been said."

"And Judge Hardy has read your petition and agrees. He thinks you've changed, learned some lessons. He has ideas for you. That's what he wants to discuss."

Jeremiah's mouth curled in contempt. "Oh, come off it, I can guess. Give up the Fenians. Give him some names so he can put more patriots in prison. Maybe, since Parnell is dead, he thinks I could bring my legal skills to the Unionists, change my political strategy to cooperation with the English. Is that it?" He began to pace, walking back and forth, silently fuming as his uncle stood, immobile, watching the movement and not knowing what to expect.

Jeremiah stopped and pointed a finger at his uncle. "I'd never fink. Never give names. But …" He moved his mouth to loosen his jaw, let his tongue moisten his dry lips and took a step back. He glanced up at the clear blue sky, and a small smile crossed his face. He said after a moment of reflection, "You know, a career in law with the Fenians' ideals, that's a way to remake Ireland. It was what I wanted most at one time, my dream, my goal. That was taken away from me, that platform in my life became no longer available. I know you didn't cause it to happen, but you damn well made sure the plan laid down by the court and by my family would be followed. Now, I'm on a new track, a new platform that I created all by myself. And I like it. I'm good at it. I'm making more money than I'd ever make as a lawyer, and I'm using my hands as well as my head. I'm a more balanced man than I ever was before." He hesitated; his whole body seemed more relaxed. "My work is here, and I'm here to stay." He shook his head, realizing, and was surprised at the realization that he'd just said. He planned to stay in America.

Ignoring Jeremiah's words, his uncle said, "Your barrister friend, Joseph Callahan, has told your da that he'd written you to finish up at Edinburgh and join him in Dublin. He thinks you have a great future in law and politics."

"Callahan I respect. He protected me, helped me. I have his letters, and I have responded to him."

"What did you say? Do you plan to return to Ireland?"

"What I said is between me and Callahan."

"Jeremiah, all these connections you have, the respect people have for you. This is a longer conversation. Perhaps we could have dinner at your hotel, meet after your work is done."

"No, I believe you've done what you came to do. You can go back with my answer. No need to waste any more time here."

"You don't plan to return to Ireland?"

"No."

"Will you at least write to your family?"

"Stay out of that. It's not your business."

"What about a visit to Boston? Come and see Aunt Sheila. She asks for you often."

"Not going to happen."

"Good God, lad, you've turned into a hard man."

"Maybe so, Uncle. But you must acknowledge that I've been taught by very hard people." His eyes did not leave his uncle's face. "And I don't intend to forget what I've learned."

They stood quietly facing each other. Jeremiah was motionless, waiting for his uncle to leave. James Knox shook his head, muttering to himself, "Can I at least see your work here?"

Jeremiah pointed him toward the open doorway and led him inside. He pointed to the arches over the windows and the carvings on the arches.

His uncle asked, "Did you do the arches?"

"No, the crew shaped the arches. I concentrated on the carvings above." He brought his uncle to the partially finished statue of St. Paul and pointed to it. "That's mine alone, there's much yet to be done."

"Good Lord, lad. This is magnificent. This is far better work than the statues and windows in our church. Do you think you could do something for St. Cecilia's in South Boston?"

Jeremiah shook his head. "No, not possible nor desirable. Mr. Vaughn has me booked for the next five years. I'm lucky when I can squeeze a week off."

"Well, lad, it's exceptional work."

James Knox walked away to his carriage. His head down, he'd done what he promised he'd do. He found the lad as requested by his brother and his wife. He didn't expect a warm greeting, but he did not anticipate the hostility the lad felt toward him, the anger at his family in Stradbally, or the contempt he registered toward the court in Ireland. He could see the young man was strong-willed and fortified by success in his new line of work. It was clear that Jeremiah was independent, didn't need anyone to help him, and was likely to be more successful than anyone in the family including himself. But what seemed to trouble James Knox was that he was accustomed to respect, to be trusted as a friend as well as a lawyer. It was clear that Jeremiah didn't like nor trust him or his wife. He didn't know what to do with that information. Should he and Sheila attempt to patch things up? Or would any attempts made be ignored. The lad certainly seemed uninterested in anything to do with his family. He'd talk this over with Sheila. He knew he had sad news for his brother and his wife, and he needed Sheila to help him with that message.

Jeremiah watched his uncle walk away and felt relief. A page turned and closed, he thought. He returned to his tools and the statue, took a deep breath, and began cutting. Chipping at the marble became the rhythm he'd left before the interruption. Soon he was lost in the movement he was trying to create in St. Paul's arm. He worked at the statue diligently for two more hours before fatigue began to worry him. *No mistakes*, he thought, *the work is too good.* No mistakes due to fatigue.

His timing was consistent with the manager of the works who rang a bell calling the end of the work day for the construction workers. He put his tools aside, wiped the marble statue clean, and studied it for a moment, thinking about his focus for the next day. He tossed his jacket over his shoulder and, joined by others, walked along the dusty road to Concord center where the broad white porch of the Concord Inn beckoned him. He swept the white marble dust off his trousers and sat on the porch, watching the sunset over the hills to the west. Gary sat with him. They were quiet at first, then Gary broke the silence. "That was some showdown you had with that man. Was it about the chapel?"

"Oh no, that was my father's brother with some news from Ireland."

"Are they still giving you a hard time there, the court and all?"

"No, today something useful happened. I think I closed that door for good."

"I and the boys were afraid we might lose you to the old country."

"Nah, it was nice to hear the judge had let up his ridiculous suspension."

"Well, you stayed so long in Italy this summer. We thought maybe you'd stay in Europe somewhere."

He slapped Gary on the knee. "Nah, you can't get rid of me that easy. I like it here. Time to put down more roots. Excuse me, I've got to try and reach a man in Worcester."

He went to the front desk and asked the clerk to secure a trunk line to Worcester. He reached the operator and placed the call, as planned, to Hamish. The young Scot was waiting in Jeremiah's apartment as scheduled at 5:00 p.m.

"Hamish, good lad, right on time. Yes, everything's going well here. I like the appraisal you got of those triple-deckers. The buildings near the college, that Holy Cross. I like your numbers and the fact that they don't need too much fixing up."

Hamish said, "Yeah, both of them are in pretty good shape, and we expect the rents to be like you said, but the bank think your rent plans are too low."

"So," Jeremiah replied, "if my offer price works with low rent numbers, it's a good deal, a safe deal. We can always raise the rents later if the market moves in that direction."

"Yes, sir," he answered. "Shall I carry the offer letters over to him? The offers we prepared on Saturday?"

"Let's do it Hamish. Can't let that cash sit around in a bank, and it's time for me to put down more roots in the US."

"That's more apartments for me to manage and fix up. I'll be comin' to you for more wages."

"I expect you will. I'll be back on Saturday. We'll talk then."

Jeremiah ended each week on Friday at 5:00 p.m. Often the construction team worked Saturdays, but he let his crew of stonemasons off on Friday. If they wanted to work on Saturday, he had no objection and would approve their hours and wages. Some men did this; others having done work that Jeremiah claimed "not quite good enough" preferred to work in his presence. It saved a lot of rework. He would take the train or some combination of trains back to Worcester, enabling him to do his studies of artwork at the library or engage in Irish football. He was amused that they called the game rugby in the United States. He made friends at the club although, with his work, he had little time for them. It was the same with his social life. He had little time to meet or befriend women. The club was all male, and many of his friends met their ladies at church.

While he made his living at Catholic and Protestant churches, he never joined a church nor went to any services. He recalled his experience with the clergy at St. Josephs in Stradbally. He was eighteen when the Monsignor O'Neill called him in for a talk. The monsignor was against his Fenian philosophy and warned him against the godless radicals. Jeremiah found the monsignor and the church in Ireland indifferent to the terrible poverty of the poor and unsympathetic to the British conditions that caused it. In a heated conversation with monsignor, the white-haired cleric told him that he was unworthy of Christ's blessings, and the monsignor would not serve him Holy Communion. In response, he told the monsignor that the church was losing Christ's message and had basically lost its way. He'd find his own spiritual path. The old man wagged a finger at him angrily as he turned and walked away. And he had found his own path, he'd go to church when it suited him. He'd visit during the week when the church was empty, sit, and think about Christ's messages in the New Testament and the messages in the Old Testament. His form of prayer was meditative and devoted to thought, he found peace and solace with this informal practice. Yet on this coming Sunday, Alice Sullivan had asked him to join her and her family at mass.

Alice was married to William Sullivan, although a young couple they were quite wealthy. He was a surgeon, and she had been a nurse at the same hospital. She had invited Jeremiah to a church breakfast on several occasions in order to meet one of her friends from the hospital. William was not against such a process but was wary of its effectiveness, especially when it came to Jeremiah Knox. He had met Jeremiah during the construction of St. Paul's Cathedral in Worcester, where his family had funded the statue of St. Paul that resided in an alcove adjacent to the altar. While William found Jeremiah a skilled sculptor, he concluded that the man was devoted only to his art. In conversations about the statue with the Sullivan family, William listened in surprise as his wife focused more on Jeremiah's bachelorhood than on the statue of St. Paul.

Jeremiah viewed invitations to parties, church socials, or other type of gatherings as awkward and clumsy. It seemed to him that married women could not stand the sight of single men, so their weekly endeavors were to introduce their single friends to single men in the best possible circumstances. A church breakfast was such a setting, and it was more of an obligation than pleasure for him.

Alice was certain that all men would be most courteous and pleasant at a Mass followed by a nice breakfast. The spiritual process followed by good food and conversation would ensure both parties ample time to illustrate their best features of character and personality.

Jeremiah leaned back in his seat as the train rattled on toward Worcester. He thought about Alice's invitation and laughed. This will be the third time. The first breakfast had been to meet her cousins, three of the nicest, plumpest young women in Central Massachusetts. Next came a fellow nurse from the hospital, a lovely morose girl who did not smile or offer any conversation throughout the entire Mass and breakfast. It was thoughtful, maybe even more than that, when friends or acquaintances introduced him to young women. Yet he was honest when describing his situation; he had no time for romance or the courting process at this stage of his career. In fact, he did not miss the companionship of woman as his work absorbed him. When he expressed this feeling to well-intentioned friends, they must have assumed that he was shy or nervous thus reluctant to meet new people. They, in this case Alice, would make it easy for him.

On Sunday, he donned his new Brooks Brothers suit, white shirt, and tie and met the Sullivan family and Connie Harrison on the steps of St. Paul's. In the exchange of greetings, Jeremiah could not take his eyes off Connie. She was nearly as tall as he, possible older, but he couldn't tell. Her hair was cut short, thick and pushed away from her face, revealing a broad forehead, long jaw, and sharp, pointed nose. She wasn't what he'd call good-looking, but she was striking.

She shook his hand with a powerful grip. "So you're the one who did the statue of Saint Paul, pointing at the statue. Where did you learn anatomy? That's a pretty sexy body you put on old Paul." She followed her observation was a raucous laugh.

He hadn't taken his eyes off her and, with a wry smile, said, "I modeled it after my own torso. That's so much more efficient."

"Oh, very good, Jeremiah," William joked. They all laughed, and Connie slapped him on the back with a large hand.

Surprised, Jeremiah glanced at her, and his eyes remained on her face.

She said, "Well, Mr. Sculptor, are all your statues based on your body? She left her hand on his back for another second or two before removing it."

"Only the males," he responded.

She eyed him as they entered the church, and out came her loud boisterous laugh again.

Chapter 17

Alice Sullivan didn't trust nature; it wasn't in her character. With a strong belief that she could change circumstances to achieve a conclusion she desired, she wouldn't allow nature to run its course. Separately, she telephoned Jeremiah and Connie, telling them they looked good together, asking if they had an enjoyable time at breakfast. She pushed forward, inviting both of them to a party she and William were having in two weeks. She bombarded them with brief notes encouraging each to see the other and repeating her desire to have them attend her party. These notes piled up in Jeremiah's mailbox as he was in New Hampshire during the week. Desperate she called Connie. "My dear, please come to the party, and I'm having no luck whatsoever in getting a response from Mr. Knox."

"Oh, Alice … why worry about him? As I recall, he's in New Hampshire and probably won't be in town anyway. He's such a character. Why bother?"

"My dear, you two were so active talking at breakfast. I think you look marvelous together and you got along so well."

"Alice." Connie sighed inaudibly, turning her head from the speaker. Here she goes again, she thought. "I am … I'm really grateful that you think of me, but you know my story. Medical school is my priority, and I don't want any male involvement to distract me from that goal."

Alice was well acquainted with Connie's ambition, but she also knew medicine. Medical school for a woman was such a long shot. Her husband's medical school at Harvard had a firm policy, no females. They didn't believe that women could withstand the rigors of the practice. She said, "I know you work hard toward that goal,

ANGELS ON A TOMBSTONE

but don't you want some insurance if it doesn't work out? Look what I did with William."

"Alice, you were an outstanding nurse. You could have gone to med school. I don't fault your decision to marry William, but you could have gone to New England Female Medical College. You could have been a doc."

"Well, you've heard my reasoning before, so it's not worth repeating, but don't you want some male companionship?"

"Of course, from time to time, I really miss it. But so many men want one or two things, and I won't give either."

"You're still on that belief ... men want sex and/or someone to do the cooking, cleaning, and laundry."

"Have you seen any evidence that there are men who have something else in mind?"

Alice laughed. "Oh, never mind, please come to the party. I'll make sure there's more than one interesting man for you to meet."

"No thank you, my dear. I have applications coming up for Johns Hopkins and Boston University. I'll be working on those over the weekend. During the week, the hospital's put us all on overtime due to the influenza outbreak."

When Jeremiah returned from Concord Friday evening, he took his stack of mail to O'Doul's Pub and sat at the corner table away from the crowd at the bar. There he saw the three notes from Alice Sullivan. He read them rapidly. They all had the same message. *Good grief,* he thought, *she's really pushing this woman at me.* He sat, sipping his Jameson, thinking about Alice's notes and Connie Harrison. One unusual woman that one. He nodded at the whiskey as he swirled it around his glass. The image of the tall women with the short hair and loud laugh stayed with him as he watched the whiskey circle at the base of his glass. His attention switched as O'Doul's door swung open. Hellos at the bar erupted, and Hamish walked in. The young Scot waved to him and walked to the table. "I have news. May I join you?"

"Of course, please sit." Jeremiah pushed out a chair from the table. "I was looking forward to seeing you tomorrow morning. But if this is more convenient, let's hear the news."

175

"The house on Mulberry Street, near the college, has gotten three bids. He likes yours but wants to talk with you first. He doesn't know you, his bank doesn't know you, and he wants to make sure you can pay."

"Why didn't he call my bank?"

"Believe me, I told him to call. He's strange. He said he doesn't trust bankers he doesn't know. He wants to see you in the flesh. Wants to hear the money's there in your own voice."

"Okay." Jeremiah pulled a pocket watch from his vest and glanced up. "It's ten o'clock. Let's walk over to his home and put a note in his mailbox with the request to meet him tomorrow."

"Can I have a Glenfarclas first?"

"Sure, I'll have a sandwich and a tall ale, then we'll go. What about the other house?"

"They like your terms and are ready to meet when you are."

They took a trolley to Lake Street and walked two blocks to the corner of Kiln and Burdell Avenue. There, on a large lot stood a three-story Victorian mansion. Looking for a mailbox or mail slot, they climbed a short set of steps toward the front door when deep, angry barking erupted from inside. The mail slot was a narrow slice in a massive front door. The wide oak portal was at least six feet wide. Jeremiah lifted the metal lid to slide the note through. The noise caused the dog to explode in anger, barking crazily.

A man's voice added to the noise. "Something out there, old boy?" Then in a booming voice, he said, "Who's out there causing a disturbance at this late hour?"

Jeremiah bent down, his mouth close to the mail slot. "It's Jeremiah Knox and Hamish McDougal. We'd like a meeting with you tomorrow regarding the property on Mulberry Street."

The door opened a crack, and a snarling Doberman, held at his collar by the strong hand of his master, continued his barking. The dog was eyeing Jeremiah's knees. His master said, "Quiet down, Beda. Easy, boy." And the dog glanced up at his master, shaking his head, and the barking stopped.

"Don't mind the dog, boys. Come in. Who's who?"

Jeremiah and Hamish introduced themselves, and Jeremiah added, "The hour's late. We simply wish to confirm our interest in a meeting as soon as possible."

"That's okay, boys. I'm ready for business anytime night or day. Albert Cassiday here." He extended his free hand.

He pushed the dog into a room off the entryway, closed the door on the Doberman who registered his displeasure with a short bursts of his angry bark. Cassiday said, "The damn dog doesn't like his sleep disturbed. Normally, he's more curious and polite." He guided Hamish and Jeremiah to other side of the entryway and into a book-filled library. He moved his square body around a big desk and sat in a high back mahogany chair. He placed his arms on a rectangular, dark-blue ink blotter and, leaning forward, said, "Tell me about yourself, Knox. Why my building and why that price?"

Jeremiah took him through parts of his background, excluding the reasons for his exile, emphasizing the unusual opportunities in the US for his skills. Cassiday laughed. "At least you weren't thrown out of your country like I was. Rich, lazy aristocrats claimed I stole from my company. Bastards."

"Well, this isn't stolen money, Mr. Cassiday. It's been earned the hard way." Jeremiah laughed.

"I've checked on you, son. Saw the article in the *Boston Herald*. I'm dealing with a celebrity here, aren't I?"

"Hardly, sir, Henry Vaughn is the celebrity if there is one."

"Modest, are you? Okay, tell me about your bid. Your man here tells me it's below my sale price but all cash. Is that right?"

"Yes, it's all cash, and it's in Worcester Commercial as we speak. We can go there together on Monday if you wish. It'll be in your bank later that day. It's that simple. My bid's good. You have the numbers."

"I like your style, Knox. Perhaps new can do more business as I sell off more of my holdings. I think you'll like the building. It's in good shape and should give you very steady cash flow."

"If I may ask, sir, why are you selling it if it's so good?"

"I'm moving to other types of real estate. I'm putting together a group to build hotels. I think that's the next big opportunity in real estate. You might be interested in investing in that someday."

"Time will tell, but right now my main focus is on my own design and sculpture. These buildings, the triple-deckers are fine for me."

"Okay, then. We have a deal." He stood up and extended his hand. "Let's meet at your bank on Monday morning. Please call this number to confirm the time." He opened a desk drawer, looked at the business card carefully, then extended it to Jeremiah. "I'd offer you boys a drink, but it's past my bedtime, so we'll have that drink on Monday." He ushered the boys, as he called them, out the door and bade them goodnight.

Jeremiah slept soundly and was awakened by the sharp ringing of his telephone. Groggy, he answered, "Who's calling at dawn. This is Knox."

"Jeremiah, I wanted to catch you before you left town again. It's Alice." There was no response, so she repeated, "It's Alice Sullivan."

"Of course, I have your three notes. Just got them as I've been in New Hampshire all week."

"Yes, so I understand. Well, it's important for you to make our party next week. You bring such life, such a difference with your work. You must come. And I believe Connie is coming."

She paused here and again, hearing no comment, rushed on. "Now, I'm not pushing you two together. There will be other lovely women there as well." She failed to mention that Connie had said no and that the other women would be married, but that detail could be uncovered later. She was certain if Jeremiah said yes, Connie would change her mind. "So you'll come? William so looks forward to seeing you as do I."

"I'm okay with that date, Alice. I'll be there."

"Wonderful." She hung up.

Fully awake now, he went to his kitchen and boiled some water for coffee. He sat at the kitchen table in his night clothes and sipped the hot drink. He made terrible coffee and made a vow to stop trying. He kept thinking about Connie and wondered if she was coming to the party. That would make a difference, he thought. He dressed thinking about her and decided to have a full breakfast with good coffee at the local diner. As he walked down Vernon Street, he thought about the conversation with Cassiday. By Monday or at some date next week, he'd own three triple-deckers and possibly a fourth by the end of the month. The cash flow from them would enable him to pay Hamish full-time and provide him a real apartment as his resident property manager. He'd talk to him about the idea this weekend. And his mind rolled back to Connie.

Tall, gawky, not terrific-looking but there was something about her. That huge raucous laugh showed great humor and spirit. Her conversation was fast, informed about the topics of the day, and curious about the work of others. He'd call her after breakfast. She'd mentioned that she roomed with three girls. One of them should be home to take the call. He checked his mailbox when he returned to his building, and there was a note to see Hamish. He descended the stairs to the basement and found him reading the morning paper.

They climbed up the flights of stairs to Jeremiah's apartment. Sitting in the Spartan living room, Jeremiah took one easy chair, and Hamish took the other. Between them was a square coffee table. The floor was bare wood, scrubbed clean, but no rugs covered the surface. The room seemed empty to Hamish, but he made no comment as he had made no comments on other visits. But he thought, with all the money Jeremiah was making, why not furnish his apartment more completely? He looked around the room. Nothing had changed in the year he'd known Jeremiah. As he looked, he waited.

Jeremiah said, "I think last night's conversation completed the Mulberry property and the bid for the Langley property was accepted too, right?"

"Yes," Hamish replied, "They took your offer quickly. Maybe you offered too much."

"Well, you studied the comparable buildings. The bank did the same, and my rent numbers work. So I'm fine with the offer."

"I'm kinda amazed on how fast you do things, Jeremiah. You've got four buildings now. How you gonna manage all that?"

"That's what I'd like to talk to you about."

Jeremiah quickly summarized his plan for Hamish, emphasizing that the young Scot was important to him and crucial in management of the properties. He explained that he needed a man to manage property improvements, secure tenants, fix problems in the buildings, answer tenant complaints, and collect rents. He offered Hamish a full-time job with a modest weekly salary and a free apartment in one of the buildings. As the property manager, he would be available to all tenants in each building to assist them when needed.

"You're offering me full-time work plus an apartment?" In a careful controlled show of pleasure, the Scot smiled. "That sounds good to me except for the weekly salary. That seems low compared to factory work I've been looking at."

Jeremiah winced. He never could detect the real meaning of Hamish's guarded smile. It was a nagging worry for him, always there. He feared that Hamish would walk off the job. He stood up and began to pace. He glanced over at Hamish and pointed to him. "You're the man I want. You're resourceful, clever in fixing things. You've got a good eye for new buildings, and people like you. I'm getting you out of the basement, into a very nice roomy apartment rent-free. Are you adding that to your salary number? Will a factory job do that?" He paused, glancing at Hamish. "Now, on the weekly salary, that's all I can afford right now. If I buy more buildings, your work will expand, and I'll increase your pay accordingly. How's that sound?"

"Can I count on your buying more buildings and me doing the lead work?"

"As long as I keep earning more than I need, I'll invest. This area is attracting lots of new people for the manufacturing work. I know you're able to get a job in one of those companies, but think of the difference. You're not chained to a machine nor a nine-to-five job six days a week. In companies like that, there'll be little opportunity to earn more or get more responsibility. I beat all of that."

"But what if you don't or can't?"

"Then you can always search out one of those manufacturing jobs. The big difference is … I'll use your skills. Those manufacturing jobs don't require much skill, won't use what you have."

Hamish stood up and faced Jeremiah. "Okay, it's a deal as long as you promise me more money as my work expands."

They struck the deal, and Hamish inquired about his own apartment. They discussed possible occupancy dates, and the young Scot bounced down the stairs to his basement lodging. He waved goodbye to it, sat on his bed, and returned to his reading. He was in the midst of *The History of Tom Jones, a Foundling* and found the changes in Tom's situation quite relevant to the change in his own prospects.

After Hamish's departure, Jeremiah stared at the telephone, sitting on the coffee table. The black instrument appeared to weigh forty pounds to him, yet he had to pick it up. He wanted to make the call to Connie yet felt hesitant. Confident in most matters, he was not confident with women, especially her. She seemed so self-possessed. Her wry comments and cryptic humor dazzled him, put him off his normal style of interaction. Yet he'd decided that the Sullivan's party would hold no interest for him unless she was there. And the only logical way to determine her plan of attendance was to ask her. That was the hard part; he'd never done this before. He did not trust Alice's offhand suggestion that Connie was likely to attend. Why did she mention that other young women would be there? Alice was too mercurial, too manipulative for him. He needed to be certain that Connie would be there. He did not want to waste his time on frivolous parties.

He picked up the phone and dialed for the operator before he could change his mind. She made the connection to the number he cited and a young woman answered. "I'm calling for Connie. Is she there?"

"Hello. Who's this?"

He identified himself and heard a chuckle as the girl hollered for Connie. "It's for you, Connie. A Jeremiah Knox."

"Jeremiah, what a surprise—hello."

He started to speak. *God this is awkward*, he thought. "Hello, Connie. I'm calling about Alice Sullivan's party. She said you're coming, and I was interested to see if that's true."

She hesitated for a second, then said, "Actually, I said no to her. I've got some work to do that's been building up."

"I had a feeling she didn't have your commitment. What a shame."

"You should go. Alice's parties are always fun. A nice way to spend a Saturday evening."

"What's this work that's been adding up? Sounds like my weekend. I probably should take your good example."

She wondered, *Tell him, don't tell him?* Her desire to do medical school seemed to turn most men off. They didn't understand the commitment or didn't want that type of woman in their life. She thought, *What the hell?*

She said, "Jeremiah, this may surprise you, but I plan to go to medical school. I want to be an MD. The applications are all due by December, so I need to get moving."

"Wow, really. There are no women docs in Worcester, are there? There were none in Ireland either. I think that's terrific. Good for you. By the way, I had to do extensive applications for law school. Would my experience be of any help?"

"I remember that you studied law, but I forget why you've shifted to sculpture. Yes." She thought it might be enjoyable to see him again and was surprised by her eager response. "Yes, indeed, I could use some help."

"Well, we can discuss my change of professions at another time, but in ways to help you, I have an idea." He waited a moment for a comment. Getting none, he proceeded. "Okay, we could meet at the Worcester Library on the afternoon of Alice's party and work on your applications. If you'd made satisfactory progress by early evening, we could go to the party."

There was silence on the line, and he thought he'd been too aggressive. His inexperience was plaguing him. He started to say, "Or …"

She said, "I think that's a grand idea, but I want to be clear, you're asking me out on a date."

Oh, Christ, he thought, *what's the right response to that?* His hand began to sweat a little. "You know, Connie. That's an American term

I'm not too familiar with. But yes, I'm asking you to join me for two events, so to speak."

"That's just grand—let's do it. It will stun Alice when we arrive together."

Chapter 18

They met at the library and found the quiet end of a long wooden table in the spacious main hall. An older man, his thin blue-veined hands holding a newspaper, was at least ten feet from them. Connie pulled a set of applications from her satchel and placed them in front of Jeremiah. He glanced at the titles on the forms and nodded. He was familiar with the questions but unaware of the schools.

He asked, "Have you considered the program at Harvard Medical School? Bill Sullivan went there, and as you know, he's very good."

"I applied there last year." She relayed the story that Harvard's decision was based on their policy, no women physicians, and the policy was firm and unlikely to change. So she was focused on applications to Boston University and Johns Hopkins University. Both medical schools had instituted programs for women. She pointed to the two folders. "These are both good programs, so let's start with Boston University. They've recently merged the New England Female Medical College into their male medical school. I like what I've heard."

When he looked at the application forms, he surprised her. He was unlike other men. He was enthusiastic and supportive of her ambition. His suggestions to various questions on the forms were informed, on target, and better than her own ideas. When he proposed a new idea to her, she wanted to touch his arm or his powerful hands in appreciation but thought the gesture could be misinterpreted. As he studied various sections of the applications, she could not stop gazing at him, finding his power of concentration fascinating. He was helping her application become much stronger than her submission to Harvard the prior year.

Once he gave her a suggestion, he watched the speed with which she incorporated his ideas. When she handed it back for him to read, he purposely made contact with her hand and said, "Excuse me." A smile followed, and they both returned to the work. The clock ticked through the afternoon as she handed him her draft answers or fresh sections to examine.

"Look at this section," she said. Handing him part of the Boston University application. "I find it confusing." Then watched him as he poured over it, his brow wrinkling, his mouth moving ever so slowly.

He caught her looking at him and smiled, then dropped his eyes back to the questions. After a few moments, his eyes flicked up for a mini-second, and found her eyes still on him. Pleased, he ignored the contact and returned to the application.

In between his review of her work or interspersed with their discussions of how to approach a challenging question, he worked on drawings from his satchel. Occasionally, she'd glance at his work, and he'd deflect her attention. Twice, she counted, he placed his hand on her arm to stop a question.

"We'll get to your questions some other day. This is your day to make progress."

She responded with a slight brush of his hand. "I have so many questions about what you do and how you do it. Is that a drawing of an altar?" She moved her fingers from his hand to the drawing in front of him.

He pushed the artwork away from her and out of her sight. "I'll take that as a topic for a second get-together."

For a second, she seemed surprised then nodded. "Okay." Then she returned to her work.

They had worked side by side for four hours, passing her prospective answers back and forth. For Connie, the time had flown. She moved faster and worked better with his comments on the clarity and persuasiveness of her written work. For Jeremiah, it was a trip back to his own applications for law school and how he addressed the differences in the questions at Trinity College in Dublin and Edinburgh and Cambridge. She put down her pen and announced that she was exhausted. It was near closing time for the library and time to catch a trolley to the Sullivan mansion and the early evening party. She closed her files on the two medical schools. She'd made more progress with his help than she'd expected. The task looked much less daunting now, and her confidence in the quality of her applications had soared with his help. She wondered where his confidence in professional woman came from. As they walked down the steps of the library, their eyes scanning the nearby tracks for a trolley, she said, "Jeremiah, you're a rare bird. Most men I meet show no interest in my aspirations, or are surprised I want something more than nursing. It's wonderful that you support top professions for women, when did that start for you?"

"Here comes a trolley that takes us near the Sullivan's house." He pointed across the street to an approaching car. They left the base of the library steps and hustled across the street to the boarding platform. Jeremiah's speed to reach the trolley was quicker than hers, and she reached for his arm and took it. He slowed his pace and gave her hand a reassuring squeeze. He liked the presence of her hand on his arm. "Sorry, a little too fast?"

They were taking deep breaths as they boarded the trolley. It was full of passengers returning from shopping, chattering away in the late Saturday dusk. As they worked their way to an open seat in the crowded car, they sat with their bodies wedged together. He liked the proximity, the sensation of her strong, long legs pressed against his.

He said, "Back to your question before our little sprint, it was my work with the Fenians in Ireland. Many of the firebrands, many of the top thinkers in the movement were women. And they were strong, smart, and very effective. Some were poets, others writers, and educators. They did more than many of the men." He told the story of Maggie McCarthy and Sheena Stearns, who had used Maggie's family sailboat to run guns from Germany to Ireland. He described how they outfoxed the coastal patrols in Germany and Ireland by picking up the arms at midnight, having a mastery of the patrol routes and supreme knowledge of the winds and tides. "I had the highest regard for those women."

"Did you have any love affairs with them?" She laughed, surprising herself when the question popped out. "No need to answer that."

He glanced over at her. "I wish." He laughed, his face blushing slightly. "The most impressive women were older, often married to intellectuals of one type or another. As I read in history, they were the type of individuals who always tend to lead political change. Some were very rich, and all were well educated. I was just a kid to them."

"I thank them for you. You're a big help."

"You don't need help. You just need a smart admissions director. I see from your records that you were at the top of your class in sciences at Manhattanville College, same in your nursing program, and you've been a surgical nurse for five years. Good grief, how more qualified can you be?"

She grasped his arm, her big hand giving it a strong squeeze. "You give me such confidence."

He chuckled. "It's deserved."

"When can I see more of your work? The statue of St. Paul we saw two weeks ago was stunning. What else have you done?"

He felt buoyed from her interest. "We could see some other work tonight if we don't stay too long at the party."

"Oh, good, let's go. That's a terrific suggestion. Let's be polite, visit with a few people, say hello to the Sullivans, then leave." She arched her eyes at him. "What do you think?"

"I don't want to offend anyone, but sure. I think we can do it skillfully."

"You're such the gentleman. Oops, here's our stop."

They descended from the trolley and walked toward the Sullivan mansion. In the distance, they could see the large house glowing with lights; soft sounds of music were drifting out into the street. She had taken his arm again, and he looked over at her and smiled.

She said, "Where do you suggest we go after the party?"

"It's not far from here. It's St. John's. They have a late Saturday Mass, so it'll be open."

"What will I see?"

"I did the altar there and the communion railing as well."

Before she could comment, the front door flew open. Alice Sullivan stood in the entryway, greeting another guest, then extended her arms to them. She was surprised and delighted. Jeremiah and Connie, they'd actually had come together. She found it hard to believe. And Connie had said no to the invitation. *Good heavens,* she wondered. How did this happen? What had Jeremiah done to convince Connie to stop her work and be social? The thoughts flew through her mind as she moved toward the couple. She'd tried for five years to get Connie interested in her husband's friends with no success. Connie frightened all men away at first meeting or after one date. She was too headstrong, too bright, often critical, and way too ambitious for most men, yet here she was with the sculptor. And Jeremiah had never displayed an iota of interest in any of her prior introductions. Her husband had said that Knox was all business, a complete artist, only interested in his work. He was all work and no play, a complete enigma. Yet she felt the challenge to bring these two unusual people together. After seeing them together at breakfast two weeks prior, she hoped they'd get along. But they were both so busy; she worried about that. And worse, for reasons she could not fathom, neither seemed remotely interested in the other. She worried they were both too independent, yet here they were on her doorstep.

"What a delight to see you two," Alice exclaimed. "Come in, join the festivities."

"Is there an occasion, an event that I missed?" queried Jeremiah.

"Only the advent of winter. It's coming, and we thought we'd better celebrate before the snow slows all of us down."

In the swirl of people, Connie made the rounds of her friends from the hospital, introducing Jeremiah as she went along. Jeremiah pulled away from her from time to time to greet people he knew from his work on Worcester's expanding group of churches and his work on civic buildings. She would wave him over to meet a nurse or doctor he didn't know, surprising herself in making it clear that she was with him. Catching him alone, she said, "Several people have asked me questions about you, and I don't know anything about you."

"Like what?" he asked.

"For example, where do you live? How did you get into your line of work? How old are you? Things like that?"

"I'm twenty-six, and for my curiosity, how old are you?"

She laughed. "I'm ancient for a single woman. I'm twenty-six also."

"And soon to be in medical school. I think that's just terrific."

Her face became quieter, more serious. She said, "That comment, you seem even more certain than you were this afternoon. What's happened?"

"I talked with Bill Sullivan. He informed me that you've done major parts of surgery with him when more than two hands were needed. You've closed up for him at the end of surgeries. He says you'll be a great surgeon, and the schools you're applying to will definitely accept you."

She grasped his arm again. "One thing I like about you is that you give me confidence."

He glanced around the room. They had been there a couple of hours, and the party was still going strong. He'd met several new people and talked with others he'd known previously. He met the mayor who knew of his work and asked him to bid on the ornamental design work for the new civic auditorium. It had been time well spent, for a party that is. He didn't like parties. The conversations were too brief, seemingly artificial, and the noise bothered his ears. But he'd enjoyed this party. He found two new design opportunities, and he'd enjoyed being with Connie.

She held his arm, saying, "There's Jean. She's just arrived. I must say hello." Before she darted off, she squeezed his arm. "I'm having a good time. I hope you are too." She glanced at him expectantly, then rushed off.

He laughed at her departing back. "I am, definitely."

Normally quiet at parties, taller than most of the men at these functions, she often retreated to a chair and talked quietly to a friend or two. Tonight, she was more animated, circulating among the crowd, talking eagerly with friends, and introducing Jeremiah at every opportunity. His presence with her provided a social connection she had not experienced previously; she found it relaxing and freeing. And finally, she found a man who was much taller than she. Most unusual. She liked that he was witty and clever in speech and rarely did he talk of his work, only if asked. He preferred to talk about ideas and was more concerned with the working and living conditions of the newly arrived immigrants from Italy, Ireland, and Poland.

Bursting with energy, she saw him separate from a conversation with a friend of the Sullivans and rushed up to him. "Have you had enough? Is it time for your showing at St. John's?"

He surveyed the room, nodding. "Yes, I guess I've met or talked to about everyone."

They said their goodbyes to Alice and Bill and ventured out to the street. Jeremiah spotted a carriage and asked the driver if he was available.

"I need to be back here in twenty minutes, Governor. Does that help?"

"Yes, indeed, please take us to St. John's. That should give you plenty of time to get back."

The handsome carriage rattled over the cobblestone streets as they nestled close to each other in the two-seated coach. He gave the driver a generous tip and bade him goodnight. The crowd had left the church; the last stragglers were walking down the long set of steps. With the evening Mass recently completed, the interior of the church was still blazing with light. The altar was brilliantly lit, the white marble glowing. The base of the rectangular altar table was strong, yet it seemed to float elegantly above the floor. The spires mounted on the table seemed, to Connie, to reach effortlessly to the domed ceiling above and beyond that to the sky. The sparkling white of the entire altar shimmered in the light. She gazed at the altar transfixed, her eyes wide.

Quietly she said, "I'm not religious, but the altar would bring the devout to their knees. It's not actually a religious piece though … Is it Jeremiah? It's a work of art. A spectacular work of beauty."

She watched him, wanting a comment or reaction. He said nothing; he was studying a feature on the left side of the altar.

"What were you thinking when you made this?"

"Don't give me too much credit here. The monsignor had seen something similar in Italy and wanted it replicated. I talked him into a design that was less busy than the Italian altar, and I added some features that I think remind people of a higher presence. I wanted them to be less awestruck and more inclined to think about their religion and how those thoughts strengthened their daily lives."

"Unbelievable," she sighed as she absorbed his comment. "Can we just sit quietly for a moment?" She gestured toward a pew near the front, and he nodded.

They sat for a few moments as she studied the structure in front of her. She took his hand, her right thumb slowly caressing the back of his left hand. She seemed lost in contemplation, perhaps unaware of the sensual gesture. He watched her from the corner of his eyes and waited a few moments.

Then he said, "I did the communion railing. Would you like to kneel there and tell me how it feels to you?"

"Of course, but remember, I'm not religious, so I may disappoint you."

They walked to the altar rail and knelt as if preparing to receive communion. She seemed a little unsure how to do this, so he led the way. She knelt beside him, her eyes asking, what next?

He whispered, "Place your elbows and forearms on the rail and relax your arms. Close your eyes for a moment."

He watched her for a few seconds. "Okay, now tell me what you feel."

"Oh my," she said, her eyes sparkling. "I'm totally at peace, so relaxed. I feel I belonged here."

She turned to face him and whispered, "Is that what's supposed to happen?"

"I've listened to hundreds of people tell me what it feels like to go to the railing. I've tried to design and shape the keeling position and the rail so an unnatural position of kneeling becomes natural and right for them. I think I've succeeded from what you've said."

Slowly she rose from her position, "Can we sit in the pew for a few more minutes?"

A priest walked out from behind the altar and began to walk down the center aisle, informing people the lights would be out in a few minutes. As he reached Jeremiah and Connie, he stopped. "Evening, Jeremiah. Evening, miss."

"She wanted to see the altar, Father."

"Magnificent, isn't it?" He shook his head and glanced back at it. "It speaks directly to God. I'm aware of God's presence every time I'm here." He turned toward the aisle again. "Night, Jeremiah, miss." He bowed quickly and continued his walk up the central aisle.

They followed him and left through the front door. A block away, they caught a trolley to her neighborhood. She was quiet on the return, and he didn't push her for conversation. She kept her hand in his, occasionally squeezing his hand as if to make sure he was still there.

She said as they stepped off the trolley, "Here's my stop. I'd invite you up for a coffee, but my roommates will be in their nightgowns, ironing their clothes for tomorrow. With curlers in their hair, they'd scream at me."

"Of course, I understand." He stood above her, gazing down at her brown hair, glistening in the lamplight.

She said, "This has been one unusual day. Great progress on my applications, I had fun at a party for a change and saw an amazing display of art and religion. It's been a lot to absorb."

"A good day, a busy day."

"All due to you. What are you doing tomorrow?" She was standing in front of him, looking up into his eyes, curious about how he might react to her question. "Are you interested in the last boat cruise on Lake Quinsigamond? Sunday's the last day before they close for the winter."

Surprised at her suggestion, he said, "That sounds terrific. I'll need some time to change plans, but if you can get free, so can I."

"I'd love to hear what I've disrupted, but can you get free by noon? We can catch a two o'clock departure at the lake. It's my favorite time to take that cruise."

"The timing's fine with me. Do you want to do more work on your applications?"

"I'd love that. But the library closed on Sundays. Where would we work? We can't work at my place. The girls would kill our productivity, and besides, we have no room to work."

"Well, this may sound a little aggressive, but I have a work room with plenty of space. We could work there if it's okay with you."

She laughed. "Sure, I'll bring my valise."

"Here's a thought. I'll meet you here, and we'll leave your valise at my apartment then go to the lake. Afterwards, we can come back and work. Maybe catch a dinner when we're done."

She smiled, seeing a side to him she hadn't seen before. The serious, logical Mr. Knox was playful, even fun-loving. She liked what she saw.

"You know what to do once you get wound up. Don't you, Mr. Knox."

He laughed, hesitated, then took a step closer. He bent down to kiss her cheek. She anticipated his gesture and moved her face, so he caught her lips. She put her hand on the back of his neck, held the kiss for a second, then pulled away.

"Thank you for a wonderful day, Jeremiah. Until tomorrow." She turned and raced into her apartment building.

Chapter 19

In high spirits, Jeremiah raced to the basement to alert Hamish that he had a change in plans for Sunday. He thought the young Scot wouldn't mind and would even prefer to have a day away from inspecting their new properties. There was no door at the base of the cellar stairs, so Jeremiah barged into Hamish's lodgings. There was a soft light near his bed, then Hamish's head rose slowly, and a fuller head of hair rose next to him. The woman screamed and dove back under the covers.

Hamish went up on one elbow. "Jesus, Jeremiah, yee surprised us. Is it an emergency?"

"No, no, Hamish. My apologies. Good night. I'll see you in the morning. Night, ma'am."

He left to a trickle of laughter, his face burning with chagrin. Knock, make noise, do something he chastised himself as he trod up the stairs to his apartment. He left a note in Hamish's mail slot that Sunday's schedule was changed. He was going to Lake Quinsagamond for the day.

He woke late with a resolve. Sunday would be a day of no work—pure relaxation except for helping Connie with her applications. He recognized the hour was getting close to eleven, so he dressed in his best suit with a white shirt and tie and went to find a carriage for rental. No trolleys today. They'd travel to and fro the lake in comfort and style. He went to a church near his building and found several carriages awaiting the ending of services. He secured one for the day and told the driver to meet him at his apartment at one o'clock.

He finished a lunch of bread and cheese then left with the carriage to meet Connie. She introduced him to her roommates, and their inspection of him was penetrating and made him self-conscious. As they left the apartment, she saw the carriage and was pleased. "How convenient, how thoughtful of you, no crowded trolleys for us today."

"I thought the carriage would give us more flexibility. It's ours for the afternoon."

"Oh, you think of everything," she teased. "Let's drop off my valise and get to the lake."

Her glance around his apartment left her speechless. He had more room than she had with two roommates. But the large living room and kitchen were barren. The living room had no rugs, no tables, just three worn-out overstuffed chairs. The sole reading lamp was tucked near one of the chairs. A pile of books stacked next to it reached the arm of the chair appearing to her like a poor excuse for a side table or lazy man's access to his books. To her, the room had the personality of a monk's cell. It was like no one lived here. His bedroom, she gave it a quick glance, was equally empty, a wide bed, no rug, and small simple curtains on the windows. She relaxed more when she placed her valise in the workroom. Here he had placed a ten-foot-long oak table, strong and handsome. There were four chairs lined up against a wall, which she surmised could be pulled up to the table. On the table, at one end, were blocks of clay and partially carved statues and a miniature altar in partial development. At the other end of the table was a large piece of drafting paper and a sketch had been started on another altar, very intricate and elaborate. Along the walls, the room came alive. From ceiling to floor, there were sketches, photographs, and paintings of statues, vases, garden ornaments, altars, cathedral towers, bell towers, stained-glass windows, buildings arches, and archways.

"Here, Connie." He pointed to the table. "Place your valise in the middle. There's plenty of room there." He brought two chairs to the table. "We'll work here."

She laughed. "Jeremiah, how can I work in here? I'll spend all my time looking at the great art on your walls. How much of this have you done?"

"Some's mine, others you'll recognize, like Michelangelo's *Pieta*, that are there for inspiration."

"Are the sketches all yours?"

"Yes."

"They're truly amazing. Beautiful. And you turn those into sculpted pieces?"

"As best I can."

"May I ask you an embarrassing question?"

"Sure."

"Why is this room so vibrant and the other rooms so ... so."

"Empty?"

"Yes, thank you."

"Well, first it was money. Now, it's not important to me. This is room where I go when I'm here. I don't live in the other rooms."

"What about guests?"

"You're my first real guest. Hamish, I've mentioned him, comes up for work, but we do that in here."

"What about a social gathering?"

"Oh, that. I have the Erin I club for some things. O'Doul's Pub or Dooley's Tavern for other parties or gatherings." He started to laugh. "Don't mistake me for a social being." He laughed again, a natural throaty guffaw. "No, no, I'm not inclined to be social like the Sullivans. Maybe someday."

"Well," she said with a hint of authority, "I'll have some ideas for you if you're interested. You have a beautiful unit here. So much potential, some of your own art. Your sketches would be dynamite in the living room."

She glanced at him and saw the wry smile on his lips. "You're not interested, are you?" She was interested in his answer but was concluding that this was a very independent man, a man used to solitude and one who didn't need elaborate to even modest surroundings.

"Not the case," he answered. "You remind me of my mother when she visited my rooms at Edinburgh. She wanted to furnish them like her living room."

"And you didn't want her help?"

"Is that a serious question?"

They both laughed. He tapped her gently on the shoulder.

He said, "We should get back to the carriage before someone else tempts him with a larger fare."

"Okay, mister, but don't think I'm through with my ideas for your living room."

She returned to her thoughts. The rooms seemed to define him, and she was determined to find out if this perception was correct. He seemed totally and completely devoted to his work, his art. There was nothing else that so dominated his being. His surroundings were irrelevant. He seemed to be other worldly. She wondered about his rugby, his Friday gatherings at the pubs with friends, his adventures with other women, his frequency at parties like the Sullivans. How did these activities fit in? Then she thought about herself. She was similar. She was devoted to the hospital, her patients, and she was consumed by her desire to go to medical school. But she loved fine clothes, which she could not afford. She enjoyed fine dining and a comfortable home like her parents. She knew she'd forgo those pleasures to become a doctor. Were she and Jeremiah so different? She thought so but was unsure.

They descended the stairs and were met by Hamish on the first floor. His smile widened his face, and he winked at Jeremiah, mischief in his eyes. Jeremiah introduced him, and Hamish bowed and took off his cap.

He said, "Ma'am," studying her for a moment. She towered over him, and his eyes swept up and down her body registering appreciation. He said *ma'am* again. "My pleasure." He turned to Jeremiah. "Don't forget the bank in the morning before yee leave for Concord."

"I have the schedule and all the papers. We're set."

"Does that mean I can start work on those buildings by Tuesday or Wednesday?"

"You'll be at the bank with me. We'll know then, but I expect yes. The banker and lawyers will make that clear."

Connie was perplexed and wrestled with what questions to ask. Who was this Hamish, and what was he doing at a bank with Jeremiah? They settled in the carriage. The black stallion trotted at a steady pace to the outskirts of the city and the long narrow lake.

The day was turning pleasant. The early morning clouds gave way to clear skies and sunshine. The autumn air was crisp, cool, but the sun warmed the carriage and streamed in through the back window. It felt good on their necks and shoulders. Connie worked on her thoughts, and finally had them straight, or so she thought.

"So you and Hamish work together? Is he a stonesmith or sculptor too? Are you doing work in a new bank building?"

"Oh no, Hamish manages this building, and he'll manage some new ones."

"Oh, so he's your landlord or your landlord's rent man?"

"Not quite." He studied her face and saw her curiosity was earnest. "I'm his landlord."

"Wait a minute. He works for you. You own that apartment building?"

"Yes, I thought you knew that."

"Well, maybe. But I guess it wasn't clear to me."

She paused again, nervous as his eyes rested directly on her. She struggled to get her thoughts straight. "So you can do anything you want with that apartment?"

"Yeah, I guess that's true. But I want to be careful so when I move it will be easy to rent."

"Well, I can't wait to give you my ideas. Are you game?"

Eventually, it all came out. As they walked the deck of the ferry as they cruised by the shores of the long lake, their conversation delved into his work, his newly owned real estate, her medical life and medical ambitions. She observed that they were very busy people, quite different than many of her friends. She learned he had few friends. Most of the people he worked with worked for him. Those over him like Henry Vaughn or Casper Soames were much older and lived in different cities. Yet he wasn't lonely. She began to conclude that he didn't know what loneliness was. She realized he was too busy to be lonely. She remarked on his travel, and he allowed that he enjoyed it.

He watched her for a reaction, then said, "It gives me variety, a chance to see new cities and towns. It enables me to understand what the people in those places need and want from my work."

He enjoyed talking about his work but understood she was after other aspects of his life. He found this confusing. In previous associations with women, no one had ever explored this facet of his character. To her probing, he admitted that he was fascinated, from an early age, by certain standards of justice or fairness. He told the story about the poor children in Stradbally and how they were turned away from his grade school because they had no shoes. He talked about his first visits at age five or six to Dublin and later to London, where he saw the fine houses, the handsome carriages carrying women in gorgeous dresses, and their children in finery he'd never seen before. He asked his father about this apparent affluence compared to the clothing and housing in Stradbally, and his father's simple answer was that the wealth was controlled by the English. He told her that from an early age, he wanted to change who had the wealth and power in Ireland. Sadly, he admitted that he'd been sent to America for his ideas, and he'd been required, in order to survive, to find a separate set of interests.

Now she understood his transfer from law to sculpture, and his accomplishments took her breath away. How did he … how did anyone shift paths like this? How hard was this? How did he do it? And now, look at him, just six years later, a substantial success as a sculptor. Her response was guarded as she searched for the right thoughts to communicate, to acknowledge what he had done. She thought it started with his early values in life, and these values were based on ideals, easy to identify, but hard to live by. She viewed him, as best she could determine at this stage of their acquaintance, as an idealist and wondered how he was adapting to his new realities. Was he comfortable with his changes? Did he plan to stay in America? Idealists, she felt, were often disillusioned and later forced into other interests to survive. Was he one of those disgruntled intellectuals? She wasn't certain, and she wanted to know. She had met a lot of men, and for the first time in her life, she was impressed with a man.

Hesitantly she asked, "Do you wish to return to Ireland, to fight for Irish independence? Do you miss your Fenian involvement and colleagues?"

"It's been hard to be away, but my friends are in exile like me or are in prison. So at the moment, it's not practical or smart to return."

In turn, she talked energetically about her early experiences in medicine and emphasized the hard facts that the average person and the poor had limited access to good medical services. She wanted to address and change that reality. She claimed to be a realist.

When she verbalized the differences between them, he wondered if she was correct. He rolled the difference between idealist and realist around in his mind and thought about it. Had he changed? He had told her that he was no longer a political radical or even a political activist that had been drummed out of him by the court in Dublin. His expulsion to the United States and the threat of punishment hanging over him if he reverted to his prior activities had altered his choices. He felt that he'd become more of a realist as he made accommodations to his past and found a different future. And this future was turning out to be quite enjoyable, very challenging and financially rewarding. He concluded that he while he was practical, he hadn't lost his idealism but didn't, at this stage, know quite what to do with it. The Americans had solved the balance of power problems with the British. His key issue in Ireland was irrelevant here.

As they walked the deck, he was struck by her drive and energy. Her commitment to medicine was as strong, if not stronger, than his passion for artistry in stone. He felt something else but didn't understand the feeling. In some way, he felt freer, more open around her. He couldn't quite express how he felt, but it was like a heavy weight had been lifted from his shoulders. He wanted to tell her this but sensed it was an unformed impression, something temporary that would vanish as quickly as it had arrived. It was too early in their association to link this feeling of freedom to her. He liked the feeling he had with her and wanted it to last. Her conversation seemed to free her too, and he wondered what it was like being her with these ambitions. She was unlike any women he'd known or courted. She wanted a life and profession of her own. In this drive of hers, was there any room for a man?

Without expressing it, she was asking herself the same questions. Could a man with his passion for work, his demanding schedule, and the travel it entailed be interested in the stable life of a home and a family? She wanted to express these questions but decided to save them until she knew him better. She thought of Sister Mary Robert at Manhattanville who taught philosophy and called attention to the difference between the bourgeois life and the life of the mind clearly preferring the latter. She thought of Jeremiah as having deserted the intellectual life for a practical life of a skilled artisan. But he did it out of necessity, she thought, so where was the real man? Who was the real man? She stopped walking and turned to face him. She looked hard and long into his face. It was not a handsome face, but it was a strong face. His eyes radiated confidence, and his long cheek bowed slightly in between his cheekbone and his jaw. She put a finger in the hollow.

She said, "Even as we talk, I can't stop thinking about you." She glanced around them. "There's no one here. Please kiss me."

He took her face in his hands, and they kissed until they heard sounds near them. She pulled her face away and tucked it into his shoulder. "I liked that," she said.

"I did too. So let's find privacy for more."

They returned to his apartment late in the day. She deposited her coat on the chair in the living room, and he could tell by the expression on her face she detested the room.

He said, "I'm gathering that you prefer the living room of the Sullivans to mine."

She laughed. "I'm that obvious, am I? I apologize. But ... for a man with your artistic tastes, that sense of style is missing in this room."

"Well, it's not important right now, is it? We're going to work on your applications for a while, then I suggest we journey over to Dooley's Tavern for dinner."

She came over to him and tugged on the lapels of his coat.

She said, "I thought we might try another kiss or two before work, and I don't want to do that in this room. There's no love seat here. And we're not going near your bedroom, so that leaves your work studio, but all you have there is two hard chairs."

"I think we'd better do this standing up." He pulled her close and kissed her. The kiss lingered for several minutes.

She pulled away, her face tucked into his shoulder, then she raised it to his lips again. Her eyes were soft, the kiss entered a dreamy state, and they held that sensation for a while. "This isn't working," she said. "How are we ever going to get any work done if we're stalled here kissing."

"I work at all hours, so when we want to stop, we can work."

"I think you have better control than I do. Right now, I shouldn't tell you this, but all I want to do is kiss you. I can't imagine getting my mind around medical school applications."

They sunk into the old stuffed chair, and amid their kisses and awkward fumbling around their mounds of clothes, practicality won out. They pulled away from each other, acknowledging the discomfort of the chair along with the recognition that their fumbling through the layers of clothes was leading into territory neither was ready for at the moment. Victorian ideals guided the behavior of both sexes at the time, and they not only recognized this but were conditioned to follow it.

She thought Jeremiah might be guided more by European values in regard to sexual behavior but found he was as careful as she. Connie judged correctly that he had abundant experience compared to her non-experience, but he was patient and respectful. She was deeply curious about intimacy with a man and wished to experience it but not just yet. This might be the man, she thought, but it was important to know him better.

They straightened their clothes and went into Jeremiah's work studio. They pulled the two chairs close to each other. She opened her valise and extracted the two applications and all her notes. She began to review them, and he watched as she shuffled the papers into some form of order. She let out a large gasp of air and studied him, her mouth taut. "Jesus." She rested her eyes on his. "My dear friend, I cannot work right now. My head's buzzing."

He chuckled. "Buzzing with what?"

"You, you dummkopf." She placed her hands beneath her chin and stared absently at him. "I can't get you out of my head."

"I guess it's like a cold or hay fever. I've got it too."

"Well, let's get out of here before we do something stupid like get naked and jump into your bed."

"Now, there's a good idea."

"Spoken like a true man."

He raised his hands in surrender. "Okay, okay, it's dinner. We'll work on your applications after dinner."

"Not here," she replied. "We'll wind up in bed, and that'll be a big mistake. It'll just confuse things."

"Where then?"

"We can try my apartment with the girls. It might work."

At dinner, she plied him with questions about his schedule for the next few weeks. It was disheartening for her. He would be in New Hampshire the coming week and going to Washington over the next weekend. He was so animated, so excited about the National Cathedral that Henry Vaughn was designing. And Vaughn wanted his work for the interior columns in the cathedral. He explained his design ideas and became lost with his enthusiasm. Delicately, she pried around his interest to determine if he actually would work in the nation's capital for an extended period of time. The cathedral was massive in scale and would take years to complete. He could be gone forever, she thought. It was a new insight into his character. He was more devoted to his work than she had imagined.

She decided on a gambit. "I understand the attractiveness of working on the nation's primary religious building, but you won't be around to see me, or I you."

"I was thinking the same thing," he replied. "How do I see you when DC is so far away? And how do I complete my other work up here in New England? Not easy, this decision."

"Have you asked Mr. Vaughn about this?"

"Oh yes, and he's totally unrealistic. He thinks I can get it all done just like I'm doing between the Connecticut and New Hampshire churches." He paused for a second as he buttered a roll and munched a corner of it. "But I can't do quality of work here if

I'm working down there. It's too far. And I have more than enough work here."

She let out a sigh of relief and hoped he didn't notice it. "I'm pleased to hear it."

"Vaughn's work in DC was very appealing to me until today. I realize that I want to see you, see more of you. I can't do that and do DC too. So I'm hoping you want to see more of me." He gazed at her questioningly.

She reached across the table and placed her hand on top of his. "That's not obvious to you?"

Chapter 20

Despite his schedule and her hospital work, they were able to see each other on a weekends here and there. While neither of them was satisfied with the frequency of their times together, they enjoyed these moments, and both wanted more. They even managed to see each other occasionally during the week as he moved between his project sites. He assisted her in her applications and was as thrilled as she when the acceptances arrived in the late winter of the new year. He took her to the finest restaurant in Worcester as suggested by the Sullivans and toasted her success with champagne and the best food on the menu. Champagne was new to him, and he guzzled it like water and ordered a second bottle. Their spirits were high and beginning to get a little tizzy.

"I've enjoyed women," he said, "but not like this. It's new. It's strange. Sometimes I'm floating on air—like now. Other times, I can't concentrate. I don't seem like myself, and it drives me crazy."

"My father always told me I'm too scientific," she replied. "I see everything in logical terms, and I've tried to see you that way. I can't. You break all my rules, my understandings of how things work. I can't concentrate either. I put the milk in the closet the other day and my gloves in the ice box. How about that?"

"Well, that's not a disaster. How about this? I gave one of my top guys at the Concord Chapel the drawings for the columns there. He came back to me, thank God, and said somewhat perplexed, 'Jeremiah, these columns won't fit in this building.' They were for the cathedral in DC."

She tossed her head back and let loose one of her boisterous laughs. "I'm delighted to hear this. Is the sensation something new for you?"

"You bet. How about you?"

"Same, I'd call it love." She glanced at him, seeking a reaction to the word and getting none went on. "But that's a daring word, isn't it? Very bold of me to use it."

She'd seen it, and others had commented on it. At all times, he maintained a poker face, an appearance of total calm and peace. Now, it unnerved her. "Jeremiah ..."

"Okay," he interrupted. "It must be love ... Definitely, it's love. I can't find the right words for it, yet somehow you've found and awakened a power and a passion in me. I've never experienced this. Never knew it was possible." He knew this sounded too cerebral but couldn't express it any other way. "I feel so differently around you. It's a wonderful feeling, such a joyous sensation."

Her shoulders slumped slightly; she leaned forward in her chair. She grasped his hand and held it tightly. She could feel a welling of emotion surging inside and rushing to her eyes. The rush of emotion was more that she could manage. "I'm sorry, this is too strong for me. All I can get out is that I love you."

They talked for a while about love, how rapidly it came for some of their friends and how hard it had been for them to find it. She wondered why it had taken her so long to find a compatible man but relaxed in the luxury that it had finally happened. Jeremiah was unique, she concluded. It took someone unusual to attract her, someone as strong or stronger than she. It was his sense of independence and the deep security it gave him that attracted her. Nothing seemed to offset his natural equilibrium. He'd come to this country under dire conditions and had carved a path of success very rapidly. Yet the very attributes that attracted her worried her.

She sipped the last ounce of champagne from the tall flute, her eyes peering across the rim of the glass. She said, "I don't want to ruin this special moment, but do you think our love can last since we're so driven by our careers? You're completely committed to your incredible work, a celebrity in your twenties no less. And I'm about to embark on a medical career that virtually no women pursue."

He didn't answer, and she fumbled her next comment, "Well, what I meant is that I'm thrilled to have found love. I want it to last."

His face was quiet, composed. He said, "We're here in America, not England or Ireland. My parents, my ancestors had little control over their lives. Their choices were limited by tradition, customs, and social class. It's different here. No one has control over what we do with our love. It's up to us." He pointed a finger toward her then back to his chest. "So we'll figure this out."

"Good God, you're refreshing and different. You're full of confidence, aren't you?"

"I'm confident that we'll do the right thing for both of us. Because ... if it's not right for one, it's not right for the other." He watched for her reaction and saw she was pleased; her smile was radiant. "So can I pivot to a new topic? Which one of these schools are you going to choose?"

"Oh, I want to acknowledge your prior thought ... what's right for one must be right for the other, something like that. I like it. I want to remember that." She fiddled with her napkin before speaking again.

"I think you know the answer to my choice of medical schools. I want to be close to you. I'm going to Boston University."

They finished the champagne, the soup dish, the fish dish, and the cherries jubilee. Feeling satisfied and slightly stuffed, they sat back in their chairs.

"Big understandings, big decisions tonight. Congratulations on Boston University. They're lucky to have you."

"That's such a relief after years of thinking about it and being rejected at Harvard and other places. It's finally going to happen." Her face became firm, her determination evident. "And I'll make it. I'll not be discouraged no matter how hard the work, no matter how hard the medical profession refuses to accept female physicians."

"I have no doubts about that," he added.

She did not acknowledge his thought. Her mind was busy with a flurry of thoughts. "But I think our declaration of love is huge too. I want to celebrate that."

He said, "We are celebrating, right now."

"Something different Jeremiah, something more demonstrative." Again, she reached across the table for his hand. Her long fingers caressed the back of his hand. "I know you've had the big experience." She blushed slightly. "You know what I mean. I want that experience too, and I want it before marriage so I know what it's all about."

The smile across his lips was soft, his voice gentle. "It's a Saturday night. Shall we spend the night at my place?"

She took his hand as they rose from the table. "Let's go."

It was the summer following her initial year in medical school when Connie saved her first life. She and Jeremiah were moving a new desk into his studio room and heard a loud commotion from the street below. Rushing to the front windows, they looked down onto a crowd of people gathered by a trolley and a horse-drawn carriage. Both had stopped. A man was on the cobblestones, and another man was hovered over him. Without hesitation, Connie flew down the stairs and into the street. Looking over the fallen man, his leg at a bad angle and bleeding profusely, she asked, "What happened?"

Someone offered, "He jumped off the trolley over there into the street, and the carriage hit him. The wheels got his leg."

Jeremiah turned away, feeling nauseous at the sight of the man's leg and gushing blood. Connie looked up at him. "Jeremiah, give me your shirt."

He tore it off. She stripped one arm into a tourniquet and applied it to the man's leg. He screamed in agony, and she tightened it with an additional two twists. "This will save your leg. I know it hurts, but we must get you to the hospital fast."

He passed out at this point, and the man with him said, "Will he live?"

Connie replied, "If we can get him to surgery fast, yes." She glanced up at the carriage driver. "Can you get us to City Hospital in three minutes?"

They loaded the injured man into the back of the carriage and raced to the hospital. The next day, Jeremiah and Connie checked with the hospital and found that the injured man would recover. They decided to visit him.

As they approached his room, they saw the patients name on the door, *Burton Milton.* Jeremiah gasped.

Connie looked at him. "Jeremiah, you're pale. Does the injury still bother you?"

He told her of the Miltons and that they were looking for him and why. She replied, "This is like Javert's multiyear search for Jean Valjean in *Les Misérables.* This is incredible, and every day, I find new dimensions of you. Well, let's get the police."

"No, let's go inside and see if he can talk."

Opening the door, they saw a stocky man, poorly dressed, sitting in a chair, staring at the wall. The man in the bed appeared to be sleeping. The stocky man looked at them. "It's you ... the doc." He stood up and extended his hand. "I thank you, the docs here said you saved his life. I'm Harry Milton." He pointed to the bed. "That's my brother Burton."

The noise seemed to arouse the injured man. He said, "What the fuck the noise?"

Jeremiah said, "It's me, Burton." He turned to look at Harry. "It's me, Harry. I'm Jeremiah Knox. I hear you want me. Well, here I am. And make no mistake, I want you."

Terrified, Harry stood up. "You, you ... saved his life. We want no more. We want no more trouble."

Burton moaned from the bed, "Wha' the fucks goin' on. Who dese people?"

"It's me Burton, Jeremiah Knox. You want to kill me. Is that right?"

"You killed my brother."

"Your brother declared war on my people. I didn't kill anyone. He died in war. That happens."

"What are you going to do?" asked Harry.

"You're both wanted for murder in Ireland, so I'll contact the police right now, and you'll be deported as soon as your brother can travel."

Jeremiah left to contact the police, and Connie stayed to talk with the brothers. When she met him in the lobby of the hospital, she told Jeremiah that the brothers were done with revenge. They were grateful that she saved Burton's life and asked her to convince Jeremiah to stay away from the police.

"Jeremiah," she said, "I'm afraid they'll run. You scared them to death."

"Well, how do you think I feel with their threat hanging over my head the past few years?"

They returned to the hospital two days later, the Burton brothers had left. Whether they left with the police or on their own, the hospital administrator wouldn't say. Jeremiah was frustrated. This was not closure for him. A visit to the police station generated no satisfaction.

The captain said, "Jeremiah, you know I can't talk about who's here, not here. All these pending cases are private until formal charges are filed."

When, after a few days, he heard nothing more from the police. He concluded the brothers disappeared as fast as they had appeared. Would they surface again? Perplexed, he wondered if Connie's right. Were they scared, were they on the run, and were they done with revenge?

Chapter 21

In her early years in medical school, they found it difficult in Boston to locate places to be together, to have sex, or even to secure long periods of privacy. Her living quarters with two other medical students was never private and hotels were very careful about signing in unmarried guests. One summer, when Jeremiah sought a vacation and wanted to share the time with Connie, he suggested they take the steamship to Nantucket. A new hotel, the Nantucket, had opened on the island, and Jeremiah wanted to lodge there and explore the old whaling town and its highly regarded beaches. He suggested they wear wedding rings to avoid the awkward questions and the possibility of being refused a room.

She arched her eyes. "We've discussed this before. Are you talking marriage?"

"No, as we agreed when you entered the program, no marital discussion until you graduate and are a fully accepted physician."

Relieved, she said, "I want to be with you, but I must give all my focus and energy to my preparation for a medical practice."

"So what about my idea? It will enable us to travel whenever we wish."

"That's clever, you're practical. As long as we stay away from Boston and Worcester and distant from the people who know us, our lovemaking, our privacy remains protected. I like that."

"Any time you're uneasy with this arrangement, we can make it permanent." He arched his eyebrows; a soft smile crossed his lips.

She sighed and shook her head warily. "You've been a gentleman about our relationship, I admire and feel the respect in your commitment. But we must be practical. I must finish what I've started, and it's all time-consuming. And you, you ... you're even busier than I am. Travel, travel, travel, and work, work, work. When would you have time for me, time for children? Between us, Jeremiah, who would cook, care for a house, do the laundries, and so on. We're not set for marriage, at least not now."

He scratched his head. "I hate to admit it, but you're right. You're as busy as I am, and that won't change. I see Bill Sullivan's life, and it's full of his patient responsibilities. Yours won't be any different. I'm afraid it will never change."

"I'm not an MD yet, so I really don't know. But as a surgeon, I may have better control over my schedule than some of the other specialties."

"Well back to practical matters, we need privacy at times. We should use a couple of rings when we're in locales where no one knows us."

She laughed. "Of course, it makes sense and gives us more freedoms from these ridiculous mores in our society."

The ring arrangement, as they called it, freed them for travel. On the steamship to Nantucket, he slipped it on her ring finger, saying, with a big smile on his face, "You're hitched for a week." When there were breaks in her schedule or his, they spent time on the island. They also visited New York and took in the plays, the symphony and operas. They took the train from Boston to Washington, where she could see his work on the National Cathedral when Henry Vaughn was not in the city. They kept their travels very quiet and maintained their privacy.

In Worcester, Connie's influence had been felt. His third-floor apartment was now fully furnished. The living room had two oriental carpets that Connie selected; she seemed to know the regions in Turkey where they were made. He liked the designs, but at the time of purchase, he was not aware of the quality and uniqueness of the rugs. It was not until he went to sell them that he realized she had selected museum quality rugs for his apartment, and he received a small fortune at the sale. She coupled the rugs with several new chairs, a love seat, and a long couch. Her style was more toward the masculine than to the flowery, feminine style of the time, and he had little hesitation in following her choices. In this manner, she transformed his empty Spartan residence into an attractive place to live. She joined him there when it was possible to do so and retain their privacy. Yet that was infrequent as her medical work was year round as was his work. In the summers, when classroom work stopped and hospital assignments filled the students' calendars, she had more time for him. His time or rather, his available time, always diminished in the summer. It was prime time to work in the Northeast as the weather enabled outside work to be done. And Jeremiah had developed a peculiar habit—he like to visit Italy in the summer and work in Pietro's studio in Siena. He often brought some of his contracted design work with him and also had enough free time to work on Pietro's projects as well. It was a locale of peace, of great artistic endeavor, a place for substantial learning, and a welcome respite from the boisterous culture of the United States. And Connie missed him. She joined him for a short visit to Siena one summer, but her schedule precluded more visits and no long visits.

Jeremiah learned that he could love a woman, and he relished the love he received in return. When he thought back to his youth in Stradbally, his lively family had warmth and appreciated each other's company. Yet it would fall apart when troubles arose, especially when he differed from his family on the politics of home rule or other legislative restrictions imposed on the Irish by the British. Or when his father didn't like the way Tommy managed the farm or when Agnes's husband refused to get maids to help her. The old man tended to dispense order rather than love. His words flowed out in a series of decisions to contain his family and to control their freedoms. Jeremiah believed that the old man promoted the idea to banish him from Ireland to teach him a lesson and that Judge Hardy and Uncle John had enabled his preference. He left Ireland, feeling no sense of love either lost or gained. It seemed like it was never there. Life was too hard in the old country to take the time to experience love, to revel in it, to have the luxury, and time to enjoy another person. Without fully realizing it, his experiences in Ireland had nudged him toward a life of solitude. He preferred that lifestyle as it was free of interpersonal complications and left him substantial time for his art. Yet

Connie had stirred a sense of family in him. It was slowly becoming a curiosity, something he wanted to know more about.

He felt more warmth in Italy with Pietro's family than with his own and wondered how the Italians captured the spirit of a close family and sustained it. He studied the daily habits of Pietro's family as if they were one of his design assignments. He walked with them to the Palio in the evenings, watched as the children scampered in one direction and another with Pietro chasing them. He liked the way the Italians stopped and talked to their neighbors as they walked around the ancient plaza, greeting each other with small kisses, touches of the arms and hands, and gentle talk in the hot evenings. In time, he thought, when it's right, he'd like that kind of life for himself.

During Connie's short stay in Siena, they visited with Countess Maria, and privately she told Jeremiah that she admired Connie. He guessed that Maria appreciated her drive and focus, yet her comment contained no enthusiasm. And Maria insisted, as she always did, that he stay in active contact with her.

He liked that he and Connie rarely argued, rarely disagreed. They saw the politics in the state, in Worcester, and in the country in a similar vein. In particular, they supported the needs of the new working classes moving into the country, the needs for minimum wages and protection in the workplace. When Jeremiah addressed these political activities, he admitted that he missed the Fenian actions in Ireland. Going back to the Fenians would rise up in his mind at strange times and linger for a while. Often these thoughts would drift away by the demanding requirements of his work and its growing rewards.

As each year passed, he saw their commitments to career and independence grow. He recognized that he continued to love Connie, but more than that, he liked her. Yet they saw each other infrequently. He thought, when the time came, when the situation in both their lives were right, they might be a good married couple.

As her fourth year of medical school came to a close, he cleared time from his schedule to be with her and her family during the graduation weekend. He'd met her family on many previous visits to New York. Her parents lived in Rye, New York, and her father commuted into the city each day on a train. His work at the Merchants Bank on Fifth Avenue had been a lifelong association as it had been for his father. He and his wife had no sons to follow in his footsteps, and he was pleased with the academic accomplishments of his four daughters, all college graduates and three with advanced degrees. He was proudest of Connie; she had endured the most difficult academic challenge and was about to become one of the first female physicians in America.

The weekend was filled with events and parties at the university. Jeremiah had learned of Connie's internship at the Presbyterian Hospital in New York in an April conversation. Now, in June, her decision to intern there versus a Boston hospital still bothered him. He drew her aside, to a corner of the faculty club, the conversational noise of faculty, family and graduates was all around them. He said to her, "Again, my love why New York and not here. We'll be so far apart."

She took his hand and gazed straight into his eyes. "It's been a long journey, and I've reached a number of conclusions which we can discuss over the whole weekend—no rush."

He was tired. It had been a difficult week, travel across three cities, and long days and nights of work. He had a ten-feet-tall statue of Jesus that was not shaping to his liking and the challenges there plagued him. "Well, frankly, I'm in a rush. I've never understood this decision and would like to."

Her eyes sharpened; her tone bristled. "It was one of the few places where I could get first-rate surgical experience. Do you think Mass General, that Harvard bastion, would give me a chance? No way."

"What about City Hospital or one of the hospitals in Worcester with Bill Sullivan?"

"Not strong enough, good enough. I'll work with the best in New York. I'm like you, Jeremiah. I want to be the best."

"To be the best, you have to sacrifice a lot. Do you really want that?"

"I've watched you now for almost four years. You are one of the best at what you do and look at your schedule. I've learned from you, and I'm ready to do what it takes."

"We've talked about this for years. I …"

"I realize that, but what I accept now is that every woman on this faculty, all the significant women physicians in Boston are unmarried or, if married, have no children. They're paying the price."

"It's a huge price. Are you willing to pay it?"

"Look, Jeremiah, we've talked a lot about marriage. I love you, but I don't want to keep house, do laundry, go shopping. I want to save lives."

"You can do both. What about Dr. Langworthy?"

"Okay, she's married and has children. I can't see how she does it."

"So, you're saying that while you love me, you don't see marriage in your future."

"I'm so sorry, but I don't." Her eyes drifted off into a space he'd not seen before. "I don't think I can give myself to this profession as I want to and give myself to marriage as well. I need to be fully engaged in one thing."

She stopped and stared at him. "I'm so muddled about this now. Sorry, so let's keep talking about this weekend." She took his hand and held it by her side. "But frankly, I don't see how you'll ever be married either, with your commitment to your work. Recently, I've come to the conclusions that you're more interested in your art than in anything else."

He stepped back, moved away from her, and dropped her hand. "You think I'm selfish? I haven't given enough time to you?"

"No, that would be selfish of me. You've taught me that excellence comes from a singular focus. You've always given that focus to your art first, and I'd say, that's your only priority."

He let out a sharp breath and muttered something unintelligible. Then said, "I want to swear, jump up and down, and curse."

She laughed; it was nervous expression and not one of her lusty guffaws. "I'm flattered to hear that, but I suggest you don't do that here. They might put you in a little white jacket."

He managed a chuckle, and they stood, facing each other. Finally, breaking the silence, she asked, "What's in that bag you've been carrying all day?"

"It's your graduation gift."

"How thoughtful. May I open it?"

"Of course, anytime. I wanted it opened at your convenience."

"Is now okay?"

"Sure, shall I collect your parents?"

"No, let's open it together. Just us."

She unwrapped the odd-shaped gift and, from the wrapping, pulled out a new, shiny stethoscope. She plugged it into her ears then pressed it to her chest, her head dropped down, her lips quivering. "Let me hear your gorgeous heart." She placed it on his chest and listened, a smile creasing her face. "Now, I feel like a real doctor. Oh, how can I thank you? How can I do that?"

With resignation and a touch of finality, he said, "You can do that by being the best doctor you can be."

She pushed the moisture from her eyes. "We'll stay in touch, won't we?"

He hugged her and said softly in her ear, "Of course."

She was never to buy another stethoscope. She wore it constantly for nearly forty years. Through her long career as a surgeon and as a professor of surgery at Boston University Medical School, it was her identification and her remembrance of him. She thought of him over the years. Whenever she fingered the instrument, she thought of what she'd given up to follow this profession. She had decided then never to marry, to give her life to medicine, and she remained steadfast in that decision. The stethoscope was a bittersweet memory of the most difficult and most important decision of her life.

Chapter 22

After four years of deep companionship, the breakup didn't strike Jeremiah immediately. A few days later, he was on the train returning to Worcester when it hit him. No longer would he see her, exchange worries, opportunities, and perspectives on the events of the day. He felt like a sodden blanket was thrown over his head. Sadness crept over him, and he placed his head in his hands. He pushed his fingers into his eyes to hold back the tears. There was no one sitting near him, and he let his sorrow out. She was gone. No longer would a phone call or visit connect them. There was no second chance. She was clear. She had rejected him for a career. He felt empty, devoid of energy, and when the train pulled into Worcester Central, he had no strength to leave the train. The conductor prodded him gently, "We've arrived, sir. Time to depart."

As he stumbled toward his apartment, his mind reached back through the past year. He admitted, as he walked with suitcase in hand, that he felt a distance growing between them during her last year in medical school. Something was off in their communication. Arguments between them, unusual in the past, had become more frequent. The conversations at graduation clarified her attitude about him, a medical career and marriage.

As the days went by, then weeks, he thought of her with less emotion. It became clear to him that marriage, for her, would only be in the way of an outstanding career. Further, he acknowledged that marriage would not be fair to her, her spouse, or children. He knew her rejection was not comparable to being expelled from Ireland; the court's finding him undesirable remained the most powerful of rejections. A relationship was different. People were mercurial, always changing in needs and interests. Her perspective on career and her decision to end their relationship saddened him, yet he began to understand her position completely. He decided then and there not to fight her choice. He'd seen her determination and thought it unfair to test it. So he accepted her decision and its consequences. He acknowledged that she wanted to move on without him; he accepted her decision.

After a few weeks, he had to admit these things happen. A fresh sense of freedom surged over him, and with weekends open, he travelled to New York with frequency taking in plays, concerts, and fine dining. Henry Vaughn's wife introduced him to several young women, and he was never without female companionship when he desired it.

The parting for Connie was different. In the days and weeks after parting, she asked, what had she done? Once settled in an apartment next to the hospital, she felt lost, and he as an anchor was not there. When she called him, he was never at his apartment. When she wrote to him, it took weeks before he replied. She began to worry that she needed him in her life. She deplored these thoughts as weaknesses, but she endeavored to reach him, to secure his support as she moved forward with her dream.

His desk, where he stored his mail, was carefully organized. There was a box for business mail, which he tended diligently and daily if he was in Worcester. If he was not in Worcester, Hamish checked this box and called him if a letter was important. A second box was important private mail. It was often empty, but once a letter arrived in that category, he gave it immediate attention. A third box was for social mail. Invitations to functions, dances, gatherings at his club and letters from friends typically landed land in this box. He got to them when he could. About a month after their parting, he moved Connie's letters from the second to the third box. Their affair had similarities to his life in Ireland, he'd concluded. He knew an ending when he saw one and that marked the point to move on.

Once Connie had asked, "Deep inside was there a block of ice or steel that anchored him?"

She noted that he never seemed upset, or worse depressed, over adverse developments. She'd concluded that being exiled from his country at a young age had matured and hardened him, developed him in ways that were quite different from most other people.

He had chuckled at her observation and replied that he did what he had to do. And for him, that was to keep moving forward, to find new opportunities. And he had moved on from Connie fairly quickly. A month later, on his annual excursion to Italy, introductions to a charming woman from Boston came early in the passage. He found that he was quite open to her flirtations. And in Italy, he visited the married Maria, and she introduced him to a sensuous young cousin. She jokingly fumed, "I'm jealous of her. This should be me, but we're the victims of bad timing."

He found these associations more social in nature, more sensual than cerebral. The differences among these women and Connie were interesting to him, and the differences were welcomed. There was a lighthearted vitality to the women that was absent in Connie, which was helping him understand the wider dimensions in female personalities. He began to think more broadly of what the perfect mate might be if there was to be one. When he examined his next six months of work, he saw the need to commit every ounce of time and energy to his projects. And more importantly, he recognized as Connie had emphasized, he was more passionate and energetic about his work than any other facet of his life. The light touch of these women fit his current interests perfectly. He could enjoy their moments together and not be drawn away from his work. He believed there was nothing missing in his life; his needs were met.

Henry Vaughn watched Jeremiah's love life from a quiet distance. He was worried that marriage would change the young man's energy and commitment to his work, particularly his willingness to travel. Jeremiah was unique in his preference to work on site, and it was one of the reasons, thought Vaughn, that his work was so consistently good. In his quiet way, Vaughn relaxed when he learned that Jeremiah and the hard-driving doctor were abandoning their relationship.

He wanted to absorb as much of Jeremiah's time as he could. In their work along the northern edge of Massachusetts, they had done five churches and two chapels together. In the growing towns along the streams and rivers of this area had come industrial mills and thousands of workers as the towns exploded in population. In these town's charming inns for merchants and tradesman like themselves had been built. They often spent evenings over drinks and dinner in such establishments to discuss their work, iron out problems, and plan ahead. A favorite of both men was the Longmeadow Inn, nestled on a hillside well above the Connecticut River. The views from the common rooms over the wooded hills to the river were rural and away from the rapid industrialization occurring in the area. They had found the inn while building the cathedral in Springfield, Massachusetts, and it became a meeting point for them when new opportunities arose in that part of New England.

Sitting on a couch in the crowded cocktail lounge, its hard wooden bench and spindle back tested Henry Vaughn's sore body. All day, he'd been standing or walking with Jeremiah through the giant cathedral, agreeing on the final finishing details with the bishop. His fifty-year-old body was sore. Although they'd been in the lounge about an hour, Vaughn moved constantly, trying to find a comfortable position on the hard seat. He had pushed Jeremiah to commit more time to his most significant endeavor, the National Cathedral in Washington. He stopped his argument for a moment and gazed around the room. The cocktail lounge was full of tradesman, the clinking of glasses. The laughter of the crowd created an ambience of noise that enabled private conversations to go unheard.

The project was intriguing to Jeremiah in scale; it was the largest church he'd ever worked on, and it had the prestige of being the nation's primary ecclesiastical shrine. But the work was intense and the schedule demanding. He would have to abandon all other leads and future work in New England. He was reluctant to do that. He was in his early thirties, ready for a little less travel and preferred the work to be in Massachusetts. He was very pleased with the altar for the cathedral in Springfield, and his work was highly praised by Vaughn and the bishop. While discussing the finishing touches to the altar and the placement of statues in adjacent alcoves, Jeremiah carefully deflected Vaughn's requests for devoting more time to Washington.

Vaughn, seeing his best arguments failing, shifted his tactics. Recently, he'd won a contract to design the Stage Chapel for a new school for girls in Proctorville, Massachusetts. Because of his attachment to the National Cathedral, Vaughn was reluctant to spend much time in this remote Massachusetts town. With two strong sherries under his belt, a warm fire to take the chill off his body, he was more relaxed than Jeremiah had ever seen him. He said, "It's grand that we could meet here and discuss the completion of the cathedral. And I wanted you to see the land and the concept for this chapel in Proctorville. It's different from what we've done at the Concord Academy and at the Gridley School. But enough similar that I have an idea."

Jeremiah took a long pull on his Jameson, stretched his long legs toward the fire, and said, "I have a feeling that I'm about to be finessed."

Vaughn said, "I'd like you to study my design of the chapel tonight and join me in the morning to see the land in Proctorville. It's for a new girl's school. If you take on this project, I'll relax my pressure on you for Washington, and you can relieve me from much of the work in this rural town."

"Is it connected by train to Worcester?"

"Not directly, but there's a train station nearby in a town called Greenfield. You'll be able to get to and fro Worcester easily."

"This sounds appealing if the schedule and my fees are about the same as in our prior chapels?"

"Yes, but let's settle on the fees once you've studied the design further. I need your opinion on the ornamentation for the stained-glass windows, the arches, and the bell tower."

Jeremiah leaned forward to speak more privately to Vaughn. "Henry, there's a man sitting across from us who's attempting to follow our conversation. Do you know him?"

Vaughn lifted his eyes and scanned the room, spotting the man. "No, never seen him."

Jeremiah stared briefly at the man then turned his attention once again to Vaughn. "Well, I'm free for a change, so I'll join you tomorrow. But I must be back to Worcester by early evening. I have someone coming in for another set of work. It never rains, just pours."

"You should be counting your blessings, young man. Not all in your trade do as well."

"I acknowledge that."

The man across from them rose. Jeremiah and Vaughn watched him as he moved toward them. He was thick in the chest and shoulders. His neck was short, giving him the appearance that his large head rested solely on his shoulders. He walked with short choppy steps, which rocked his body from right to left. He extended his hand. "Gentlemen, forgive me, I interrupt, but overheard—impolitely I acknowledge—some of your conversation. Am I correct, you, sir"—he pointed to Jeremiah—"that you are Jeremiah Knox, the designer and sculptor of altars? You're doing the altar for the bishop of Springfield, in the new cathedral ... yes?"

Jeremiah and Vaughn stood up; Jeremiah extended his hand. "Yes, the altar is mine, but the beauty in the cathedral is due to this man." He nodded toward Vaughn. "Meet Henry Vaughn, the architect and genius behind that cathedral and many others throughout the east."

The short stocky man shook Vaughn's hand vigorously then glanced back to Jeremiah. He said, "I've wanted to ..."

"I'm surprised you know my work," Jeremiah interrupted.

"Please excuse me, sir, but I'm John Driscoll, a builder, and my friends call me Jackie." His legs and arms had stopped moving, but he seemed possessed with nervous energy. His body fidgeted as if he wished to rush away. "I'll come quickly to the point. I'm building my second church in Northshire just up the road from here." He pointed north with a thick forefinger and brought it back to his side. "And last week, I was in Springfield with the bishop of Springfield and the monsignor of my parish. They showed me the altar in the cathedral. The monsignor and I want that type of altar for our church."

Jeremiah nodded. "I see."

Driscoll said, "This is not the place for me to ask or talk. I have no appointment with you, but can we meet some time?"

"Of course, my schedule's atrocious, but ..."

"The bishop says you live in Worcester. I can take a train there. You let me know, and I'll meet you."

They exchanged addresses and telephone numbers although Jeremiah indicated that mail was the best method to reach him as he was rarely near his phone. He thought about the town and liked the idea that it was near Vaughn's project in Proctorville. Perhaps it could work if he liked the Stage Chapel, he could combine the two projects. It would be easier travel on him than his normal long distances between his work sites. Yet this was a different type of connection. Normally architects like Henry Vaughn or a major financier like Harold Cawley or Casper Soames contacted him for work. This was a contractor or builder; he didn't know what to think.

The trip to Proctorville with Vaughn was productive. Jeremiah could see the chapel would be similar to those at the Gridley School and Concord Academy. Both were widely popular and appreciated; the design the Proctorville trustees had selected was similar to those buildings. But Proctorville was remote in Northwest Massachusetts; it was not close to other work Jeremiah was considering.

He was reading the Sunday newspaper in his apartment when the phone rang. He gave it a disgusted look, a disturbance to a nice, quiet day. After three rings, he picked it up. "Knox here."

"Ah, delighted to catch you, Mr. Knox. Sorry to disturb your Sunday, but I figured this was a good day to find you. It's Jackie Driscoll calling."

He talked fast and nonstop, a style Jeremiah never liked. Jeremiah had to stop him and ask to repeat a phrase or idea that had not been rendered clearly. At the conclusion of his speech, there was a pause. "What do you think?"

"Mr. Driscoll, I believe your idea of seeing your church before suggesting one of my altar designs is a good one. The size of your church surprises me. It's for a thousand people, a large altar under a hundred-foot ceiling. That's huge. But when is the question? My work does not take me near Northshire."

"How about a weekend, say next Saturday or Sunday? You can train in by noon and leave on the five o'clock. You'd be in Worcester by six or seven."

"You know the train connections better than I. Let me look at my schedule, and I'll call you back later today."

He had thought of rejecting Vaughn's offer at the chapel in Proctorville. It was too inconvenient and the fee too small. Driscoll's project was large, but he might have to push hard for his standard fee. He was thinking about Driscoll's conversation when the phone rang again.

"Henry," Jeremiah said, "good to hear from you. I was just thinking about that Proctorville project."

"Jeremiah, the pressure is on in Washington. I'm in a bind on the Proctorville chapel. I need your help there."

"Well ..."

"What I'm willing to do is increase your fee by 50 percent to encourage you to relieve me there. Will you consider it?"

"I understand. Yes, I'll consider it. If I can secure one more project in that area, I'll do your chapel. I'll settle that down in the next few days so I can give you a hard answer by next weekend. Is that soon enough?"

They agreed on a time to talk. Jeremiah picked up the phone and called Jackie Driscoll. Driscoll was delighted in Knox's rapid response. He had seen Knox's work not only in Springfield but in churches and in Catholic seminaries in many New England cities. For some time, he wanted a Knox altar in one of his constructions. He had sent letters of inquiry to Knox on previous occasions, and always the response was that he was fully scheduled. The visit to the cathedral in Springfield had increased Driscoll's resolve, and meeting Knox by accident at the Longmeadow Inn had confirmed his desire to engage the man. And the monsignor had loosened the purse strings. They could afford Knox, the church, and altar size should be sufficient to attract his interest. Driscoll bristled with enthusiasm when he heard Jeremiah's voice on the phone.

He said, "Mr. Knox, does this mean you'll come for a visit?"

They settled on a time the following Saturday, and Jeremiah started to think about combining the two projects. Could that be done? He concluded that he'd have to see the Northshire church first. He was curious about the church; Driscoll indicated that it was largely completed on the exterior. Why had they waited so long to arrange for the interior finishing, especially the altar? Had other sculptors turned down the work? Well, he'd find out. But he felt certain that he wanted to do Henry Vaughn's chapel at the girl's school in Proctorville, so if this work in Northshire came to fruition, it could be a good package for many months. The package would enable him to tell Vaughn he was not available as a full-time sculptor for the National Cathedral. As he prepared for his Saturday trek to Northshire, he placed his well-worn book of sketches of altars and statues in his valise. He'd show Driscoll and the monsignor a range of altar designs, give them plenty to think about.

Driscoll met him at the train station. The Northshire station was a yellow-brick structure, a rambling wide building with a long wooden platform. At the center of the platform stood Driscoll waving his arms toward Jeremiah. The wind from the train jostled his hat, and he held it in tight grip with one hand as he waved with the other. He led Jeremiah to a carriage. As they climbed in, Jeremiah noticed it had been well used. Spittles of mud were on its sides, and the upholstery was worn. They trotted up a broad and long main street with old red-brick shops constructed on either side. A green strip separated the east and west lanes. Main Street had a slight upward slope that rose into a gentle hill at the end. On the crest of the hill was the church, St. Steven's. It was massive red-brick structure, a surprise to Jeremiah, who knew about the seating capacity of the church but did not expect such a large building.

It stood at the top of the rise dominating the street, a gloomy Gothic structure that looked more like a fortress than a church. Its narrow stained-glass windows gave the appearance of gun slits rather than ecclesiastical portraits. The building soared upward, several stories high by Jeremiah's quick estimate, and the twin spires at the entrance to the church were hundreds of feet in the air. The exterior was too big for the town, thought Jeremiah, and not pleasing to the eye. Driscoll, now joined by the monsignor, opened the wide double doors, and they entered a dark, stark interior. The narrow stained-glass windows allowed a modest amount of blue-tinted light into the body of the church. The cavernous altar space at the end of the central aisle was empty. Driscoll and the monsignor walked Jeremiah to the site of the altar, and they walked around the open space. Jeremiah removed a tape from his valise and began to measure length and depth of the space as he examined the setting of the altar in relation to the other space in the immense room. He walked back and forth from the altar to the main aisle and back to the altar. He remained quiet, making measurements and drinking in the interior dimensions of the church.

Driscoll watched him pace, examine, measure, and pace again. He was getting nervous yet was unsure how to begin a conversation. He walked with Jeremiah trying to gain his attention.

Finally, Jeremiah stopped and faced Driscoll. He said, "The church is large as you said, but ..."

He was about to say, "I'm sorry, this altar setting isn't my style. I'm not the right person for this design." Basically, he found the church unbearably dreary, and he could not imagine that any of his altars would bring the light and vibrance he sought to create in a church.

Yet he had stopped midsentence. A bustling of noise interrupted him. He, Driscoll, and the monsignor glanced to the entryway and saw three women walking into the church and striding confidently down the central aisle.

They were talking energetically, and one of them was pointing to the ceiling then the walls. She was the older one and walked with a purposeful gait. She was tall and slender, and beside her was a woman about the same age who was doing all the talking, her head following the arm of the other woman. The third woman was the tallest of the three yet much younger. Unlike the other two, she was quiet, almost serene. Her eyes took in their conversation, and in contrast to their purposeful walk, she seemed to glide down the aisle.

As they approached the altar, Jeremiah saw the younger woman more closely. He tried not to stare or let his gaze linger too long. That was difficult. He'd never seen someone so beautiful.

One of the older women spoke, "Jackie, we're on our way to the station. I thought we'd drop by and see what the sculptor has in mind for the altar."

As the introductions were made, the women who spoke first was Driscoll's wife, Stephanie. The other older woman was her sister, Clarisa, and the youngest was her daughter, Amelia. Driscoll appeared annoyed at the intrusion, but the monsignor was all manners and courtesy. He welcomed them and referred to the altar in Springfield they wished to replicate. While he talked, Jeremiah continued to steal glances at the young woman who he learned was called Milly. She caught one of his glances and returned it with a lovely smile displaying a wide mouth with very beautiful white teeth. Her smile was dazzling, and he looked quickly away.

Driscoll gathered his manners; he said, "Well, ladies, the monsignor and I would like Mr. Knox to build an altar here exactly like the one at the new cathedral in Springfield." He seemed at a loss with the three women and added, "Milly, when is your train to Springfield?"

She knew her father wanted to get rid of her, her aunt, and mother. He never liked them bringing their artistic ideas to his projects. She said, "It's in about an hour, plenty of time." She turned her attention from her father to Jeremiah. "Mr. Knox, I've seen your altar in Springfield. It's quite elaborate, ornate, and beautiful."

He wasn't sure if she was admiring or criticizing his work. He replied, "Miss Knox, thank you for the comment on beauty. On ornate or elaborate, the altar simply adheres to the overall design of the church."

"Milly"—Driscoll put his hand lightly on her arm—"when did you see it?"

"Oh, we took a group of our students to see it. The bishop invited us. Mr. Knox was not there that day."

"Well ..." Surprised at his daughter's knowledge, Driscoll added, "As Mr. Knox can see, the church is done. All those architect meetings are over. We just need the altar."

Jeramiah turned to Driscoll. His smile was warm. "That's a problem for me, Mr. Driscoll. I haven't worked that way. My work has always been closely tied to the overall design of the church. The inside and outside must work together."

Milly tapped her father's hand. "Daddy, I'm not exactly sure what Mr. Knox is saying, but I believe that the altar for the bishop's cathedral is too grand, too elaborate, and not suited for a smaller local parish church like St. Steven's. I think he's saying the same thing."

Her aunt was listening with great attention. She added, "Jackie, when Milly and I were in London and Paris a few years back, we saw gorgeous churches, elaborate altars. But that was for cities. We're a small town."

Driscoll's mouth turned down; he glowered at the two women then turned to Jeremiah. "Do you agree with them, Mr. Knox, this church is not worthy of one of your altars?"

"There's no such thing as worthy or unworthy in designing the interiors of churches. It's a matter of artistic fit. One does not put a single marble table in the bishop's nave in Springfield, nor does one put the bishop's altar in a church with a twenty-foot ceiling and fifteen pews."

Driscoll was getting exasperated. "Monsignor, you've been quiet. You want the Springfield altar, right? What are you thinking?"

But the three women were ready to talk. They had no interest in hearing from the monsignor. Leading the fray, Driscoll's wife stepped in. "Mr. Knox is right, Jackie."

"Steffy, he hasn't said the bishop's altar's wrong."

"What I want to say is that those cathedrals in Europe like the one in Chartres or Reims or the one Clary mentioned in London, St. Paul's. They have windows, lots of them. You need windows to have big altars and statues. Don't you, Mr. Knox?"

Jackie Driscoll had never been to Europe, never seen the cathedrals the ladies referenced. They knew more than he did of the range of architectural designs, and his wife had always been critical of his "dour brick buildings" as she called them. He was a contractor and a good one. None of his buildings collapsed or had slanting floors, and he always came in on budget. He wished he'd never sent Milly on her excursions to Europe, and then she took her aunt and his wife on subsequent trips. He'd created his own nightmare. He wasn't sure what to do next, so he called on the monsignor again. "Charley, you have the bishop's okay for the church, altar, and statuary. Do we go ahead as originally planned?"

"The ladies have some good points, Jackie. I would like to hear Mr. Knox's thoughts."

All five people focused on Jeremiah and waited; he met the eyes of each person before he spoke. "Mr. Driscoll, monsignor, the women have a very valid point. For this church to have a large altar, like the one in Springfield, the nave needs much more light. They're right—there's a need for more windows."

Milly gave him her dazzling smile then glanced over at her father. She said, "See …"

"Now hold on," Driscoll said. "There's no way the roof can be safe if we place more or bigger windows on the walls. The walls won't hold the roof."

Milly wouldn't give him an inch. "Let's see, Daddy, Chartres was built in the late thirteenth century, same for Reims and Notre-Dame de Paris. St. Paul's in London, if memory serves me, was built in the fourteenth century. Hundreds of years ago, all of them with higher roofline than St. Steven's and windows all the way to the top. If they could figure out how to support a roof, then …" She let the phrase dangle.

Jeremiah shook his head, his admiration evident. He watched her face as he spoke, "Mr. Driscoll, monsignor, as the church now stands, it is fine. It will be a wonderful place for worship. But my style and rather expensive approach is not what this church needs. You could be very nicely served with a simpler altar, quite lovely and at vastly less expense than what was done in Springfield."

"Christ, lad. Sorry, Monsignor." Driscoll glanced at the monsignor chagrined that he used construction language. "I've never had anyone turn down work before. Is there any way we can change your mind and get the Springfield-type altar?"

The monsignor placed his hand up to slow Driscoll down. "Jackie, Mr. Knox, I'd love to see a brilliant altar here. One that would inspire people to worship. One that would make them feel closer to god. You've done that in Springfield. Would a smaller-scale altar have the same effect? Would you do a small-scale altar?"

"I've done them before and may do them again." He paused to organize his comment so it wouldn't seem insulting. "My experience has been to combine what I do on the exterior of the church in bell towers, window structures, and other external ornamentation with the design of the altar. They all fit artistically, so if I do the exterior work, then I like to do the interior work too, regardless of size. Your exterior is completed and is not similar to my style. You'll find others better suited to match what's been done."

The monsignor persisted, "Could we do a complex, highly artistic altar here, a Springfield-type altar even if it's not exactly similar to the exterior design?"

"You have the space. That's important, and there's ample room for a large altar. And you can change artistic styles." He paused for effect. "That would not be my preference. However, if you want an altar like the one in Springfield, there is another important factor, and that is the light. I'd need to bring in Henry Vaughn and the structural engineer we worked with in Springfield to see what can be done to retrofit the upper walls. You'll need to add more windows and maybe even expand the lower windows."

Chapter 23

Driscoll stood in the nave, unsure how to proceed. He wanted a Knox altar, and the young man was passing up the work. He thought, more windows, how, where, what would they look like? He'd never constructed a church with two levels of windows or windows taller than five feet.

Milly, watching her father fret and at a loss for words, saved him as she and her mother often did. "Mr. Knox, can this Mr. Vaughn and the structural engineer visit St. Steven's? I think we need them to propose ideas on how to increase light in the church."

"Oh, Milly, Mr. Vaughn is from New York, a big shot and very busy. He wouldn't have time or interest," Driscoll said.

Jeremiah interrupted, "If I may, I'd like to ask a question."

All five heads turned to him. "Of course," Driscoll replied.

"Mr. Driscoll, what's the thickness, density of the walls, at the base and on to the roofline?"

"There about two feet thick. Need to be thick to withstand the snow and storms here."

"That's the thickness of the walls at the Duomo in Siena, and the Duomo is much taller than your structure. I believe you can add more windows if you wish."

Before he could finish the sentence, Milly had chimed in. "Daddy, that's the depth of the walls at Chartres, Reims, and other churches built centuries earlier. They have tons of windows."

The monsignor had begun to smile. "I think I can get the structural engineer the bishop used ... He'll come." He shifted a sly smile toward Jeremiah. "Mr. Knox, can you convince Mr. Vaughn to see the church?"

"It's possible. We're considering work on a chapel in Proctorville. When we're there, he should be okay with a short visit here." He turned to direct his next thought to the monsignor. "Having worked with him, he may have ideas that will alter the exterior of the church. Are you willing to entertain that?"

"We'll know when we hear his ideas." The monsignor clasped his hands and rubbed them together. "When can we coordinate the next visit?"

Driscoll appeared perplexed. "We're not done yet. I want a commitment from Mr. Knox to do the altar and a start date for the work."

Jeremiah replied, "I understand your need to get started, but let's proceed as the monsignor suggests. Let me secure a date for Henry Vaughn, and I'll get that to you and the monsignor. Then we can match the timing of the two experts."

"Oh, how grand. Can we meet Mr. Vaughn too?" asked Clarisa. Stephanie and Milly nodded in agreement. "It would be so nice to have a church as grand as the cathedral in Springfield." Clarisa had grasped her sister's hand; her broad smile radiated enthusiasm.

Jeremiah glanced around at the group. "I think we have a plan." He reached down to pick up his satchel. "I'll try and catch the next train."

"Mr. Knox, you can't go. We don't have a deal, a contract."

"We're not there yet Mr. Driscoll. The next step is to see what's possible. Are additional windows feasible? What will they cost, and does the monsignor's parish want to do what Henry and I recommend?"

Driscoll shook his head, clearly unhappy. Nothing was rock solid for him. There was no closure as more planning and thinking was needed. His construction work was under review and on hold.

The monsignor could see his distress and clapped him on the back. "Jackie, this plan makes sense to me. I'm willing to wait and see what the experts say. If we can have more light and with that a more beautiful altar, then I'm willing to wait."

Jeremiah pulled a timetable from his jacket. "I see there's a train to Springfield in an hour. I'd like to catch that if I may. I'll get back to you with the dates for me and Henry Vaughn."

Stephanie said, "Milly, that's the train you're taking. Am I correct?"

"Ah yes, Mr. Knox, you'll see more of the Driscolls than you bargained for. That is indeed my train," said Milly.

"I welcome the company." Jeremiah was delighted with the news. He'd see more of her, get to know her better. He'd be able to know if she had a suitor or was planning marriage. He was surprised at himself; it was only a first meeting, yet he was very attracted to her, a most unusual sensation for him. It usually took several evenings with a woman before his interest was aroused.

They travelled to the station in Driscoll's carriage. Stephanie and Clarisa asked numerous questions of Jeremiah about his other projects and how he came to be a sculptor. Milly was quiet during the ride to the station, and he wondered if she had any interest in him or his history.

When they arrived at the station, the women kissed Milly good-bye and asked her to say hello to Carl for them. As they boarded the train, Jeremiah placed Milly's small overnight bag next to his on the rack above their seats, and they sat together. She turned to him, gave him her wide, stunning smile and said, "Now I have you all to myself. I can get the real truth, can't I?"

He was amused. "What truth would that be?"

"Oh, I think you know. Really, be honest, you don't want to do St. Steven's, do you?" She waved a lovely hand at him. "I don't think you do. You're just being polite. I've seen articles and photos in the Boston Sunday papers about your churches and altars in Worcester and the private school outside of Boston. The cathedral in Springfield, that's more your style, isn't it?"

"Hmmph," he mumbled. "My favorite altar and statuary was my first. It was a small parish church on the outskirts of Worcester, St. Suzanne's. I've done more elaborate, more difficult work, but that's not what it's about for me."

"What is it about then?"

"It's about the people, the community, and what they want in art to connect them to a higher being, a loftier level of thought from their day-to-day lives. I design to inspire, to please, and to bring them to a different place." He stopped for a moment, taking in her lovely face and thought his next statement might be presumptuous but decided to make it. "And I take on projects where my work fits in and supports the overall artistic concept of the building."

She seemed pleased, he thought, because she gave him that gorgeous smile then became quiet. Her silence continued for a minute or two, so he opened his valise and began to review some of his sketches. He was thinking about St. Steven's and what altar design might fit the sanctuary if higher windows were possible. *Am I arrogant?* he wondered. *Is St. Steven's an ugly duckling that won't grow to a beautiful swan? Is it not suited for one of my altars?* As he thumbed through his sketches, his new focus seemed to attract her attention. He could feel her head next to his shoulder. He glanced down at her.

"Sorry," she said, "I bumped into you. May I see?" She pointed to his drawings. "What are those sketches? They're marvelous."

"Sure, they're my sketches of different altars I've done or altars I like and might do in the future. They're my reference points, and I show them to the architects when we're discussing a project. It's a way for them to see what I can do and if that fits into their concept for the interior space."

"You drew these?" She gazed at him intently.

"Yes, of course." He returned her gaze, a bit confused. Did she think he ripped them out of some book?

"They're remarkable. You're an artist too. You could make a living being an artist. How did you get to sculpture and stonecutting?"

He faced her directly then laughed; it was a long laugh. "Oh, that, well that's a very long story."

"I'd like to hear it."

"Oh, good grief no, it would bore you to death, and the train ride's not that long."

"The article about you in the Sunday paper years ago said you were from Ireland. Did you study sculpting there?"

"How about you? What do you do in Springfield?"

She was surprised at the rapid pivot in the conversation. Why wouldn't he talk about himself? For reasons illusive and unusual to her, she wanted to tell him about her life. "Okay, I'll tell you, but I'm aware Mr. Knox that you're mysterious. You're dodging my questions." She wagged a long elegant finger at him, the nail perfectly shaped. "And I believe you want to stay that way. I think you've got something to hide, have you?"

He laughed again. "Please, what do you do in Springfield?"

She told him of her education at Smith College and her teaching at St. Agatha's School, a private school for girls. She taught senior English and French and was a dorm mistress. She went on to describe her ambitions to be head mistress of a school, and she was studying for a master's degree at Harvard in the summers.

"Now how are you going to do all that when you're married and have children?" he asked.

Her mouth became firm, and her voice dropped into serious tones. "Who said anything about marriage, children? My ambition is in teaching and running a school."

"Well, your mother and aunt mentioned a man's name. I just thought …"

"Oh you did, did you? Old Carl, they all want me to marry old Carl. He's been around forever, steady, capable, and so … I'm being unkind but so boring."

"So you don't plan to marry him or anyone?"

"Oh, I expect I could marry someday, but I haven't met him yet. I wonder if he even exists." She stared straight into his eyes. "I see no wedding ring on your hand, what's holding you back?"

He stretched his long legs, trying to find more room in the confined space. "Good God, this carriage is cramped. My story is that I work too hard, too long, and have had no time for courting or that sort of thing."

"All work and no play makes Jack a dull boy," she teased.

"That's probably true. But on the other hand, I love my work. I can't wait to get at the stone and see what comes out."

"Do you really want to do my father's church?"

"Persistent, aren't you? You really do want the truth, don't you?"

"Yes, and although I don't know you, I believe you'll tell me the truth. That's why I asked in the first place."

"No … I'm sorry." He glanced at her, hoping for understanding, perhaps sympathy. "The place doesn't inspire me. Normally, I work with architects as they design the church, and I can say yes or no early on. You father's place is finished." He saw that her dark-blue eyes were riveted on his face; she was fully attentive. "I dunno. Maybe if Henry Vaughn can design some attractive windows near the roofline and maybe redesign the lower windows too, it could provide an atmosphere where the altars I like to do would be artistically pleasing."

"Thank you for your honesty." She shuddered.

He asked, "Are you okay?"

"Yes, sorry, but you reminded me of our home." She gave him a humorous expression indicating a bad taste. "You should see it one day. It's like the church, dour red brick. It's more like a mausoleum than a home." She paused to laugh. "St. Steven's, the downtown office buildings, our home, it doesn't matter. All his buildings are the same. He's never worked with an architect. There are none in Northshire, so mother and I were delighted when we heard you were coming. We wanted to hear what you had to say."

"Well, he's a hell of a builder. That church would withstand a major artillery attack."

She laughed. "Mr. Knox has a sense of humor, nice. Could we look at the sketches in your book to see which altar might work if more windows were added."

"Could you call me Jeremiah, and may I call you Milly?"

"Yes, as long as you promise to return with Mr. Vaughn—not forget about Northshire and this church."

"Of course not, I gave my word to take a second look. Henry and I will be back, but that doesn't mean the parish can afford the changes or want to do them."

They poured through the book and compared the altar in Springfield to several that Jeremiah thought would fit better in St. Steven's. She noted that her preference was different than his, and this discussion occupied them until they arrived in Springfield. He helped her down from the train, and as she stepped onto the platform, she asked him, "Do you think I could see, could visit some of the churches you've done?" As she waited for his reply, a man rushed up and hugged her.

Beet red, she said, "Jeremiah, this is my friend Carl. Carl, Jeremiah, the sculptor who did the cathedral here in Springfield."

Carl extended his hand, which Jeremiah took quickly, and said, "I'm off. Must sprint for my train to Worcester."

He tucked his valise under his arm and walked away as Milly called after him. "I'll see you and Mr. Vaughn when you propose the changes to the church."

Absently, he waved back as he walked down the platform. He searched the board for the track information and found the train to Worcester and, moving quickly, boarded it as the conductor was hollering, "All aboard!" He looked back up the platform, but she had left. Damn, he admitted, she unsettled him. He was not ready to part; he wanted the conversation to go on longer. Then came this Carl. Well, damn it. Normally, it took several meetings, several dinners or parties before interest in a woman developed for him. Was it her beauty? She was as tall as her father and had her mother's slender figure. Her jet-black hair flowed in waves to her shoulders, framing a long face with high cheekbones, an elegant nose above a wide mouth. Her lips were thin in a rich color that brought out her sensuousness. Her beauty was exceptional, but there was more. There was her ease in talking about art history, her quick grasp of artistic differences, her relaxed command of the situation in the church. She was not the buyer or decision-maker, so why did he want to keep talking to her? There was so much unsaid, incomplete. Did she mean it when she asked to see some of his altars and churches? If it were true, how would he arrange it? He had no address or contact information on her.

He moved restlessly in his seat and tried to focus on the rugby game the next day, and that didn't work. Her face flashed in front of his eyes. He pulled out his notepad and started to list the action items for Hamish on the rental properties. He stopped mid-list. His mind kept wandering back to Amelia, Milly. What a wonderful name.

Carl carried Milly's bag to his carriage, trying to gauge her mood, having a sense that something was awry and afraid to ask. He said, "So that's the sculptor. Somehow I expected an older, wizened man. He's quite young."

She didn't look at him; her eyes were focused on an unseen object straight ahead. She said, "Yes, so surprising ... young, tall, confident, and commanding. He sure surprised my father. Can you imagine someone telling my father that his building was ugly?"

"He said that?"

"Not that blunt. It was skillfully done, but he made it clear the building wasn't fit for his altars."

"Good God, Milly. He's quite arrogant."

"That would be one conclusion, but he doesn't come off that way. It's more pure confidence. It's more like he wants to do the right thing artistically."

"What happens next? I assume your father will find some other stonemason or sculptor for the altar and statues?"

"No, Mr. Knox promised to come back with a couple of people and illustrate how to alter the walls for more windows, more light, and more beauty. I think he'll come back. He seems to be a man of his word."

"You seem to like him."

"I do, he ... well, he's interesting." She wanted to admit that she found him fascinating, but she was not ready to acknowledge that he'd made a strong impression.

Carl said, "I'm curious. Why did you introduce me as your friend? We're way beyond that, aren't we? We're nearly engaged."

"Carl"—she glanced at him, her eyes pleading—"please don't rush me. I'm not ready for engagement and all that follows."

"Well, I'm ready," he said. "We're both twenty-five, and time's moving on. My law practice is going well. I love you, and we've been courting for a year and a half."

"You're a dear, Carl, and patient. But if you're ready to settle down, I don't want to hold you back."

In Jeremiah, she'd seen characteristics not evident in the law-yers, doctors, and businessmen that had been attracted to her. They all had educations, professions, and family backgrounds that she wanted, but in each case, something was missing. The sturdy, pre-dictable future they offered seemed humdrum to her, and no one provided the lively chemistry of physical attraction. She had thought that sexual attraction was overblown and rarely happened; it had not occurred in her young life, but she was looking for that type of spark. When she saw Jeremiah Knox, she was very aware of his physical presence. He reeked of a magnetism she had not previously experienced. He wasn't handsome in any conventional way, but his presence was powerful, and in his profession, he took risks in art and in business. He made that clear to her father. He'd pass up guaranteed work to do what he wanted to do. She was beginning to feel an interest toward Jeremiah yet was realistic to know that her flash of interest could quickly vanish when she got to know him. But she wondered, would she ever get to know him?

When Jeremiah arrived in Worcester, the need to complete their conversation plagued him, and he thought of himself as a man of action. He concentrated on the options to contact her and praised the development of the telephone. He waved his hands over the instrument as a form of benediction then placed the call. He called St. Agatha's; it was Saturday evening, and he planned to leave a message for her. The operator tried Milly's rooms but, as he expected, no answer. She took the message that he was sending her the sketches of the altars they both liked. Would she please continue to think about them? The school's evening operator dutifully recorded the message and gave Jeremiah the address to send the sketches. She advised Jeremiah that if he wanted to talk directly to Amelia, he would have to make a telephone appointment. He thanked her for the information but deferred on that option; his travel during the week would make that difficult.

He contacted Henry Vaughn on Sunday to coordinate the next meeting in Proctorville, and Jeremiah discussed the technical and artistic challenges with the St. Steven's project. Vaughn was intrigued by the design of St. Steven's and agreed to visit Northshire with Jeremiah; the dates were set. Jeremiah assembled a small package for Milly, including the drawings and a note specifying the date and time for the meeting at the church. Although it was a Thursday, he hoped he'd see her and get her thoughts on what he and Vaughn would propose.

When she returned to her rooms at St. Agatha's, Milly saw the message from Jeremiah. Her dinner with Carl had been enjoyable, but it took her more time than she would acknowledge to banish her thoughts about Jeremiah. His long face and frame rushed to her mind as she quickly read the note. She sat at her desk and drafted a reply. It was brief, as brief as his; she expressed enthusiasm about receiving the sketches and hoped the date for visiting St. Steven's was on a weekend day.

After his conversation with Vaughn, Jeremiah composed letters to the monsignor, Driscoll, and Milly, indicating the date and time of the St. Steven's meeting. He requested confirmation from each and instructed Hamish to read incoming mail from these three people. Jeremiah would call him to secure their responses. He was departing to Washington that week to work on the columns in the National Cathedral. It was a week of long hours; he went to his hotel, exhausted each night, almost too tired to eat. Toward the end of the week, he contacted Hamish to review his mail.

Over a crackling telephone line, Hamish said, "I have the response from a Mr. Driscoll and a Monsignor Cummings. They can make the date with you and Mr. Vaughn. The third response is a little strange. It's from a woman, a Miss Driscoll, who signs it, 'Best wishes, Milly.' Who's this Milly, Jeremiah? Are you holding out on me?"

"More on that later, Hamish, but what does she say?"

"She says, and I quote, 'Regrettably, Jeremiah, it's a school day, and I have classes that day and supervise our tennis instruction that afternoon. I cannot make it. Can we find a time to talk about what you and Mr. Vaughn conclude and what altar you prefer if that is the conclusion.'"

"Oooh, that's unfortunate."

"Unfortunate, aye. I suspect romance here, am I correct? She has lovely handwriting. Who is she?"

"She's the daughter of the builder and the one in the family with some artistic taste. She wants to be part of the decision to select an altar for a church in Northshire."

"And she's got your interest?"

241

"She's made an impression, old friend, but time will tell. Our geographies may be in the way here."

"Not if you do the church in Northshire. St. Agatha's in Springfield, not far away."

Jeremiah sat on the train to Worcester on Friday evening. It had been a long week, and he looked forward to a week in Worcester. He arrived in Worcester near midnight and tiredly open his mailbox as he entered the building. His spirits rose immediately. There was a letter from Milly. He found new energy as he bounded up the three flights to his apartment. He placed his luggage in the front room and tore open her letter. Initially, he sighed in disappointment. She could not make the Thursday meeting and was not available that evening. She provided one line of delight. She decided that his altar preference for the St. Steven's was superior to hers. She agreed with him and would lobby her father and the monsignor for his choice if he and Vaughn believed the church was a possible site for a classic altar.

He read on, then read it for a second and third time. In the last few lines of a fairly short note, she asked in her elegant handwriting:

Dear Jeremiah,

You been so kind, so open-minded with my father and the monsignor on matters of art that are new to them. You've educated them, my mother, my aunt, and especially me. Yet I feel my education is incomplete. In that regard, do you think I could visit one or more of your churches in the near future? It would help me better understand how to support your cause with the monsignor and my father. And since I'll miss you next week, perhaps this will give us the opportunity to exchange our ideas.

My best wishes,
Milly

He placed the letter down and resisted the impulse to write a response. He do it in the morning when he was fresh. He had to think, and he was too tired to do it now. He slept soundly and woke late for him. He glanced at his watch; it was ten o'clock. He remembered her letter and read it for the third time. He finished his coffee, scooped up the last of his oatmeal, and placed the dishes in the sink. He'd wash them later as an idea came to him at breakfast. He'd invite her to Worcester so she could see St. Suzanne's, his first church, and St. John's and St. Paul's, two of the larger churches he had done later. The altars and the statuaries were his designs and sculptures. They would give her a view of the variety of work he'd done. And she could be back at St. Agatha's by early evening. If she wanted he could supply a chaperone. Alice Sullivan was a willing guide to Jeremiah's friends when visiting the city.

He alerted Hamish that mail from Milly might be coming during the week and to look for it. His week had been planned for McGuinness's shed, but the headmaster at the Gridley School had requested a visit to discuss a set of head carvings for their library. He called Hamish from Gridley on Thursday. "Any letters from Springfield?"

Hamish replied, "No, none yet. But, Jeremiah, does she have your telephone number? Your phone's been ringing off the hook the last few days."

"You've given me an idea. I'll call her."

He'd returned to Worcester that evening and called the school as soon as he arrived. The operator was beginning to get acquainted with calls between Springfield and Worcester, a source of delightful gossip. She was exchanging her exciting news with fellow employees of St. Agatha's. The chaste, aloof Miss Driscoll has an admirer who name was not Carl. The operator obliged Jeremiah, "Mr. Knox I'm ringing her rooms, I believe she's in."

"Oh my, how delightful," she responded. "I thought I'd never connect with you since the mail is so slow."

"Here I am and delighted to catch you. How've you been?"

"I'm in a tizzy here, papers… exams, my tennis team—it never ends, but I don't have to travel like you do. That must be inconvenient."

"I don't think of it. It's part of the work." He forced the conversation forward. "How about a visit next Sunday. Is that a possibility? Alice Sullivan, one of my friends, is most anxious to meet you and is pleased to serve as a chaperone."

"I guess you were away when I called. My answer is yes. I can catch a train to Worcester around nine and the return train around five. Is that enough time?"

"Yes, indeed. After travelling that distance, I'd love to take you to dinner, but if you need to get back, I understand."

"I'm so pleased I can see your work before my father and you meet again. I think my opinions may soften the old goat."

He laughed, and before he could say more, she said, "Wonderful, we'll meet at the Worcester train station." She gave him the time and train number and quickly signed off.

Chapter 24

She stepped off the train. Her eyes swept the platform, and a radiant smile appeared when she saw him. He was fifty feet from her car and could see her step down, but he'd see that smile a mile away. He waved, and she moved toward him, greeting him with European kisses on each cheek. He was used to this custom with his Italian acquaintances and fell into the process easily.

He pointed to a carriage a hundred feet away, "Your coach awaits."

"Yours?"

"Heavens no. With my travel, the horse would get arthritis from inactivity, and the driver would turn to drink."

She chuckled at his response. "So where are we headed in this fine carriage, Mr. Knox?"

"First things first, my lady—would you like some refreshments or a ladies' room?" Once the pleasantries were settled, they climbed into the rented coach. Comfortably seated, she was dressed in light spring clothing, pinks and whites in a long flowing dress. A wide-brimmed hat with a sharp purple sash accentuated her outfit. For a schoolteacher, he thought she dressed well. He wore his normal warm weather outfit—white twill pants, an off-white jacket, and a white shirt with an open collar. A beige Panama hat sat on his head. He saw her review his dress and seemed to approve. She expressed no opinion, nor did her eyes reveal her thoughts.

He described the flow of the day in terms of chronology. They'd start with St. Suzanne's, then progress to St. John's, then St. Paul's. He started to describe the reasons behind the chronology but didn't get far. When he mentioned that his first sculpture opportunity came from the death of a little girl, she began a flood of questions.

"You came from Ireland to work in a stone quarry? With your talents, why did you come to the US?"

He glanced at her and said, "As I mentioned on the train, that's a long story and a boring one. Aren't you interested in the art?"

"Of course I'm here for the art, but I want to know about the artist too. It's only natural, don't you agree? If I were showing you my school, you'd probably want to know why I chose teaching or teaching French. Wouldn't you?"

"Of course … Well." He shook his head. How to start? What to admit? What to hold? His reluctance came from a surprising source. Although he hardly knew her, deep down he wanted to impress her. If he withheld information now, the avenues of deceit would be uncovered if they spent more time together. "Okay, this will take a little time, and I'm open to your questions."

She studied his face and realized he was troubled. She wondered if she should rescind her questions—his life was none of her business. Or was it? What drove her to know more about him? Then she knew. Despite Carl, regardless of Carl, she was very interested in this man. As his story unfolded, her attention never wavered. She was fascinated by the decisions that shaped his life in Ireland and in the United States.

When he concluded that stone work was viewed by his family as temporary, he saw consternation on her face then added, "I'm guessing at the last part because my uncle thought, as soon as the five years were up, I'd return to law school."

"Why didn't you or don't you go back? What prompts you to stay?"

"It started with Suzanne's gravestone, then her statue, and just grew from there. One good opportunity turned into another, and success came. I found I loved it." He completed the Suzanne story and how it led to a connection with Henry Vaughn.

She held the handkerchief to her face. He could tell his story had an impact as her voice was unsteady, struggling for its normal tone. "My god, what a story. How did you do all that … rejected, tossed to hard labor? You must be made of iron." She placed the handkerchief in her pocketbook. "I've never heard of anyone overcoming such adversity. It's very moving."

"I was afraid of this, of upsetting you. I've given you too much background too fast."

"No ... no, when I first met you, I knew you were different from others. I didn't know what caused your special attributes, what trials you must have faced. Again, please excuse my active inquiries." She attempted to smile, and it was slightly brighter. "I'd like to meet Mr. McGuinness, your first boss."

"It's Saturday, so he may be hard to find. Why don't we see the three churches and go to the McGuinness works if we have time left over."

While he chatted about the church of St. Suzanne, she thought about her first impressions of him. In Northshire, he was very confident to the point of arrogance; it was obvious that he was deeply schooled in art and sculpture. His determination was evident, and his independence was even more obvious. Yet in their first meeting, she had missed his courage; she saw that now. It made her wonder if his courage was also a limitation; it was so strong that it gave him the capacity to go alone. It enabled him to live alone and be successful alone. He needed no one, perhaps trusted no one.

As they toured the churches, her eyes grew wider and wider, admiring his work. To her, the altar in St. John's was stunning, larger and more complex than St. Suzanne's, more like the altar she imagined for St. Steven's. She prayed at the altar and wondered why he did not appear to join her in prayer. Instead, he knelt in silence, staring at his work. At St. Paul's, she paused by the Pieta, and after a moment, he began to walk toward the altar. She grasped his arm and pulled him back. He had told her the Pieta was fairly recent; construction workers repairing the floor near the statue had damaged the original. She appeared transfixed by the mother and child, and he waited patiently until she was ready to move. She prayed a long time at the altar of St. Paul's; he wondered if she was ever going to finish her prayers. He thought she must be very religious and wondered how she'd view his unorthodox religious philosophy.

She took his arm as they descended the long steps from St. Paul's. She glanced up at him. "I think you were influenced by the French designers in this church. Am I close?"

"Yes, well done. I tried to blend some of the ornate work in the spires after a church in Lyon. Then there are some touches of the Florentine in there too, especially the angels. The Pieta, you know where that came from."

"So, let me see. I have your work in Springfield plus these three churches and I must admit, I'm emotionally spent. It's like a day in a grand museum. Too much art always overwhelms me."

"So what will you do with all this information?"

Her look was one of a wise old owl. It was at once coquettish, slightly sexy, and a tad mysterious as if she was withholding a secret. She said, "I have more information than you'll ever imagine. I have what I came for. I have plenty of ammunition to push my father and the monsignor toward one of your more ornate altars, like the one in St. Paul's. That is, if you and Mr. Vaughn can make the alterations you want and the church accepts and can pay for the changes."

He wondered what she meant by more information than he could imagine but was hesitant to ask. Between their visits to St. John's and St. Paul's, he'd enjoyed their lunch at Dooley's Tavern, the Saturday lunch crowd friendly with their hellos to him and most gracious to Milly. He probed more into her life and found strong ambition to be a leader of a school, to publish a text on better ways to learn French and to travel abroad on a regular basis as he did. She asked if he thought Western Massachusetts was a backwater. He was vague, saying no place on earth was a backwater as long it was important to those who lived there. Stradbally was quiet, but Dublin was not far away. Northshire was not that far from Boston. He liked the mix of urban and rural settings, and she had agreed.

For Milly, the visit was transformative. She wanted to see his work, but mostly, she wanted to know him better. In their brief encounter in Northshire and on the train to Springfield, her interest was piqued. This was unusual for her. Most men did not impress her, and she wanted to get to the source of her interest. Was it simply curiosity, his European manners, his strong presence, or was it his unusual skills or his character? Now she had, at least, partial answers to these questions. He was fiercely independent, a trait she admired yet found unsettling. She thought about similar figures in history or in literature, individuals where their work was their life, while lovers and families were of secondary importance. She felt he was in this category and possibly explained why he was nearly thirty and not married. Yet she didn't know if he was kind or thoughtful or cared about others—values that were important to her.

At lunch, she listened as he had described his one big romance. She understood the reasons for their parting. Neither would bend from devotion to their career. Yet the basis for their parting bothered her. Was he all thought, all principles with a limited heart? Or given his disappointments with this woman, with the people in Ireland, with his own family—did he trust people? As the day went on, his qualities and his physical appeal continued to grow increasing her interest despite her concerns. He was so different than Carl. She wanted to see more of him and was perplexed on how to do that unless he decided to do St. Steven's.

She asked him, "Jeremiah, after you see my father, and the monsignor next week will you call or write about the decision? It means so much to me."

"Indeed, I will," he replied. "I hope you'll talk to your father about the altar and the need for light." He stopped for emphasis. "Light is essential for the altar to have a big impact on the religious experience."

"We do agree. Don't we on the preferred design?"

"I think so." His smile was tentative; he was holding something back. "I always discuss my design with Henry, Mr. Vaughn, as his ideas always improve mine."

"I'm apologizing here, but I've seen more imagination today then I anticipated. Your ideas are way beyond anything I can contribute. I trust you and Mr. Vaughn totally."

He acknowledged her compliment yet remained quiet as they walked along the grounds of St. Paul's. She was long in the legs and had no trouble in staying with his fast strides. They moved briskly through the lush gardens at the rear of the cathedral. He spotted a bench beneath an oak tree and suggested a brief respite from the hot sun.

She sat quietly for several moments, and he let the silence continue. Finally, she turned to face him. She said, "You've given me so much to think about. I'm a bit overwhelmed." She laughed. "Does that surprise you?"

"You've seen a lot today and have been a most impressive observer, but it is a lot of information."

"I have many thoughts and more questions, but I need time to assemble them, get them to be more coherent. So I'm wondering, when will I see you again or have a chance to talk with you?"

He wondered if this was about the church, or was it something more personal or a little of both? "My schedule is a little unusual right now. I'll visit the church with Henry next week, and then I'm off to Italy to work with my Italian colleague, Pietro, on two statues were doing for a church in Montepulciano. If we get the work with St. Steven's, I'll start the altar in Siena with Pietro then come back to Northshire in October to start work there."

"Hold on for a second, I'm lost. If the monsignor and my father accept your ideas, you'll start the altar in Italy? Why there? What about the windows?"

"The altar we both like is quite large and will be built in three sections. The most complex section is the middle piece, and I want Pietro with me on that part. I've decided that we'll complete that section in Italy and ship it to the US when it's done. The two side sections will be done in the McGuinness shed. The windows"—he waved his large hand—"they can be done at any time."

"You'll be in Italy from now to early October?"

"Yes, that's the plan. I'll start Henry's project in Proctorville the first week in October, and if your father and the monsignor approve the windows, I'd plan to start working in Northshire the same week."

"So I won't see you for two months. We'll not have the opportunity to exchange our ideas?"

"We can exchange them by letter. If you'd like?"

He saw a look of dismay on her face and wondered, does she want to see more of me? What about this Carl? He wanted to ask the question but held back.

It had been an exciting day for them, yet neither was ready to admit interest in the other. Her appreciation of his work meant a lot to him. He was impressed with her sophistication, lively personality, depth of knowledge in art history, and captivated by her beauty. He was challenged, given his schedule, to see any woman on a consistent basis. Connie had been perfect; she was as busy as he was. Yet he was convinced he'd make St. Steven's a workable project if for no other reason than to see more of Milly. It might be a dreary mausoleum, but he was certain he could transform it. Foremost in his mind, he would have the opportunity to know this woman better. Time would tell if this interest was sustainable.

For the first time in her life, she had been moved by a man and was dazzled by the uniqueness of his artistic spirit. He was unlike anyone she'd met before. She knew with more conviction than she'd known anything in her life that she wanted to see Jeremiah again.

Finally, she said, "That's a long time. I guess letters are the only option."

"I agree," he said. "Letters are a poor substitute. Today was a treat for me, and I'd like it to continue." He peered down into her eyes. His gaze was known as penetrating, yet he saw that she met it with calm focus. Pushing his curiosity about her into words, he added, "I'd like to see more of you regardless of what happens at St. Steven's. Is that acceptable to you?"

She pulled back a step, her radiant smile replacing her serious demeanor. "I'd like that very much."

He took her hand; his strong fingers laced into her long fingers. The sensation of his touch pleased her; she could feel the coarseness of his hands and their immense strength. He led her to the carriage, and they travelled to the station. They walked to her train, and as she was about to board, she faced him.

With their faces close to each other, he said, "Until October," and leaned forward to kiss her.

She met his lips eagerly then said, "Please write." She kissed him again, then her face became serious. "What if you don't do St. Steven's?"

"I'll come to Springfield as soon as I return from Siena, St. Steven's or no St. Steven's. I'll be writing and will give you the dates."

Chapter 25

The following week, the meeting with the monsignor and Driscoll went well for all parties, except for Driscoll. Jeremiah knew he promised to communicate the decision to Milly, but he didn't. What held him back from writing letters he could never explain, but a lifelong aversion of putting pen to paper characterized him. Milly learned of the decisions on the windows and altar from her father, yet she didn't blame Jeremiah for lack of communication. She assumed he was terribly busy.

Driscoll was not pleased because the walls of his building would be altered. Yet he secured a new contract to replace the existing windows and to insert new windows below the roofline. Jeremiah suggested designs for the lower and upper windows. Vaughn agreed and put them to scale. The structural engineer studied the drawings, reviewed the structure of the walls, and approved the changes.

Driscoll was shaking his head. "I don't see how I can get an arch shape from my existing windows. The bricks won't hold a peak. And arched windows near the roofline, that's tricky."

Jeremiah sketched how the bricks should be cut, shaped, and showed him a photograph of an English church where the brick was done in that manner. Vaughn assured him that this window design and placement was common and would be structurally sound. The windows would direct light to the altar, he asserted, light that would bring the altar to life.

Driscoll said, "You may have to cut those bricks yourself, Mr. Knox. I don't have men to do that. I'll have to wait until you return."

"I think you'll be delighted with the change, Mr. Driscoll, and I'll do whatever needs to be done in October."

Driscoll was still grumpy. He growled, "My daughter, Milly, showed me the altar she liked. Apparently, the two of you have talked about this." He gave Jeremiah a grudging glance.

The monsignor said, "I'm delighted for Milly's involvement. This altar is more elegant, more dazzling than the bishop's. I'm delighted with it."

Vaughn added, "Jeremiah has selected the perfect marble for color. The light refraction off the altar will brighten the entire interior."

"The monsignor clapped his hands together. I think we have a deal. Do we all agree?"

Heads nodded and the monsignor saw he needed to take charge. Driscoll was stunned or overwhelmed with the redesign of his walls. It was as if he was insulted or felt his work was judged to be inferior. The monsignor sought to boost his spirits. "Jackie, this will enhance your reputation and be a landmark for miles around."

Driscoll looked as if he'd been thrown from his horse. He moved his body awkwardly, reflecting some form of internal and external pain. "I don't dare start these windows until Mr. Knox guides my men on what to do."

Vaughn inserted, "As you all know, Jeremiah's off to Italy." He glanced over to Jeremiah, who nodded. "I've drawn the windows, defined their spacing. If you want to start before Jeremiah returns, you have the drawings."

The monsignor asked Jeremiah, "When do you return, and when can you start the altar?"

"I'm back in late September. I should be able to start work here in early October. If we get the contracts done and the payments in place, we can start one section of the altar while I'm in Italy. I plan to work with my Siena crew on the midsection of the altar. They're the best team for that."

The monsignor beamed, "This is wonderful. What's the completion date?"

Jeremiah said, "The central altarpiece will be the slowest part of the overall project. Any statuary will come after that. I expect we may have an altar for you by next June or early summer?" He faced the monsignor. "Is that acceptable?"

"Yes"—his expression indicated little enthusiasm—"I'd hope we have the new altar for spring weddings." He glanced expectedly at Jeremiah.

Jeremiah shook his head. "Not the altar you've chosen. I can do a simpler one for the spring, but you've chosen one far more elaborate. And I'll not rush the work. It will be premium quality."

Vaughn laughed. "Gentleman, meet Jeremiah Knox. You have a combination of the best of things and the worst of things. You have the best sculptor in the United States, and you have the worst at accommodating pressure or influence—he'll do it his way or not at all."

Jeremiah jumped to his defense. "Henry, you make me sound impossible."

Vaughn gave his protégé a clap on the back. He said, "Gentlemen, Jeremiah has never disappointed me on any project by being late, having budget problems or delivering quality below what was promised. In fact, he's generally ahead of schedule, below budget, and the quality is consistently among the best in the world. But ..." He smiled at Jeremiah once again, his hand still resting on the young sculptor's back. "He's going to do it his way."

As they walked away from the church, Jeremiah said to Vaughn, "I've learned a lesson here."

Vaughn stopped to face him. "Oh ... I've got to hear this."

"Don't be cute, Henry, this is a big compliment. Please never let me take on a project without an architect. The church is built like an armory or factory. Your windows will help, but ... I dunno."

"I agree, Jeremiah. The clergies of the world don't buy an altar from a catalog. I don't know why that was done here. The bishop in Springfield should have stopped the monsignor before Driscoll was hired. We don't know what happened." They had descended the long wide steps from the church and stood on the sidewalk. Vaughn stopped and faced Jeremiah. "One more thought, maybe two. I know you're taking this on to make a good year for you with the Stage Chapel. I truly appreciate what you're doing for me in Proctorville.

You know that, right?" He saw Jeremiah nod and, with a smile on his face, said, "There must be another reason you're taking on this project. It's more than avoiding a long stay in Washington, isn't it?"

Jeremiah blushed, and Vaughn clapped him again on the shoulder. "Ah, it's a woman. She must be some kind of beauty. Is it Driscoll's daughter?"

Jeremiah fought off a big smile. *Old Henry*, he thought, *so insightful, never misses a trick.* "You know, I prefer work in the northeast, and it's hard at times because I prefer to work on your projects. They are the best—exquisite churches. I will work on the National Cathedral, but I need to do this one. I need to find something out."

"It must be very important." Vaughn laughed. "Because this is a church neither of us would ever touch."

"You know, Henry, if the flow of light from the upper windows does what I expect, I believe our individual contributions will transform the place."

Vaughn nodded, his face quiet as he studied Jeremiah. "You may well be right, and I hope you get an answer to your quest."

Jeremiah parted with Vaughn at the Northshire train station. Vaughn headed back to New York while Jeremiah returned to Worcester. He thought of Milly as he packed for Siena, and before he boarded the SS *Geneva*, he sent her a brief letter.

She was packing her bags for her summer program at Harvard. It would be busy, she thought, and would keep her mind off him. He'd given her Pietro's address, and she planned to write him often.

When Jeremiah arrived in Siena, he was flooded with work from Pietro's backlog of projects. Pietro was having a banner year, and he'd saved some of the most complex work for Jeremiah. In his mind, there was no peer equal to Jeremiah for intricate carving on altars and small statues. While Jeremiah worked on the design for the St. Steven's altar, even Pietro was impressed with its elegance and high degree of detail. It was clearly one of the most elaborate and difficult altars that he and Jeremiah had undertaken. Jeremiah and Pietro travelled to Carrera to select the marble for the altar. Several tons were sent to McGuinness for the two sidepieces; the marble slabs for the massive centerpiece were delivered to Pietro's studio.

Upon returning from Carrera, Kinga Biasi extended a cablegram to Jeremiah. He opened it with care and a degree of apprehension. It was from his mother, his father had died, a heart attack. Could he come home for the funeral? He called Callahan to be assured his return was okay with the courts then called his family. He'd arrive in two days.

When he stepped off the train at Stradbally, the haunting beauty of the town struck him. Even the old train station, its gravel departure platform and the simple construction of the station house had a charm that he'd missed. As he strolled toward the awaiting carriage, the lush green of the town square, the rolling hills leading to the cove, and the Irish Sea took his breath away. He inhaled the damp air tinged with the scent of the nearby sea. As it tickled his nostrils, he realized how much he had missed the town. Surprised at this jolt of familiarity, he gave the driver the address of the family home. He stayed in his old room in the large stone home; memories of his last night before deportation surged through him. During the day, he walked the land as he had done so many years ago, and what secured his attention was the slow, quiet movement of the people in this tranquil valley. He had forgotten its beauty; it had been taken away from him so quickly. He compared the surroundings of Stradbally to the hustle and bustle of Worcester. He viewed the difference of the urban crowds and noise to the timeless peace of the village, the energy of the Americans in contrast to the gentle pace of the Irish.

At the wake and later at the funeral, Joseph Callahan, with light flecks of gray at his temples acknowledging the passing years, urged him to return. He emphasized that the time was ripe for another movement toward Irish independence.

Callahan said, "Maybe it's not law for you anymore, but as a sculptor or businessman, you can lead the movement in Dublin again. The hotheads are gone, and a more intelligent strategy, like you advocated before, could make a big impact."

Jeremiah listened politely. Inwardly he felt pleased to be acknowledged after all these years, but as he asked about his friends in the movement, the answers were troubling.

His brother Tommy said, "Many have left the country, either forced out like you or they left because there was no work. In the paper recently, they said over a million people have left in the last ten years."

"Jesus," Jeremiah murmured. "What does one do for work if everyone leaves?"

"Ahh, there's always somethin' to come up, you know," Tommy added.

Jeremiah was not sure. While daily life and the extraordinary beauty of his town had a surprisingly powerful effect on him, it was the limited possibilities of interesting work in sculpture that held him back. That he actively toyed with the idea of returning stunned him, but the quiet charm of Ireland compared favorably with the boisterous energy of America. He was perplexed. A touch of nostalgia gripped him, and he worked on the idea ... Could he fit in again?

As he prepared to return to Siena, he sat at the kitchen table with his mother. She grasped his strong hands in her long delicate fingers and said, "It's been wonderful to see you even on this sad occasion, but I want to talk heart to heart with you."

He studied her calm, intelligent face, the blue eyes that always sparkled. "I welcome that, I've missed your wise thoughts for too many years."

"I know we haven't communicated much over the years, have we? Your da and I weren't much good at that. But I want you to know, Jeremiah, I'm pleased you've found success and happiness in the new country. And I have a thought."

"You always surprise me, go on."

"I know Mr. Callahan would like you to return as would many of your friends in the movement. They need you, I see that." She paused and held his hands more firmly. "But that'd be wrong." She stared hard into his eyes, letting her thought sink in. "The time is not ripe in the movement toward independence. There's tremendous strife among the factions here in Ireland, and the British are still adamantly against it. There will be much more bloodshed. I'm afraid, very afraid, you'd wind up in jail again or worse be killed. I'd never see you again, and I couldn't stand that."

Softly, her hand next to her eyes, tears fell down her cheeks. "I know I should have come with da to America. That's our fault. But if you'd like, I can come to America, and I'd like to. I know you can come back and visit. I'm hoping you'll do some visits." She wiped the tears away.

He was so surprised; he was speechless. The thought of returning to Ireland was troublesome, and she'd made her reasoning clear, and it helped him.

He said, "I did not expect that perspective, Mother. I do have obligations in America. I have a big project that I must finish." He chuckled watching for her reaction. "And I've met a woman that I'd like to know better."

"What … what's she like, this young lady?"

He described Milly, how they met, and the project at St. Steven's. They talked for hours about his life in America, and she conveyed a strong interest in a lengthy visit now that Sean had passed away. He was surprised by the warm greetings of his brothers and sister as they greeted him at the wake. The hearty exchanges with his Fenian friends added to a sense of family and community that were missing for him in America. He talked to his mother about these experiences; she smiled at him and patted his hand.

She said, "If this Milly becomes a strong interest, I want to meet her before you offer marriage, so I'll definitely be coming to America soon."

The death of his farther, the return to Ireland, and the accumulated body of work at Pietro's studio consumed Jeremiah's time. He poured into the work at the studio contributing to Pietro's projects, as well as working on the intricate designs of the middle section of the St. Steven's altar. He rose at six every morning, had his coffee, pastry and eggs at Silvio's Café nestled on a block off the Palio, then worked tirelessly into the early evening. Chipping away at a design, he'd mutter, "I must write to Milly." But his energy and time for such social matters evaporated every day. Evenings were full of five-course dinners with a rich Barolo or a sharp Chianti then deep sleep.

Interspersed with his travels with Pietro, he spent a long vacation week at the Rimmini Beach with Maria, the count, and their children. The count was aging fast, and Jeremiah worried about Maria's joke of being an early widow. Maria and Jeremiah walked the beach, the warm waters of the Adriatic swirling over their feet and talked about marriage and his thoughts of Milly. She was delighted with his newest prospect chiding him for waiting so long to be serious with a woman. She admitted to having an adverse view of Connie when Jeremiah had brought her to Siena. That night he began a letter to Milly describing his long talk with Maria, but it was unfinished when he returned to Siena, and it was never completed.

Milly wrote faithfully every week in July, and with one letter in return, she felt annoyed, wondered if he had dropped interest, and she stopped writing as well.

In late August, he and Pietro were sitting in an outdoor cafe, facing the Palio, watching the crowds wander by. They quaffed tall glasses of beer to calm their thirst while the sun set behind the buildings and the air cooled as the shadows extended toward their table. A figure emerged from the shadows and approached them.

His strong Irish voice boomed as he walked to their table, "Jeremiah Knox, the woman at the shop told me you'd be here drinking as usual."

As he came closer, Jeremiah saw the face of Jimmy O'Farrell. Stunned, he stood up and greeted his old friend, "What in the world are you doing here?"

"Joseph Callahan told me about your recent trip home. My sympathy over the death of your father, Joseph also told me where to find you."

"Why, what ... I'm confused. What are you doing here?"

"Slower, Jeremiah, hello ..." O'Farrell turned to Pietro. "You must be Pietro. I'm Jimmy, and I worked with Jeremiah many years ago."

"Got us all deported you did," added Jeremiah. They all laughed.

"I've come from Germany as you know. I'm there because I still can't return to Ireland." He spoke to Pietro. "They forgive very slowly in Ireland if at all."

Jeremiah said, "Well, they let me back and want me to return. But it's a little late for me to return to law school."

"That's why I'm here. Callahan wants you back for the cause, but he said you saw no work for yourself in Ireland. Is that the reason you won't return?"

Before Jeremiah could reply, O'Farrell added, "I've got an idea and a piece of news for you. First the idea, come to Germany. You can do this sculpture work that's made you famous. There's tons of work in Germany. The country's expanding, and we can get involved with the workers' movement. And maybe bring those workers' programs to Ireland, which would be your task."

"Jesus, Jimmy, you don't waste time with your pitch, do you?"

"We don't have time in the fight, Jeremiah. We've got to act quickly. Several years ago, I asked you to come to Germany. Now I'm doing it face to face. I'm convinced you can serve the Irish cause from Germany plus do important work in Germany too. So there."

"So what's the news? Your friends the Milton brothers … you knew they tried to kill some of ours in Dublin, right? Then they ran to the United States to find you. Our Fenian comrades in New York wanted them bad. Guess what, they found the dumb bastards in jail, a place called Sing Sing in New York. Seems like the Miltons tried armed robbery on a liquor store in the city, and one of them, on crutches with a broken leg, couldn't get away fast enough. The police caught them, put them away. The one with the broken leg died in the prison, apparently from infections in that leg."

"And the other brother?"

"He's still in that Sing Sing, been there a long time. New Yorkers apparently don't like armed robbery."

"Jesus." Jeremiah shook his head. "Good riddance."

Pietro laughed. "Signore Jimmy, who are all these crazy people? Are all of Jeremiah's friends a bit crazy, no? These gangsters, this McGuinness in Worcester, totally crazy, you, others in America … what's with you people? Jeremiah, by temperament, belongs in Italy. He loves it here. We do great work. What's this work you talk about … Fenians, revolution? No thank you. Art is good, no politics in art."

O'Farrell pulled up a chair and sat across from Jeremiah. "I'm sorry to intrude, Pietro, but I haven't seen this man since we were both sent out of the country. I want to work with him again."

Jeremiah sighed. "Jimmy, I hope you can stay a while. I'd like to hear what you're doing, but a few reality pieces first. I have a contract that will take me at least a year to finish, that's in America. We're working on part of that contract here." He pointed to Pietro. "Second, I like America. It's been good to me, and I've done well. Can't do what I'm doing in Ireland. People are leaving like rats on a sinking ship. I can't imagine there's much new building work there."

"You can do your sculpture in Germany as I said, big need, think about it."

"My turn," Pietro interjected. "You can do that here, my friend, as I've said many times. You even speak the language now."

Jeremiah glanced at both men. "I won't say no, but I can say not now. I have a ton of work and obligations to complete in the US. I love Italy, I miss Ireland, and I should visit you in Berlin, Jimmy. But later. What you say does intrigue me."

They had dinner every night for several days as Jimmy supplied Jeremiah with the actions of the communists and socialists in Germany and his prediction of its spread to England and Ireland. In his opinion, it was the time to get into the movement. Pietro, realizing that Jeremiah might consider returning to Europe, wanted him to join his studio as a full partner. The discussions went late into the evenings and contributed to the many reasons why Jeremiah's communications to Milly had gone to zero His sojourn in Italy was mixed with his daily work at Pietro's studio, offset with project work as far away as Bare on the Adriatic and Biagio on Lake Como. In between those projects, they delivered statues they'd completed for churches in Bologna, Florence, and Milano. By late September, he was not ready to leave Siena, but Pietro had excellent command on the design of the central altar section, and Jeremiah needed to start the Stage Chapel with Vaughn. On the side sections, he wanted to check the progress in Worcester to see if Biasi's crew needed help from him. On board, he drafted letters to the monsignor and to Driscoll describing the schedule for work from October forward. If Driscoll had not started work on the windows, he wished to meet him October 1st to start work. In his haste, he neglected to draft a similar letter to Milly.

Chapter 26

October 1st was a Wednesday, a school day, and Milly was not there when Jeremiah met with her father. The two men discussed the changes to the lower windows, and Driscoll asked Jeremiah to create the first window as an example to his men. They placed the scaffolding beneath a window and, under Jeremiah's guidance, cut the brick away from the stained glass, extracted the stained glass window and lowered it to the ground. Then they removed bricks, one by one, five feet above the existing window frame. Jeremiah, working with a pile of bricks on the scaffold, cut them, then placed them carefully cementing each in place. He formed an arch curving from the original square top of the window to its new apex, gracefully pointed, five feet higher.

Driscoll watched from below, took off his cap, and said, "Mr. Knox, come down. We need to talk."

Jeremiah descended the ladder joining Driscoll near a stack of bricks. Driscoll, his hand on top of the bricks, said, "That's grand, Mr. Knox, your cutting and shaping is most impressive, but I can't count on my men to do that. They don't have the experience."

"If that's your decision, that's okay with me. They're your men. I don't want to deny them work."

"What'll you do? Do you want to do all the windows?"

"No, no—I like what I've done, but you're paying me far too much to do brickwork. I'll bring a team of McGuinness's men from Worcester. They'll be here tomorrow, and they'll have all the lower windows done in a week."

The surprise on Driscoll's face nearly caused Jeremiah to laugh. Driscoll blurted out, "Well, I'll believe that when I see it, but you have my approval. No change in cost. We're substituting your people for my people."

"No, no. If your people can't do it, the monsignor needs to know this. He needs to pay the difference between your men and my men, it might be higher." He paused for emphasis. "Given how slow your men are, it might be lower."

"Jesus, you're a tough man, Knox." He thought, damn, the cocky young pup had insulted his building and was now insulting his workers. He calmed down to say, "I estimated two months of work to do the upper and lower windows. What's your estimate?"

Jeremiah glanced up at the walls. "I can believe it with your crew. With McGuinness's cutters and my direction, I'd say a month at the most, so let's stay with your cost on this. If we do it for less, we bill what you would have billed. If we run over, we eat it. How's that?"

Driscoll took off his hat and wiped his brow. "You're something else, you really are. It's a deal." He extended his hand. "I'll tell my boys to go home."

Jeremiah's estimate was generous. Once McGuinness's crew arrived on site, they had removed and extended the height of eight windows on the north and south walls, a total of sixteen new openings in one week. Jeremiah sighed in satisfaction and promised them a bonus for the speed and quality of their work. To get the placement and spacing of the upper windows at the roofline correct, the lead foreman asked Jeremiah to outline the shape of the windows and mark his outline in chalk. His team built the scaffolding, over a hundred feet high, so when Jeremiah stood on the floor of the scaffold, his head was at the edge of the roof.

On the following Saturday, Jeremiah was standing at the top of the scaffolding. The wind was blowing his long hair. The breeze ruffled his blue work shirt and billowed his tan twill work pants. His hands held the blueprints for the tall, narrow windows at the top of the church. He studied the prints then examined the brick wall. He tucked the blueprints into his pants and pulled a piece of chalk from his pocket and began to sketch the outline of a window. He was the only workman on site and was using this day to define the windows for the McGuinness crew on Monday.

Driscoll had driven his wife, Stephanie, Clary, and Milly to see the shape of the lower windows completed during the week. The former windows were now holes in the wall, their shape held by wooden frames. The stained glass for the new design had been ordered but was months away from delivery. Even as open spaces in the wall, Driscoll had to admit that the taller, tapered windows made the church appear more handsome, more welcoming. It softened its overall appearance. As they stepped out of Driscoll's carriage, Clary saw Jeremiah perched at the top of the church, his brown locks blowing in the wind.

She said, looking up, "Who's that way up there?" She waved an arm at Jeremiah. "Yoo-hoo up there." She kept waving. "Hello!!" She turned to Driscoll. "Jackie, I think that's Mr. Knox, whatever is he doing up there alone and on a Saturday."

Driscoll shook his head. "Well, Jesus H. Christ," he muttered to himself. "It is Knox, but what the hell is doing at the top of the scaffold?"

Jeremiah saw them and waved. "Hello down there. I need a few more minutes, then I'll come down."

Milly saw him, the glorious head of thick brown hair. His absolute comfort of standing on a narrow platform hundreds of feet above the ground was so definitely Jeremiah Knox. It made her knees weak, and she hated the impact he had on her. She'd not heard from him in two months, and she had not expected to see him. It sent shivers through her body. She had tried to forget him and had begun to listen to the attentions of Carl once again.

After weeks of constant pushing, Carl had worked his way back into her life. Now, she felt stirred to her inner being by the sight of Jeremiah standing high above her, and she abhorred the sensation she felt.

She saw him sketch the outline of a tall, narrow, peaked window. The opening was a thin spear about a foot or two wide and as tall as Jeremiah. She could see from his drawing, the window alone would be a brilliant addition. The light it would provide to the sanctuary would be everything he claimed. He moved about ten feet on the scaffold and drew another one, identical to the first window. He put the chalk in a pocket and came down the ladder of the scaffold.

When he reached the group, Driscoll extended his hand. "We've interrupted your work. You shouldn't have come down."

"It's okay, I can use a break. It's good to see the shape of the windows from here. See how it works." He pointed to the chalk sketches. "What do you think?"

Milly thought, *The bonehead.* He was all about the work. He didn't even say hello. Did he even realize that she was there? His mind was only on the windows. He had no idea who was with her father. She asserted herself, pushed past Clary, and moved toward him. "The travelling Mr. Knox, we'd thought you'd fallen off the end of the earth."

He gave Milly a warm smile, stepped toward her, preparing to kiss her on both cheeks.

Her severe look froze him; she took one step back, extended her hand, stopping his movement. She said, "Well, at least you're alive."

He shook her limp hand. Well, that was cold, he thought. Why, what had he done? Was it the lack of letters? He stepped away, a faint look of disdain, and through tight lips, he said, "Obviously, I'm alive and haven't fallen off the earth." He moved away from her and extended his hand to Stephanie and Clary. He pointed to the shape of the lower windows and asked, "Any impressions on the shape of the lower windows? It's hard to tell without the stained glass."

Clary said, "Oh, I think they're a great improvement already. The building looks more churchlike, don't you think?" Her enthusiasm was evident, Stephanie agreed, and Driscoll smiled, content.

Milly remained quiet. She watched Jeremiah with hooded eyes. She wanted to say more to him, but he was ignoring her now. Clearly he was angry, probably confused by her statements. She was muddled. Why had she said that? Why so rude? Could she undo the unpleasantness of her greeting? She said to the group, "Since we're headed to lunch, perhaps Mr. Knox would like to join us?"

Quickly he replied, looking at the others, ignoring her. "Thank you and no. I have fourteen more windows to sketch up there." He pointed to the windows he had previously done. "And I don't want to delay the crew when they arrive on Monday. Since your here Mr. Driscoll, any thoughts before I climb back up?"

Driscoll said, "No, Jeremiah, I like the sketch you've made up there. I'm looking forward to see if the opening threatens the roof."

"The windows won't begin to test the structure. Your walls are too sturdy."

Stephanie had been quiet; she was worried about her daughter. She decided that something had happened between Milly and Jeremiah. She knew Milly had visited Jeremiah to see his altars but was unaware of any association beyond artistic inquiry. But she surmised something had occurred. Milly's rudeness was uncharacteristic; she had been hurt, but how, why? He seemed so friendly and warm toward her, and she was most unpleasant. She gave Jeremiah a warm smile. "Your ideas, your work is daring and bold, isn't it? I see you walking casually hundreds of feet in the air like it's nothing. Drawing on a wall like it's on the ground right in front of you. Remarkable." She shook her head.

"Mrs. Driscoll, your thoughts are kind. This elevation is minor compared to my work on the Duomo in Siena a few weeks back. My fellow sculptor, Pietro, and I were hanging off the ceiling in canvas seats, pulled up from below to repair small sculptures in the dome of the cathedral. We were much higher than this scaffold and hoping at the time that the fellows holding the ropes didn't have heart attacks or decide to put their hands in their pockets." He laughed.

"You did sculpture hanging off a ceiling in a chair?" asked Clary.

"When you think about what needs to be done, as long as you're comfortable, the position doesn't matter." He thought about his aching back and tired arms, but those were not worth mentioning. He went on, "Pietro reminded me that Michelangelo painted the ceiling of the Sistine Chapel hanging a similar way. A hammer and chisel is vastly easier to manage than paint and a brush. I have no idea how he could paint lying on his back."

He waved his large hand at them. "Mr. Driscoll, sorry—still not used to calling you Jackie—I'll be back on Wednesday and Thursday.

See you then." Ignoring Milly, he turned his back and headed toward the scaffold.

Well, I'll be goddamned, he thought. *Wow, Milly.* He'd misread her, his mistake. He thought she had real interest in him, apparently not. Now he was stuck with this project for a year. He had looked forward to seeing her, and his disappointment turned to anger. He swore loudly as he climbed the ladder. Never in his memory had he been so rudely treated by a woman. As he mounted the scaffold, he thought, well, this project would give him time to consider living in Europe. Which country would make the most sense? His thoughts trailed back to his mother's conversation. Ireland was in disruption and dangerous. "Do not come back," she warned. Callahan was more optimistic as was O'Farrell in Germany. And he could work in Italy. He and Pietro were strong partners. He was free now to entertain these thoughts, free to give Europe serious consideration.

He thought, as he marked out the windows on the brick wall, *I shouldn't rush to conclusions, but what happened? Why was she so distant, cold?* Before getting enthusiastic about living in Italy or Germany, he needed to—wanted to—talk with her.

As they climbed into the carriage, Clary exclaimed, "It was so nice to see, Mr. Knox, and see what the upper windows will look like. Oh, I like him, so charming and pleasant and willing to explain things to us in ways we understand."

Milly gave her aunt a disgusting look then studied her hands; they were slightly shaking. Her mother tapped her on the arm. "What's going on, Milly? You were not quite yourself out there. You're angry with Mr. Knox, aren't you? Your hands are shaking, and you're a little red in the face."

"It's nothing, Mother. Maybe we can talk later." She gave her mother an appreciative smile and patted her arm.

Chapter 27

Jeremiah was still on the scaffold when the Driscolls' carriage rolled by, their lunch completed. Driscoll's driver honked the carriage horn, and Jeremiah waved. He was tempted to send Milly the Italian salute for disgust but laughed at himself. She wouldn't get it, and it would be a childish pique. He resolved to contact her once back in Worcester; this time he'd write.

When he was in Worcester, Hamish had ideas for him. Several new buildings were for sale, and several lots on the outskirts of the city looked promising for new apartments as the city expanded. He saw the buildings and walked the land. They went back to his apartment and pushed the numbers. The land opportunities had the biggest potential for profit, but the greatest risk. He put the work papers aside and told Hamish they'd go over them again the next day. The investments appeared attractive, but a new problem had appeared. Should he continue to invest in America when the lure of Italy, Germany, and Ireland beckoned? The power of his experience in Italy and Ireland during the summer continued to command his attention.

Inside, Jeremiah was still angry at himself and at Milly. He knew he should have written more, but he acknowledged that wasn't him. And he thought she could have handled his lack of attention, his lack of communication in a better manner. Well, he mused, maybe Milly was like Connie——tough, determined to see things her way. Maybe—he frowned—he was doomed to select tough, independent women yet eventually fail at getting close to them. The fault could be his. It could be theirs, but whatever it was, he was not getting close to any woman.

As the days went by, his frustration with her did not diminish. He hardly knew her. Why was she still on his mind? What was he missing? He decided to write, assuming a letter would get her out of his system. He went to the desk that Connie had given him on his twenty-eighth birthday, pulled out his fountain pen, and wrote.

Dear Milly,

When I departed for Italy in June, we seemed to share a growing interest in each other. I had high hopes for seeing more of you upon my return.

As I look back on those three months, my work in Italy and the death of my father totally absorbed me. Unfortunately, upon my return, I continued to allow fresh demands on my time to consume me, a flaw of mine. Perhaps I love my work too much, and I failed to inform you of my plans. My apologies.

Also, I should have notified you about my quick visit to Northshire last Saturday. It was a last-minute decision, and I apologize for that as well. Did my poor communication over these months prompt your cold response? Or was there some other cause? I don't know what happened, but your contempt, or was it indifference, whatever it was, it was obvious.

I've been through difficult times as you know, and despite that extensive experience, the basis for your rejection eludes me. However bizarre, I accept that your interest has changed.

Sincerely,
Jeremiah

He read the letter over several times, pulled an envelope from his desk drawer, and sealed it. He'd mail it Monday. He sighed deeply.

This was a loss, a disappointment, and maybe he was to blame. Perhaps she'd thought long and hard about his Irish troubles and concluded that he wasn't right for her. Even in that case, he thought, most women would convey their thoughts more pleasantly, more directly. But a woman who acted like she did, giving no reasons, he didn't want someone like that in his life.

He put his hand to pen again and wrote two more letters. One was to Joseph Callahan and the other to Jimmy O'Farrell. He said he planned to work in Italy next summer and would take time to visit Dublin, Stradbally, and Berlin. He looked forward to continuing the discussions that were held weeks ago. He intimated that a return to Europe was possible.

On Monday, he travelled to Proctorville and started work on the Stage Chapel. He sensed the bell tower and other structural features that Vaughn wanted would be easy to do. He organized his part of the work and interviewed several stonemasons to support the carving of the window frames and the ornamental work at the crest of the bell tower. It was going to run smoothly, better than St. Steven's, and this pleased him. He called Henry Vaughn in New York with his first progress report on the project. He was in no mood to return to Northshire. "Henry, we're off to a fast start. I may even have some time for the National Cathedral."

"Now, Jeremiah, it's not nice to tease an older man. Seriously though, the Stage Chapel goes well?"

"Better than that. Your contractor has a full understanding of the design and the blueprints are very clear to him. He'll make zero mistakes, and I'll be surprised if he falters in any way. So that makes my tasks easier too."

"Terrific, so where's this free time coming from?"

"From the church in Northshire. By the way, your windows make all the difference there. Actually, it's going to look like a church."

"Delighted to hear, but where's your time coming from?"

"It sounds like you do need me in DC?"

"You have no idea, but you haven't answered my question."

"It's just as we talked. At St. Steven's we've gotten the light problem solved with the changes to the windows, so I'll do the altar in Siena and Worcester and ship the finished sections to them."

"Ah, I see. The second reason for doing it has evaporated, I'm guessing. Miss Driscoll is no longer in the picture?"

"Right, I have no idea what happened, but when I came back from Italy, I found a hostile stranger. I'm done there."

"Okay, keep me posted when you have a free week here and there. There's some spot work I'd love you to do." He paused. "While I have you on the line, Jean and I are having a party in a few weeks. She'd love you to come. Some pretty interesting friends of hers will be there—we'll introduce you to Emily."

"Send me the dates, and I'll put it on my calendar. I'll have more for you on the Stage Chapel in a couple of weeks."

He put down the phone and remembered his commitment to Driscoll. He'd promised the builder that he'd be in Northshire midweek and decided to use that date to inform him of new working arrangements. Instead of working in Northshire, he'd do all the altar work in Worcester and Siena. Driscoll and the monsignor could visit at any time to review progress, make suggestions, and have their questions answered. He planned to tell Driscoll that the side altarpieces would be delivered to Northshire first, the centerpiece from Italy last. By late December, he expected to be in Northshire to cut and place the marble floor of the sanctuary. He planned to lay the floor the week or two before Christmas. He scanned over these plans and thought the schedule would work. He was curious if Driscoll would have any questions or problems with the plan.

When he and Driscoll met, Jeremiah was delighted with the upper window openings. The placement and spacing was perfect, the size ideal for the large walls. They enhanced the exterior appearance of the church beyond what Jeremiah had expected. He walked the interior with Driscoll. The midday light flowed down onto the sanctuary as Jeremiah had predicted. The altar that he and Milly had selected would be completely bathed in the light from above. He measured the area where the streaks of sun hit the floor and knew his altar would be a perfect fit. It was almost too good to be true.

Driscoll was perplexed that Jeremiah would not spend much time in Northshire with a second project a few miles away. Jeremiah explained he'd save the monsignor considerable money by limiting his travel expenses and that of his Worcester crew. Driscoll acknowledged the practicality of Jeremiah's approach but said that the monsignor, the missus, Clary, and Milly would be disappointed by his absence. They all enjoyed his company.

Jeremiah laughed. "Kind of you to say, but you and the others can come to Worcester at any time to see the work as it progresses."

Late in the week, he returned to Worcester to see a letter from Milly. He read it quickly, somewhat puzzled by the last sentence.

Dear Jeremiah,

I've taken pen in hand several times, wanting to respond to your letter but uncertain how to do so. This attempt will have to suffice.

You certainly didn't mince words; your message was clear about my behavior. It appears I owe you an apology. Here it is. I apologize—it was not my best day.

However, with all due respect, your letter was rather cold and abrupt. In fairness to a friendship we had begun to cultivate, I feel strongly that we should at least have a conversation face to face before we terminate all communication. Please let me know when you're next in Northshire, and we'll find some time to talk.

Best regards,
Milly

He read the letter a second time to make certain he missed nothing. She still wanted to talk, but why? That was surprising, but she gave no reason why. Her behavior at the church remained bizarre to him. And her letter was abrupt and cool, too cool. Why would she

273

want to talk? Although she appeared strong and stable to him on first meeting and during their day in Worcester, he had begun to wonder if his initial impression was wrong. Her letter, blithely ignoring her odd behavior and finding fault with his letter, indicated, actually confirmed for him, that she had character complications he didn't understand. He put her letter aside and decided to forget her. What he saw at the church on Saturday was probably the real Milly. Best to leave this alone.

He replied:

> Dear Amelia,
>
> Your request for continued conversation is understood but a difficult request. My schedule is horrendous, and I will not be in Northshire or Springfield in the near future. I will let you know when I'm in the area but have no idea when.
>
> Best regards,
> Jeremiah

As time went by, she remained on his mind. For him, she was perplexing and annoying. She'd pop up in his consciousness, yet he could not explain why. Perpetually logical, this was not familiar territory. He could think of a hundred reasons to ignore her, to continue to date others, yet it was Milly who came to mind, not any of the ladies in Worcester or Henry's friend, Emily, in New York. Yet when he pushed her presence to the corners of his mind, she'd pop back up.

When she read his letter, she was disappointed at first then concluded he had no further interest. He seemed so warm at one time and now so cold—such an enigma. She still wanted to talk with him and hoped that they would see each other in Northshire. She wanted clarification on the lack of communication over the summer. Was he just absent-minded, or had his interest flagged? She wanted to engage him. It would help her clear her mind, answer the question of why his presence stayed with her. In the interim, she turned her attention back to Carl, assuming Jeremiah an unlikely suitor, she began to consider Carl's proposal of marriage.

In early December, Jeremiah informed Driscoll it was time to lay the marble floor in the sanctuary. The geometric pattern he'd designed was intricate, and he would personally supervise its installation. It was a wintry day when he arrived. Snow had begun to fall, and a light breeze swirled the snow, stinging his eyes and face. St. Steven's was bone-cold inside. The central heating system was unable to combat the draft from the windows, boarded over, and leaking gusts of air and flakes of snow. The work went slowly. The men wore gloves, mufflers, and heavy coats and were still cold. Jeremiah was particularly well protected. He wore a bearskin Russian cap in addition to his gloves, a heavy coat, and fur-lined boots.

The monsignor joined the men and watched with interest as the cement floor rapidly disappeared as sections of red marble slid between slabs of cream-colored marble, creating a wide checkerboard pattern across the vast floor. "Oh dear," said the monsignor. "The altar will cover much of that beautiful design."

"Oh no," Jeremiah assured him, "the celebrants and communicants will see much of the floor."

"It's too beautiful to walk on," said the monsignor, blowing on his hands freezing in his light gloves.

Biasi answered him, "Not to worry, Monsignor, the floor will last for centuries even if you said Mass on it every day."

Jeremiah rose from his knees and went to the monsignor. "We'll finish later today, and I'd like to leave a gift for you and the Driscolls at day's end. May I leave them at your residence?"

The monsignor continued to blow into his gloves, trying hard to find warmth. "I'm going to the Driscolls for dinner. Would you join me and drop the gifts there? I know they want to see you."

Jeremiah was hesitant. "I can't stay long. I promised the boys." He waved his arm at his crew busily at work. "That we'd have a few wee ones at the hotel to celebrate the completion of the floor."

"I understand. We can take my carriage, and after you leave your gifts, my driver can take you back to the hotel. The Driscolls will be disappointed you can't stay for dinner. And why gifts? No need to do that, Jeremiah."

"It's my tradition to thank those who seek me out for projects. This is a good time to remember my good fortune is due to you and others like you."

By day's end, the snow had begun to accumulate. The early snow showers had formed into a howling blizzard. The monsignor was slipping in the ankle-deep snow when Jeremiah offered his hand as the older man reached the carriage door. Gales of snow whirled around them, and Jeremiah hoisted his bag of gifts onto an open seat. The monsignor patted the bag and glanced across the carriage to Jeremiah. "A nice sentiment, Jeremiah … very nice indeed."

The monsignor's carriage had difficulty mounting the small rise on Jackson Street; momentarily stalled, Jeremiah and the monsignor left the carriage and slogged through calf high drifts to the Driscolls' front door. They were covered in snow; an inch or two of the white fluffy had accumulated on Jeremiah's cap. His coat, muffler, and the bag carrying his gifts were blanketed as well. He appeared like a white Santa Claus. Stephanie opened the door with Milly right behind her.

Stephanie asked, "Who's the large white ghost behind you, Monsignor?"

"Ah, I bring many surprises. Let us unrobe and you'll see."

Hats and coats were removed, snow was shaken out the door and the tall, lanky frame of Jeremiah appeared. While Jeremiah searched to place his sack of gifts, Stephanie blurted, "My goodness, it's the missing man. Look, Jackie, Clary, Milly … it's Jeremiah. We heard you might be here for the floor. Is that what finally brought you back?" She shook a finger at him in jest. "You haven't been in Northshire since that day in October when we saw you high on the scaffold. You've been avoiding us."

"Just working hard, Mrs. Driscoll." His smile was easy, creasing his face still slightly moist from the snow. He wiped it with his scarf. "I came to finish the floor of the sanctuary. It was completed today." He patted his twill pants and heavy wool sweater. "I've come from work. Please excuse my clothes."

Jackie came forward and pumped his hand. "Damn, Jeremiah, I thought you'd be done by late tomorrow. You and your crew, you work so fast. I'm sorry to miss it."

The monsignor was expansive, waving his arms in enthusiasm. "Jackie, you must see it. It's exquisite beyond description. I don't want to cover any part of it with the altar."

Forgetting the past connection between his daughter and Jeremiah, Driscoll said, "Jeremiah, you remember Milly." He gestured to his daughter standing quietly to the side, biting her lip. "School's out, and she's here for the holidays."

Milly stepped forward to greet him, planning a European greeting. Jeremiah was faster. He bowed, a short quick movement, then stepped back, his hands at his sides, and said, "Merry Christmas, Amelia." He didn't want her cold rejection again and felt his bow was polite if formal. He was about to turn his attention to Stephanie and Clary, wishing them happy holidays when Milly moved closer to him.

She extended her hand, the back of her hand up. He didn't bend to kiss it. He took her elegant hand and gently released it. He extended his hands to Stephanie and Clary and said, "I can't stay long and don't want to interfere with your festivities, but I bring a few holiday thank-yous. My crew awaits me at the hotel, and I don't want to delay their drinking."

The monsignor said, "What he means is that we're delaying his drinking." The monsignor extended the word *his* for several beats.

Laughter ensued, and Jeremiah was directed to a couch in the living room near a roaring fire. After the chill of the church and the ride through the driving snow, the fire felt good and warmed him. Stephanie brought him a cup of heated wine. He sipped the spicy drink slowly. Nodding his appreciation to Stephanie, he said, "Do you mind if I distribute my little tokens then make a not too subtle but rapid exit?"

The family arrayed around him in chairs. The monsignor sat next to him, his square body crowding Jeremiah. The room was warm, crowded with a towering Christmas tree fully decorated with candy canes, silver icicle strips, colored balls, and lighted candles.

Beneath the tree, a galaxy of brightly wrapped presents pushed up against the lower branches of the tree and spilled out to the living room floor. Jeremiah waved a hand at the tree then turned to the clergyman. "Most beautifully done and first the monsignor," The monsignor opened a wrapped bottle of Jameson and then a box of Cuban cigars. He expressed delight as Jeremiah said, "The bishop in Springfield said you were partial to these items, and I thought they might be appropriate to ease the pain of my tearing out the walls of your church."

The monsignor was delighted with the gifts, grabbed and shook Jeremiah's arm. He said, "Now all my secrets and bad habits are out. I'm ruined."

Amid the laughter, Jeremiah reached into his bag and brought up two packages similar in shape to the monsignor's. He reached over and gave them to Driscoll. "To my other boss who I still have trouble calling Jackie, a small testament for putting up with the endless suggestions, alterations, and travels of your hired sculptor." Driscoll opened the present of Jamesons and a box of Cuban cigars.

He pulled them to his chest. "I'm not sharing these with anyone." He sniffed hard to hold back his pleasure from this unexpected gift.

"To the ladies," Jeremiah announced. He drew three packages from his bag and distributed them. "Stephanie, yours. Clary, here's yours. And, Amelia, this is yours. For the ladies, I thank you for your interest and support of all the changes in the church and particularly for the initiative to press for a truly original altar—an altar that I think will please all of you." The women opened their gifts to find elegant silk scarves woven in Siena, each one bearing a different floral design and a wide mix of colors. Clary jumped to her feet, swishing the scarf around her neck in a stylish fashion. She pranced around the room to everyone's delight as one who was ten years younger. She came over to Jeremiah and gave him a big kiss. Milly and Stephanie, more reserved, came to Jeremiah with European kisses. He rose and claimed, "I should depart before your wine keeps me by this glorious fire and you start asking me hard questions about the altar."

A flurry of protests arose over his departure, but he moved quickly to his coat and hat. He smiled while maintaining, "I must go. My crew awaits me." Milly followed him to the door and grasped his hand. "Jeremiah, in your last letter, you said you let me know when you're in the area. And here you are, no warning."

"Sorry, Amelia, I'm just not good at these things."

"And you never came to Northshire after October. Why? I asked for more conversation." There was a pleading tone in her voice, her eyes on his as she held fast to his fingers.

He looked down at her hand; her long fingers were laced into his. He was locked to her and not getting away. He thought, *No visits were a surprise to her—is she dense?* "I guess I didn't see the point. You'd dismissed me pretty clearly in October."

She said, "I realize now, better than in my letters, what I did and how it affected you." She continued to stare hard into his eyes, intermittently biting her lip. "You're an immense puzzle to me, and I believe I puzzle you as well. I don't know why it's taken me so long to say that." She tugged at his hand, her eyes imploring him. "I want to talk with you. Can we do that? There's so much more to be said."

He sighed and realized she'd just done something that was hard for her. "Amelia, I didn't inform you of my schedule for Northshire, because I didn't understand what there was to discuss. I can say yes to 'let's talk,' but I'm not sure why and have no idea how or when. Now, really—I must run."

"Can you call me Milly again, and will you let me work on that?"

He had one step out the door, and the snow billowed in the entryway. "Sure … I'm sorry, but I must go." He waved goodbye and exited toward the monsignor's carriage.

She kept the door open, waving as he trudged through the blizzard to the snow-covered carriage, the horse snorting and shaking his head at the blinding flakes.

Without looking back, he climbed in, wrapping the heavy blanket around his shoulders. The carriage headed back to the center of town and the warmth of the hotel bar. *An unusual departure,* he thought, *what's on her mind?* He wondered if he'd hear from her. It didn't matter, he thought, foremost on his mind was his work and whether to return to Europe.

Slowly she closed the door. She tried, she thought, and couldn't read him. So hard to understand. She had no idea if any of his original interest remained. Yet he gave her a gift, although her mother and aunt got the same gift. She sighed. What did she expect? He agreed to talk, but she wondered, what if he had no interest in talking to her but was too much a gentleman to refuse. It didn't matter, she concluded. She couldn't get him out of her head. She had to find out what he thought of her. If it were nothing, it would free her to consider Carl's proposal more seriously.

Carl's pressure was mounting; he wanted to announce their engagement over the Christmas holidays. His persistence, almost annoying, was driving her to talk with Jeremiah.

Chapter 28

At dinner, the monsignor waxed on about the floor of St. Steven's and what he called Jeremiah's unusual characteristic. "The singularity of the man's focus is astounding. Couldn't get him to talk while they laid the floor no matter what I said or asked. He paid no attention. He concentrated only on his work, getting the design lined up perfectly, never seen anything like it."

Clary had been quiet during the meal; she had not yet removed the scarf Jeremiah had given her. She fingered the tassels at the end of the scarf gently and glanced around the table at her family. She said, "Monsignor, that's not true. He's not singular in the least. His mind roves over many topics and in interesting ways. For example, the poor in Northshire have caught his attention. And you've all seen that he's not afraid to express his mind on the design of St. Steven's. What's singular about him, if that's the right phrase, is that he has exceptional focus. He wants what he's doing to be the best, and he fears no one, bows to no one in the pursuit of excellence."

Milly glanced at Clary. "When did the topic of the poor come up?"

All eyes turned to Clary, and they stopped eating as they gazed at her.

She gave a little laugh. "I was at the church earlier today, looking at the progress on the floor of the altar and saying a little prayer for my late husband. Jeremiah entered with more marble for the floor. He came to me and asked who were the people huddled on the steps of our city hall. I told him that's where the poor go to get a slip for groceries. He said, 'Why do they need to line up in public like that? That's humiliating.' There's much better ways to help them. And he described a program they have in Worcester. It's very clever."

Stephanie placed a hand on Clary's arm. "We've talked of him before Clary, and you described him as intense in his opinions and set in his ways. You wondered why he was not married at age thirty or so."

Clary patted her sister's hand then glanced at Milly. "No, no, Stephanie. Not set in his ways but more … I'll use the word *particular*. He won't do something until it is just right for him, no compromise whether it's a helping hand to the poor, an altar, a statue, or I imagine, a woman." She gave a quick glance toward Milly. "I'm guessing he's never found the right woman, and he won't compromise."

"I'll say he's particular, actually damn peculiar to me," Driscoll inserted. "He didn't like the church then decides to do it, says he'll work in Northshire then changes the work location to Worcester. Now we have to go there to see it. Damn inconvenient."

The monsignor glanced over at Driscoll. "We're going to Worcester next Wednesday, right?"

"Yep," Driscoll answered. "Three days after Christmas. Well, I really can't complain. He's ahead of schedule, wants to show us his progress."

"Very thoughtful of him to give us the cigars and Jamesons," the monsignor added. He liked Jeremiah and knew Driscoll was trying to find ways to dislike the self-assured sculptor who basically found his church unappealing. The monsignor was bothered by the same issue but couldn't bring himself to hold Jeremiah's opinion as a grudge. He couldn't put his finger on exactly what he liked, but the young sculptor gave him comfort, confidence in the quality, and beauty of the altar. In character, he found Jeremiah to be unusually direct. He had no fears about being honest and was surprisingly nonreligious. The last part puzzled him yet amused him. How could he do such exquisite ecclesiastical work and not be a strong Catholic?

Clary glanced at both men. "Jeremiah mentioned that the two side sections of the altar were coming along nicely. Is that what you're going to see? If so, I'd like to come."

Driscoll rubbed his head. "I dunno, Clary … it's …"

Stephanie said, "Aha, a conspiracy. You're hiding something from us. I think we should all go. After all, we women influenced the choice." She waved her hand at her husband. "I'll change that to we made the altar decision. We truly have a vested interest." She turned her attention to her daughter. "Milly, interested?"

"Definitely, Mother."

The monsignor chuckled loudly. "Jackie, it looks like we have some delightful company for our journey next week. I wonder what Mr. Knox will think of our little surprise party."

Milly bit her lower lip and thought, *I'll make certain it's not a surprise to Jeremiah*. After dinner, she had the strong desire to telephone him and thank him again for the gift and inform him of the gaggle of Driscolls coming next week. She knew he was in Northshire's lone hotel, drinking with his crew of masons so she sat at her desk to draft him a letter. In it she mentioned the forthcoming visit and that she was looking forward to seeing him. She asked if it would be possible for them to have a dinner alone on the day they arrived. She knew she'd have to manage the evening arrangement with her parents and Clary; they would be surprised, possibly confused, and quite likely offended by her desire to dine alone with Jeremiah.

Unaware of Milly's plans, Jeremiah was at work with Antonio Biasi. The side sections of the altar were taking shape. The high spires with their intricate lace work were ready for Jeremiah's chisel. At noon, he put down his tools, and McGuinness walked up to him.

He said, "Join me for some cheese and bread. You need a break."

Jeremiah eyed him suspiciously, "Somethin' on your mind, boss? When was the last time we broke bread together?"

"Too long ago, and yes, I have something on my mind."

"Go ahead, I've got a feeling I'm gonna get screwed."

McGuinness's grin broke into a hearty laugh. "Now some people I know are easy to screw, but you ... I doubt anyone's ever screwed you. And I wouldn't know where to start."

They both laughed; Jeremiah said, "It looks like my Northshire altar has crowded out a lot of your other work. Your guys are all jammed in that corner over there." He pointed to a cold drafty end of the shed where a group of men in coats and gloves worked on a set of gravestones side by side.

McGuinness was eating his sandwich, and his laughter interfered with his chewing. He said, "I'm giving you the best space 'cause you pay better than any of my normal clients. You get the best workers too. What I have in mind is to build you space. Your own space."

"How would that work?"

"There's excess acreage on this lot. You'd pay rent for the land and building. You'll have access to my workers, but it will be your own studio." Like we've been doing, but you won't have any space problems.

"It's very kind of you and worth much thought."

McGuinness expected a quick yes. He gazed at Jeremiah, worried. "Is there another offer or arrangement you'd prefer?"

"No … well, actually, I'm considering spending more time in Europe."

"Permanently?"

"Possibly." He watched for McGuinness's reaction.

McGuinness held his speech, his eyes searching Jeremiah face for clues to this surprising statement. He said, "Something happened hasn't it? If you want to talk about it, I'm here. But, Jeremiah, don't go. Your future is unlimited in this country. I can't imagine a better future anywhere else."

"There's many ideas afloat. If there's to be a change, you'll be the first to know. As you know, you've been instrumental to my success."

McGuinness stood up and offered his hand. "Take your time, my friend. We've come a long way in a short time, haven't we?"

"Indeed, we have. I never expected I'd be in this position when I arrived at your shed fourteen years ago."

"Well, let's get a builder for some estimates. I'll work out some rent numbers, and we'll get started. It'll give you an alternative to Europe and give me time to convince you to stay." He walked around his cramped space, a big smile on his face. "I like the idea of you next door. Your own studio so to speak. I like it."

That night, her letter in hand, Jeremiah called the Driscoll house, and Amelia answered, "Well, hello, Amelia, so pleased to catch you."

"Likewise, Jeremiah. Did you receive my letter?"

"It's in my hand. McGuinness and I are delighted that the whole gang, so to speak, will visit."

They bantered about the altar, Jeremiah emphasized that there was much work to be done. He mentioned that they would be working the stone on that day and asked if the group wanted to see the artisans at work. Milly's interest in seeing Jeremiah at work was high, and she conveyed her interest but could not comment on the interest of the others. Then she moved to her main question. "Jeremiah, in my letter, I suggested dinner for the two of us. Is that possible?" She was sitting in a chair next to their telephone. The chair creaked as she moved, trying to find a comfortable position for her slim body. One hand was on the phone, and the other, with fingers crossed, was in her lap.

"I hope I'm not being too bold by asking you to dinner."

"No, not at all." The words came out slowly. He was perplexed by the request. She wanted time alone. Why? "So it's just us?"

"Yes, is that okay?"

He knew she wanted to talk, but what was the topic? He remembered that she had gripped his hand hard after he left his holiday gifts. She had pleaded for a conversation. Her gestures surprised him then as her desire to dine confused him now. He returned to his initial thought—what's she thinking? He wanted to ask yet decided he'd save the question for dinner. "Does your family or the monsignor need any dinner or hotel reservations? I can do that if it's helpful."

"No, they have their travel and accommodations all settled. By the way, the monsignor wants to see your statues in Worcester. I suggested it, and he's called the clergy at St. Paul's and St. John's."

"Well, that's nice of you. If he wants my assistance, let me know. Otherwise, we'll see you on the 28th at the train station."

He met them with two rented carriages. Sorting out who wanted to ride with whom created a jumble of conversation, which Jeremiah watched with amusement. He hadn't realized the altar created such interest among the women and concluded it must be due to his holiday gifts. But the Driscoll clan and the monsignor all had other motives. Each wanted a private moment with the sculptor to present their latest design ideas. Stephanie and Clary had brought books on altars in Europe to show Jeremiah they had special interest in floral motifs on the spires. Milly wished to confirm their dinner arrangements while Driscoll wanted assurance that the sections could be shipped to Northshire without breakage. For his part, the monsignor was planning to encourage Jeremiah, with a little more cash if necessary, to add statues to the sides of the altar to distinguish it from the bishop's altar in the Springfield. Jeremiah opened the doors to each carriage, assisting the women into one carriage and the men another. To their surprise, he avoided conversation by climbing up to the driver's seat of the men's carriage, merrily chatting with the driver until they reached McGuinness's shed.

Jeremiah ushered them to the area where two side sections were protected under large sheets of canvas. He removed the covers; the white marble spires were beginning to take shape. As they gazed at their shape, Jeremiah explained the ornamental designs he and Biasi were placing on the side of each spire. The questions flew at him, and over the period of an hour, he'd explained the design and accepted several of their suggestions for details he and Biasi could easily accommodate. He knew from the questions and requests that they liked the work; in fact, they were in awe of the unfinished product.

When they had become quiet, Jeremiah said, "Wait till you see the center section of the altar. It's much taller. It's very dramatic and will fill the large sanctuary perfectly."

Driscoll went to the marble and tapped it with his fingers. He said, "This is looking good, Jeremiah, but I don't see how you're going to get all those intricate patterns on this hard surface."

"Patience, Mr. Driscoll, patience. They're all inside waiting to be brought out, you'll see."

They talked about the schedule to finish the sidepieces and the centerpiece. Jeremiah admitted the centerpiece was going more slowly, and he needed to get back to Siena to accelerate the work. It was late afternoon when he offered the carriage to take them back to their hotel; Amelia demurred. She wanted to stay and watch Jeremiah work. He acknowledged her request by bringing a stool for her to sit near the altar's side section. Once she was settled, he began to work the edges of the spire, first one side then the other, carefully balancing the design on one to match the design on the opposite side, back and forth. She noticed that he was carving angels, one on the left side in the center of the spire and one on the right side also centered in the spire. They appeared to be looking or pointing at each other, and she sought confirmation of her observation. She asked him about the angels. Were they similar to the two angels on a tombstone that he'd carved years ago? He grunted a monosyllabic reply. She asked other questions, but his concentration was so great she realized her queries were unwelcomed distractions. She noticed after one leaf or part of angel was carved, he'd stop and look at it, maybe rest for a minute or two, then begin again. Often, he and Biasi would stop and share thoughts or problems then continue, always in their own world. She'd never observed such total concentration, and it fascinated her. Yet deep in her mind she wondered, how different was the artistic personality from a personality like hers? She wondered if she would be compatible with someone dominated by these traits.

She knew now, as she watched him work, that her impulse to talk with him privately was right. She had to make a decision about Carl's proposal. This man, this Jeremiah Knox, who seemed to show no interest in her, was nevertheless in the way. She wanted to know that her interest in him was well founded. She had to address the gnawing sensation that his arresting presence in her mind was real, that Jeremiah Knox was not a shimmering fancy to slip away once she knew him better. Then she had to know—the uncertainty bothered her deeply—did he have an interest in her? Months ago, he seemed to desire a closer association, then he disappeared in Italy. Was his interest fleeting, now over? Their dinner conversation couldn't come soon enough.

Milly worked hard to convince her parents to dine without her at their hotel. She made it clear to them that she wanted to get to know Jeremiah and that would be best done alone.

Driscoll appeared surprised. "You're interested in this chap, this stonemason? What about Carl?"

Her mother was less surprised and smiled at her daughter. "How nice, Milly. Is this a final test? Is this a way to know if Carl is right for you?"

Milly said, "This dinner will tell me a lot about the best kind of man for me."

Driscoll, a scowl still on his face, said, "A stonemason. Milly, I'd pictured you with a man like Carl, a lawyer."

Her stare burned into his face. "Father, it's not the work, it's the man, and I haven't found too many men that I admire in Western Massachusetts. And besides, it's clear from his work, very few can do what he does. He's a sculptor, an artist."

"Well, gosh darn, Milly, artists tend to starve."

"Not this one," countered Stephanie. "Look at his fees for the altar, Jackie. You showed me the numbers. His fees are more than any doctor or lawyer makes in a year. And this is just one of his jobs."

She turned to her daughter. "Are you interested in the young man, Milly? I told you that he was interested in you."

"I know you did, Mother, but I didn't believe you and still don't. I felt you had misread his interest, guessed incorrectly. What you saw was his natural curiosity. He's interested in everything, as Clary said, but I don't believe he has a real interest in me."

Stephanie helped her daughter dress for the evening while Driscoll sat grumpily in a chair, reading the local newspaper. When Jeremiah arrived to take her to dinner, he noticed a heightened interest and cordiality in their greeting. The lingering stares, the compliments over his red silk paisley scarf, and his top hat were too obvious. He smiled and offered a nod of appreciation. Connie's parents had similar behaviors, and this type of comment made him uneasy. Flattery, no matter how well delivered, made him question its sincerity and purpose. Were they really commenting on his clothing, or was there something else going on? He didn't know. He didn't flatter in return; it was against his grain. He wanted to compliment Milly, who looked exceptionally lovely, but he would save his observations for their moments together if they seemed appropriate and welcomed.

In the numbing cold of late December, they walked briskly from the hotel. Their breaths exhaled soft white clouds in the dark air as they walked two blocks to the Armitage. The sidewalks were cleared of snow, but occasionally, a patch would appear and crinkle under their feet. He made no attempt to hold her arm for safety or comfort. She shivered slightly, and he said to her, "That's the restaurant just ahead. You'll be warm in no time. It's considered one of the best in the city. Let's hope we like it."

"You haven't been here previously?"

"No, it's new to me."

How could one be so casual? she wondered. During the afternoon, he handled her family and the monsignor with ease where his work was on display, thousands of dollars involved. Now he seemed totally relaxed with her while she felt full of tension. Yet he did this all the time. He did a different sculpture in an unfamiliar city, in another country month after month, year after year. Facing new people with differing demands, where did this confidence come from? These questions flitted through her mind as they were seated at dinner, and the tuxedoed waiters asked their preferences for drinks while explaining the menu. She wanted to ask her questions, and each time she began, a waiter arrived to fill their water glasses or to bring her a sherry and a Jameson for him. She laughed. "I've been trying to get a question out, and they keep arriving. I didn't realize that you attract a lot of attention."

"Oh, don't be silly," he admonished her. "They're coming to see you. You're the attraction."

"But you're so at ease with a constant flow of strangers. Does that come from your travel?"

"Never thought about it. Perhaps."

"But your travel and constantly working with new people is amazing to me. How do you do it?"

"I'm not sure what you're asking."

"For instance, is it a joy to see new places or a burden?"

He gazed at her for several moments. What did she want or expect from this question? He said, "For fourteen years, I've worked in different locales to build altars in churches. I've never found that to be a burden."

"It never became a hardship, never interfered with other aspects of your life that were or are important."

289

Again, he took his time in responding, thinking of Ireland, Italy, and Germany, sipping his drink and wiping his mouth with the lily-white napkin. "Most of the people I've worked with and respect have frequent travel and demanding schedules too, so I never thought I was any different."

"I see." She sank back in her chair and appeared thoughtful for a moment. The waiter arrived with their dinner dishes, and she glanced up at him, offering a radiant smile. "Thank you," she said. "It looks delicious."

She parried with her food, pushing the filet of flounder around with her fork to the point where he asked her, "Amelia, is the fish not tasty? We can send it back."

"Oh no, and please call me Milly," she replied smiling. "My minds in another place, and it's hard to concentrate on eating."

He decided to let her comment sit and resumed carving small slices of roast beef, which he devoured with great relish. He had the sense that she was deliberating some large topic but was unsure how to proceed. Twice he glanced over at her, breaking the quiet impasse with small remarks on the quality of his meal. She smiled weakly in return. Whatever she wanted to talk about wasn't coming out. She must have a delicate topic but doesn't know where to start. He felt he should help her along, break the ice so to speak.

"Milly, if I may, how do you and your fellow teachers maintain a hearty social life in a girls' school?"

"Oh, it's not easy, Jeremiah, but we manage. Our families make introductions, and last year, our Latin teacher introduced me to her cousin Carl—you met him—who was quite charming."

"When you're as busy as we both are, it's hard to meet new people." He added, "I depend on my friends for introductions or invitations to balls or other social functions."

"Do you frequent balls and similar festivities, Jeremiah?"

"Not frequently. Often they're in Boston. Mostly I don't have the time to get there."

"Given your travels and devotion to your career, do you ever see yourself settling down into a more sedate life?"

"I had a good friend. We saw each other frequently for a few years, and we had this conversation often. She concluded that to have a demanding career and to excel in it, one needed to give every ounce of energy and time to that work. No real settling down so to speak."

Here it was, she thought. Finally, she discovered his reluctance to show her interest to become more involved. Perhaps that woman doctor had turned him sour on women and marriage. Had he'd concluded that his career demanded a monastic life as well? She took a deep breath and thought, *Be very direct.* "In the final analysis, did you agree with her decision?"

"She's doing something quite unusual. She's become one of the few female physicians in Massachusetts and a surgeon at that. In terms of a decision, the more I thought about it, the more I realized it was the right decision for her. I can't see her doing all the family things while being the first female physician in the east."

"You talked of her when I visited in the spring. She sounds most impressive."

He nodded but said no more.

She waited for more conversation about this woman, but none came. She wanted more, so she motored on, "Do you think a demanding career like yours would interfere with a desire for family life?"

His smile was wide. *So this is what it's about,* he surmised. He reached across the table and took her hand. "Now, you're a highly educated woman, Milly. What about Ulysses? What about Mark Antony? What about Rochester from *Jane Eyre*? If I remember that novel correctly, it depends on the woman, doesn't it? Some women have considerable influence on a man's career."

She liked the feel of his hand. She twisted her hand so she could lace her fingers with his and said, "Your hand is so strong. Is that from your work?"

He said, "I think that men—and I can only speak from the men I've known or read about—are capable of great love, great devotion, and great work. I believe they can combine all these facets of life."

"Were the men you worked with in Ireland married? What were those women like?"

"In the Fenian movement, many of the men were married. Often, the women were more capable, smarter than the men. Some of the men were famous writers, intellectuals, and their wives were their equals. In fact, many of the women were more interesting, more effective than the men."

"I can tell. You miss Europe, all the political action there. That's why you go back every year, isn't it?"

"Yes, in a way I miss it, yet I love what I'm doing here."

"Would you consider going back, full-time I mean?"

He gave her hand a squeeze and pulled them both closer together across the table. His eyes fixed on hers. "Milly, if we decide to get closer as a couple, it will be important for you to know my thoughts on work, where I see my future."

"Jeremiah, I'd like us to be closer as we discussed last spring. Can we forget what happened in October? Can we start now? I'd like to know what drives you, pleases you."

He released her hand and pulled away. He leaned back in his chair and thought, *Here it goes*. He reminded her that he'd described his commitment to work in America when they met on the spring. Now, he told her of his conversations with Callahan, O'Farrell, and Pietro, the European opportunities. When she asked about the challenges in each country, he was precise and insightful of the risks and what he'd lose by leaving America. He saw her emotions sway from quiet reflection to laughter as he described each character and his experiences with them. He was unsure what she thought as they finished their coffee.

She took his arm as they walked to the cloakroom and gazed at him as they bundled into their coats and walked out into the cold night. They took a few steps away from the hotel. A light dusting of snow had begun, and it clung to their coats and placed a white crown on their hats. She stopped, once away from the lights of the hotel, her breath exhaling a slight mist in the cold air. She waited until his expression became a concern then tucked her head beneath his hat and gave him a long kiss, holding him tightly at his shoulder. She liked his response, so she held the kiss even longer, then took his arm, and they continued walking.

"To what do I owe that great pleasure?" he asked.

"For sharing your life with me, being open about your future. For being a remarkable man, I dunno, many other things too."

His hat had been pushed awry by their kisses, and he adjusted it, glancing at her as they continued their walk. He said, "My interests or aspirations as I view them, they don't frighten you?"

"Not at all. And if you'll let me, I'd like to be part of what you decide. I'd like to keep talking about your aspirations as you call them."

"I should add," he said, "that your kiss was exquisite … I think you're an amazing mix of beauty, brains, and charm to the likes I've never seen. Your flexibility over my next steps in life amazes me."

She flicked her eyes toward him as she walked straight away. "Is it safe to say we plan to see a lot of each other?" Milly asked.

"That's a safe statement from my side."

Abruptly she stopped and faced him. "You'll write to me often and come to Springfield or Northshire on weekends when possible?"

"I don't like to write as you know, but I will try. Better yet is for me to come to Springfield or Northshire on weekends and you can come to Worcester on occasion."

"Only with chaperones, and that's not easy to arrange."

"Okay, we'll do it the easiest way at first and perhaps get more inventive later."

She took his arm once more and began walking. Her pace picked up as she shuddered in the cold. "I just want to see more of you regardless of how busy you are."

"And I, you. We'll make it happen."

Chapter 29

The New Year began with a gala party at the Parker House in Boston. The Sullivans agreed to host and chaperone Milly. She came to Worcester two days before the festive evening to enjoy more time with Jeremiah. It was her last free days prior to the start of winter term at St. Agatha's. She assembled a near trunk load of clothes to cover the formal party at the Parker House and the myriad functions and parties that Jeremiah had arranged. Her mother accompanied Milly to the Sullivans, and Jeremiah planned to travel back to Northshire with her as he returned to work on the alcoves adjacent to the altar at St. Steven's.

Over the holidays, Jeremiah was flooded with mail from well-wishers and from those inquiring about new business. The population in the New England states was exploding, and the immigrants wished to continue their religious rituals. New churches and seminaries were being planned throughout the region. In addition, the rapid growth of industry had created a sizable bastion of wealthy patrons who wanted statues in their homes, fountains in their gardens, and art museums in their names. Jeremiah was awash with opportunities to bid on these new projects. He tried to select those that were closest to Northshire, but that was not simple. Many of the more interesting opportunities in size, beauty, and significant fees were farther away. Inquiries came in from Portland, Maine; Providence, Rhode Island; Bristol; and Stamford, Connecticut, all substantially distant from Northshire.

While in Worcester, Milly saw another side to Jeremiah. With the Sullivan carriage at her disposal, she and Alice Sullivan made a tour of Jeremiah's apartment buildings, or three-deckers as he called them. She met Hamish and his wife. She met some of Jeremiah's tenants. She read his Christmas letters from his sister, brothers, and mother in Ireland. She was surprised by the formality in the family letters and heartened by the warmth she observed from his apartment tenants. He seemed different with his tenants, chatty, engaging, more sociable than he was at work.

As she and Alice Sullivan toured Worcester, she counted ten buildings owned by Jeremiah. Being good at numbers, she began to calculate his income from the apartments. She had assisted her father with his business accounts, and if her numbers were remotely close, his income from these units alone dwarfed her fathers. And that did not include his fees from the altars and other ecclesiastical sculptures nor dividends from his investment holdings. Now, she knew for certain he was a solid businessperson as well as an artist. And he had showed her warmth in their recent meetings, but she remembered the chill from his indifference in the fall. She saw a range of dimensions in his character. He was as cool as a cash register in his business decisions yet wildly imaginative and intuitive in his sculpture, warm in personal associations at one moment and cold as ice at other times. She'd never seen such discipline and drive in person, yet he could be casual and relaxed as well. At thirty-four, she wondered, would any of these aspects of his character change? Should they change and in what direction would be best for her? She knew, if they were to marry, some aspects of his daily, weekly, and yearly behaviors would have to change; but would he be willing to make those changes? She wanted a man at home. She wanted to continue to teach. She wanted children. Was he that kind of man? Did he want that kind of life? The one character feature that worried her most was his commitment to his art, his work, and the incredible demands of time, energy, and travel it placed on him.

While these thoughts would capture her attention for a moment, they would disappear as rapidly. The evening at the Parker House was divine for her. The food, champagne, and fine dancing filled her with joy. They talked that evening and on through the next day about their appreciation of each other. The talk was more formal than Milly expected. Jeremiah was careful about his feelings and emotions while she was eager to talk of her blossoming love.

To Jeremiah, it became clear that she wanted a formal declaration of a courtship.

He was unused to the custom. Connie had never sought such a declaration. They discussed what this meant to her, and she emphasized that he would have her complete attention, and she wanted the same in return. She wanted to see him on most weekends and always when he worked on St. Steven's. To him, she was refreshing, a delightfully different type of woman from Connie or others he knew. So he was inclined to meet her wishes for frequency and predictability of visits, yet they seemed unnecessarily structured to him. With her precise arguments, she explained that his demanding schedule required this type of organization. Her thoughts made sense to his logical mind. So he agreed. He made these commitments with the full intent to honor them, to keep them. Keeping true to his word turned out to be more difficult than he expected, and unfortunately, she noticed.

A request for drawings came from the Archdiocese of Providence, and Jeremiah was fascinated. A new church was being constructed upon a hilltop near Brown University. It was large in scale, over a thousand seats, designed to attract the growing population of the nearby neighborhoods and the students at Brown. The bishop had seen several of Jeremiah's altars and had a strong interest in bringing one of his designs into the city. The scale of the altar and the numerous statues on the altar and along its sides combined into a substantial project. The negotiations were lengthy. The Bishop was a skilled and tough negotiator and contested Jeremiah and the lead contractor on material prices, labor costs, and on Jeremiah's fee. The daily work, once it began, required more attention than Jeremiah had planned to provide. The bishop insisted that Jeremiah do all his stone carving on site and held back payment when Jeremiah ignored the request.

Workers at the church often saw Jeremiah stooping over and talking heatedly to the shorter more burly bishop, both faces red, arms gesturing energetically and eventually bodies turning away, each still muttering to the wind. The arguments focused on Jeremiah's presence at the site. The bishop wanted to see him work, to view the altar emerge from flat blocks of marble to a finished, shimmering place for worship. He would take no chances that the clever Irishman would have the work done by lesser stonemasons at his shop in Worcester; he trusted no one. The one who lost in this test of wills was Milly. For many of the months that spring, Jeremiah was in Providence during the week as the final work in Northshire did not need his attention. On weekends, he was tired and frustrated by the bishop and wanted to be in Worcester, attending to his other projects and interests. In the long run, the bishop did Milly a favor. His management attitude ground at Jeremiah in a way that caused him to reconsider how to address and deal with difficult clients. No longer would he readily accept an intriguing project until he learned the nature and character of the client. He knew he had to master the skill to detect the good from the difficult clients.

As the months in the New Year wore on, Jeremiah was working twelve to fifteen hours a day to finish the work in Northshire and to make needed progress in Providence. He had to complete much of his own work in Providence before early July when he was scheduled to go to Italy and complete the central altarpiece for St. Steven's. When the work started, he told the bishop of his commitment to Siena, and the bishop agreed as long as certain progress was made in his church. As the months rolled by, Jeremiah was getting more and more concerned that the bishop's sense of progress may be different than his.

These worries spilled into the courtship of Milly and Jeremiah. As the end of June neared and the passage to Italy was imminent, she said, "I want you to reflect and think about the past six months. We pledged time together, and that has been less than I'd hoped. Is this a one-time problem that will never happen again? Or …" Here she paused for emphasis and waited for his complete attention. "Has it happened before, but wasn't a problem for you because you were not courting?"

His eyes down, he glanced away from her. He said, "I'll think it through, but I'm worried you might be on to something. Tough jobs do happen and take more time and attention than I want. It might be just part of this business."

"How will you know whether it's just the bishop or whether it was the same in the past too?"

"I plan to look through my records, and my memory's pretty good on every job I've done. Plus, I want to read about other sculptors and their patrons. What problems did they have?"

"That's good. I'll miss you this summer, but in the fall, we'll resume this talk."

"Are you certain about Siena? You can't get there this summer?"

"It will take me from my graduate studies, and I'd just be in the way, making your life even more miserable than it's been this winter and spring."

Each time he had these conversations, he thought about his discussions with Connie about the demands of difficult careers. He dug deep into his memories. What was life like for his professors at Edinburgh? Did the sculptors in Italy and France have wives and families? What about his own family and the families of the Fenians? The wave of memory he sought began in a trickle and then became a flood. One feature that emerged was his own family's life. He'd largely ignored it when he left Ireland. But as he thought back, he remembered the early years when his older brothers and sister teased him yet protected him. He recalled the mirth and vitality of family dinners with everyone talking whether in agreement or argument. The noise was boisterous and rich with life. His current life was aesthetic in comparison. He'd grown accustomed to the bachelor life, its solitary pleasures, its tremendous freedoms; yet when he touched these family memories, he knew his current life was absent the companionship and love a family provided. He was surprised to find that he missed some the old family interactions.

In repose one evening, he laughed, thinking of the odd mixture of personalities in his family. His oldest brother, Tommy, whom he always considered the family idiot, was a good farmer, had become a good husband and father, yet was a wee narrow-minded on topics apart from his Angus herd or the barley crop. And Timothy, dear sweet Timothy, the priest, all piety and philosophy, quiet and humorous, always supportive of Jeremiah's ideas even when he disagreed. And his mother and father, he shuddered now at how often he challenged their beliefs with his radical thoughts for Ireland while they fought for their Unionist positions. Yet he acknowledged that their love for each other was always evident, always there. It was a strict and formal family, but it was welcoming and thoughtful as well. He had turned against family life without realizing he'd done that. They had not supported his Fenian interests, so he ignored their existence. Even today, over a decade later, he could not forgive or forget what they'd done and not done. Yet he decided he needed to reconsider his family situation. It wasn't all bad, and his inner feelings were recognizing a truth he had pushed away. He realized that he needed to separate his Fenian activities from the life he had with his family. They had backed off from him and he from them, but the exile to America was due to his decisions, not theirs.

There was good in his family's life, and Milly reminded him to think more deeply about his views on family life, on a wife, on children. She emphasized the importance of family life to society, to physical and mental health, and that it could make a career richer, not poorer. On the last point, he had his doubts, but he needed to give the idea more thought. He had told her about his exile to the United States, and she was not surprised, mentioning other families in the state that had come from political problems.

After ensuring that he had left that part of his life behind, she quickly put aside her worries about his political ideas. He was in a country where those battles had been fought and won a century before. She was more interested in how he viewed a family given the disappointments with his own. It was an honest conversation that became a running topic with them. Each weekend she saw him, the lively banter about daily vignettes would eventually drift toward life together and what that would look like, what that would mean. He learned that she had given family life extensive thought and had a well-developed philosophy and an even more detailed sense of how the days, weeks, and years would be occupied. He'd not given any thought to such matters and left each session with her overwhelmed with information to digest. And as he took his train to one destination or another, he would think about her thoughts, but eventually, he'd drift back to the work to be done. His excitement came as he thought how to improve the fine detail on an altar or statue, how to make the designs in a bell tower evident from a great distance. How to use a new hand drill and make it part of his skill set intrigued him more than the thought of how to best educate their children. *That kind of daily living detail will work itself out when the time comes,* he thought.

When he departed for Italy in late June, he had the long steamship trip to Genoa to think about these matters. Milly had given him a set of notes on her thoughts of how her work would continue when they married, how to manage a household, and when to have children. He chuckled at the organization of her topics, like lesson plans at her school done completely in her neat handwriting. Each day, he'd take a set of pages to an easy chair on the deck. He'd plunk down with a blanket at the ready, prepared if the wind became chilly, and read with fascination her detailed and precise thinking on the nuances of a married life. Did other women think this way? Certainly Connie didn't. Connie preferred to live spontaneously and alone rather than unravel the large burdens and the unfathomable mysteries that came with a spouse and children. She claimed a career in medicine was hard enough. Why put more on one's self?

As the ship pitched through the waves, he walked the decks, letting these thoughts spin through his mind. He became a solitary figure strolling the decks, tipping his hat to fellow strollers but rarely engaging in conversation. On stormy days, he'd bundled up in a slicker, and with his head down, he'd push through the wind and occasional spray to drive his thinking to a conclusion. Was marriage right for him? Would he be right for her given his muddled perspective on marriage and his devotion to his art?

When he finally reached Siena, he knew Pietro's experience on the mix of marriage and sculpture would be helpful and sought to include his long time artistic colleague in his deliberations.

Before he settled down to work in the studio, Pietro said, "These letters anticipated your arrival here. One from a Mr. Callahan in Dublin and another from the crazy man in Berlin, O'Farrell." Jeremiah read them quickly and put them aside to read more carefully later. Both letters encouraged his visits to Ireland and Germany as he had promised when he left last year. He sighed. How would he explain this interest to Milly?

Pietro's studio was as dusty as in previous visits despite his intentions to clean it. Jeremiah couldn't understand how the stonemasons accomplished skilled work amid the clutter of statues, vases, fountainheads, and ornaments arrayed around them yet stunning statues, tables, and friezes emerged each day. The Northshire altar stood in a back corner, covered in chalky dust, surrounded by saw horses and two six-foot-tall vases. Jeremiah entered the room and shook his head. He was greeted by a cluster of hellos in English and Italian and many claps on the back. They walked to the altar, Pietro explaining what had been done and where he thought Jeremiah should concentrate his efforts. He handed Jeremiah a long-handled feather duster and left him to clean the altar and prepare it for work.

Jeremiah was dressed in his work clothes of rugged leather shoes, heavy twill pants, a long-sleeved white cotton shirt, and a cotton jacket. He removed the jacket, rolled up the sleeves of his white shirt, and began to clean the tall structure. He could see where they left work for him. They hadn't touched the delicate filigree along the sides of the spires nor the carvings of the figurines in the tabernacle. He yelled over the tumult in the room, "This looks good, Pietro. Tomorrow and together, we'll tackle the spires. Can we do that?"

In blast of Italian mixed with a few English words, Pietro hollered across the room, "I'd prefer to discuss the design of the figures for the tabernacle and work on those while you do the spires. Your great height is an advantage there, and you work the delicacy of filigree better than I." They agreed to a work plan, and Jeremiah returned to dusting the altar.

That evening, after a dinner of seafood pasta, veal scallopini, and a creamy panna cotta, the children were whisked away. Jeremiah and Pietro sat at the long, rough board wooden table. The two men sipped a hearty Tuscan grappa, the musty bottle in front of them, while Kinga toyed with a sweet Prosecco. Jeremiah sipped the grappa and let it slowly leave his mouth. The sharp bite tickled his throat, and he let the pleasure and the burning sensation linger. He extended his long legs under the table, and fully relaxed, he said, "It's a perfect time for me to ask you a personal question."

Over the years, Kinga and Pietro had many dinners with Jeremiah, and his conversations centered on his work with Pietro, the art in Italy, or the politics in both countries. Their eyes widened, and both sipped their drinks, awaiting a surprise. In his many visits, Jeremiah had rarely talked of anything personal. They knew very little about his life outside of his work in sculpture. Pietro had confided to his wife that their friend was a private man, a man who preferred solitude.

"Like a monk?" she had suggested.

And he had agreed with her in part but reminded her of Connie, whom he'd met on trips to Worcester. "Brainy and bossy" was his observation. In prior visits, he mentioned to Kinga that his cousins and the Countess Maria had enjoyed Jeremiah's company and confided that he was no monk. So he laughed at his wife's insights and offered the thought that Jeremiah liked many women and did not prefer to be saddled with one.

While Pietro was still sipping his grappa, Kinga said, "Of course, with us you can ask anything."

Jeremiah placed his glass on the table and stared at the clear liquid. It was half gone. He said, "Since I was last here, I've met a woman. She's the daughter of the general contractor for the church in Northshire, the congregation that wants the big altar." He stopped to ensure they were following him. His eyes told him they were riveted to his disclosure. "She's talking marriage, and I, for a change, am listening."

Kinga appeared to be jolted from her chair. She sat straight up and simply stared at Jeremiah. She was lost for words. She started to speak in Italian then tried English, and nothing coherent emerged.

Pietro broke the silence. "That's good news, in fact wonderful, if it's the same for you."

"It is good. I'm very happy yet full of questions."

"Like what?" Pietro asked.

"Well, my big question is how do you maintain your incredible work when you have wonderful Kinga here?" He pointed at her with the glass that was wrapped in his hand. "Then there's the five children, your workers, and the work that takes you to Rome, Cetona, Pisa, Montepulciano, and so on."

Pietro waved his hands, his face expressing surprise. "I could never do this alone. They sustain me."

Jeremiah turned to Kinga. "How do you manage when he travels to Rome for several weeks or comes to the US for two months?"

"It's not easy, Jeremiah," she replied. "I miss him. I miss the help in the house, but I have my sisters and cousins to help, so it all works. But most importantly, his work brings him joy, and that joy comes to live in our home."

He thought about Milly and wondered if she would respond in a similar way. He would ask her and tell her of this conversation. He liked Pietro's answer. Apparently, it gave enormous energy to his work because his family believed in what he was doing. This response was so different than Connie's philosophy that demanding work requires one's full attention and that focus should not be diluted by mundane matters, such as the bourgeois values of family life. To Pietro and Kinga, a family life enhanced what he did artistically. As the conversation went on, Jeremiah listened to Pietro's rambling philosophy of how one's immediate family was a microcosm of the larger family who were uplifted and gratified by the glory of a church's interior. He explained that the art in a church took this family of Catholics to a different place, a better place once they entered. The beauty of the surroundings gave the celebrants relief from their daily strife, enabled them with art that was not part of their everyday life, and transported them to see the divine, to see life as something much larger than their own direct experience.

He listened with full attention. He had not had this conversation with anyone in the United States. He would bring these ideas to Milly.

Pietro asked, "Does this woman—what is her name, Jeremiah? Does she believe as we do? Would she agree with what we've said?"

"Amelia, Milly to me, that's her name. Very beautiful and a teacher." He stopped to sip his drink. He inhaled it a little too fast and coughed. "This is quite strong Pietro but so good." He raised his glass toward Pietro, and his friend poured a little more into his glass. Again, it was half full. "I'm not sure. This is a conversation we must have."

Pietro regarded him with a solemn face. "My friend, I've known you for more than a decade. You're strong in will, an example to all in determination and in your dedication to the stone. Important too …" He wagged a finger at Jeremiah. "You're fixed in your ways. She must understand this, agree with how you do your work, or there will be nothing but misery ahead. And in this vein, is she aware of your interest in living here or in Ireland or Germany with crazy O'Farrell?"

Kinga interjected, "Ah, now, Pietro, don't confuse the man with so many topics. Let's talk about the work. I don't agree with all the projects you take on, and I don't agree with the travel on some of them. But largely you're right. I do believe in what you do and that your work lifts the lives of others. And for that, a lot can be forgiven."

Pietro stood up, walked over to Kinga, and placed a kiss on her forehead. "Thank you for keeping me balanced, my dear, but Jeremiah needs to think of where he wants to live in order for his art to soar as well as how to make a family life complete."

Chapter 30

Progress on the St. Steven's altar moved rapidly with Jeremiah present. The elaborate and decorative filigree along the sides of the spires came alive under his chisel. He and Pietro made trips to the Duomo in Siena to the seminary in Montefollonico and to the basilica of San Pietro in Chuisa. There they were refreshed and convinced that their decorative work was consistent with the work done in those cities and as good, if not better. In conversations with Pietro, Jeremiah worried that the Northshire altar would not be an aesthetic fit in such a drab church. It was too formal and elegant for the brick structure. Eventually, after considerable conversation about churches in Italy, where the exterior was simple or commonplace and the interior brilliant, they agreed that the St. Steven's altar would bring excitement and life to the dour facility.

In the evening, they purchased a bottle of chianti and one of grappa for the train ride back to Siena. They opened the chianti and quaffed it, thirsty from the dusty hike from the seminary to the train station. The hot sun of the July day, along with the olives, cheese, and bread and the gentle rolling of the train, lulled them toward sleep. Jeremiah broke the sleepy atmosphere with the grappa and the sharp taste of the wine revived them. They talked excitedly of finishing the altar and preparing it for shipping to New York in the fall. Jeremiah planned to telegraph his plans to the crew in Northshire and scratched out the notes as the train moved toward Siena.

As he reviewed the draft of the telegraph, he put it aside and prepared a second missive to the bishop in Providence and to the crew there, guiding them on completion of the project.

When they arrived in Siena, they were met by Kinga. Her presence at the station was unusual as she rarely left the house. She had a telegram in her hand. She said, "This seemed important, so I brought it with me," as she handed it to Jeremiah. He rarely received telegrams, so he was surprised until he opened it. It was from the bishop in Providence.

Mr. Knox:

Have stopped all work and all payments for wages and materials until your return. Current work is not at your contract agreement and standard. I find you in breach of contract. Return immediately.

Bishop Cronin

Pietro and Jeremiah talked all evening over the strategy to complete the Northshire altar and the implications for Jeremiah's hasty return to Providence. He telegrammed the bishop the next day and gave him his arrival date. He would return as quickly as a voyage could be arranged. Deep down he resented the approach the bishop had taken. He knew and agreed to Jeremiah's Siena trip. Also, he knew that the Providence altar was ahead of schedule, and the remaining work did not require his full attention. He had completed all the difficult carving prior to departure.

He learned, upon his return, that two sections of the altar had been damaged and needed rework. A ladder and part of the scaffolding had collapsed against one of the side spires, causing modest damage. In the bishop's mind, the only person capable of the rework was Jeremiah. When Jeremiah inspected the damaged sections, he did not agree with the bishop's assessment. His fellow artisans could fix the damaged section easily. Uncharacteristic of Jeremiah, he brought his attorney to his first day back in Providence to inspect the damage and to agree to the schedule for repairs. The attorney was more effective than Jeremiah expected. The bishop was afraid of adverse publicity, especially of a lawsuit for unpaid wages for the workers, and a new schedule was rapidly settled.

As they left the bishop's opulent office, Jeremiah's dour face expressed no satisfaction with the agreement reached. The bishop said, his hand extended, "It's only fair and just that you finish the work."

Jeremiah stared at him and ignored the outstretched hand. "I don't need this work, not at all. And it doesn't require my skill to fix the damaged section. You overreacted, ignored our agreement for me to work in Siena, nor paid my workers. That violates our contract, which I now view as invalid. I'm no longer obligated to you. If you do not pay my workers today, my lawsuit will come fast." He waved his large hand in the bishop's face. "The newspapers will have a field day with you for failing to pay our labor force. I'll leave my attorney to work with you on the payments. I'm done." He turned on his heel and left the room.

The bishop, red in the face, his hands shaking, halted the lawyer; he grasped the attorney's shoulder. "He doesn't mean that, does he? He will do the work, won't he?"

The attorney glanced at the hand on his shoulder and gently removed it. "I'll settle him down, but my guess is that he'll ever do another project for you. I'll place the schedule and back-wage agreement we reached into a letter; I want you to sign it. When you've signed it and the past wages have been paid, then Jeremiah will continue the work. You do your part, and I'll make sure Jeremiah finishes the work here." He turned and followed Jeremiah out the door.

Jeremiah went to the church and inspected the altar again carefully studying the damaged section. The side of the spire had been cracked by the collapsed scaffolding, and the tips of ornamentation on the side of the spire in the shape of tiny crosses had been knocked off. The damaged section was about three feet in length by his estimate. That estimate was far different from the bishop's claim that the entire spire of ten feet had been destroyed. Jeremiah conferred with the stonemasons on site, each in fear of being fired. He relieved their worries, saying the problem was minor and these things happen. He assured them that the back pay would be forthcoming within a day or two. The bishop had agreed to it fifteen minutes ago.

He saw the faces of the masons had relaxed, so he turned his attention to the work. "Let's concentrate on how to repair the damage." Alternative fixes were discussed, and Jeremiah took the most radical solution. He thought that cutting away the damaged section and replacing it with a newly carved piece would be faster and be of higher quality than repair of the damaged crosses. He said, "We can do a new section faster than we can make and mount replacements."

When the bishop arrived on the scene, the stonemasons turned their backs on him, so he addressed Jeremiah. He complained that the seams of the new section would be evident to any onlooker, and Jeremiah replied, "Look at the base." He paused, pointing his fingers at the side columns, ensuring the bishop's eyes followed his hand. "Look at the spire on the other side. Please show me the seams."

The bishop stared at him then went to the altar and pointed to two apparent lines. His finger rested on a seam most evident to him.

The stonemasons began to laugh. The bishop looked at them, confused. Jeremiah walked to the altar and painstakingly showed the bishop that there were no seams where his hand rested.

Then he said, "You haven't noticed these seams, have you?" He pointed to the seams where the side sections of the altar joined the central section. Jeremiah stared at the bishop until the prelate looked away and nodded in satisfaction.

With Jeremiah's return, the work in Providence moved more quickly. The men accelerated their pace in his presence. Pleased at the speed of the work, Jeremiah proceeded to Northshire to finish the St. Steven's altar railings.

Milly had spent part of the summer at a graduate program at Harvard and was at home, visiting her parents before the school year started. Letters and telegrams had informed her of Jeremiah's change of schedule, and she was delighted.

Awaiting him on the narrow porch of her parents' house on Jackson Street, swinging in the hammock while reading a book of Robert Browning's poetry, she rose to greet him. She raced down the steps, brushing his dusty pants with her hands, "Oh, so grand." She hugged him and kissed him eagerly. "I hope it wasn't too awful with that ogre of a bishop."

"This is one of the delights of coming back early. I'm away from you for less time."

"Tell me everything from the arrival in Siena to today's surprise appearance." She sat him beside her on the hammock and linked her fingers into his. She noticed he winced when she moved his right hand. "Are you injured?"

"No, but it's odd. I hurt the hand in Siena. We were lifting a large block of marble and one of the men stumbled. I put more force into the stone to prevent it from falling, and I felt pain in my wrist. After a day's work, it tends to get sore, like now."

"I'll rub it and make it better. You'll see I'm indispensable."

He laughed. "I'm beginning to see that, but I didn't need my wrist to send me the message." At the moment, his wrist seemed unimportant, but the pain would subside for a time then reappear. It never went away.

With the Providence altar nearing completion, Jeremiah began to place all his attention on the elaborate and ornate altar in St. Steven's. He and Pietro had agreed that the top of the spires would be done last and would be done on site in Northshire. This decision was practical as the slender and intricate carvings at the top would be in jeopardy during a long voyage to New York as well as the transportation from the port to Northshire. Too many hands, too many movements worried both men, and the final work on the central altarpiece would be exclusively Jeremiah's. The shipment from Siena was expected in late December or early January.

As the summer ended and before fall classes began for Milly, she directed her full attention to Jeremiah. She believed she knew his intentions. She wanted them to be explicit. On late Sunday morning, they walked down Jackson Street away from her house. Armed with a picnic basket and a bag with a blanket, they left the road to climb the hill above the street. The hill overlooked the downtown area of Northshire, and in the distance, they could see the Connecticut River. On a good day, the river sparkled in the sunlight. She nudged his shoulder. "It's so beautiful." She pointed to the river. "This is one of the most beautiful spots in the whole state."

"It is lovely here, so private, so quiet."

"The peacefulness is one of its attractive features, don't you think?"

"I fully enjoy beautiful places like this." He took her hand, his long thumb rubbing the back of her hand gently.

"Would you like to live here?" She watched his expression, carefully awaiting an indication.

His reply came quickly; there was no hesitation. "Oh, I love my visits here, but that's because of you. I prefer to live in more active locales like a Worcester or a Boston." He turned to face her. "You don't, do you? I mean live here … You're much too vibrant for such a small town."

She nodded and remained quiet, reached into the bag, unfolded the blanket, and placed it on the ground. He set the picnic basket on the blanket and opened it to a brace of wrapped sandwiches, bottles of root beer, and a canister of chocolate cookies. "Well, look at this!" he exclaimed.

"I could live here," she repeated. "With another degree, I could teach at Smith, a trolley ride away."

He removed his hat, placed it on the blanket, and fixed his eyes on her. "Could you live in Worcester?"

Her eyes widened. "Why, Mr. Knox, I do believe you just proposed. Are my ears deceiving me?"

He turned red. The flush came quickly and disappeared as fast, but she noticed it. "Yes, I guess it is."

"Yes, my ears are deceiving me, or yes, you proposed?"

"It's the latter. I believe you know this, but I can make it formal. Would you like to be my wife and come to Worcester and live with me?" He laughed. "I can offer a life in Siena, Dublin, or Berlin if you don't like Worcester."

His gazed remained fixed on her face, and she met it without blinking. She seemed surprised at his words but said nothing. She leaned forward and kissed him eagerly. She held the kiss for a long time, and they fell back on the blanket, merging their bodies. The sun shown down on them and kept them warm. He held her tightly, and they rested, feeling the other's breath on their cheeks. She pulled her head away, studying his face.

She murmured, "Such a nice face. I haven't answered, have I?"

"No, I guess not. Do you have an answer?"

"Of course, it's yes, a dramatic yes, and I have a ton of questions about how or where we'll live together. And are you serious about living abroad? You've talked about it. Is it a serious possibility?"

"I'd like to talk with you about Europe. Take our time. Give it real attention."

"Oh my," she replied and glanced down at her hands. "Here I am thinking about Northshire or Worcester or you're thinking about Europe."

"Okay, I'll start with Worcester, and then we can go on to more serious question you have. There's some very nice houses there, I'm sure we'd find one we both like."

She sat up, her hands in her lap as she gazed out toward the river. "Other than Worcester or, my golly … Siena, the big question for me is your work. I want to be with you, see you every day, raise the children with you. I worry that will be very difficult since you travel every week."

"I understand my work does take me all over New England, recently even down to Washington."

"That's my point. Have you thought about what that means, what that does to a marriage?"

"Look, I think you know this, but it bears repeating. It's important for me to do something worthwhile, that is of value to others not just myself. I had that initially with my Fenian work. I was making a strong contribution to the Irish people, and after much reflection, I'm satisfied that work is over for me. You know that story. Now, I'm satisfied that my work in sculpture is not only worthwhile. It is of great value to hundreds of thousands. And secondly and equally important to me is that I do it well. I'm better at my art work than I was as a political activist."

She gazed at him quizzically.

He grasped her hand and brought his face close to hers. "For me to be good in marriage, good to you and our children, I must be able to do my work."

"I understand," she said hesitantly. "In fact, I've never heard anyone describe their relationship to work so well. It's quite profound. But what if your work limits the marriage. That makes it hard to flourish."

"Before we marry, we should come to an understanding of how I can do my work and satisfy your needs as a wife and mother. Then as time goes by, we should always talk about how that's working."

She gazed up at him. "I like that, Jeremiah. Let's start there." She paused. "I don't want to shock you, but I have some initial ideas."

"No surprise there."

"Well, do you think you could work mainly from a studio?" She put her other hand beneath his hand, enclosing it in hers. She gazed into his eyes. "I've studied this at the library. Many of the great sculptors like Michelangelo, Bernini, Donatello worked mainly from their studios."

The intensity of her eyes unnerved him, and he turned his head away. He knew her observation was only partially true. These men had worked away from their homes too. "It's hard to do an altar in a studio. It's done, but it's much easier on site as you can see from your father's church." He paused for a second. "But I've never thought about it. Let me think about that and we'll talk more."

"You're wonderful Jeremiah. So many talents, yet it's the so many talents that make it complex. You know, how we'd live together."

"Does that bother you?"

"No, no … I agree with what you said earlier. We'll talk, we'll plan, and I hope adjust when we need to."

He was less certain. He knew she'd hit a big issue for him as it had arose with Connie. How to manage a demanding career and have a predictable home life, a good marriage. Yet he could feel the stirrings of a solution but could not quite define it. He had his concerns about working at building sites. It required train rides every week, sometimes two and three trains a week plus multiple hotels and their watery soups and uneven cuisine. He would not miss some of the travel. Maybe he could find a way to reduce the frequency of it. And then there were the difficult clients like Bishop Cronin, not often, but they did appear. Also, he was beginning to realize that his wrist was sending a message. How much longer could he be a first-rate sculptor if the wrist worsened? Should he reduce the number of engagements per year?

He was certain of one part of his life. He was past the point of viewing a solitary life as the best life. He wanted a life with Milly, and the question was, how to make that happen so it is good for both of them? He thought back to his days in the Kilmainham Gaol, revisited his many conversations with Maria, with Connie, and how the twists and turns in his life had always been managed alone. He felt ready for a partner in life.

A life where love was not only possible but there every day. A part of life that he had missed since he left Ireland fifteen years ago.

He put his arm around her and held her tight. "I didn't plan this well, did I? I've not gotten down on my knees. I've not asked your father for your hand in marriage. I have no ring of engagement. I think I've violated all proper procedures."

She kissed him on his cheek. I'm a Smith girl, very modern. These things all get sorted out in time. "Plus I'd like to select the ring with you if that's okay."

They walked back to her home in the late afternoon, the chill of fall air replacing the warmth of the midday sun. They had agreed to wait until dinner to inform her parents of their plans. At the round dining table with the Wedgewood china and the Suffolk silver settings, Milly announced that they had some news then took Jeremiah's hand. He talked about their desire to marry and sought their blessing. Stephanie jumped from her seat and hugged her daughter and kissed Jeremiah on the cheek. "I hoped this would happen," she said. Her hands all aflutter as she waved them at her husband and alternately waved them in front of her face.

Jackie Driscoll rose and kissed his daughter and shook Jeremiah's hand. "Welcome to the family, Jeremiah, but I have a few questions. Like where will you live? Could you live in Springfield or here?"

"We've agreed it will be Worcester, Daddy," Milly replied.

"Oh, I wished it would be closer, but we understand, don't we, Stephanie? Would you live in that apartment of yours or in one of your other buildings?"

Jeremiah said, "We need to talk about what we want. There's many possibilities." He turned to Milly. "Maybe I should sell one or two of my properties and buy us a house. What do you think of that?"

There was silence and then exclamation. Stephanie exclaimed, "So exciting. Milly, you might be able to pick out your own house right at the start of the marriage. Oh, how wonderful."

"As I think of it now," Jeremiah added, "it would be nice for Milly and I to have our own home. A place for her piano, a hobby room for her, and so on."

"And room for lots of children," Milly chirped.

They all laughed and later discussed the date for the announcement, plans for an engagement party, the date for a wedding, and the conversation lasted for hours. Still in the back of Jeremiah's mind was Milly's question about sculpture, their life together, and the serious demands of travel if he continued to do altars.

What Jeremiah confirmed in these family discussions of engagement and wedding plans was that Milly excelled in driving a conversation to the ends she sought. Yet she attained her goals without rancor, or in Jeremiah's words to Hamish the following week, "She does it without breaking all the furniture." He marveled at her skill as she negotiated her way through her mother and father's preferences. He waited patiently for her to turn her attention on him. He didn't have to wait long.

Chapter 31

It was an unusual time for Jeremiah; he had only one active project, the altar for St. Steven's, and it needed his full attention. He relished the time he was spending with Milly, and she was eager to express her appreciation.

"You know, Jeremiah, you've been in Northshire almost full time for the past six months. I see you all the time. I like that very much, and I'm very used to it."

"That's because the centerpiece of the altar arrived from Siena. I stopped my other work because the top spires were not done and were so intricate they needed my full attention." He chuckled. "And it gave me a great excuse to spend all this time near you whether in Springfield or here."

"I'm serious, Jeremiah. I don't want that to change."

"It's been wonderful. However, you know, that can't last."

"I've been thinking about this since our last conversation. I waited a long time to marry, and I found what I want in a man." She extended both arms toward him. "You're it, you're perfect. But I want my man to be with me, near me, an integral part of my daily life."

She saw his resignation and had sufficient confidence to ignore it. "Well, my darling, we're just starting this conversation, but will you consider focusing on studio work?"

"Right now, I don't see how I can do the intricate work on spires without being on site or at least near it. It's what I love about this work, and it's made my work unique."

Undeterred, she pulled forward in her chair, seeking to be closer to him. "I was thinking about your friend, Pietro, in Siena. He works from a studio in his own house. You could work from your studio at the McGuinness address."

"I could do more from there, no doubt. But I couldn't do everything. I'll have to think about it."

"You could shift to doing just studio sculpture, like the statues that you do so well. Or the fountains or other smaller ornamentations."

"But it's the large works, like the altar here, that's made my reputation."

She moved back in her chair, sitting up straight, her posture perfect. "I know, I realize that. However ..." She watched him. He was curious and patient with the conversation, so she took a deep breath. "Let me go back nearly twenty years. You were studying law, an outstanding student with innovative political ideas for your country, and that got taken away from you. Your platform for life removed by a judge at the tender age of nineteen. Okay, I'm right so far." She smiled, giving him the opportunity to interrupt. "So you created a new platform of sculpture in Worcester. Now you can create another platform in the same field but more specialized, just do statuary."

Normally slouched in a chair, he had come forward and was about to speak. Deep inside, he felt uneasy.

She sensed his inner reserves organizing for an argument. Yet it didn't alter her intuition that this was the time to release her ideas, thoughts that would guide their life together. She saw the growing intensity in his eyes, and she met them directly. "Jeremiah, you proved then that you could switch from intellectual work to a combination of artistic and intellectual work from law to sculpture. You did it with no trouble. I'm convinced you can do anything."

He relaxed slightly, a quiet release of breath that even he didn't notice. He lifted his hands. "Okay, okay ... I hear you."

He wondered, how long had she held these thoughts? Why were they not revealed earlier? Was she afraid that he'd stop seeing her? He wet his lips and sat back in his chair. "Do you have more ideas on studio work?"

"If you did that, we'd be together most of the time. I can find a teaching position in one of the schools in Worcester. Alice Sullivan has one of her boys in a marvelous school, and she'll introduce me to the headmaster."

He nodded, and she believed he was listening, taking her ideas seriously. "We'd have lots of time for walks, talks, having children, and having ample time to play with them. We'd become involved in the cultural activities in Worcester and so on. Activities that you have no time for now."

"Milly, my dear, your compliments on my statues are most pleasing to hear, but I'm no Donatello, Bernini, or even a Pietro Antonino. Yet my altars are unique; it would be hard for me to stop that work."

"What about your apartment buildings? You'd have more time for them."

"Those are business investments, building capital for our retirement. They're not central to the purpose of my life."

She moved forward in her chair; her color was rising. "I'm not an expert on sculpture, you know that, but in my opinion, your work in statuary will be valued and appreciated with the best in Europe and the US. Henry Vaughn told me that, by the way."

She watched him as he rose from his chair; he seemed preoccupied. She could tell he'd gone into his own head, and when that happened, all conversation was over.

He motioned for her to remain seated. "You've given me a lot to consider. I need to walk, get a little fresh air."

He politely dismissed her offer to accompany him on his walk. He needed to be alone with his thoughts. Obvious to him was that she'd been thinking long and hard about how to make a marriage work. And he wasn't clear how to think about it. As a solitary man, he had to answer only to himself. In every crisis he faced in life, he'd done it alone. He didn't need to think about others as he made decisions on his work. Connie had never been a factor or consideration in his decisions about what projects to choose. With Milly, he was facing a more complex life, and it was now apparent that he must decide if the benefits of a married life exceeded the benefits of his solitary life. Connie had chosen the solitary life to avoid this type of conflict and compromise.

He secured his hat and coat and waved to her. "I'll be back shortly. Just need to clear my head."

She knew her man. He needed time to think, and she wanted him to do that. Yet the nervousness in her stomach would not settle down. Had she moved too fast, too aggressively on the idea of limited travel with the shift to studio work? She was a secure woman, and she had confidence in her strategy. "I love it when you go to your head. What comes out is always for the best."

He acknowledged her last thoughts with an absent wave as he walked from the house on Jackson Street to a main avenue that led to the center of Northshire and the location of St. Steven's. He mounted the steps of the church and gazed down the hill to the bustling traffic on Main Street. It wasn't that her ideas were wrong, but they shifted the balance of what he wanted to do. His mind was not in the same place as hers.

Recently, he'd been concerned about two developments. There was the drop in demand for churches that had Henry Vaughn constantly worried. He claimed immigration had peaked, and the need for new churches was going to decline and with that the need for Jeremiah's altars. The uncertainty of the demand for altars was something outside of his control and impossible for him to calculate, although if that work fell off, Milly's worry became irrelevant. Then there was the new factor. It had emerged recently and was very present in his mind, the growing pain in his right hand.

This ailment perplexed him most of all. He rose one day; it seemed like months ago, with a stiffness in his wrist and hand. He ran warm water over it in the morning, and it loosened up. One night, after a long day of carving the Providence altar, the pain came at night and wakened him. It was a sharp pain causing his fingers to tingle and his wrist to throb. It lasted a while and interrupted his sleep. Eventually, after flexing his fingers, circulation returned, and he was able to sleep. The next day, the demands on his carving were less, and the problem did not occur. It had been this way now for several months. He wondered, after fifteen years of sculpture work, if his hands were going. Could it be that he had damaged the tendons or nerves in the wrist and hands? Was it likely to be progressive and get worse in time?

After the problem occurred again, he sought the advice of a physician who specialized in the joints of shoulders, elbows, wrists, and hands. He suggested that Jeremiah take several months off from carving and then carve to the point of fatigue or to the early stages of pain, then stop. With his contracts, Jeremiah could not take three months off from work, so he tried to pace his efforts more carefully and stop when pain was felt. That seemed to work and had become his pattern of work in 1905.

He turned away from his view of Main Street and opened the door to St. Steven's entering its cavernous interior. The clerestory windows above the altar brought beams of sunlight to the white marble. The altar was taking shape and beginning to glow in the bright light. There were two workers shaping the edges of the altar rail. They nodded to him. Their chisels chipping at the marble, they continued to work. He walked to the ladder at the back of the altar and mounted the scaffolding. He reached the center spire and studied it, picked up a cloth off the wooden plank of the scaffold, and wiped a section clean. He saw what worried him and began to rework a delicate arch. Quickly, he lost his worries as he worked, and his thinking became focused only on producing an elegant section of the central spire. The hard work cleansed his mind, and in its recesses, he began to grasp a way to have Milly in his life and to define a different life, a life that was more diverse, more socially active, yet a way of living that enabled him to maintain his work in sculpture. These thoughts, as they swirled through his mind, began to intrigue him rather than dismay him.

Without fully realizing it, he'd spent hours on the scaffold, and the shape of the lower part of the spire was much more to his liking. He dusted it off and stared at it, pleased. He dropped the rag to the plank and lowered himself down the ladder to the floor. The other workers had left; he'd heard their goodbyes and barely acknowledged their departures. He left the church, locking the massive doors, and stepped out into early evening. It had become dark without his notice. He picked up his pace and ambled back to Jackson Street and entered the Driscoll home.

Milly rushed to meet him, hugging him then pulling away to face him. "You've been gone too long. I was about to send father to search for you. Are you angry with me? Please say no."

Shyly he smiled, "Of course not. As usual, I became too engrossed in my work and was on the scaffold all afternoon."

"On a Saturday, why, darling?"

"Others were there too. The altar just draws us to work. And it's a good way and a fine place for me to think."

"That's what worried me. You thinking and I'm not aware of your thoughts."

He placed his coat in the hall closet and gently grasped her elbow. "Let's go into the living room, and I'll give you a brief summary of my thoughts. Particularly, your ideas on my career."

"Remember, I just asked that you consider my thoughts. We have plenty of time to discuss what you do and what I do. We're both facing big changes."

Briefly, he described the two major themes that were influencing his work, his opinions on the economic trends, and the problems with his hand. She listened with care and offered no comment, saying that she had more ideas, but they could come later.

Her heart was lightened considerably by the fact that he listened and was giving her view of his profession serious thought. She knew she had a well-defined vision of a good marriage, a balanced marriage between two intelligent people. She wanted him to share that vision and to add to it, make it even more complete, more interesting. But to do that, she knew that he'd have to change his world of sculpture from one of constant travel, an itinerant stonemason by her father's definition, to one of studio work. Her challenge was to convince him that this change, would benefit her life, yes, but that his life would be improved as well.

She had been sitting next to him on the love seat tucked into the back corner of the living room. She leaned over and kissed his cheek. "I can see why you were a great law student. You examine all aspects of a situation. You're very comprehensive. By the way, we're having dinner here as you know. Maybe you'd like a few moments to clean up before Gladys brings in the sherries?"

He rose from the seat, stretching his long arms over his head and flexing his right wrist, getting the soreness out of it. "Yes, I'll wash up quickly and put on some better clothes." He regarded his pants and saw dust on one leg. "Gal, darn, when I see the altar I forget how I'm dressed and just get to work. I've made a mess of these fine pants. I'll get something clean and fresh."

"Your smock protects you most of the time, but you do forget, don't you? When you see the stone, you see what needs to be done. Why, you could be in your best suit, and you'd pick up the hammer and chisel."

He shook his head as he ambled toward the stairway and to the guest bedroom. "I guess you've gotten to know me pretty well."

She knew her ideas had taken hold. This was good, she thought. It was time to try one more idea and then leave her marital and career thoughts alone to stew, to gain age and ripeness, to let him find his own perspective. He had to get there on his own; she was confident of that. Or he'd bolt as he did with the female doctor. She'd concluded that he was the one that gave up on that relationship even though the woman was strident. She did not want to cast herself in a similar way. She did not want to lose this man, but she wanted him aligned with her view of a good marriage.

Jeremiah and Milly were married in April of 1908, the first marriage in St. Steven's. Jackie Driscoll was a proud father that day and even more proud of the church he'd built. He claimed to all that would listen that he had it finished for his daughter's wedding.

The honeymoon was a surprise to Milly. For a couple that shared every thought, every worry and had thoroughly explored how to be a married couple, Jeremiah kept one secret. He felt she'd never agree to the expense of a honeymoon in Italy, so he plotted the trip alone with the occasional help of Pietro. The first-class voyage on the Mauritania was the first step, the second was a week in Venice at the Gritti Palace, and the third was a week in the Chianti region with a villa in Siena as their base. April was bright in Tuscany. The red poppies on the rolling hills were beginning to bloom; the vineyards were waking up from the long winter, releasing their leaves. The farmers tilled the lush fields, giving the sleepy towns a rush of new energy.

People began to bustle more in the markets, linger a little longer, saying hello to friends with much touching of hands and kissing of cheeks. Milly was enchanted.

Pietro told her they would have a small party to mark their wedding. A few of Jeremiah's friends from his work in Italy wished to celebrate the couple. But first Cardinal Grimaldi wanted to offer a small mass in their honor, and Jeremiah explained to Milly that the cardinal was a bishop when he met him, and the clergyman had guided him to exquisite altars in Italy and introduced him to Pietro. The late afternoon mass was to be followed by a small gathering at Pietro's villa.

Milly's head spun in all directions as she saw a crowd moving into the cathedral. "Who are all these people?" she asked Jeremiah.

As he surveyed the crowd at the Duomo, he was surprised as well. There were hundreds moving into the church, and he recognized all the men. "This is Pietro's concept, or an Italian's idea, of a small gathering." He laughed. "You'll meet them at Pietro's. They've worked with us at various churches."

The joyous, happy Italians overwhelmed Milly as she was hugged, kissed, her arms and hands touched, held by women and men that worked with Jeremiah in Siena and in other cities and towns. She met Maria, who was delighted that Jeremiah found such a beautiful and talented wife. Milly laughed heartily at Maria's story that she was holding out for Jeremiah, waiting for her aging husband to die, and now her plans were demolished.

He was equally surprised, actually stunned at the reception, its boisterous, ebullient ambience. Their wedding and reception in Northshire had been a lovely, small affair, sedate with a quiet formality. There was Milly's family, a few of her college friends, St. Agatha colleagues, Jeremiah's mother and his sister, and a smattering of Jeremiah's friends, including Hamish, Biasi, and McGuinness from Worcester.

Jeremiah spotted Pietro and approached him. "How did you do this? It's spectacular and so joyous. So many of our fellow workers and the cardinal." He repeated, "How did you do this?"

"It was simple, my friend. When I told my people of your marriage, their immediate reaction was that when you came to Siena, we must celebrate. Then it exploded spontaneously." He waved his arms in the form of a big explosion, nearly spilling his prosecco.

"What about the cardinal?"

"Ah yes, he heard about it from Maria and telephoned me. He made it clear. You needed a mass from him." He laughed. "He has a deep appreciation of your gifts, as he calls them. He's impressed with your cold logic, but mostly he's interested in your soul."

Jeremiah laughed. "My soul, aye." He clapped Pietro on the arm. He gathered Milly, and they circled the crowd in the large tent, thanking everyone for coming and for their good wishes. In each stop, Jeremiah was reminded that Pietro had a new project in coming up. Would he be joining the team of artisans? The cardinal took him aside, insisting that he join Pietro to reconstruct the damaged cathedral in Pienza.

Overcome with joy and exhausted, Milly and Jeremiah fell into each other's arms after the dinner. Milly pulled away from him, holding both of his hands in hers. She asked, "You mentioned this several months ago, but I didn't take it too seriously. The folks at the reception all expect you to come back for Pietro's work in Pienza."

He said, "We've discussed this before, and guess what, the cardinal has raised the money, so the project has become a reality. You've asked about my seriousness of living in Europe. Well, here's a decision point. They want to start in the next six months, so it's up to us."

"What do you want to do?"

"It looks like this to me. My work in New England will be done by early summer. Vaughn has tried to interest me in a large church in New Jersey. Given these two opportunities, I'd rather work in Italy than in Trenton. If it's here, we'll be together every day versus seeing each other on weekends if I'm in New Jersey."

"Those two projects are the main opportunities now?"

"Yes, oddly it's been a quiet time. That will change. It always does, but that's the situation at the moment."

"You really want to live in Italy for a while, don't you?"

"Yes, I'd love to give it a year or two. And the timing of this project in Pienza is perfect on my current schedule."

Milly tugged on his sleeve. "Now that I'm here, meeting all these people, I'm getting more comfortable with the idea. Actually, I'm getting excited."

"We'll talk again in the morning and perhaps over the next day or two. But if you're comfortable, I'll tell Pietro and the Cardinal that we'll be back to do the cathedral."

"One more promise, Jeremiah, as your mother indicated at our wedding and my colleagues concur, this is not the time to be active with political movements in Italy, Ireland, or Germany. You'll stay away from politics. Do we agree?"

"We do. I think it's finally dawned on Callahan and O'Farrell that I've been away from their squabbles and wars for too long. I'm out of touch, so I'm as free of them as they are of me."

They relaxed into a warm embrace that led to intensive love-making. Milly was certain the special closeness they felt that evening would bring them a child. Despite the confidence she felt, her expectation would not be realized. It would take more time.

Well, before the wedding, Hamish had offered to find a home for the married couple. Jeremiah thought a small house for the two of them would be perfect. He would, with diminishing reluctance, leave his apartment after fourteen years. Hamish escorted Milly and Jeremiah through the three "best" houses on his list. They were stunned at his selections. The houses were large, much larger than Milly's family home in Northshire.

Hamish, sensing their surprise at the size of the properties, said, "You must look ahead. There will be children, maybe lots of them. And this is such a bargain." He escorted them through the twelve-room mansion on Linden Street. The rooms were spacious. Tall windows faced shrubbery and trees. The high ceilings combined to please Jeremiah with the feeling of open space. The house gave him a sense of freedom.

Hamish added, "The owner is moving unexpectedly and has priced it to sell quickly."

Jeremiah put his arm around Milly, his eyes seeking the corners of the vast living room. "How many servants will you need to manage the place, my dear?"

She shared his joy. "Well, let's look at the kitchen and the second floor, then I'll tell you."

They purchased the twelve-room house and had it furnished while they honeymooned in Italy. With furniture in every room and a wall removed on the second floor to create a working area for Jeremiah, the house had a comfortable feeling for Milly. At first, she was taken by the formality of the spacious living room with its tall marble fireplace, French doors opening onto an outside patio, and her baby grand piano lending the final touch of elegance to the room. Eventually, she preferred the sitting room with its French windows overlooking the gardens behind the house. Access to the room was from a side door in the kitchen or from wide double doors, normally closed, from the living room. The sitting room would become her favorite location for reading, knitting, and a simple mahogany desk in the center of the room would become her place for work.

Life in the new home was short-lived as they prepared to embark for their stay in Siena. As Milly finished the school year, they packed and departed for Italy in late July. In many conversations, they had discussed the duration of the stay and had agreed a year at the minimum and three years at the most. With his interest in political movements gone, Jeremiah concluded that a permanent stay in Europe was unlikely, but he planned to keep his eyes open.

Married life settled in slowly and enjoyably for Jeremiah. His former routine of living alone, preparing his meals, or having a quiet evening alone with his books or at the Worcester library was gone. He adjusted to Milly's presence. Her bubbling conversation was ever present. Her laughter and her evening piano exercises filled the spacious villa on the outskirts of Siena with joy and companionship. Her life in Siena was as full as his. Cardinal Garabaldi had secured a teaching position for Milly at St. Angelina's, a school for girls, where she taught English and French.

In their vacations from work, they travelled to Berlin, Dublin, and Paris. With Jimmy O'Farrell in Berlin, they marveled at the beauty of the city by day and by evening listened to the debates in the cafes that often became heated between the socialists, the new group of communists, and the faithful adherents of the Kaiser. Tempers flared, and fights broke out occasionally. The same was true in Dublin, where civil unrest was even more strident.

Milly remarked to Callahan as they sat in a cafe off Rutland Square. "There seems to be so many factions in disagreement over who's to rule, how to rule. Will it ever get sorted out?"

"What's true here, as you observe, is true throughout Europe," Callahan replied. "Change is needed, and it will come. But I'm afraid," he added, "it will not come without bloodshed, without war. Perhaps you and Jeremiah are better off in America even though we need him here."

In the evening, in the quiet of their hotel room, Jeremiah said, "I'd never realized, as I have now, that America was so different. Yes, we have ethnic and cultural differences and rivalries, but basically we get along. We solve these problems through our city councils, our courts, our clubs, and not by brawls or gun battles."

"I'm relieved," she replied. "I've been worried that you'd want to stay in Italy or Ireland."

"No longer, I see too much unrest in countries and between countries. There's too many dangerous ideas floating around. The push of nationalism is going to cause a big war or many smaller wars. There are too many restive ethnic groups in Ireland. The same is true in Northern Europe and in the Austro-Hungarian Empire. These conflicting interests need to be reconciled."

"It's surprised me too. It seems so different than when I visited as a student many years ago."

"Don't get me wrong. I'm no rush to leave. I want to finish my work. This may surprise you, but I look forward to Worcester again. How about you?"

"I agree. I'm enjoying this stay immensely. It's been a highlight of my life, but I look forward to our life in Worcester."

Toward the end of their second year, the final touches to the altar and the statues throughout the cathedral were completed. Cardinal Garabaldi gave the dedication Mass followed by a lavish dinner at the rectory for the construction staff. Pietro and Jeremiah were hailed with many toasts. For Jeremiah, it was another step in his work. He felt his skills continued to advance. This altar and the statue of Saint Sebastian were among his best. There seemed to be more life in the figurines; the altar appeared to beckon the congregation to its altar rail. He was eager to find opportunities in the United States for his new ideas.

Before leaving for America, Milly and Jeremiah took an extended tour of Northern Italy, spending the last two weeks at the Grand Hotel Tremezzo on Lake Como. By the time they had packed up the villa in Siena and said their farewells to Pietro, Kinga, and their friends, Milly began to feel stirrings of life within. When they boarded the ship to New York, she was one month pregnant.

Chapter 32

After two years in Italy, Jeremiah returned to his own studio, freshly constructed, on the McGuinness property. While in Italy, work in the United States climbed from its slump. Vaughn and other church architects had saved sections of their churches for Jeremiah. He came back to a full slate of opportunities. He attempted to work more in Worcester, yet he still travelled to Washington for work on the National Cathedral and to other towns in New England for the finishing touches on altars. His work in stone regained its high demand, and as agreed, he selected his projects after consultation with Milly.

Due to his travels and Milly's teaching, they hired a maid, Milandra, who lived in a two-room suite on the third floor. She was a widow in her middle thirties. Her only child—a son—was in the army; her husband was dead from an industrial accident years before. In the movement of African Americans from the cotton fields in the south to the industrial work in the north, she had migrated with her husband from South Carolina in 1894. A tall, bulky woman with a strong set of opinions was to entertain, cook, wash, and keep 52 Linden Street immaculate for years. Gardeners, an occasional coachman, and other household employees would come and go, but Milandra was the heart and soul of the house, dependable, loyal, and imaginative. Her views of the world, Worcester, all politicians and the friends of Jeremiah, and Milly were a constant source of wisdom and entertainment.

To Jeremiah, time flowed by like a gentle river. It seemed as if he met Milly yesterday, yet suddenly there were children. Milly gave birth to John Francis, named after Jeremiah's grandfather, in 1910, and Mary came shortly thereafter in 1912. Both children drained Milly of energy, and she responded slowly from the birth of each.

Her physician told her no more; her body couldn't take the strain. At first, she tried to return to teaching but needed, under doctors' orders, to rest. She postponed her teaching until the children had reached the ages of five and three. Once back into the world of teaching, she would take advantage of the long summer vacations, visit her parents in Northshire, and take a month in gray shingled house in Siasconset on the island of Nantucket. The rambling house was on a bluff above Sconset beach facing the open Atlantic. The cool breezes off the Atlantic gave the family relief from the heat and humidity of Worcester.

While they were in Northshire, Jeremiah visited on weekends, and the family took long hikes on Mount Tom or along the grassy hills and streams in the back of Jackie Driscoll's property. Picnics along the streams were favorites of Milly's and the children; a basket of sandwiches, jars of root beer, and bags of cookies accompanied them in Milly's rucksack. Often, on the hot humid days, they cooled their feet in the chill waters of the rushing streams, tossing the water onto their faces and over their heads on the hot and humid days.

After the birth of John Francis, Jeremiah curtailed his visits to Siena and brought the Italian artisans to the United States for work. He loved Italy and wished to return, but the needs of his family kept him in or near Worcester. His complaints were few. After so many years in solitude, he enjoyed family life. His wife was a delight to him, and his children gave him a sense of family he had long ignored. The strife with his family in Ireland had slowly diminished skillfully assisted by Milly; she helped close old wounds. Jeremiah's betrayal in Boston had been put aside but not forgotten. The bitterness of that experience, as he saw it, had colored his view of family life. Milly's loving nature brought harmony and joy into their marriage, creating a life he never knew was possible.

He wanted a month-long trip to Italy to be part of their experiences, but he decided to wait until the children were older. Milly, relieved, concurred in his choice, and as a family, they enjoyed their vacations in Massachusetts.

When Milly became stronger, she suggested a trip to Ireland and Italy, but events in Europe began to interfere with her ideas.

In 1914 the hostilities in the Balkans expanded onto the entire European continent, and the Great War began. Jeremiah's plans to visit Siena or his family in Ireland were placed on hold. Little did they realize at the time their plans would be suspended for nearly five years. During those years, demand for church work and other ornamental sculptures declined. Milly was delighted. Jeremiah was home more often, and he and Hamish purchased another group of triple-deckers, bringing his total buildings to twenty. He spent considerable time negotiating the purchases, refurbishing the buildings, and managing the financials. The cash flow was substantial, his bank account swelled, and his stock market holdings increased. While pleased with these developments, he waited patiently for news of new church constructions or substantial rework in older churches.

Pietro suffered the same fate, and his finances were challenged when his oldest son chose to go to medical school rather than go into his father's studio. The war involvement of Italy was sufficiently disruptive to ecclesiastical projects that Pietro had no work for long periods of time. In letters back and forth, Pietro was afraid to travel to the United States because of the submarine danger for all ships, including passenger ships. Jeremiah loaned his old friend money for his son's education to be repaid when times got better.

When the war ended, business in Jeremiah's altar work increased again. He planned to take projects that required travel infrequently, and he tried to schedule the work when Milly was with the children in Northshire or Nantucket. In 1920, his cousin, Benji—the eldest son of Jeremiah's uncle John—contacted Jeremiah. In a long letter, he wrote that his church, St. Cecilia's in Boston, had a devastating fire, and a portion of the altar had been damaged. Would Jeremiah be willing to let bygones be bygones, since the despised uncle was now dead, and build the church a new altar? Milly encouraged him to take the project.

He settled in a small hotel near the church. Its twenty modest-sized rooms with a desk, a bathroom with a newfangled shower satisfied his simple needs. He was especially satisfied that there was no fussing at the front desk over his dusty clothes at day's end.

On a quiet Monday evening, he walked twenty blocks to dine at the Union Oyster House, often his evening destination for a meal. He recalled his first meal there in 1891, the day his uncle's promise of a legal apprenticeship was withdrawn. It was nearly thirty years ago, he mused. The changes in his life flew through his memory. As he sipped a cold beer, his thoughts shifted to Nantucket. It was late July, and the family trip to Nantucket was but a week away. He welcomed the thought of the island's cool breezes as he returned to the hotel. The evening was hot and humid. The wind off the Charles River had a putrid fragrance, and he was perspiring heavily when he entered the lobby. He wiped perspiration off his brow and greeted the desk clerk. The clerk responded in a quiet fashion and extended a white envelope to Jeremiah.

He said, "Mr. Knox, good evening. Here's a message for you."

Jeremiah read the message while walking to the elevator. The shock of it was in its brevity. It was from Stephanie, his mother-in-law, "Call immediately."

He greeted Atmos, the ancient elevator operator, a short black man with cotton-colored hair immaculately dressed in a crimson tunic with matching pants. His smile was warm, yet he saw the concern on Jeremiah's face and avoided conversation. He waved Jeremiah into the lift, pulling the cable with his white-gloved hand. "It's the third floor, isn't it, sir?"

It wasn't a question. Jeremiah had discovered after two days at the hotel that Atmos knew the floor of everyone after one ride in his elevator. A remarkable memory, he thought, then he drifted to Stephanie's message. He'd talked to Milly the night before; she had told him that she felt drained from the heat, unlike any fatigue she'd ever remembered and that Mary had the sniffles, but otherwise, everyone was fine. John Francis was busy as ever, driving everyone nuts. The long-distance operator connected him quickly. After the third ring, Jackie Driscoll picked up.

Driscoll said, "Ah, Jeremiah, we've been awaiting your call. It's not good. Let me get Stephanie."

Now alarmed, Jeremiah thought, *What could be the problem? Why wouldn't he say what's not good?* He had a sudden sense of foreboding, unusual for him.

Stephanie breathed heavily into the phone as if she'd been running. "Jeremiah, thank God we've found you. You must come immediately. They're sick, very sick."

His heart was racing. "Stephanie, please slow down. Who's sick? Sick from what?"

"I've taken them to the Codman-Trumble Hospital here. They had vomiting and very high fevers that won't come down."

For God's sake! "Who, Stephanie, who?"

Breathlessly, she said, "Milly and Mary, they had a tired feeling like a cold then came the fever, and I couldn't get it down with any of my remedies. Mary was red hot and starting to get jumpy."

"Jumpy—what do you mean? Convulsions?"

"Yes, Dr. Clements was here, and he went with us to the hospital. Can you come right away, Jeremiah? I know it will be a comfort to Milly, Johnny, and Mary."

"Of course, I'll be on the next train west. Once I arrive, I'll go straight to the hospital. You say John's okay? You're sure?"

"Yes, he's with us and has no fever, no sign of what they have. He's asleep in the guest room."

In recent years, summers in Massachusetts had experienced a series of urban illnesses; polio and influenza panics had come and gone. Jeremiah felt it was the heat and poor sewage systems in the cities that caused these problems, so he was pleased and slightly relieved when Milly wanted to take the children to rural settings like Northshire or Nantucket. He boarded the train with a sense of doom. He couldn't shake the fear he heard in Stephanie's voice. "The fevers won't go down." As much as he tried to read on the ride west, he couldn't concentrate. He put his book down and paced back and forth between the cars. He'd never been sick, never been a patient in a hospital, and the thought of his wife and daughter suffering was extremely frightening to him. Fear was not an emotion or state of mind that often came to him. He couldn't think of the last time he was actually afraid. But his wife and daughter were in the hospital with runaway fevers. Fear seared through his system, and he was unable to control his anxiety.

After he transferred to the train to Northshire, he began to relax. He was thirty minutes away from the town, and he could finally take action. He'd go straight to the hospital, go right to the medical staff, and get a detailed briefing about the mysterious illness and the recovery timetable. He told Stephanie not to meet him. He had urged her to go to bed. He'd see her in the morning after he visited Milly and Mary at the hospital. It was 2:00 a.m. when he reached Codman-Trumble Hospital. Despite the hour, his energy was at an all-time high. The bleary attendant at the reception desk guided him to the second floor and the physician on duty. On the floor, there was a beehive of activity as nurses rushed from room to room. Gurneys jammed the corridors. Families had gathered in the lounge in teary clusters, heads down. There was the sense of an epidemic here; Jeremiah shuddered at what he saw.

Entering the small office, the doctor sitting at a desk in his long white coat was bathed in pale light and writing on a tablet. The sterile color from overhead lamp gave him a ghostly appearance, a ragged look from endless hours at the hospital. He rose from his desk, gesturing Jeremiah to the chair. "I'm Dr. Adams. Please sit, Mr. Knox. The front desk and Stephanie Driscoll said you'd be coming. I know you've come a long way. Please sit."

Jeremiah said, "Thank you, Doctor. How are they? Can I see them now?"

Dr. Adams walked closer and stood beside Jeremiah. He took a slow breath, bowed his head. "There's no easy way to say this Mr. Knox." He paused to stare directly into Jeremiah's eyes. "They're gone." He waited, fighting off his own exhaustion, watching Jeremiah, then placed a long thin hand on his shoulder. "Several hours ago, the fevers spiked, reached a level we were unable to control. Mary's came on more rapidly, but within no time, both had become delirious." His eyes searched Jeremiah's face. "We did everything possible, but I am so sorry ... we were unable to save them. Your wife died about two hours ago, and an hour before that your daughter died."

Jeremiah sank into a chair, unable to register what he'd heard. He dropped his head into his hands for a few seconds then looked up at the physician, red-eyed. "Gone, both of them? No, I can't believe this. I can't accept it. I talked to Milly two days ago. She was a little tired."

"This was typhoid, a typhus fever, and they are fierce. It came on fast to them, faster than I've ever seen before, a virulent disease." He sighed deeply. "We have several cases. It's ..." He shook his head.

"Oh god," Jeremiah moaned, "I can't believe this. I left them healthy, vital ... just a few weeks ago." He mumbled into his hands, his mind unable to fathom the death of his girls. Grief had begun to take hold, unrelenting and tenacious. "They came here to get away from the diseases that afflict Worcester ... in the summers." He stared up at the doctor, tears streaming down his cheeks.

"I'm so sorry. We did all we could to bring down the fever, but ..."

He choked out the words. "How could this happen? Oh my god," he muttered.

"We think it was some bad drinking water, water that became polluted. We've had many cases as you can see from the beds in this ward." He waved his arms in the direction of the corridor filled with gurneys. "Mrs. Driscoll said they had a picnic on a hill near some streams. We think the streams must have carried the disease. Nothing else they did would bring this bacteria to them."

Jeremiah glanced up in surprise. He rose from the chair, horrified, and lashed out at the doctor. "They drank from one of those streams on the Driscoll property. What! Is that what you said?"

Stunned, the doctor watched Jeremiah carefully. "Apparently, that's what Mrs. Knox said to her mother."

Jeremiah rarely cursed and never in public or in front of his family or strangers. But now, he struck out again. "Well, goddammit to hell. I told her, told the children to never drink from streams or rivers. They're all getting polluted from these companies putting bad things into the water."

"Mr. Knox, I hear you. This is terrible, but actually we don't know. The problem is more likely to be animal waste in these rural streams. We've had typhus cases last year and this year with similar misfortunes."

Jeremiah had sunk back in the chair, his head buried in his hands again. He was muttering, "Gone, gone," shaking his head back and forth.

Doctor Adams said, "Mr. Knox, I have a few pills for you to help you sleep. Tomorrow at some point, when you're ready, the monsignor has offered to help you with the arrangements to take them to Worcester to schedule the wake and funeral. Do you think you could handle this tomorrow?"

Jeremiah, numb, nodded and stumbled out of the office. He had no idea how he reached the Driscoll's home, but he opened the door and sank onto the couch in the living room. It was the same couch where, many years ago, he had distributed his Christmas gifts to the Driscoll family and the monsignor. He swallowed two of the pills and laid back, praying for sleep.

Stephanie rose at six to find Jeremiah on the couch, her eyes red and swollen from an evening of sorrow. She must have slept, she thought, because she had not heard him come in. Let him sleep, she decided, but her movements were heard. He lifted his head, rubbed his eyes, trying to remember where he was and the horror that awaited him on this day.

"Stephanie, is that you?" And he told her what happened.

She went to him and sagged into his arms. They held each other for a few moments. "Oh, Jeremiah, I don't know what to say. There are no words. It's unbelievable."

Gently he pulled away. "What happened? They were okay a few days ago."

She stared into his chest. "If it could have been Jackie or me, we'd gladly traded places."

He sighed. "I know ... I know." His head hung low, still struggling to accept the magnitude of his loss, he glanced down at her. "And I haven't even asked about John Francis. He's okay, yet he was with them."

"Yes, he's so fine, so strong. He never showed the slightest hint of infection, cold or fever. He's like you Jeremiah—very strong. Milly and Mary, I guess they were more delicate." She let out a sob and started crying.

"What does he know, Stephanie? Have you told him anything?"

Solemnly she said, "No."

He reached for her, and they hugged again. Stephanie gazed up at him. "I'm not being fair. I should be comforting you, not you, me."

He sat on the couch and remembered thinking that being deported from Ireland was the low point in his life or being cast into the stone quarries of Worcester was horrible. Those experiences were minor compared to the deaths of Milly and Mary. He sank back in the couch, staring at the walls. The thought that kept plaguing him was, how would he recover from this? Yet he knew, as in the past, he had his work, and now he had John Francis as well. The thought raced through his mind then back out again. How would he raise John Francis alone? Milly had been the anchor in the family, now this.

They decided to wait until breakfast before telling John Francis. He came down to the kitchen, bubbling with energy. He was getting long and gawky, the tallest kid in his class, his thick brown hair cut short for the summer. Ignoring the bowls of cantaloupe and blueberries sitting next to his cereal, he rushed to his father and hugged his waist.

He said, "Papa, what brings you here a few days early?" He glanced around the kitchen. "Have Mommy and Mary come back from the hospital?"

"Come here, son."

Jeremiah placed his arm around his shoulders and hugged him. John Francis searched the sad face of his father. "There's something wrong, isn't there? They're not here." His eyes darting back and forth between his grandparents and father.

"Johnny," said Jeremiah. "I have very sad news. They're not coming home."

"What are you saying? What are you telling me?"

"They've gone to heaven, Johnny. They're with the angels."

"You mean they're dead? Both Mommy and Mary died?"

John Francis studied his father's face in disbelief. He's had friends at school that had lost a parent; in several cases he had lost classmates to illness or accidents. Childhood and adult deaths were not new to him, yet this was his mother and sister. He'd never see them again, never play with his sister again. They'd never be with him and his father in the surf at Nantucket or on the playgrounds of Worcester. He began to cry, his whole body shaking. Jeremiah held him and fought back his own tears. John Francis clung fiercely to his father, unwilling to sever the physical connection. It was days before he'd willingly leave his father's side.

Milandra came from Worcester to assist with arrangements and to provide solace to John Francis. After lengthy conversations with the Driscolls and Monsignor Cummings, Jeremiah decided the funeral service would be in Worcester while the burial would be in the family plot in Northshire. Jeremiah worked with stonemasons in Northshire, masons that had worked with him on St. Steven's years before. In their workshop, he put his entire being into the tombstones, his despair and grief driving him. He fashioned two four-foot-tall granite markers. This was different for him, smaller in scope than the altars and statues that he had built his career on, yet it reminded him of the work he had done for the Cawley family years before. The tombstone that had launched his career.

He was careful with his design of the angels. He knew Milly preferred aesthetic simplicity, and he kept it that way. As a final touch, he etched their names and their dates of birth and death. Mary was eight; Milly was forty-one. He wanted to etch small laurel wreaths at the base of the tombstone, laurel being Milly's favorite, but put his chisel down. *Let the space be open*, he thought. *Let them float uninterrupted to heaven. Milly would like that.*

Jeremiah needed brace of humor and perspective at this trying time, and it came from an unexpected source. Through Pietro, Maria learned of Milly's death and telephoned Jeremiah. The conversation lasted for many minutes, then she shared a thought that brought a moment of levity to both of them.

"Jeremiah," she said, "remember, I was supposed to widow first. Now, my dear old count continues to surprise us all by living forever, and your young wife has departed early. What are we going to do?"

"Thank you for that, seeing our lives in a broader perspective. I needed that."

"Do you want me to come to the funeral?"

"Oh"—he paused—"no … no, so kind. It's too far, and I'd be terrible company." He stopped again. "You know, my plans are to be in Siena next summer. I plan to do that and bring my son with me."

"Most wonderful. I'll see you often. Then you must come to Rimini for a few days. The count is too ill to travel, so it will be the three of us—you and I and John Francis. We'll go to our villa, swim, enjoy the sun, and relax. I'll help you recover."

"It's hard to believe, but I feel better. You've lifted my spirits. Thank you for the call."

The day was dark with clouds threatening rain. The crowd on the grassy hillside of St. Steven's cemetery was dressed in black and moved in slow, deliberate steps to the gravesites. Occasional nods of heads were the only form of recognition among the mourners. There were a few chairs for the Driscoll family, and once seated, Monsignor Cummings gave a short eulogy. The crowd came from Milly's St. Agatha's colleagues, her fellow teachers from the Buckley School in Worcester, friends from Smith and Northshire, and her friends from Worcester. Patiently they stood in an informal line to offer condolences to Jeremiah, John Francis, and the Driscolls, then slowly made their way to a post-burial reception at the Draker Hotel. Jeremiah and John Francis were the last to leave. Jeremiah murmured his last goodbye to Milly and then to Mary, their graves side by side. John Francis leaned against his father's leg, glanced up at him, tears streaming down his cheeks.

Jeremiah smiled down to his son. "We have to find a new path, Johnny. I've found one before—two times in fact—and we'll find a new one now."

"Is it important to find a new path, Father? Can we do that without Mommy and Mary?"

"When you've had a great sadness like this, it's important to find a new direction to get you busy again and make you feel better."

"I don't feel better now."

"You won't, son. It takes time." Quickly he flashed back to his deportation, the abandonment of his family and country, that first lonely train ride to Worcester. He thought, sculpture sustained him then; may it sustain him now. He rubbed the top of his son's head. "But we'll find a new path together. Mommy and Mary would want that." Side by side, they stood gazing at the exquisite *angels* carved above the names of Mary and Amelia.

John Francis looked up to Jeremiah. "Father, those *angels on the tombstones* are welcoming Mommy and Mary to heaven, aren't they?"

"Yes, they are, son. Come ..." Jeremiah took his son's small hand. Slowly they turned from the graves and walked toward the awaiting Pierce Arrow.

Chapter 33

The new path forward was elusive for Jeremiah. For several days, he and John Francis stayed with the Driscolls in Northshire. Jeremiah had trouble sleeping, and the recurring dream of falling into a dark well shocked his slumber into a soaking sweat. In despair, he spoke to Stephanie one morning as he munched on a blueberry muffin. "What I can't understand is why this dream keeps reappearing." He searched her face, seeking some reason, some understanding.

She said, "Now that I have you alone for a few minutes, I do have an idea or two."

He nodded.

"Well, I think this dream reveals a fear, perhaps a fear of being smothered by your responsibilities. It's been several weeks. You need to get away from here. Away from this place of death."

"But …"

"Yes, Jeremiah. You need to get back to work. Your sculpture drives you, sustains you. Let us take care of John Francis for a while."

"He does like it here, doesn't he?" He stopped, scratched his head. "But Johnny will feel like I'm abandoning him. He's lost so much already."

Stephanie said, "He likes us, likes it here. I think being close to where she died will be good for him. At least for a few weeks."

"Stephanie, do you honestly think he'll be all right with my leaving?"

"He'll understand that you're doing what you love and need to do. And he can play in the fields and streams he loves. You'll have plenty of opportunity to talk with him, plus you'll see him every weekend, yes?"

"Definitely."

"Let's talk to him when he comes down for breakfast."

When Jeremiah returned to Worcester, the dream did not go away; it reinforced what he already knew. He had no idea how to raise a son alone and manage his work. He was in constant demand. The work was difficult, time-consuming, and required travel. Raising a son was hard and so important. Could Milandra do it? Would the boy accept her? He wrestled with these thoughts at night, and when the dream found its way into his sleep, he'd bolt upright, sweating with worries.

Months later, he spoke to Milandra about caring for John Francis. She said, "Yes, sir, Mista Jeremiah, I can do dat. He's a good boy. He be easy. But I'm tellin' you, as sure as I'm standin' here, that boy's gonna need a momma. You best be thinkin' about gittin' married agin', you hear."

Her advice paralyzed him, stopped him cold. It was too soon. It was impossible to *think* of replacing Milly. The thought of marriage unnerved him. Connie had refused him; Milly had died. His own family had let him down. Personal relationships were fragile, often breaking. The whole concept of family spoke of heavy responsibilities that seemed to head down a road to disappointment and loss. He wasn't ready to hear or act on Milandra's admonitions.

That didn't stop her from trying. The following evening as she placed his supper in front of him, she said, "Now mebbe gittin' married agin is too soon. Mebbe a year or so of grievin' be okay but afta that ... time to be doin'."

His eyes, ringed with dark circles, gazed up at her. He couldn't shake the sadness he felt. "I can't think of it just now, Milandra ... It's gonna take time."

"Oh, I knows I'm pushy, but you best be thinkin' of it, you knows ... for the boy. Mrs. Sullivan been a-callin', you listen to her. She'll guide you to the right woman when the time comes."

Alice Sullivan watched Jeremiah from the moment he returned to Worcester and talked with him frequently during the year. It was a long year for Jeremiah and John Francis, but with Milandra's buoyant spirit and the energy of other friends, they plugged along through the school year. To Alice, his grief was evident. She knew that grieving was different for each person. Some took months; others much longer. She wanted to help him yet not push him.

When she and Bill saw them off for their summer trip to Siena, Milly had been dead for a year, and she prayed that the change in scenery and culture would be a boost to both of them. The excursion to Italy was new to John Francis and exciting. His spirits soared as he ventured on hiking and camping trips with Pietro's sons. Their visit to the Rimini, with Maria and her sons, was marked with sailing and swimming in the Adriatic under blue skies and a baking sun.

After dinner one evening, Maria said, "The old count is in his late sixties, is quite sick but still here. My timing, our timing couldn't be worse."

Jeremiah sipped his grappa, gazing at her fondly. "We've been close friends, and now we've gone further, yet distance separates us from permanence in our relationship, and our marital decisions haven't helped much either." He laughed. "You're right Timing never worked in our favor. Yet this summer, this week here." He shook his head and sipped from his glass. "You've given openly, freely, and by your warmth, you given me the gift of life. I feel alive again. A heavy burden has been lifted off my shoulders. I'll cherish this week for the rest of my life."

When they returned in late August, Alice knew the summer in Siena had been good for both of them. Jeremiah was tanned, rested, and looked vibrant. John Francis was bursting with energy. Jeremiah spoke with animation about the help from Pietro and Kinga and, with unusual fondness, from the help of Maria Fazio. He was in better spirits, and John Francis seemed eager to return to school. She helped Jeremiah enroll John Francis in a Sunday school class at St. John's. Their son Andy was in John Francis's class. Alice managed the coffee hour in the church's rectory for the parents of the children.

As the parents assembled in the rectory, she spotted Jeremiah and brought him a cup of coffee. "Ah, good to see you and John Francis as well. How's he doing?" She handed him the cup and patted his shoulder.

"It's gotten better after the trip to Siena. Yet"—he paused—"we miss Milly's presence, especially as a mother. I don't have a lot of answers ..."

"They'll come in time, Jeremiah. Please talk to some of the other single parents here. They have stories and ideas on how to address many of your questions. And you can always count on Bill and me."

He circled the room and spoke to a few men and several women. As the Sundays rolled into October, November, December, more and more widows were sufficiently confident to approach him. He pushed himself to show interest in their conversations, and he wondered why this was so difficult compared to the comfort he felt with his work. There was no question in his mind that he was totally happy and absorbed with his hands on the marble. Quite simply, it was hard to transfer that attitude to his home life. Gradually, he recognized that the division between family life and work had always been with him. The ups and downs of family life, even its joys with Milly, seemed to be at a different level than the satisfaction and rewards of creating a work of art. He knew this would get in the way of a new relationship. How could any woman know and accept his way of life? Milly did, but she was entirely different from others.

At home and after Siena, John Francis emerged from his cocoon of sorrow as he became engaged in more demanding schoolwork and became an enthusiastic participant in after-school sports. He was eager to tell Jeremiah of his daily exploits, and if Jeremiah was away for a few days, John Francis would save his stories for the weekend. Jeremiah worried, after each telling, was the boy getting enough from him? Was he being a good father, the right kind of father? Yet it was all he could do, given his work.

Milandra, in her direct way, reminded him, "Mista Jeremiah, the boy's been good at school, at sports, but he be lonely too. And he's so smart. He says to me ... he worried about you ... you bein' lonely. How 'bout dat?"

"Milandra, we couldn't survive without you." He smiled at her wide face with the dark-brown eyes. "With you, John Francis, and my work, I'm hardly lonely. I have no time to be lonely."

"Oooh, Mista Knox, you be lonely, I knows … you jus' don't recognize it yet. You need a missus just as he needs a momma."

Jeremiah laughed as she walked away, muttering, "I knows, I knows."

He thought about her insights all week and on Sunday. Alice Sullivan approached him, tugging along a slender, blonde woman of average height with a round, pleasant face. "Jeremiah, I'd like you to meet Martha Chandler."

"I gather you're new to our church, Mrs. Chandler. Welcome."

Alice said, "She's just moved here from Boston to work in the admissions office at Holy Cross, and here's a surprise, she knew Milly."

"You knew Milly?"

"Not really, Jeremiah. We were in the same class at Smith, but she had a different major, lived a different dorm so we knew each other by sight, no more. She was lovely and had the reputation of being very smart."

Jeremiah felt a sinking feeling, and he fought to appear energetic. "Yes, Milly had a lot of light bulbs up top. Kept us on our toes, she did."

Martha laughed. "I like the light bulb analogy. My late husband was the same way."

"May I ask what happened?"

"Like you, I lost my husband and a son to the influenza epidemic of '18. I'm not sure you ever get over it, but I've learned to live with it. Finally, I had to leave Boston."

"I understand … Would you like some more coffee?"

Initially, their loneliness connected them. Then walks in the park, Sunday concerts, and occasional movies moved them toward a solid companionship. Martha met John Francis, and after a year, a fast friendship grew between them. Watching this happen gave Jeremiah courage that she might be the mother Milandra was suggesting. When he talked about his interest in pursuing the relationship to Bill and Alice Sullivan, they were ecstatic and supportive. Yet he was troubled. He was not in love with her the way he had been with Milly. He was very comfortable with her. He was supported by the enthusiasm of his friends, and his son enjoyed her companionship. Without a powerful love, should he ask her to marry?

One evening, after their stroll through the park, they went to their favorite restaurant for an early dinner. Halfway through the desert, Martha placed her fork on the plate and brought both hands together. She cleared her throat to get Jeremiah's attention.

He noticed and waited.

"Jeremiah," she began, "we've known each other for over a year, and I believe I know you fairly well. Pardon my assumption, but I think you've got something on your mind. All evening there's been a slight tension in you, like you're holding something back."

"Well ..."

"You can tell me if I've read you incorrectly ..." She hesitated. "But I hope you realize a woman's intuition is 95 percent accurate." She fluffed her napkin and laughed.

"Martha, you need not worry about your accuracy. You're right, I do have something on my mind. It's been troubling me. That is, how to bring it up. As you've said, we've been together over a year, and for me, it's been most enjoyable."

He paused for a moment, watching for her reaction. Pleased, he went on. "You know ... you're a wonderful woman. I care for you deeply, and my son has taken to you enthusiastically." He reached for his glass and sipped the water, his hand trembling slightly. "I can imagine sharing my life with you. However, it's complicated, isn't it? We've both been married, and this is different."

She reached forward and took his hand. "Jeremiah, stop twisting yourself into a pretzel. Please pardon my candor, but ... if you're asking me to marry you, the answer is yes." She didn't wait for his reaction. "You see, I've wondered about us too. Where might this relationship go? I would be honored to share the rest of my life with you and John Francis. I cannot imagine a finer companion." She lifted her hands in the air. "Now, if my intuition is wrong, if this is not your intent, then I've really stuck my foot in my mouth."

He laughed and settled back in his chair, holding her hand. "You've always been a bit ahead of me on these matters. You're on the money. Yes, I do want to marry you, and have you in my life."

"You said something about it being different. Of course, it'll be different than our prior marriages. We can't hope or want to duplicate what we had before, but knowing you as I do, I believe we can create a marriage built on respect, understanding, and a beautiful companionship."

"This is wonderful, but I must remind you that my work is very demanding. Might that be difficult for you?"

"Of course not." She laughed again. "I accept you with full awareness of your commitment to art."

On their honeymoon, they travelled by train to New York and Washington. He showed her his work in several churches in New York, and they spent several hours in the National Cathedral in Washington. He pointed to the renovations he was asked to make in the cathedral, and she jostled his arm. "You're preparing me for being away, aren't you?"

"I want to show you what projects fascinate me, challenge me."

"I don't know why you do these churches. Why not focus on pure sculpture for art galleries, museums, and so on? Your work is that good."

"I prefer religious art because it's seen by more people and can hopefully inspire them, please them. I don't want to make art only for the art lovers or educated elites. I want my work to touch everyone."

"I see." She gazed at the altar he was to work on, then looked up at him. "I knew what I was getting into when I said yes. My late husband was very busy, a lot like you." She tugged at the sleeve of his coat. "You do your work, travel as you need, and I'll take good care of the home front."

He thought of Ian McCracken's statement as he often did, "Only art endures," and leaned over to kiss her cheek. *Thank God*, he thought, *that I have the skill to do it.* "I know I'm single-minded, and I appreciate your understanding of that odd characteristic or forgive it." He laughed. "I'll take either."

She said, "We have work to do to give John Francis a fine start in life, and I'm sure we can. But you'll need to give of yourself to him and to me."

His gaze rested steadily on her eyes. "I will."

Epilogue

September 1947

Milandra had stacked their mail on the long table in the entryway. Returning from a weekend in New York, they opened the door and were struck by the size of the pile. "It never stops," moaned Martha. "Let's look at it later."

Jeremiah nodded as he flipped through the pile then stopped. "Well, look at this." He held the odd-shaped envelope high. "It's from Pietro. It's been a while. I wonder what he's up to."

"I'm tired and have no appetite for the mail," she replied as she placed her coat in the closet then turned to Jeremiah. "Yet I'm curious about Pietro. Why don't you open his letter? The rest can wait."

Jeremiah took the letter into their living room and sank into his favorite chair. He opened the envelope, smiling as he read. He was relieved; Pietro's letters during the war spoke of hardships and the deaths of old friends. The saddest was the death of Maria and her family; the family's villa was destroyed by bombs. All were killed.

He put the letter down then turned to Martha. "Pietro says we must come to Siena as soon as possible. He's very insistent."

"Good grief. The war's barely over, and Italy's a mess. What's he have in mind?"

"Hmm, that's my concern. He doesn't say. Maybe it's his health. He's in his early eighties now."

"Let's send Pietro a cablegram and get to the bottom of this."

They sent the cable, and the return cable was as equally mysterious. Pietro claimed it was most important that they come to Italy as soon as possible. He hadn't seen them since 1938 before the war.

He admonished them that it had been nearly ten years, and they were getting older.

Jeremiah and Martha had to laugh at the "getting older" comment. They were both in their mid-seventies and feeling their age. Pietro, several years older, seemed to have more energy than they did. Pietro had presented a challenge as he often did, and Jeremiah took the bait. "Martha, my dear, I think we should go. We've been stuck in the US since the war began. It's time to travel, visit Europe again. Maybe tie it into a side trip to Ireland."

They notified Pietro and planned the trip for early October before the weather turned. Martha was reluctant to fly on the Pan Am Clipper, so they travelled by ship as they had done so many times in the past. Arriving in Genoa, they were struck by the damage to the city. Shattered buildings everywhere, stones were stacked on street corners and in vacant lots. The people on the streets wandered through the rubble. Their clothes were old and worn, their faces haggard, their bodies sagged, burdened with the weight of their losses.

As they travelled by train to Siena, the devastation in the rail yards was still evident, although the trains were running with some predictability. The train station in Siena and the surrounding yards were still being cleared of bent tracks and demolished buildings from the Allied bombing raids of '44 and '45. Churches and apartments near the rail station had been damaged, walls missing, roofs crushed, and not as yet rebuilt. Jeremiah shuddered at the thought of seeing the destruction of the Maria's villa.

As he stared out at the broken buildings, Jeremiah said, "Why would Pietro want us to see this? I wonder what happened to our work."

Martha had the same reaction. "But we don't know. We'll see."

As they left the train station, they saw men and women huddled on sidewalks and curbs, begging passengers for small coins, any coins at all. Pietro saw them, frantically waving his arms. He broke past the beggars, his eyes radiating warmth. He greeted Jeremiah with a hearty handshake, then grasped his shoulders and gently shook them. Bending over, he hugged Martha. "You haven't changed in ten years"—he pointed to his snowy-white hair—"while we've aged one hundred years during the war." He waved the beggars away, impatient, irritated. "I'm sorry, it's embarrassing, but some people haven't figured out how to survive in the aftermath of the war. Too many Italians have given up." Then he changed his tone. "But I'm confident the country will come back. You'll see that tomorrow when we visit Rome."

"Rome?" Jeremiah asked.

"Yes, tonight we dine with a few of your old friends, and tomorrow we take the train to Rome. You must see the recovery in Rome and, particularly, the repairs on one of the historic churches. It's one you worked on, and I believe you'll be pleased."

Jeremiah placed his hand on Pietro's shoulder. "You've suffered mightily during the war, I can see that. I've read that there's been considerable loss of great art. How will Italy ever recover from what's been destroyed?"

"That's why it's important for you to be here. I wanted you to see what's been lost but also what we're doing to restore what's been damaged or destroyed."

When they arrived in Rome, they made their way through the streets to the church of San Giovanni. Jeremiah observed that Rome seemed less damaged than Siena. The power and beauty of the ancient church captured his attention as it had thirty years earlier. When they stepped inside, he turned to the right, looking for the statue he'd done those many years ago.

"See"—Pietro pointed to the statue of St. John in the entryway—"it's as if you finished it yesterday. It survived the war, as did this church. It was meant to last. It was God's will."

"When I think of the original sculpture, I'm humbled that my work stands in its place. I never thought it was quite as good."

"Ah, but, Jeremiah, the original collapsed with age. Yours is superior. It has come through the bombings, survived a war. Yours has endured, and I wanted you to see that."

Jeremiah stared at the statue for a few moments' pleasure coursing through his mind. As he designed and carved St. John, he never gave thought to its longevity nor its capability to withstand bombing. He nodded to the statue and gently touched the arm of the saint.

The three of them walked slowly down the central aisle of the church with Jeremiah and Pietro pointing to minor repairs that they had made on the columns and the pulpit, pleased that their interior work had required minimal attention and had survived the war.

At the altar, Pietro looked at his watch and said, "Now we'll go and view some of our work that didn't make it through the war."

"Oh, wonderful, my friend. What are we going to see, a headless saint, one-half of an altar?"

Pietro, glanced at his watch again, then laughed. "You'll see."

Their taxi rattled through the streets to the Galleria Nazionale d'Arte. As they entered the building, Jeremiah asked, "This is an art museum. What are we doing here?"

Pietro walked them through several rooms of paintings by Picasso, Kandinsky, Klee, Matisse, and other moderns. The rooms were empty of art patrons. They reached a long rectangular room where paintings and sculptures were mixed. They paused in the open doorway and saw a large group clustered in one corner. Pietro said, "Let's see what they are looking at."

He pointed to the crowd facing a large sculpture. As they approached the group, a tall man in a well-tailored blue suit turned toward them and began to clap. Others in his group turned to face Jeremiah, Pietro, and Martha and began clapping as well. As they walked toward the group Jeremiah was able to secure a better view of the sculpture.

Pietro nudged Jeremiah with his elbow as they walked. "I may be wrong, but that looks like your statue of Thomas Aquinas, doesn't it?"

Jeremiah strained his eyes to peer at the statue. "What's it doing here? Who are these people, and why are they clapping?" As they neared the group, Jeremiah could see a table covered with white linen adjacent to the statue. On top were dozens of wine glasses and bottles of champagne in ice buckets.

Pietro said, "It's a long story, but they're here to celebrate you."

The tall man stepped forward, his hand extended. "I'm Nino Formicella, curator of art here, and I welcome you and your work to our museum."

Stunned, Jeremiah shook his hand and held it for a moment. "I'm astounded, actually speechless why me, why this statue?" He gestured toward the statue. "I did this in Bologna years ago."

"Around me," Formicella said as he pointed to the men and women standing near him, "is our monuments staff. They have travelled the country to save important works of art from the ravages of the war. In Bologna, the cathedral was demolished by bombs or dynamited by the Germans. We don't know the real cause, but by some miracle, your statue survived. We thought it belonged here because it's so unique. We believed that it should be seen by many not just those in Bologna. We have placed other works of yours in different museums—one in Siena at Pietro's request, others in Milano and Napoli. Today, we gather to thank you for your contributions to our culture, to our country."

Jeremiah placed his hands together and bowed. "I thank you. I thank all of you for this recognition. I'm simply a humble sculptor." He halted, swallowed hard. "To be recognized in this outstanding museum is beyond my comprehension."

Formicella smiled. "We had trouble finding you. Locating the artists behind the damaged work has been a challenge for all of us. With Pietro's help, we were delighted to finally locate you. Let us have some champagne to celebrate and to get better acquainted."

They clinked glasses, and Jeremiah moved through the crowd, making introductions and thanking them for selecting his statues. There were pats on the arms and back as they joked with him, telling stories of dishonest artists who claimed it was their work or the local priests whose churches had been demolished but refused to release the sculptures.

Jeremiah moved close to Pietro and raised his glass high. "I'm lost for words, my friend, but I give you thanks. I give you my boundless appreciation for making this happen and for all that you've taught me and for all we've done together."

Pietro took him by the shoulders as the others watched, and said, "We did great work together, but the main reason your large statues were good was that you're so tall." They both laughed. "You could reach where I needed stools, ladders, and an elevator."

Amid the laughter, Martha sidled up to Jeremiah and reached for his hand. "I always knew you did museum quality work and believed your work would endure in the churches of the US, but this! Oh, Jeremiah, there could be no greater honor."

He nodded, struggling to hold back the emotion that coursed through him. "Most unusual for me, Martha, but today I'm without words."

She said, "I know, I understand, but I'm puzzled by an odd thought. I'm curious about the Irish. What will they think when they see this recognition and the body of your work?" She paused, staring into his eyes. "Yes, I do believe that they'll regret the day they sent you into exile."

He gazed at her and thought he'd left Ireland so many years ago. He'd gone from a day laborer in a stone quarry to "angels on a tombstone," from that single, simple tombstone to presence in museums. His smile was serene. "I wonder."